ON THE ERADICATION OF SMALLPOX AND THE INTRACTABILITY OF RACCOONS

JAMEY GITTINGS

On The Eradication of Smallpox and The Intractability of Raccoons

Published by Attila Press, 2025

ISBN: 979-8-9921827-3-6

Printed in the United States of America

Visit our website at www.attilapress.com

ALSO BY JAMEY GITTINGS

Knock Three Times and Ask for Attila

Meat of the Horse

Jane

For Amanda, for no good reason

CONTENTS

Note on Language and Spelling

The reader will note that I have omitted the apostrophes on words such as *em, comin, goin, hangin,* and the like. I feel these are legitimate words in their own right and thus represent legitimate speech. That to signal them with an apostrophe demeans them and relegates them as inferior or bastardized forms of other words. Much like the asterisk did to Roger Maris' home run record. I hope I offend no grammarians.

All other forms of misspelling or grammatical errors may be viewed as shortcomings of the author.

Foreword

I wrote the first pages of this novel over 20 years ago when I still had faith in progress. Since then, faith is no longer my default. At the time of writing, two of my greatest heroes were John Lewis and Robert Moses, who were folded into the narrative. Moses as a rough model for Bob More, the protagonist's half-brother, and Lewis as the name for More's dog, named after his own personal hero. The references were meant as a tribute to both men. Since then, the two have become icons in our present turbulence, Lewis becoming as close to a saint for us secular folks as we have. In the publication of this second edition, I have had cause to question the appropriateness of the inclusion of these men. Upon reflection, I have kept both in place. First, because they play important parts in the original story and to remove them out of a faux veneration would weaken the intent of the tale. Second, they were written with a respect and tribute that has not changed. It would grieve me if either would view this as a form of disrespect.

I believe the storyline is as relevant today as when it was first begun twenty years ago and first published eleven years ago—perhaps more so.

JG, July 2021

1

The Last Job in Town

You don't know me, unless you read a little book I wrote as a Harvard undergraduate—unlikely, but more on that in a moment. My name's Ned Alexander; I'm a minor screw-up, or a major ne'er do well, whichever way you want to look at it. My time at Harvard was less than distinguished, as I graduated on the nine-year-plan. My only redeeming achievement was a little book I wrote about my summer travels in Wales pursuing the ghost of Dylan Thomas. This book, complete with exercises in Dylanian self-destruction, spoke of the alienation and disillusionment of youth in the early '80s, received a limited literary approval, and fielded a sympathetic audience of like-minded, semi-estranged college students. Its greatest notoriety came when it was used as a textbook in a number of freshman English courses, at Harvard and other universities. However redeeming of my intellect, it did little to justify my overall poor academic performance, and I drifted from course to course and major to major without distinction.

The only way I got into Harvard in the first place is that I come from parents of illustrious, though esoteric, fame. My mother is a sociologist famous among scholars of Appalachia and popular educators. She has a penchant for doing real work, with real people, which was an extreme handicap when it came to climbing the academic ladder. For her, integrity on her own terms was enough, again a fatal flaw for an academic. When my parents met, my mother introduced herself as she always does: "I'm Helen from North Georgia—North Georgia, you know, has always been an abolitionist stronghold." That pedigree, and Helen's youthful and energetic beauty, was enough for my father, who, in the only active pursuit of his life, married her within the year.

My father was a literary critic who dabbled, most often against his will, in diplomacy. The son of an old-moneyed New England family, he drank in erudition with his mother's milk. Indeed, mother's milk remained an important theme far into his adulthood, when he resigned from a stint in the United Nations after his country was the only vote against restricting the advertising of infant formula in the Third World that was contributing to an appalling rise in infant mortality. His early erudition, along with his mother's milk, was distilled into a fine liquor at the best prep schools and Ivy League institutions.

His voice and manner lent an intoxicating quality to his opinions and arguments. He was one of the few people I can call an intellectual, with that rare ability to speak with meaning to anyone, on any topic, in any situation, without appearing pompous. This ability was also the source of much of his unhappiness, since he was continually pressed into service on some diplomatic foray at the request of childhood and college friends who seemed to constitute much of the government.

"God damn it, Ned," he said shortly before his death, "I should be aging gracefully, moldering on the wine rack that makes up the faculty of our finest institutions, instead of making powerful people who have behaved badly feel better about themselves." Two months later, he was dead, the result of a bomb explosion at American University in Beirut, where he had been sent to infuse a little sanity into a world controlled by people behaving badly.

The major benefit of Harvard is not a good education, though it's there for some. No, Harvard, as it turns out, is the absolute best university for finding a job. Not because people at Harvard are smarter; everyone with any sense after their freshman year knows that there are tons of people who are smarter than they are. And it's not because it has such an illustrious faculty. No, it's because everyone thinks that Harvard is the best university, and consequently Harvard graduates, or students, think they're smarter than everyone else. If people know you're from Harvard, they'll hire you so they can tell you what to do and feel good when you screw up. I learned this lesson early on and have made somewhat of a profession of advancing my career through minor screwups.

If you work a construction job, someone will say, "Hey, Harvard, go get me a ballpeen hammer. No, not that one, that's a framing ax. Jeez, do I have to tell you everything?" If you make pizza, you hear, "Hey, Harvard, that last crust was a little doughy, so leave the next one in a little longer." Then: "Hey, Harvard, the crust looks a little burnt. Gosh, can't you guys do anything right?"

"No, sir," you say as you smile stupidly. You can work there forever.

As I said, the only way I got into Harvard was through my father's connections. My poor performance was again buffered by the university's esteem for him, and whatever the reasons, though I was constantly on probation, they failed to throw me out. Upon his death, this esteem transformed into martyrdom, and I knew that whatever I did, or didn't do, I would be allowed to drift through the halls of the school with impunity.

Scaring myself with *Twilight Zone* visions of an endless existence at Harvard, I went looking for help from my father's best friend, the Brazilian poet and radical educator Umberto Conway. Conway was a professor who had been living in exile from his native country for twenty years. He was also my godfather, having christened me, so the family legend went, with a bottle of tequila at a nondenominational ceremony marking my birth. As the story goes, Conway emptied the contents of the bottle over my forehead in the garden. Some of it splashed into my eyes, and I cried for the next hour. Whatever the truth of the tale, Conway has since served the function of godfather. I confided my fears and asked him for help.

I don't know if all poets are great listeners, but Umberto was, and he listened for more than an hour, making only grunts and sighs. When I finally rambled into silence he said, "So you want my opinion." It was not a question, so I remained silent. "I'll give it to you, because your father was my greatest friend and also because your problem is relatively simple."

He went on, his R's rolling syllables of thunder. "Most fundamentally, your problem is that you have been pursuing reputable disciplines: literature, history, sociology, even biology. These are disciplines that require both rigor and respectability, and you, Ned, are not respectable. Moreover, you are not respectable by choice. Since I have known you as a little boy, you have refused respectability, seeing a conflict with your own independence. If you wish to pursue an academic career, it must be one that is not completely reputable. Although you respect, admire, and even, in your own way, aspire to intellectual pursuits, you choose to live between the cracks of the academic disciplines. In short, you refuse to pay the price of respectability." Smiling at my discomfort, he continued. "The answer is simple. We need a disreputable discipline that you can commit to. I know of three taught here at the university. If you had a pirate's soul, rather than just a pirate's style, I would recommend business—we have a fine business school—but your sensibilities preclude this. For the same reason, political science is not an option. I recommend journalism." He said this as if there were nothing more to say. And as there was nothing more to say, I left.

Journalism indeed proved to be the semi-respectable discipline with room for both independence and literary rigor, as prophesied by Conway. I threw myself into the course requirements and soon graduated. The degree required no great theoretical or academic foundation, had few doctrinaire components, and best of all was mobile. One could, I reasoned, write anywhere, then for any reason pack up and go anywhere else. Thus, I found myself in need of a job in Tucson, Arizona, in the early winter of 1997.

There were two major papers in the southwestern town of just over 500,000—the *Sun* and the *Times Review*—along with a few local cultural and business tabloids. I tried the personnel offices of all of them and found there were no jobs for an itinerant, inexperienced journalist at the time. I was told, euphemistically, that they would let me know if anything came up. I was not yet dead, however, and still had my trump card to play. I spent some time reading the two major papers and liked the *Daily Sun* the best. I paid attention to the reporter's bylines, the names of the editorial staff, and their editorial positions, although no names were tied to the editorials. I also wrote a number of letters to the editor under assumed names, delivering them in person to the main desk. This allowed me to skulk around and do a little observation of some the people whose names I was learning. One letter even got published. It was about a high school baseball coach whose players got caught ordering beer at a Pizza Hut after an away game. The coach was fired, I thought unfairly, and my letter pointed out the long and respectable association of baseball with beer, and I signed my assumed name followed by the title *Milwaukee Brewers Fan*.

Following the successful beer theme, I hung out in a few of the bars near the *Sun*. An editor named Mike Halloran was a regular at Famous Sam's, across the street. I sat at the bar and listened to Halloran talk to members of the *Sun*'s staff. Everyone seemed to defer to him, and I liked his humor and rough manner. I didn't know exactly what he did, but after listening to him for a couple of days, I was ready to make my move.

The next morning, I went to the *Sun* and found Halloran. I knew his desk from previous scouting expeditions. He was standing outside his office and talking to a young woman who was alternately waving her arms and pointing at him, looking frustrated and upset. Halloran's manner was calm as he walked away from the woman, who continued to point where he had been standing. After he had put some distance between them, and she did not follow, I approached.

"Mr. Halloran," I said. "I've been an admirer of the *Sun* for a long time, and I'd very much like to work for you."

He looked up from the copy he was reading. "Who are you?" he asked evenly.

"My name's Ned Alexander, and I've just graduated from journalism school," I said, delivering my words carefully.

"Have you gone to the personnel office?"

"Yes." I said. "But they're really the last to know, aren't they? And I'll take anything, it doesn't even have to be a standard job. So I thought I'd come to you."

The young woman had now moved closer to us, and it was evident that she was waiting for me to leave. Her shoe tapped the concrete floor as she stood with one hand on her hip and holding copy in the other, in a perfect dramatic exercise of someone exhibiting impatience. Halloran, though not unaware of her, continued with me. I silently thanked the young woman whose presence I was sure prolonged our conversation.

"Did you notice the weather today?"

"Ah, yes," I said, slightly thrown off balance.

"It's seventy-two degrees out there in December. Other parts of the country are freezing their asses off." He paused. I waited, not knowing where this was going. "Everybody wants to work at the *Sun*. I probably get twenty inquires a week from reporters wanting to live here, admiration for the *Sun* aside."

I now understood where it was going, but I continued anyway. "Yeah, but they all probably want real jobs. I'll take anything." Halloran smiled not unkindly. By now, the tempo of shoes on the concrete floor had increased to double time, and the young woman's knuckles were white where they drove into her hip, as she fanned herself with her copy. He looked at her, then back to me. I could have kissed her.

"Sorry," he said, in what was meant to dismiss me.

It was time to play my card. "Damn," I said, looking down and gently kicking the floor. "I guess a journalism degree from Harvard isn't worth the ink that's used to print it." I had worked hard on that line and delivered it smoothly. I turned slowly to walk away.

"Harvard, is it?"

"Yes," I said, turning back. The women's fan increased its speed, no longer mere theater; it was now becoming necessary as a functional cooling device. Again, I could have kissed her.

"Ever do any crime reporting?"

"Quite a bit," I lied. Actually, I had done almost none.

"Well, Barbara there," he said, pointing to the woman who was quickly becoming a caricature of silent fury, "is unhappy with her assignment. She's drawn an aesthetic and moral line in the sand and dares me to cross it. So, Harvard, I have a job for you, if you want it." I waited. "You want it?" he asked, raising his voice for the first time. Barbara, who had been listening to our exchanges all along, stood up straighter with his words and looked directly at us. "Yes, I do," I said, trying to sound both earnest and confident. With my words, Barbara turned quietly and walked away.

"She's really pissed now," he said. "But she's class and not about to show it. Come on, Harvard, I'll tell you about your job." We walked to his desk, and he pointed for me to sit.

"How do you feel about capital punishment?" "I'm mostly against it."

"Mostly against it," he said, repeating my words and stretching them out in parody. "Well, America's mostly for it, in fact, seventy-seven percent mostly for it by the latest polls. How mostly against it are you? Seventy- seven percent, perhaps?"

"I don't really know, I haven't given it a whole lot of thought," I answered honestly.

"Your view on the death penalty is not really the point. Have you heard of Eugene Redway?"

"The murderer? Yeah," I said.

"Yeah, the murderer," he repeated—more parody. "Well, my problem is that Barbara is pretty much against capital punishment one hundred percent. She's been covering the story, and covering it well, too. Anyway, unless there's a stay, which doesn't seem likely, Redway dies tonight in Florence. It's Barbara's job to cover it, and she's been selected to view the execution. Her idea is that we should cover the story without viewing it. Take a stand, if not against the death penalty, against what she calls catering to the ghoulish sensibilities of the masses, if I have that right. Fact is, I think it's an interesting idea. A bigger fact is our responsibility to the seventy- seven percent of Americans who are mostly for it.

"You begin to see your job now, don't you? If it were just up to me, I'd side with Barbara and aesthetics, but it's not. And if I don't make some attempt to cater to the ghoulish sensibilities of the masses, I get in trouble with my supervising editor. And frankly, I don't know where I stand on this issue, so when I get into trouble, I want it to be something I really care about. So, the job, Harvard, is this: You cover the execution for the *Sun*, and Barbara writes the piece the way she sees it.

"If you're a lousy writer, then I won't use your piece, the managing editor will be mildly pissed, but at least I can say I tried. Barbara will be happy, and we'll strike a blow for aesthetic journalists everywhere. If your piece is any good, then we did our duty by the masses, and Barbara's piece still gets its licks in." He relaxed into his chair and said, "So Harvard, what do you think? It's probably the last job in town."

His last question was rhetorical, so I said nothing, and I spent the rest of the morning and afternoon going over the file that Halloran had provided me. Most of the articles I read bore the byline of Barbara Solomon. Halloran was right that they were good, and surprisingly balanced, given the strength of her convictions. I saw no more of her the rest of the day but periodically gave her thanks.

I hadn't paid much attention to this story. Despite what I'd told Halloran, crime work never interested me much, my preference being for articles on politics, international policy, urban social problems, stuff like that. Though I had heard the name Redway recently in my recognizance reading of the *Sun*, I had been unaware of the crime spree he had participated in at the time eighteen years earlier or of its nature. While I was ecstatic about the way my employment had taken place, the fact that I was to see a human being killed in a few hours gave me a creepy feeling, and I did my best not to think about it. This was a bit difficult since I was busy arming myself with as many facts as I could.

Solomon's stories focused on the debate between those advocating for Redway's execution based on the heinous nature of his crimes and those opposed to the death penalty on ethical, religious, or moral grounds. There was little or no discussion of possible innocence, or of redeeming activities of Redway while in prison that might mitigate the severity of the sentence. Also in the file were articles written at the time of the crimes and the original trial. I sat at a little wooden desk built on a scale appropriate to a third- grader, feeling like I was in high school detention, as I took notes on an ancient typewriter.

I don't really type, being brought up on computers, but it seemed the thing people would expect, so I hammered away, paying more attention to my rhythm than my accuracy, which was laughable. I noticed that the keyboard, or whatever it's called on typewriters, was dusty and probably hadn't been used for a while. I told myself that maybe I did have the makings of crime reporter.

In the back of my mind, I reviewed the nature of the fragile employment agreement between Halloran and me. Fundamentally, I was being used as a device to promote a kind of domestic harmony between Halloran and his reporter. And though she was unhappy now, this compromise would work to her advantage in the end, and Halloran knew it. My worry was that perhaps he had no intention of publishing my article. "But," I told myself, "I'm a hell of a writer and the quality of my prose would make it impossible not to use it." Pursuing the ghost of Eugene Redway would be easier than pursuing the ghost of Dylan Thomas, I reasoned. And so, with arrogance to the rescue, I thought little more about it.

After a couple of hours, Halloran called me back to his desk and told me that everything had been set up for me to attend. When he gave me an I.D. pass that said *Sun* and told me to get my picture put on it at the personnel office, I began to feel a little easier about the reality of my position. "Listen," he said before dismissing me. "What I want from you is an account of the execution, how he looked, what he said, times of events, that stuff, I don't want you to do a lot of background. We'll leave that to Barbara. Can you do that, Harvard? All I want is accurate observation and competent writing. This isn't the *Daily Weasel*."

Through all of his instructions I had been nodding along earnestly, but with this last comment my head snapped to a halt, and I looked straight at him.

"Yes, sir," I said. The *Daily Weasel* was an underground newspaper I had written for both during my time at Harvard and after graduation.

It specialized in exposing unjust social conditions around the Boston area, did political commentary, and had a limited but educated readership. As I stood up to leave, I saw a photocopied page from the Weasel with an article I had done on housing scandal in Roxbury. I had been surprised when my name appeared correctly on the I.D. pass since I had said it only once when I introduced myself. Now, it seemed that in the space of a few hours, he not only knew my name but also had done some checking and read some of my work. Halloran may have looked and acted casual, but it seemed he missed little.

"Redway's in Florence State Prison, which is about an hour and a half from Tucson. He's scheduled to die at midnight. I want you back here with your story written by three o'clock tomorrow morning. Can you do that?"

"Yes," I said.

"Good. And afterward, Ned, I'll buy you a beer at Sam's, and this time you can sit at my table."

Again, I did a double take, then turned to write an account of how a dead man, not yet dead, comes to die. I walked out of the offices of the *Daily Sun* much different than when I walked in, holding my incompetently typewritten notes in one hand and clutching my I.D. in the other. For me, it was the last job in town.

2

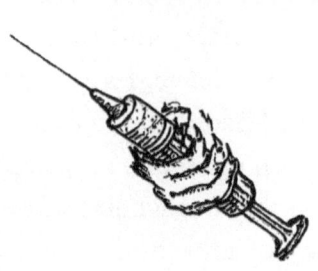

A Poor Case for Opponents

I had never paid much attention to the details of real-life murder. When I thought about it at all, it took the form of Agatha Christie-type stories. Even my exposure to this kind of fiction was limited. I did, like everybody else, enjoy a good whodunit on TV or at the movies. Stuff like *Murder on the Orient Express* or *The Maltese Falcon*. Real crime, I had long been convinced by my father, was perpetrated by powerful people with armies, slaughtering countless souls in scenes of unimaginable horror, leaving little mystery about who the killers were, and with little thought of justice or chance of retribution.

I found individual murders, even modern serial killings that people found so fascinating these days, to be not only unseemly but also for the most part uninteresting cultural perturbations. I never bothered reading the daily crime serials that made up a good part of the news. Even deaths and murders involving celebrities were, for me, uninteresting, and I paid little attention.

This attitude, I realized, was not a great background for an incipient crime reporter, and I told myself that I really would have to pay more attention. I recalled the words of my first-grade teacher, Miss Hopkins. "Edward," she would often say, wrongly assuming that Ned was short for Edward, which it's not. "Edward, you're a bright boy, but you have a messy mind." The woman was perceptive, I reflected, as I made my preparations to leave town.

Everything I knew about Redway was from Barbara Solomon's stories and from the two earlier accounts that were in the file. Redway and two others, known as the Reach brothers, had broken out of prison and gone on a killing spree that stretched across fifteen days, three states, and six victims. The nature of the killings was particularly brutal and mindless. The two earlier accounts in the file laid out the crime spree in excruciating detail that focused primarily upon the murders and the ensuing capture. Solomon's articles, while recounting the original saga, focused primarily on the battle between the district attorney's office and opponents of capital punishment who were seeking a stay of execution. Woven into her account in the form of dialogue between the two parties were all the details of the crimes and much of the pathos from both sides of the issue.

The main protagonist on the punitive side was assistant district attorney Roger Burwick. Had I not been given some insight into Barbara Solomon's point of view, I would have thought her work demonstrated a marvelous mosaic of journalistic objectivity, but as I reread parts of the narrative, a feeling emerged that Burwick, and his words, were used as a literary device—a strawman, to balance the issues presented by the other side. Solomon recapped the story of the eighteen-year-old crime in graphic and passionate detail, using Burwick's words almost exclusively. Interviews with Redway's attorney, his family, and Redway himself provided a counterpoint to Burwick's official stance. In one article, Burwick answered his critics by recounting how Redway killed a baby held between the legs of his pleading mother. At the end of the piece, Burwick was quoted as saying, "This is not a good case for the opponents of capital punishment."

On the other side of the debate, the Reverend Dr. Shirley Moran of the West University Christian Church grounded her arguments in the New Testament. Her logic was basic: *Thou Shalt Not Kill, Jesus is Love*, that kind of stuff. When set against the fiery words of Burwick, the mood of the country, and Halloran's seventy-seven percent, the Rev. Moran's theology rang out as anachronistic—an old-fashioned holdover from a time passed. I could almost hear people saying, "Yeah, yeah, we've heard all that stuff before, but we're way beyond that now." Her persona emerged as rather bland, and she was by far the least dramatic figure in the articles, yet I felt a certain sympathy with the Rev. Shirley Moran that I did not feel for the others. Bland and armed only with homilies, she exhibited courage as she stood up to the righteous indignation of the majority. The only photo of Moran in the file showed a frail-looking middle-aged woman with short, light hair as she addressed her congregation. "Well, Shirley, you're probably the only player in this minor drama with honest motives," I found myself saying out loud, briefly suspending my mistrust of religious organizations.

Tuning from the particulars of my assignment, I addressed the issue of fashion: What does one wear to an execution? Is it like a funeral, warranting a dark suit, perhaps? It's the West, so maybe jeans and a denim shirt, the working-class-hero look? Who could I ask? My father would have known. Halloran, maybe. "Ah, by the way, Mr. Halloran, what does a budding crime reporter wear to an execution?" In the end, I compromised on khaki slacks, a blue button-down Oxford shirt, and a tweed sport coat. I put a tie in my pocket just in case it later seemed appropriate.

By then, it was late afternoon and I wanted to get on the road, having made most of my fashion decisions. I grabbed a notebook and my laptop computer, then drove toward the town of Florence, wanting to get there before dark. Taking the Catalina highway to state route 77, I drove north twenty miles from Tucson and turned west on the Florence highway. To my back were the Catalina Mountains, a light mist hanging over them. In front of me, the lowering sun emerged from beneath the orange cloud cover. Looking in my rearview mirror, I saw an almost perfect rainbow framing the mountains, the most beautiful I'd ever seen. Later on, I would hear that this phenomenon was common, but at the time I took it to be an omen. An omen of what, however, I was not sure, but it added to the auspicious nature of my task. The creepy feeling began to return as I drove on.

The Florence highway is a two-lane desert road that slowly gains altitude, providing vistas of lush desert vegetation. I continued to look into my rearview mirror as the rainbow faded and grew smaller as I increased my distance. On the first stretch, there were signs identifying a variety of Sonoran desert plants: palo verde tree, catclaw, mesquite tree, yucca, and barrel cactus all flew by as I read each sign as a diversion from my thoughts. Farther down the road, I passed the Tom Mix Monument, which is a memorial to an early cowboy movie star who was killed when he lost control of his sports car and drove into the dry river that now bears his name.

For some reason, I stopped at the memorial. A two-dimensional bronze statue of Mix's horse, Tony, was placed high on a pillar of native stones. The stationary Tony was riddled with pockmarks from the bullets of less famous Western gunslingers. I counted thirty-two—one for every year of my life. Tom Mix was from an earlier era than my cowboy heroes, but his name was familiar to me, as he represented the genre of early Western films. His name had become a dead metaphor for old cowboy movies. I winced at the unspoken pun, and the drama of the death I was about to cover returned. Now, at least, I had two omens to counterbalance any inevitability, the natural beauty of the rainbow at my back; fate and capricious death in the ghost of Tom Mix to my front. Whatever happened tonight would surely fall somewhere in between. "Don't get morbid. It's just an assignment," I told myself with what I knew to be pseudo professionalism, and I got back into my car. As I drove on, I no longer looked in the mirror at Tom Mix or the rainbow.

Approached from the east, the Florence town limits sport a few abandoned buildings and lots of cactus I now knew to be teddy bear cholla thanks to the roadside instruction I'd received from the signage along the way. Moving on, I began to see some signs of civilization, mostly in the form of mailboxes clustered around the mouths of dirt roads; a few rooftops showed themselves in the distance above the desert vegetation. The sun was setting now and a yellow light heightened everything it touched. The fuzzy spines of cholla looked iridescent in the light. A large water tower sprouted from the horizon and grew steadily taller. It was my first view of the prison.

As I approached the Florence State Prison from the highway, I mused that it looked more like a giant farm, albeit one wrapped in chain-link fence capped by razor wire. The only motion was a lone tractor dragging a plow- like thing across barren red earth. The sun was now beneath the horizon, and the orange light had changed quickly to red. Then, just as quickly, all color drained away, leaving the grays to highlight only dark silhouettes. There was no sign of an entrance, so I drove around the perimeter of the fence. The farmland around the prison was extensive, and it took me far out into the desert. Various unnamed crops appeared and ended in geometric plots. Back around to almost where I had started was a break in the chain link with a drive leading to a group of buildings I took to be the entrance. It was approaching six o' clock, and the winter light was almost gone.

As I approached, the end of the driveway looked more like a campground, or a swap meet, than it did a prison entrance. RVs of various sizes formed small enclaves, their windows bright and showing activity inside. I parked my car away from the others and, feeling very much like an intruder, got out. Lawn chairs sat around folding tables, the scenes lit by gas lanterns. Coffee brewed on camp stoves. Small groups of people talked quietly, warming themselves with propane heaters. There was little laughter. Although I was met with eye contact and a number of somber smiles, no one seemed curious as to who I was. It was as easy to identify the various camps as it was to identify the desert vegetation along the highway, since signs marked each grouping, identifying their sympathies. A van from the West University Christian Church was in one of the larger groups and sported banners that proclaimed *God Is Love* and *Thou Shalt Not Kill*. Other groups displayed signs of varying sophistication, *Justice for the Victims*, *Justice for the Innocent*, and *The Innocent Have Rights Too*. A quick survey of the signs revealed the two operative words were *Love* and *Justice*, though nowhere were they used together. It was love on one side and justice on the other. I wondered if this represented some sort of true dichotomy. I wondered if I came back with a sign that proclaimed *Love is Justice* or *Justice is Love*, how that would be interpreted? Which side of the issue would I be on then? It was almost six hours until midnight and I was told to be at the gate no later than 10:30, so I had more than four hours to explore the town.

Every reporter has a forte, and one of mine is bars. Or rather, my specialty is getting information from people in bars. Many journalists have expertise in getting information from people, by asking astute questions, baiting people so they'll say things they hadn't intended, listening well, paraphrasing what is said to them and giving it back to the person as if it were an answer or a commitment. I've found that particular bars will yield particular information to a large extent irrespective of the individuals sitting inside. I would come to learn very soon that this is what the behavioral psychologists called stimulus control.

Coming back into town from the prison, I picked up a hitchhiker, a boy who looked to be about fourteen who was carrying a skateboard. "Where you going?" I asked.

"Into town to skate," he said. "If it's all right, you can let me off at the Burger King."

"Burger King," I said noncommittally.

"Yeah," said the boy, who introduced himself as Jeremiah. "It's new—it's the best thing that's ever happened to this town."

I dropped him off to his polite thanks. From Jeremiah, I had learned that there were three bars in Florence, the Giddy-up, My Office, and a bar outside the town near the private prison where the bikers hang out. My Office and the Giddy-up were on the same side of Main Street, about half a block apart. They looked pretty much the same, wooden fronted buildings done in a Western style. I started with My Office, which looked the seedier of the two, though only slightly. I had an Easterner's view of what a Western bar should look like, and My Office did not disappoint. I walked into a large room dominated by a long wooden antique mahogany bar, two pool tables, and a mural of a gunfight in progress that covered the entire back wall.

Two girls sat at the bar, while two middle-aged men alternately shot pool and sat at the bar drinking, filling their glasses from a pitcher of beer. The four seemed to know each other but did not appear to be couples. The bartender introduced herself as Rayanne and asked what I would have.

"I'll have what they're having," I said, pointing to the two girls who were drinking a Mexican beer.

"One Corona coming up," she said. One of the girls looked over and smiled.

I took this as my lead. "Everybody excited about tonight?" I asked her. "What about tonight?" said the girl who smiled. She was blonde with short hair and dressed in tight shorts and a tank top, slightly overweight but pretty.

"The execution," I said. "You know, Redway."

"Oh that," she said. "No, not really. Mostly everybody only wants to know what he's having for his last dinner."

"What is it?" I asked.

"Haven't heard yet. You're not from Florence?"

"No. Would you two like another beer?" I said, trying to dodge the question. She looked at her bottle.

"Thank you," she said politely. I ordered three beers that appeared almost immediately from the expert hands of Rayanne. "I'm Kim, by the way, and this here's Carol." The other girl at the bar nodded at me. "So," she continued, "where you from?"

"Boston."

"Huh," she said, remaining in control of the conversation. "You a reporter or something?"

Hey, I thought, *I'll ask the questions around here*, but instead I said, "Kind of, but more of an *or something*. I'm interested in capital punishment, and I might try to write something about it."

"Huh," she said again.

"What do you do?" I asked quickly, trying to regain possession of the interview.

"I work at the Burger King, and part time in the prison outlet store."

Bingo, I thought. "I hear that the Burger King's the best thing ever to happen in this town."

"What? Where'd you hear that?" she asked, surprised. "Oh, just a hitchhiker I picked up earlier tonight."

"Huh. Yeah there's really not much to do in this town." One of the men playing pool howled defeat. "Come on, Kim, we're up," Carol said.

"Doubles," insisted the man who howled. "Go ahead and break." Kim broke, sank nothing and returned to her seat beside me.

"It must be interesting working in the prison store," I said.

"No, not really. Hardly any people come around unless it's like today." "Today was busy?"

"You being a reporter now?" she asked.

"Yeah, a little bit I guess. I hear that Redway does knitting," I said, repeating what I had read in one of Solomon's stories.

"Crocheting," she corrected. "Actually, does some real nice work." "What kind of stuff does he make?"

"Sweaters, placemats, potholders, baby blankets, that kind of stuff," she answered, studying the pool table.

"You're up next, Kim, we've got the little ones," Carol said. Howler stalked around the table hunting his next shot.

That would be one secure baby swaddled in a Eugene Redway-crafted baby blanket, I was thinking as Kim sat down again.

"I suck at this game," she said. In response, I offered her another beer. "Thank you," she said as the beers again appeared. "You gonna write about this?" "I might."

"Well, you know, he did some real nice weaving lately. Somebody got him a small loom like the Indians use, and he started to do pictures, only they weren't Indian designs. Instead they were pictures around the prison yard, guys playing basketball, farm scenes, tractors, the water tower."

"Did any of his stuff sell?"

"Not hardly at all until they said they was gonna kill him, then it all sold. We could have sold ten times what we had. After they did a story about him crocheting in the newspaper, people kept coming in asking for stuff he made. The manager told us to take orders and get paid in advance. It was only a joke," she said with a smile that was not malicious. "Yeah, we sold the little bit that was left today, mostly small pieces, potholders, early stuff before he got really good. Everything but a pair of deerskin gloves. People bought all kinds of stuff today. Didn't matter who made it."

"Would you girls please get some of your balls off the table so I can see to shoot," Howler interrupted. The balls looked pretty even to me. Howl shot and missed, and it was Carol's turn. She sank two of her balls before she scratched the cue ball on her third shot and had to relinquish the table. There were fewer little ones than big ones on the table now, and Carol sat down at the bar looking satisfied. "Your shot, champs," she said to the guys.

"Why didn't the gloves sell?" I asked.

"Too expensive, I guess. We've had them about a year. He made them from some deerskin and did a real nice job, not work gloves but for fancy dress. I might have bought them myself, only they're too big. Never made anything like em again. Too hard, I guess. Excuse me," she said, setting down her beer and taking up her cue.

"How much are they?" I asked when she returned.

"The gloves? A hundred dollars. Like I said, too expensive."

"Listen, Kim, if I give you the money now, will you send the gloves to me in Tucson?" I was beginning to feel the effects of the beers and figured I better move on. Another scream and I looked up just in time to see the eight- ball roll into a pocket while Howl danced in disbelief.

Kim squealed in delight. "Set em up, chump."

"What does he do?" I asked her, nodding at Howl. "Oh, Rudy? He's a guard at the prison."

"So, is that all right about the gloves?" I asked again.

"Sure." I gave her the money and my address. "Thanks for the beers. I'll see ya," she said as she moved to the break the balls set up for her by the much-defeated Howl.

I moved on down the street to the next bar, the Giddy-Up, about a half a block away. As I approached, I saw a man leaving the bar. He wore a dark suit and sunglasses, and despite the dark, looked like the pictures I'd seen of Burwick, but I was too far away to be sure. If it was Burwick, I was really sorry to have missed him. Inside, the Giddy-Up was larger in scale but of similar motif to My Office. Scattered among the pool tables, foosball, and video games were tables where a fairly large crowd of people ate, drank, and talked. I took a seat at the bar and ordered a Bud. The bartender, also a young woman, did not introduce herself as Rayanne had done. Ours, it seemed, would be simply a business relationship. OK by me, as she looked a little intimidating, probably doubling as a bouncer on occasion. I paid what I was told to with a simple thank you while she said nothing.

I scanned the room. Most people looked like they were winding down from work. A few of the men wore business suits, but most men and women were dressed in jeans. In a corner, a woman sat alone at a table, and she looked familiar. It took me a few seconds, but I walked over.

"We haven't met," I said, "but my name's Ned Alexander." "Yeah, I know who you are," Barbara Solomon replied. "May I sit down?"

"I hope you're a lousy writer," she said in response to my question. I took this as permission and sat down across the table from her.

"I'm not," I said without apology. "And neither are you. I've read some of your work." She ignored both comments.

"Halloran says you wrote a book, went to Harvard, and worked on a thing called the *Daily Weasel*." What she didn't say, but didn't have to, was "big deal."

"Where did you go to school?" I asked, trying to turn the conversation away from me.

Her green eyes widened and she glared at me.

"Arizona," she said, just waiting for me to say something.

"That's a very good school," I temporized, not knowing a thing about Arizona.

"It's not Harvard, OK, but I learned how to write, and you don't know a damned thing about it."

I wasn't sure if "it" referred to writing or Arizona, but I was quickly finding that this was not a woman to be patronized.

"OK, look," I said trying again, "I want to state from the beginning of our relationship that you're probably a hundred times smarter than I am and a much better writer."

She smiled slightly at this and said, "I am a hundred times smarter than you, and we don't have a relationship."

"Yes, we do," I said. "I'm your buffer."

"What?" She was still irritated but for the first time displayed an interest in something I said.

"Your buffer," I repeated. "Halloran has great respect for you, so he hired me as a compromise that would allow you to do things the way you wanted and still meet what he sees as his professional obligations. I wish somebody thought that much of me. You really don't have any right to be angry at Halloran, or at me." She listened through my little speech, and at its finish seemed to relax a little.

"OK," she said. "Sorry."

"Nothing to be sorry about. I'm just hoping this will lead to something more permanent. Can I buy you another beer?"

"I have beer," she said, picking up a half-full pitcher from a small table beside ours. She filled her glass, then reached over and took my near- empty beer bottle and filled it from the pitcher with what was an incredibly steady hand, directing a small stream into the narrow opening of my empty beer bottle from a good foot above without spilling any. Quite a trick. She returned the empty pitcher to the small table alongside of us where sat an empty glass. I was becoming quite the detective.

She looked at her glass, drank about half, and placed it hard on the table. "Damn, I hate these people."

"What people?" I asked.

"People who think that killing people is a good idea," she said. "They're so stupid." Her green eyes flashed.

"People like Burwick?"

"Yeah, people like Burwick, like Rosenthal. Like all the politicians who hold it out as a solution, and like all the dumb sons of bitches who vote for it." She looked down at her beer glass, drained it, and set it down gently on the table. She looked suddenly tired, the fierceness all but gone.

I've noticed that there are some people who are so intense that they are hard to look at. You don't really see these people—what you see is their intensity, their energy. Trying to describe them is like trying to describe the features of a fire. I realized that Barbara Solomon was like this. It was only now, in this moment of quiet and fatigue, that I could study her features. I stared at her. She was truly beautiful. It was a beauty that can only be achieved when accompanied by intelligence and passion. There was compassion there in her face, but it was a fierce compassion devoid of any pity. Unlike the previous fire, what I now saw was the glow of embers, a soft aura, but one hotter than the flames.

I shook myself from these thoughts. "Rosenthal?" I said, mostly to break the silence.

The flames shot up again and the green eyes blazed. "Yeah, Rosenthal." I had forgotten about Rodney Rosenthal until she mentioned him in her litany. Rosenthal was a professor of sociology at the University of Arizona who, fifteen years earlier, had written a book called *The Last Rage*, about the Redway and Reach crime spree; he and his book were referenced in one of Solomon's articles. From what I gathered, Rosenthal graphically described the crimes and focused on Redway, continually making reference to his extremely high IQ. I would only later read the book. Rosenthal was interviewed in the article and quoted as saying that Redway was the worst kind of manipulator, someone incapable of remorse. He was quoted: "If ever someone deserves to die, it is Eugene Redway, and he indeed deserves to die."

"Rosenthal's a sociologist," I said a bit provocatively, and Barbara responded.

"Yeah, academic dumbshits are the worst." Meeting sociology with sociology, she continued, "Like child abuse and wife beating, some types of ignorance have no social class, or economic distinctions."

"Your articles don't reflect this perspective. You treat all these people evenly in your stories."

"That's my job. I'm trained as a journalist, and I'm paid to report the news. But that's not who I am. Some people may be their jobs, but I'm not one of them. If you work on the crime beat for very long, you inoculate yourself pretty quickly against dumbshits. Halloran said you haven't done much crime reporting."

"I've done some," I said, scaling back my earlier lie. Mercifully, she didn't probe further.

"Want another beer?" she asked. The pitcher was almost empty. She poured the remainder of the pitcher into her glass and downed it in one gulp. "I do," she said, answering her own question, and walked to the bar with the empty pitcher without waiting for my answer. She returned with a full pitcher and an empty glass, filled it, and handed it to me before filling her own. She set the pitcher on the smaller table beside the abandoned glass.

Someone across the barroom waved to her, and she waved back, smiling warmly at a middle-aged guy in gray slacks and a blue blazer who was just sitting down at a table with about seven other men who were all talking loudly. "Who's that?" I asked.

"Rosenthal. All the dumbshits are here," she said. I turned to look again while she held her smile until Rosenthal joined the others in revelry.

"Who are the others?"

"Reporters and minor Justice Department types. The guy in the jeans and denim shirt on the far side is Ray Block, our counterpart for the *Times Review*. He's a real asshole. If you stick around any time at all, you'll get to hate him. He's a smug little bastard with an IQ of about 50." She laughed, her intensity dimming as though fueled by damp wood. "More beer?" she asked, filling her own.

"Last one for me. We still have to write our stories." "You do. Mine's written," she said.

"How can you write it ahead of time. It hasn't happened yet?"

"Sure it has," she said, "this thing's been over for months. All I have to do is wait around for the facts to catch up with my story. If something else happens, I'll change it. But it won't."

"Sounds cynical."

"Well, crime reporting can be a fairly cynical enterprise, and the death penalty is the most cynical of them all." She reached for the pitcher and filled her glass, and I quickly put my hand over mine.

"Why are you so against the death penalty?" I asked, hoping for some facts or statistics that might be useful in my article.

Sparks appeared in the green eyes again. "Because it's a form of collective murder, it's premeditated, it's savage, and it's completely avoidable. So- called rational people sit down and choose to kill."

"Where does Eugene Redway fit into this scheme of bastards?" "Redway's irrelevant," she said simply.

"What?" This was not an answer I had expected.

Barbara smiled at my surprise and said slowly, so that someone even as dimwitted as I would be able to understand, "Redway and all of his kind are irrelevant to this scheme, as you call it." Still speaking slowly, she continued, saying, "I don't know what Redway is, he's been called a monster by Burwick and the others, he's been called a lost soul by Dr. Moran and her followers, and I don't disagree with either of these claims. Eugene Redway is a thoroughly horrible human being and should be kept away from society forever. I can't fathom the things he did. But then I don't try too hard, either. I have convinced myself that I have little in common with him. Whatever Redway is, he has little to do with me, and I don't, under ordinary circumstances, care much about him. But I do care about me, and the people that surround me in my society. I am like them in ways that I'm not like Redway. So, when they commit acts that resemble his, I get worried and I get angry." Solomon's words had been picking up speed, now she slowed down again as if talking to a child. "You see, Redway is the focus of a passion that ends in murder. He is only an object in the same way, I believe, that his victims were irrelevant to the motivation of his acts."

"So, the point is, killing in any form is wrong?"

"No, that's not the point at all. The point is that when Redway kills he presents a unique problem that society needs to contend with. When collective members of a society kill, when they have other options, society injects itself with a poison. The poison is cumulative. It's like a virus that incubates and then reproduces itself."

The conversation had turned a bit academic, and I felt I was being lectured to. "So, no one deserves to die? Is that your position?"

"Oh, no," she said. "Lots of people deserve to die. But killing should be a singular act performed by an individual for personal reasons. Done not out of righteousness but out of human frailty." She paused for just a moment.

"And I'd never come down against human frailty." Her features dissolved into heat, no more damp wood. This was a fire made from diamonds.

These were strange answers, in some ways, intimate answers. Barbara Solomon had opened up a small window and I had been allowed to peek in. I would find that this was a rare occurrence, one that would not soon happen again. "Thanks for the beer and the conversation," I said, getting up to leave. "Time's getting on, and I have a story to write. I'll see you later."

Solomon said nothing. The fire was back to wet wood. Ray Block came toward our table, and Barbara Solomon smiled. But the smile was all smoke.

3

A Hitch in the Get-a-long

I stepped out onto the street, my watch said it was ten o'clock, and the coldness of the night felt good after the closeness of Barbara Solomon and the Giddy-Up. The air smelled sweet with an organic scent I took to be alfalfa. I wondered if Eugene Redway could smell it. I wondered how many corridors the air that transported the smell would have to travel down before it reached him—how many other human beings got to breathe it first. The minutes were counting down.

Halloran had said that I should be at the prison office by ten-thirty for some type of briefing. The streets were quiet as I got into my car and drove the short distance across town to the prison parking lot. What had seemed earlier like a small-town swap meet now seemed like a street market in New Delhi. People were everywhere. Fires burning in portable barbecues, people talking, eating, drinking, placards and banners everywhere. The atmosphere was more like a carnival than a funeral. Unlike earlier, many people laughed and talked loudly. Beer and wine were prominent on many tables.

Parking near the mouth of the entrance, I walked the distance through the crowd. A group of young men and women sang softly to the music of a guitar behind a table ablaze with votive candles, their youth and the light making them look like something out of a Victorian painting. Their handwritten banner read: *When Will We Stop Killing People to Show People That Killing is Wrong?*

I made my way through the crowd slowly. My watch said 10:10, so I was still all right with time. I spied a colorful banner, bright yellow with a black-and-white yin and yang symbol and something next to it that from my distance looked like a map. A meditation sect protesting the death penalty, I thought. As I moved closer, the man standing behind the banner saw my interest. When I came within speaking distance, he asked, "Would you like to sign our petition?"

"What is your petition?"

"It's to stiffen the death penalty," he said in all seriousness.

"What?" I said to one more surprise in an evening of surprises. "How do you stiffen the death penalty?"

"We're the Ying Lon Society," he said, not answering my question directly. "We base our position on ancient Chinese law. It is a code that has stood the test of civilization for thousands of years." He was a handsome man dressed in a dark suit, and I must have stared at him as if I'd opened the door to a Jehovah's Witness from Hell. He saw my consternation but continued. "Look," he said, "we feel the death penalty should be both a punishment and a deterrent. There are many ways to die. The Chinese code prescribed a number of death sentences as punishments for a variety of crimes. We feel, as they did, that the punishment should fit the crime. Capital punishment, as it exists now, is not sufficient to either of its purposes. It really doesn't deter others, and it is most often insufficient punishment. Ying Lon believes it should be augmented. Some of the Chinese deaths took as long as four days. They were public and conducted in an open square for all to see. We feel this system should be introduced into our penal system, with some modern adaptations, of course."

"Oh, of course," I found myself saying like a character in a Samuel Beckett play. "What you're talking about is torture."

"Nonsense. What we're advocating is effective penal reform. My name's Jerry Boyle, I'm the president of the organization," he said, handing me a brochure. "Read what we have to say and get back to us. I'm sure you'll find it interesting."

As I made to leave, I glanced down again at the banner. What I had taken to be a map was in fact a diagram of a human figure sliced apart at various angles into puzzle pieces and covered with patterns of incisions indicated by dotted lines.

I wondered how I could work this into the just-the-facts piece that I was directed to write. *Boy*, I thought, *Halloran's seventy-seven percent are getting gypped with me when they could have Jerry Boyle and the Ying Lon Society*. I stuffed the brochure into my jacket pocket and moved on through the crowd to the office door. A woman in uniform looked at my virgin press pass, checked a list, and directed me to a small conference room. Around twenty chairs were set out looking toward a table and podium at the front of the room. In the back was another table with pitchers of water and plastic glasses. Five people were already there. No one I knew. I poured myself a glass of water and sat down. A crowd of about seven people walked in, and I saw that they were the group from the table back at the Giddy-Up. For some reason, I became interested in their exact number, and I counted them. Yep, exactly seven.

I had read that baboons could count to five. When baboons would rob certain African cornfields, farmers with guns would go out into the fields to scare them away. The baboons would run, and the farmers would make a great show of leaving. One of the farmers, however, would stay back, hiding in the field to shoot the returning baboons when they thought the coast was clear. The ploy was foiled with three, four, and five farmers, because the calculating simians knew there was something amiss. It was only when they upped the ante to six diabolical farmers that the baboons were fooled. Seven. That was a lot better than the baboons, and I was feeling pretty cocky, evolutionarily.

I've always been amazed at my capacity to entertain myself. Here I was waiting to be briefed on the etiquette of viewing a man about to be killed by society, and I was counting groups of spectators and thinking about the mathematical powers of baboons. One recent girlfriend had told me that it was a real talent to be able to set your sights as low as I did. The remark had hurt at the time, but hey, I could sit here and take solace in the fact that I could probably kick ninety-nine percent of all baboon's asses on the Graduate Records Exam.

The baboons were not entirely irrelevant. The book was called *African Genesis* and was written in the early 1960s. It made the point that man was a territorial animal with a number of evolutionary skeletons in his closet. One of the chapters, titled *Cain's Children*, talked about the road to modern humans. The book was important in its time and set the stage for biological controversies still raging at Harvard and elsewhere. I read the book when I was a teenager, and it made quite an impression.

"How you doing?" Ray Block said as he sat down next to me, scaring all my baboons away. "Name's Ray Block, I work for the *Times*."

"Ned Alexander, *Sun*." We shook hands.

"Barbara says you've done a lot of crime reporting back in Boston for an underground newspaper called the *Daily Muskrat*?"

Solomon was right. I already hated this guy. It gave me a good feeling, though, that she was perpetuating my crime legend. My initial impulse was to correct him, saying it was actually Cambridge and the *Daily Weasel*. But I said, rather, "Yeah. That's correct."

"Really?" He said not getting the response he had expected. "The newspaper was really called the *Muskrat?*"

"Yeah. We would say that we specialized in in-depth reporting and fat tales," I answered without smiling.

He knew I was goofing on him but was unsure of how to call me on it without admitting that he had deliberately tried to bait me.

I saved him from his dilemma by asking, "This your first time covering an execution?"

"No, this'll be my third. I covered the Byrn execution, first time they used lethal injection in Arizona, a real botched job. Took em twenty minutes and three tries, while he all that time flopped around like a fish on a line. Made great copy."

"Wow," I said, duly impressed. "When was that?" January '95, he said and I made a mental note of the date. "Must have been awful to watch."

"Yeah. Awful. Look, it was nice to meet you, Ted. See ya later." Then he was gone, off to talk to some people in the back.

I glanced down at my watch, then around the room. It was nearly eleven and the room had filled to about fifteen people. I didn't count them, content to let my earlier victory over the baboons rest.

A middle-aged woman walked to the podium as everyone quickly took a seat. The woman identified herself as the prison public relations officer. As her assistant passed out a press release, Roger Burwick walked in. It was a star's entrance, and he stood in the front and off to the side. He didn't have on the sunglasses, and I was still unsure if he was the man exiting the Giddy- Up, but I was becoming more convinced.

The PR officer introduced herself as Daisy. She said that we would be taken through the main prison building and transported in vans to the execution building, where we would pass through a series of checkpoints and metal detectors. We were to empty our pockets of all metal objects, keys, coins, etc., at the first checkpoint, and we were allowed no electronic devices. There were to be twenty-five people to witness the execution if the governor did not grant a stay. All other appeals, said Daisy, had now been rejected.

In addition to members of the press, the judiciary, and the invited guests, members of the victim's and Redway's families would be attending. Dr. Shirley Moran was Redway's spiritual advisor and would remain with him until the final moments. The list included Redway's sister, and a father and mother of one victim, as well as a sister and brother of two other victims, along with their spouses. There were several names that I did not recognize, but one I did was Jerry Boyle, as an invited guest of the governor's office. Maybe I had a shot at a quote after all. Our groups would be kept separate until everyone gathered in the viewing room.

Daisy moved on at a competent clip. "We ask that silence and decorum is maintained at all times and the dignity of the proceedings be respected." It sounded more like we were going to a graduation ceremony. She continued, "You may ask questions after the execution, but if people choose not to answer, their privacy will be respected." She placed a heavy emphasis on the word *will*. She threatened no contingencies, but as we would be deep in the bowels of a prison, it seemed unnecessary—I would certainly behave myself. She then gave a brief and antiseptic outline of the procedures we were about to witness. "Are there any questions?" she asked us. A member of the Baboon Seven asked if they had any indication that the governor would intervene. "We have no knowledge of any such intervention" was the terse reply.

Fat chance! The embattled Governor Simon was currently being tried on twenty-two felony counts of fraud concerning his business dealings both before and while in office. He would in no way align himself with other criminals. His situation was more the type of reporting I was used to doing, and I had followed the story with interest. It was testimony to apathy, or to a keen sense of irony on the part of Arizona voters, that they chose not to recall their governor. While in the first four years of office, he had filed bankruptcy after transferring most of his assets to his wife, who was worth a reported twenty-five million dollars, defaulted on ten million dollars' worth of personally guaranteed loans, and managed the state as a fiscal conservative. He was reelected, and in his fifth year he was indicted by the federal justice commission. I took great pride in the fact that governor P. Wellington Simon was a fellow Harvard man.

I felt a certain kinship with Simon since, between the two of us, we encompassed all three of Umberto Conway's semi-reputable disciplines. But whatever the governor was or wasn't, he would be no friend of Eugene Redway's this night. Solomon could safely file her story with no amendments. A few more questions came and went, and we were informed it was time to go. Daisy turned on her high heels and we, The Children of Cain, followed her noiselessly from the room.

We all moved through the halls in single file behind the competent Daisy, her high heels the metronome orchestrating our cadence. Burwick strode right behind her in perfect time. I had tried to work my way through the line to get close to him, but I was stalled in the middle of the pack.

It was much like an unfriendly airport, or customs at the Gulag. The person in front of me was the only woman, besides Daisy, in our group. I identified her from the press release as Sandra Warren, an assistant from the prosecutor's office. We were given baskets in which to put our metal items and asked to write our names on a card with a grease pencil. People filed quickly through the metal detector while guards stood on either side. A large man a few people ahead of me undid his belt and removed an enormous buckle.

"Zuni bear fetish," he said, handing it over to the guard. "Got over a half- pound of silver in it. Don't want your machine to have a heart attack." He laughed as he walked through the detector gate. As Sandra walked through, the machine made a sound like a church bell had been dropped down a flight of marble stairs. She jumped, produced a formless noise, and dove back through the entrance of the gate, as if she expected a trap door to open. "Keys," said the humorless guard, extending a large hand. Assistant prosecutor Warren fumbled around in her purse for what seemed to be a long time before producing a fob with a handful of keys. "Name?" asked the guard.

"What? My name?" Warren asked.

"The name on your basket, so I can put the keys in it," said the guard, forced into a complete sentence.

"Oh. Sandra Warren." "Step through again."

Yeah, Sandra, how do you like it on the other side? I thought as I moved through the metal detector, keeping my eyes on the floor and looking closely for any subtle signs of a trapdoor.

We moved without further incident through the other two checkpoints, out of the building, and into an open yard, where two gray vans waited. For a second time, I was thankful for the cold night air. Half the group got on the first, breaking after Sandra Warren. I was the first one to get on the second. The vans drove a short distance through two heavily guarded gates and stopped in front of a small block building. Being the first in, I was the last out. Two other vans were parked alongside ours. Our group stood around the front of the entrance, unsure of what to do next. I put my hands in my coat pockets against the cold. Discovering my tie, for some reason, I decided to put it on. Respecting the dignity of the proceedings, perhaps. My hands shook, and I told myself it was the cold. My stomach felt sick, and I told myself it was the beer. The creepy feeling from earlier in the night returned. Daisy now moved to the back of our group and along with three guards shepherded us through a door. Just off to the left, people filed in from the top of the room, ushered by more guards. The room had five rows of five seats and looked like an art theater. It sloped gently upward, providing each observer with an unobstructed view. A large rectangular curtain was at the front. By the time I made my entrance, there were only two seats left, both in the front row next to each other on the aisle. I sat down in one next to a small, frail bespectacled woman who looked to be in her late sixties. She looked directly at me and smiled. Extending a delicate hand, she said in a remarkably robust voice, "I'm Emma Johnson, Gene's sister." *Redway's sister!*

I took her hand, and I thought it was shaking, at least I hoped it was hers, but I couldn't guarantee it wasn't mine. "I am Ned Alexander. I am pleased to meet you."

"Why are you here?" she asked.

"I am a reporter for the Tucson *Sun*." I've noticed that when I'm in awkward social situations that I have a tendency not to use contractions, using *I ams* and *do nots* where I never would otherwise.

"Oh." She looked at me and smiled again. "You have nice eyes," she said.

The seat next to mine moved, and I looked over to find Dr. Shirley Moran. She smiled at me and said hello, then reached across me to grab Emma's hand in both of hers.

"How's Gene?" asked Emma.

"He's doing fine, Emma. He's prepared." The dim light glistened in their eyes.

Both women now had rested their hands in my lap.

"Would you like me to move so you can sit together?" I asked.

Emma sat up. "Oh no, you stay where you are. I've forgotten my manners. Reverend Shirley Moran, this is Ned Alexander, he's a reporter for the Tucson *Sun*. Shirley is Gene's spiritual advisor." I marveled at Emma Johnson. Perhaps a good definition of grace is remembering your manners a few minutes before your brother is about to be killed in front of your eyes.

"Nice to meet you," said Dr. Moran politely. Behind us, I heard the sound of quiet weeping, and a low male voice. More guards had filed in and now stood at the back, where the projector should have been.

With the curtain open, it looked even more like an art theater. The movie had started and everyone's attention was fastened to the screen. Redway stood erect but bound to a board secured at anatomical intervals from the forehead down to the ankles. His arms were slanted downward at about a forty-five- degree angle to his perpendicular body. Had they been at right angles, he would have looked Christ-like. Instead, he looked like an astronaut strapped to an incredibly small rocket ship. The astronaut image did not end with his configuration but was enhanced by a plastic tube inserted into his arm. The tube draped across his right shoulder. The plastic line that would deliver his final sentence formed a catalytic arch almost touching the floor at its apex or nadir, I can never remember which. From there, it curved gently upward until it was joined to three more plastic lines that diverged from a group of cylinders, holding different-colored liquids, mounted on the wall. Around these a man in a white coat fussed.

He turned to face the audience. A large name plate on his breast identified him as Dr. ArnolD Flowers, M.D. Dr. and M.D. seemed to me a little redundant, but along with the lab coat and the stethoscope around his neck, the bell secured in his pocket, the state wanted to be clear that this was a medical procedure done by a professional. I wondered how he had bamboozled his Hippocratic oath.

The cylinders set side by side on the wall, looked not unlike an understocked bar with inverted liquor bottles waiting to dispense premeasured amounts of alcohol on demand, and Dr. Arnold Flowers, M.D., was the bartender. Despite myself, I wrote the dialogue:

"Gene what's your poison?"

"Well, Arnie, make mine tequila. Naw, on second thought, I'll go out on Jack Daniels."

"OK. Jack Daniels it is. One lethal dose of Mr. J.D., comin up."

The absurd little play was ended with a sudden pain in my hand. I looked over at Emma, who was squeezing my left hand with both of hers. I felt ashamed at my mental wanderings. I put my other hand on hers as she continued to squeeze. Her gaze had not left the window. Nice eyes and all, I noticed I was quickly losing my journalistic distance. The dimmed lights in the viewing room now went up, and there was the cackle of audio being turned on.

"Mr. Redway, is there anything you would like to say?" came a voice from speakers somewhere in the ceiling.

Redway scanned the room from left to right as if reading a book, slowly looking at everyone. He stopped for longer periods at certain faces. Among them were the family of the victims. I wondered if his pause was because he recognized them or because he didn't. It probably only took two minutes, but it seemed like hours. His eyes scanned the first row and settled on his sister, who was still holding my hands. Then to me, looking right at me wondering who the hell this guy was holding hands with his sister. I was afraid he'd ask. He looked down and said, "I'm sorry. I'd take it back if I could." His gaze shifted to Moran. "Thank you." Then he looked long at his sister. "I love you," he said. He then turned to the guard to signal that he was through. The audio cackled off.

Things happened quickly. As Dr. Flowers attended to his bar, two guards attended to Redway's rocket and adjusted it to an angle midway between vertical and horizontal. An eyeless hood was placed over his head. As Dr. Flowers stepped over the drooping line, he caught his foot on it and nearly lost his balance. He coiled it three times to take up the slack. He checked the connection between the single line and the three connecting lines and nodded. He then set the coiled line on the top of the board near Redway's head—the nose cone of the rocket. He then turned back to his console of cylinders.

As he turned, the board to which Redway was strapped slipped slightly, and the three coils of plastic line slid off the top and settled around the neck of Redway's hooded head. The astronaut's line now looked like a hangman's noose. The line was almost horizontal and contained little slack. A few of the viewers gasped. His back to Redway, Dr. Arnold Flowers, M.D., started the pistons of the death machine that slowly forced the various chemicals into the line that terminated in Eugene Redway's bloodstream. Almost as the pistons began to move, the board slipped again, this time into a full horizontal position. The already taut line had no place to go and was ripped from its connection with the other three. Dr. Flowers whirled around to stare at Redway's prone form, whirled back again to look at the three lines that now dripped poison on to the linoleum floor of his operating room. With cat-like quickness, Arnold Flowers dove at his machine and the pistons halted.

The dignity of the proceedings was in shambles. Gasps, cries, and *oh my Gods* were everywhere. Emma uttered a cry but altered neither her gaze on her brother nor the force on my hand, which was now numb from lack of circulation. The surreal quality of the drama was heightened by the lack of sound as it unfolded silently before us. One of the guards mouthed an unmistakable "shit." Redway wriggled what little he could, and Emma began sob in short convulsions. In a period of sudden quiet from the rear of the theater came a stout chuckle. "Whoa, that's what I call a hitch in the get-a-long!"

Still holding tight to Emma, as if I had a choice, I turned to stare at the person who spoke. It was the man who had taken off his belt buckle at the first checkpoint. Dressed in a white cowboy shirt with pearl snap buttons, his rubicund face and small eyes glistened in a good-nature way out of place. He looked, to my eastern prejudice, like the perfect good old boy.

The decorum shattered, I ventured a question to Dr. Moran. "Who's that?"

"Jack Stroud," she said between tight lips. "The governor's ombudsman to the Justice Commission. Imagine that."

The rocket board was quickly righted and positioned by the two guards, and the connections once again secured by Flowers. The pistons began their movement toward the floor. The lines filled and merged with the contents of Eugene Redway's bloodstream. The unsecured parts of him, which were free to move, fluttered briefly, then lay still. Dr. Flowers pulled his stethoscope from his pocket and listened at his heart, then at his wrist. I wondered if stethoscopes lasted longer if they have nothing to hear. Moving away from Redway, he pulled himself up to his full height, looked at the guard, and shook his head in a pantomime that no one could misinterpret. The curtain closed.

It was dead silent for a few moments, then people began to shuffle their feet, sniffle, blow their noses, and disengage from their seats. Daisy suddenly appeared, barring the exit, and directed us to return to the vans.

"Please return in the same van you came in" was her instruction, as if you could tell one from the other. Emma still held my hand, but the strength was gone. I knew I should be asking journalistic questions but said rather, "Are you OK?" Pretty stupid question. Still gracious, she ignored it.

"I'm twelve years older than Gene. When he was four, I was sixteen. He was such a cute little boy; we used to play soldiers on the front porch. He had these lead soldiers, American Revolution. The British soldiers were all painted red with black hats and the Americans were blue. We would line them all up against each other. I would always insist on being the Americans. Gene didn't care. Then we'd start making shooting noises and knock the soldiers over with our fingers. The Americans would always win, of course. When all the British soldiers were knocked over, Gene would smile at me and say, "Soldiers all gone. All gone, Emmy." She looked up at me and smiled, her eyes sad but clear.

"Where was this?" I asked. Another reporter's pearl.

"Oregon. Portland."

I was saved from asking more inane questions by Dr. Moran, who moved gently between us and, taking Emma's hands, said, "It's time for us to go."

4

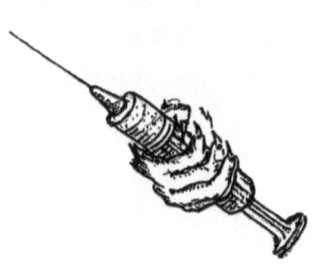

Hand in Glove

ll gone, Emmy. And then Emma was really all gone, and I was alone. The trip back was a reversal of the forward procedures. We collected our various items at the first checkpoint. Jack Stroud strapped on his ingot of Zuni silver. We were expertly ushered out by Daisy, who vanished when the last visitor was escorted through the door. The room had now filled with members of the press not fortunate enough to be part of the elite twenty-five.

Burwick, dark glasses in place, was back in his element, quelling the flood of questions with a waving of his hands that, with a bow, would have been a salutation. He was all smiles as the crowd quieted to let him speak. "Ladies and gentlemen, I can just say that Eugene Redway was pronounced dead at twelve-fifteen this morning. Just let me say that after seventeen long years, justice has, at last, been fulfilled."

"We heard that there was a problem with the procedure. That it had to be started over," said one reporter.

"No. That's not true" was Burwick's quick response. "There was a brief interruption of the procedure that was corrected within seconds," he said glibly, dismissing the hitch in the get-a-long. I thought of the diving Dr. Flowers. Maybe it had been only a matter of seconds.

"What actually happened?" came one question.

"Did he suffer as a result of this?" came another. Burwick stiffened at this one.

"No. Not at all. This is a case, if ever there was one, where the punishment fit the crime." He hesitated for an instant and added, "Fit the crime, hand in glove."

More questions. One victim's sister said that it was the end of a long agony and that she felt some measure of justice had been done, but it could not ever be enough to fill the void. I thought of the remedy offered by the Ying Lon Society. The mother of another victim just sobbed. There was no sign of Shirley Moran or Emma. Jack Stroud was asked if the governor was pleased with the execution. "Well, you didn't see no stay of execution, now did you?" was his rhetorical and jocular response.

I had all I needed, and I moved into the parking lot. Those keeping vigil were still there for the most part, and I moved quietly between them toward my car. At the entrance to the parking lot was a new table that displayed T-shirts. On the front of the shirt was a picture of a large syringe with three drops dripping from the needle. Underneath the picture sported the co- opted slogan: For All You Do This shoT's For You. Manning the table was the star-crossed pool player and prison guard, Rudy. I walked over.

"Seen you earlier tonight at the bar," he said in recognition. "Yeah. These yours?" I asked.

"Uh-huh. Made it up myself, you know from the beer commercial. For all you do, this Beer's for you."

"Yeah, I got it. "

"Been selling like hotcakes, made over three hundred dollars so far. Want one? They're only ten bucks."

I did the math, making any baboon proud—thirty souls kindred with Rudy. "Maybe later," I said. "They let you sell these as a prison guard?"

"Yeah, no problem, I just can't wear my uniform."

I wanted to ask if he ever won a pool game, but by then he was attending to two teenagers waving ten-dollar bills in his face. Unlocking my car, I saw a dark convertible BMW approach, and behind the wheel was Roger Burwick and what I took to be a woman in the passenger seat. Then in a flash of bright light it was gone, just leaving an impression.

My friend and fellow Harvard screw-up Mad Michael had a theory about BMWs. The theory rested on the tiny grille that he said was made to resemble Hitler's mustache. According to Michael, BMWs were Hitler icons representing devotion paid to him and Nazi ideals by a group of wealthy and influential international capitalists, just biding their time for another try. I thought the theory amusing and relayed it to Conway as a joke one day. He thought seriously for a moment and said it sounded plausible to him. A couple of weeks later, after some reflection and discussions, he said that Mike's theory was most likely correct. After the events of the evening, this recollection gave me the shivers.

It was now just quarter to one and Halloran wanted my story by three, an hour to drive and an hour to write it. I had made few notes, and as I drove, I mentally organized the major points of my story. At Tom Mix, I stopped to pee. In the moonless sky the stars were spectacular. I returned to the car, started the engine for the heater, and under the gaze of Tony the wonder horse and a trillion stars, on the very spot where Tom Mix's spirit left his body, I wrote the story of how Eugene Redway's spirit left his.

Halloran had said one thousand to fifteen hundred words, and the story clocked in at thirteen-eighty, and I was pretty well satisfied. I gave a brief account of Redway's exploits, taken mostly from Solomon's work, and recounted those present. Told who they represented, and what they said. I included a small version of Emma's toy soldier story and reported Redway's last words. I used self-control with Jack Stroud's hitch in the get-a-long, and used his words to describe a malfunction of the restraining board that loosened a line that had to be repaired. I ended the piece with Burwick's quote about the punishment fitting the crime like a hand in glove.

Take it all around, and I was happy with my work. Halloran wanted competent reporting and solid writing, and that's what I tried to give him. If this really was the last job in town, I wanted to keep it for a while. I titled my story *Hand in Glove*. It didn't matter, though, since reporters usually don't write their own headlines. This is done by headline writers, and my title was merely a bookmarker for me. I pulled into the *Sun* at a quarter to three, looking forward to that morning's beer.

Halloran was at his desk drinking coffee. "Right on time, Harvard," he said as I handed him my disc. He took it, stood up, and motioned me to stay seated. "Coffee's in the corner," he said as he left. I sat drinking coffee until he returned, waving a hard copy at me.

"Not bad, Harvard, not bad. I took out the part about the Ying Lon Society; it's a side issue here. But good work. I've never heard of them. It will make a good feature story. Have you seen Solomon? She's supposed to be here."

"No. Not since earlier last evening," I said. "Didn't she turn in her story?"

"Yes, she faxed it in, but she's supposed to be here, and it's not like her to be late." By then it was four-thirty.

Halloran left again and I sipped more coffee. It had been a long day, and I was looking forward to a collegial beer and a long sleep, waking up to my first Arizona byline. I wondered what time Sam's opened. "Any sign of Solomon?" he asked on his return. I shook my head. "Son of a bitch," he said. "We have some kind of situation at El Palomino, looks like a murder. Son of a bitch," he said again more quietly. He thought for a moment, then said, "Well, Ned Alexander, ironman of crime reporters, you're on again."

El Palomino, I learned, was a golf club and resort to the north of Tucson. Flashing my no longer virgin press pass, I was directed across the lobby and out past an enormous free-form swimming pool to a set of bungalows on the edge of the golf course. Light was just beginning to show over the mountains to the east. One of the bungalow doors was open, and two hotel security guards were standing around. I showed my pass to the guard who approached me.

"You *Sun* guys are fast. You're the first one here, even beat the police. You're in luck, too, this one's a real doozy." I would later learn that I owed my temporal advantage to a network of "little people" that Solomon cultivated in a variety of places. A laundry boy who had noticed the open bungalow door had called in the story for Solomon, and in her absence, it had defaulted to me.

"What happened?" I asked.

"Have a look. It's like nothing you've ever seen before," said the young security guard.

Actually, it was just like something I had seen before. But that didn't prepare me. In a setting of elegance, sitting on a Queen Anne chair, was a dead Roger Burwick, naked except for his boxer shorts. He sat with his back to the curtained picture window that made up the south wall of the bungalow. In his left arm, just below the elbow, was an intravenous line that traveled up his arm, across his chest, looped three times around his neck, and joined to three others connected to three large plastic cylinders pinned to the curtain at his shoulder. The plungers were pushed to the bottom of the cylinders and bubbles could be seen, indicating that there had been fluid in the plastic lines. On his right hand, the one with the line, he wore a smooth, brown leather glove.

There seemed to be no sign of a struggle, an overnight bag lay open on a rack, and a clothes bag hung on the open closet door. A glass half full of amber liquid rested on the coffee table, at Burwick's flaccid right elbow. "What the hell is this supposed to mean?" said an ununiformed man. He read from a small white card. "Act in conformity with that maxim, and that maxim only, which you can at the same time will to be universal law." When he finished, he looked accusingly around the room. It seemed the police had arrived.

"I know that," I heard myself say out loud, forgetting that reporters should neither be seen nor heard if possible.

"Who are you?" the reader asked. And not waiting for an answer, he ventured another question: "How'd you get in here?"

"It's Kant," I said, ignoring his questions. "What?"

"Immanuel Kant. The philosopher, it's his first moral axiom. It means that no one should commit an act unless they are willing to be treated in a similar fashion." The quote was right out of my childhood. One of my parents' closest friends was the radical theologian and social activist Reinhold Niebuhr. It was Niebuhr who introduced my father to my mother, who was one of his students at the time. Uncle Rein was a frequent guest in our house. Kant's Universal Moral Axiom was one of his favorite principles, and it was fed to me like vitamins from an early age.

"Who are you?" he asked again. This time, he waited for an answer, which I supplied. "Well, Mr. Alexander, if you know something about this, you had best tell it," he said.

By now, other reporters had begun to filter in. Lieutenant Hickey, for that was his name, turned to a uniformed officer. "Let's clear this place until we're finished."

For a guy with little close-up experience with death, I'd had a banner day. Two human beings transformed from life to death before me within a five-hour stretch. Three people, if I counted the ghost of Tom Mix. It had been a long day, but I was wide awake now. I left the bungalow and walked back through the lobby and out into the parking lot. After a few minutes of searching, I found a black convertible BMW, looking a lot less like Hitler in the soft light of dawn. It was locked, of course, but the rear window of the convertible top was not fully zipped. I was probably tampering with evidence just by walking around it. I looked through the windows. His sunglasses rested on the passenger's seat. I used a pen to further unzip the window and reached through the back and unlocked the passenger side door, again using my pen. I pulled my jacket over my hand and opened the door.

Burwick's dress and manner may have been impeccable, but his car was a pigsty of paper cups, fast-food wrappers, newspapers, and other stuff. I poked through the garbage but found nothing interesting, my heart beating like a jackhammer all the while. It was getting steadily lighter, and I needed to get out of there. I zipped up the rear window and pushed the button of the glove box, expecting it to be locked. It flew open with a force that made me jump. In the box was a roll of white computer paper. Despite a heart that felt like a fist pounding me on my back from the inside, I unrolled the paper and read:

> *The need for retribution through death seems to be a universal that was again exercised by the state of Arizona when convicted killer Eugene Redway was put to death yesterday at midnight.*

I read on for a few paragraphs, then skipped to the end. The article was signed Barbara Solomon, Tucson *Daily Sun*, Florence, Arizona, twelve- twenty-five a.m. The word *universal* made me shiver when I compared it with Kant's axiom. I folded up the article and stuck it in my inside jacket pocket, closed the glove box, and locked the door. The car looked to me just as it had before. With knees so weak I thought I would slump to the pavement, I moved away from the car as quickly as I dared. I took an indirect route back to the lobby and returned to the bungalow.

A small crowd had gathered, and the area around the door to the bungalow had been cordoned off. "Just get here, Sport?" said the ubiquitous Ray Block, at my elbow.

"Yeah," I said. "What's up?"

"You remember Burwick, the assistant attorney general?" He paused for drama.

"Yeah," I said. As if I would have forgotten after three hours. "He's in there, dead."

"Wow," I said.

"You'll get the hang of it, kid," he said. And then he was gone to talk to someone else.

After lots of milling around and shifting their feet, the reporters became attentive as Lieutenant Hickey emerged to give a brief statement. He said that the dead man had been identified as assistant district attorney Roger Burwick, who was the apparent victim of murder by person or persons unknown. He said the exact means of death was still to be determined, but initially it looked like poison. Somebody asked if there had been a note.

"No comment" was Hickey's response. He looked right at me when he said this, as if daring me to say something. No need. Despite a barrage of questions, this was all he would say.

Walking through the parking lot back to my car, I glanced over to the BMW to see a group of plain-clothed and uniformed personnel meticulously inspecting it. My breathing became shallow as my heart began to pound. My knees weakened as I thought of the implications of what I had done. Despite myself, I touched the paper in my coat pocket to make sure it was still there as Ray Block moved alongside me.

"They say there was a note with some philosophy quote on it. Did you hear anything by any chance?" The question again was intended to be mostly rhetorical, but I surprised him. Happy for a diversion from my runaway metabolism, I said, "Yeah, I heard two officers talking off to the side. They said there was a note that used a quote from Hegel's *Philosophy of Right.*"

"Who?" he said.

"Hegel. He was a German philosopher that had a big influence on Marx." I wanted to say "Karl, not Groucho," but I resisted. "He felt that the synthesis of power was not fixed but determined by society and should be used to achieve what was right."

"Huh, guess they teach you that old stuff at Harvard." "Yeah," I said. "They're real sticklers for that old stuff." "Well, thanks, Ted. That's your real name, isn't it? Ted?"

"Yeah, that's right. My father named me after Ted Williams. My full name is Ted Williams Alexander. He didn't even bother with Theodore, just went straight for Ted."

"Yeah, well," he said.

Having regained my biological homeostasis, I left him looking at his newly written notes to sort out what Frederick Hegel and Roger Burwick had in common.

Back at the *Sun*, I reported to Halloran and told him that I thought I could write a hell of a story, being the only reporter to have seen Burwick and the interior of the bungalow.

"Do it," I was told.

I sat down at the child's desk, having been assigned no other, and wrote the story. My chief pleasure as a journalist is that I write fast and easily. Having been exposed to the written word since the womb and read to incessantly until I could take over for myself, I have little trouble putting events into an understandable written order. It doesn't mean I always do it, just that I can when I want to. And I did it then.

I told the story of Burwick beginning with his statements about Redway being a poor case for the opponents of capital punishment. I contrasted his position to Shirley Moran's, relying heavily on Solomon's earlier pieces. I described the scene outside the prison, juxtaposing Jerry Boyle, the Ying Lon Society, and Rudy and his T-shirt booth, to the candlelight, *Jesus is Love* vigil keepers. I described the apparatus used to kill Redway, the hitch in the get-a-long and the three loops around his neck. I reported the hand-in-glove statement and went on to describe Burwick's murder as a macabre reflection of the evening's earlier events, and of the bizarre manifestation of Burwick's fateful simile. I told of the note left at the scene, and quoted Kant's Universal Axiom and worked hard to limit innuendo. Finally, I reported that Burwick had been observed leaving the prison at about twelve-thirty that morning with an unidentified passenger of unspecified gender.

The whole story took me little more than an hour. It was a bit prosy in places, but take it all around, I liked it, and I was confident that no one else could match the details. It was too late for the morning edition, but I submitted it to Halloran for his review. As I awaited his judgment, I read the morning paper. My story was on the front page and carried the byline Ned Alexander, *Sun* Staff Reporter. My elation gave way to surprise as I read the headline. *Hand in Glove: Redway's Execution Hailed as Fitting Punishment.* Next to my story was Solomon's. I took the newspaper into the bathroom, shut the stall door, and pulled my purloined copy from my coat. The article in the newspaper read almost word for word with what I'd found, editorial changes probably counting for the slim difference. Solomon's headline read: *The Need to Kill—An Unfortunate Universal.* I winced at the word *universal.* Between the hand in glove and the image of universality, our headlines foreshadowed pending murder. I soon found out that a new headline writer had been assigned to both our articles, and the *Sun* had not yet time to kill his lyrical sense. His name was Eric Lee, and I would come to like him.

Halloran returned with my story. "Good work," he said again. "I'll get it online. Anyone else have this stuff?"

"I don't think so," I said. Then I briefly recounted the circumstances. He picked up the paper on my desk.

"Christ," he said. "Who wrote these headlines? Looks like we've got a serial on our hands." He had no idea. Still forgetting nothing, he said, "Come on, Ned, let's get that beer before it's happy hour."

5

.067

With half a pitcher of beer poured on top of thirty waking hours, I slept like a dead man and awoke twelve hours later to darkness. It was early evening, and I went out and bought the afternoon *Times Review*. A small article on the front page told how Assistant Attorney General Roger Burwick was found dead under mysterious circumstances. It reported Burwick's statement to the press and that after leaving the prison he had not been seen again until he checked into the El Palomino. Police were not commenting on the cause of death until the results of the autopsy were complete, but Burwick was thought to have been poisoned. It was also reported that a note had been found with the body, the substance of which was a quotation from the German philosopher Frederick Hegel from his *Philosophy of Right*. Ray Block had used a philosophy dictionary and presented a brief biographical sketch of Hegel and a synopsis of his *Philosophy of Right*, presented the Hegelian Triad of Thesis, Antithesis, and Synthesis. He then speculated fuzzily what it might have to do with the murder.

I felt a twinge of guilt at my deception, but as Ted Williams Alexander, I chuckled. In honor of the Florentine skateboarder Jeremiah, I grabbed a hamburger at Burger King. Then went to the *Sun* to see if I still had a job or if I'd dreamt the whole thing up.

"Hello, Mr. Alexander," said the receptionist. "You have a message in your box." I was directed to my "box" and read: "If you get here before me, Patty will show you your desk. Be here by seven a.m. tomorrow. Have you seen Solomon?" The note was signed Mike at one-thirty p.m. Patty, it turned out, was the receptionist, but she didn't know anything about a desk, so she told me to take any empty one. Each desk was partitioned off into a little cubicle. Several people bustled in their cells, but Solomon wasn't one of them, and I knew no one else. I found an empty desk, played around with the word processor a little while, explored the electronic archives, and when no one showed up, I went home for more sleep. The last job in town, it seemed, was real.

I woke up early, and at five-thirty I bought the morning paper at a convenience store. My article led on the front page carrying the headline *Assistant Attorney General Found Dead in Unusual Circumstances*. I was pleased to see the editors had left it almost entirely intact. I ate breakfast, drank more coffee than usual, read the article and byline another three or four times, and was installed in my cubicle looking reporterly when Halloran, true to his word, walked in at exactly seven.

"Well, Harvard, shit has hit the proverbial fan," he said, smiling. I waited. "Ray Block just called and he's mad as hell. Thinks you set him up. That true?"

"Not precisely," I said. "More accurately it was Ted Williams," and I relayed the story.

"Good job," he said, laughing. "But watch your back from now on. Block's a little bastard. The other call is a bit more serious; it's from Lieutenant Hickey. He wants you in his office immediately. Says he's contemplating charges for withholding evidence. He's bluffing, but he's also mad as hell. Best get down there and smooth his ruffled feathers and see what information you can squeeze out of him while you're there."

"Still no Solomon?" I asked. He shook his head.

As I left, I met Solomon at the entrance. She appeared tired, her hair looked like she slept on it wrong, her clothes were clean but didn't seem to hang on her quite right. "You OK?" I asked. "You look terrible."

"Thank you," she said as she breezed by me.

As the door closed behind me, I could hear Halloran bellowing, "Where the hell have you been?"

Hickey was with two other plain-clothed officers when I walked into his office. Immediately turning red, he dismissed the two men, then took hold of the newspaper and punched what I took to be my article. "What is this?"

"What do you mean?" I said in a flash of rhetorical wizardry. "Where did you get this information?"

"Which information?"

"The information in your article, you idiot. Sit down!" he said, turning a deeper red and hitting the newspaper again. "And why have you been concealing information from me?"

"I've kept nothing from you. If you remember, I told you at the scene what the quote meant, and you responded by throwing me out."

Paying no attention to my defense, he said, "Where did you get the information about a second person leaving the prison with Burwick?" For a second, I debated saying that the information was confidential, but I decided against it, figuring that with my intellect I could only handle so much deception without getting it mixed up, so I would

63

tell the truth when there seemed no clear advantage in lying.

"I was the one who observed them leaving," I said finally. "Was it a man or woman?"

"I don't know," I lied. "It was just a quick impression, and then his headlights blinded me." That part was truthful.

"Well, what was your best impression, man or woman?" he pushed. "I really couldn't say."

"How do you know it wasn't a big German shepherd, then?"

"I didn't get the impression that it was a German shepherd. I got the impression it was a person. I don't know what else to tell you."

Dropping the topic, he said. "What do you think the note means?" Given a serious topic, I took it. "I think it was somebody who has studied some philosophy. It's rather obscure stuff. Not the kind of thing given to *Bartlett's Quotations*." Hickey nodded. "Go on."

"The irony is pretty clear. Here Burwick comes on as a champion of capital punishment, saying the punishment fit the crime hand in glove, and not three hours later, he's executed in what looks to be a similar, albeit do-it-yourself fashion, with his hand in a glove. By the way, do you know the cause of death?"

Ignoring my question, he said, "What do you think Burwick's crime was?"

"Smugness maybe?" I said incautiously.

Hickey jerked to life, suddenly interested. "Who do you know that kills people for smugness?"

"I don't know anyone who kills people. At least I didn't before last tonight." He gave this a quick thought but let it pass, grasping my meaning. "Why did Ray Block think the quote was from Hegel's Philosophy of Right?" he asked.

"I gave him the information, and he didn't corroborate his sources." "Why did you do that?"

"I don't like him much."

"Yeah, he's a prissy little bastard, ain't he? Watch your back from now on." Hickey looked up, but he didn't smile. "Hope you confine your obfuscating of information to reporters. I expect any information pertinent to my investigation to come to me directly. Do you understand me?" He continued without time for a response. "If you find out that Burwick's passenger was a German shepherd, I'll expect a call. If I read about it in the newspaper, I'll haul you in, Mr. Alexander." I could tell by his manner that the interview was over.

"On what charge?" I asked, getting up to go. "Animal slander," he said without looking up.

Despite our relationship, I liked him. It seemed with Lieutenant Hickey, I would only have to watch my front.

On my return to the *Sun*, I received a call. "Ned? This is Kim. You know, from the bar," she said to jog my memory. The pool game seemed a long time ago. "You gave me a hundred dollars for the gloves Redway made. You remember?"

"Yes," I said, wondering how I could have forgotten.

"Well, they're gone. When I came into the store, they were just gone and there was no record of their sale. Strange ..." She trailed off. "I'll send you your money back, of course. I'm terribly sorry."

"That's OK. Look, just hold on to it and see what you can find out, maybe they were misplaced and they'll show up," I said without much hope. "Kim, I'll be in touch in a day or two. Don't worry about the money yet, just call if anything turns up." I thought for a moment then said, "Do you think you could recognize the gloves again if you saw them outside the store?"

"Sure," she said. "They're made of deer skin, and the leather has these little wrinkles all through it, not like anything I've seen. Why?"

"Thanks Kim, I'll be in touch," I said and hung up.

I thought another minute. Then I dialed Lieutenant Hickey. He wasn't in, or at least wasn't taking calls, but I left a message with his secretary for him to get back to me. I reasoned that if the glove found on Burwick was in fact Redway's, it was key information. The image of Redway's gloved hand reaching out from the grave to his executioner held a good deal of drama, and was a hell of a story in itself. And the only way I could see to establish this fact was to put Hickey in touch with Kim. It also put me directly back into the investigation, but I felt that it could do little harm and was worth the risk. As I was going over the possible implications of my actions, Halloran called me to his office.

Halloran sat with his feet up on his desk, Solomon across from him. He motioned me into the empty chair next to her. "You'll work as a team on this one," he said.

Solomon sat up straighter. "I don't work as a team," she said sullenly. "You do on this one," Halloran said simply as he looked straight at her.

Obviously, she knew him well enough to leave it alone. He continued. "I want background on Burwick and his dealings, and I want an interview with his wife if possible. Barbara, you'll take the lead on that, but I want Alexander along. Check law school buddies, colleagues at the attorney general's office. You'll report to me this evening. Check on the results of the autopsy. Now go. And Solomon, you *will* work as a team." We left without further word.

"What's next, boss?" I said to Solomon cheerfully.

Barbara looked as if she'd bitten into a rotten apple and was looking for a place to spit. After a moment, she swallowed hard, what I guessed was her pride, and resolved herself for what was to be in her estimation a bitter meal. "I'll get the interview with Burwick's wife, you call the coroner and get what you can. We'll meet back here."

"OK," I said. "But I think Halloran wanted me to be in on the interview with the wife."

More rotten apple: "Look, working as a team doesn't mean we function as Siamese twins."

"I still need to be at the interview," I said.

Swallowing hard again, she said, "OK, just call the coroner."

"Right. Anything else I can do?"

"Stop looking so happy."

The results of the autopsy were in. Burwick died from a combination of chemicals similar, though not identical, to those that killed Redway, the cause of death being, in the end, heart failure. Also found in the analysis of the chemicals were trace amounts of dirt and sand. In addition to traces of alcohol was the presence of a powerful sleeping medication. I asked where the dirt and sand had come from. The coroner said it seemed to have come from the cylinders themselves. I asked him further if he could tell if Burwick was unconscious from the sleeping medicine before his death. The coroner said simply that it would be impossible for it to be the other way around, now wouldn't it? As I was feeling like an idiot, Lieutenant Hickey came on the line.

"What's up? You find the German shepherd?"

I told him of the gloves and Kim. He was interested and asked, as I had expected, how I came to know about them, and why I would want a pair of hundred-dollar gloves made by a murderer. I answered truthfully and as best as I could. The part about why I wanted them sounded pretty lame, even to me. I didn't really know why I wanted them, and I said so.

Then it was my turn. "Look, lieutenant, all I'd ask is that you let me know what the result of Kim's identification is before anyone else."

"I don't make deals, certainly not with reporters," he said.

"I'm not asking for a deal, only a little mutual consideration. Do you ever engage in consideration?" Not waiting for his reply, I hung up the receiver feeling pretty well satisfied. If the lead proved to be worth anything, Hickey might ruminate on the advantages of consideration.

I met Solomon at the front desk. She said she'd had no luck

getting in touch with Burwick's wife, but two of his colleagues at the attorney general's office had agreed to see her. I could see no harm in her pursuing those interviews on her own.

"OK, I'll follow-up with some other things," I said.

She paused, then asked, "Did you talk to Hickey today?" "Yeah," I said. "Twice. Why?"

"Did he say anything about my ... our articles?"

"He questioned me on the second person in Burwick's car and tried to get me to say whether it was a man or woman."

"What did you tell him?" "That I couldn't tell." "Nothing about my article?"

"What about your article?" I probed.

"Anything. Oh, never mind," she said. And with her usual irritation having come back, she turned and left.

There were two people I wanted to follow up on. And I was glad to be alone. I pulled the pamphlet on the Ying Lon Society from my pocket and dialed the number. After a number of rings, I got an answering machine that began cheerily — "Hello, fellow social reformer." I left a message for Jerry Boyle. Figuring the society was probably only an answering machine in his house, I also left my home phone number. I had better luck with the second call. After I'd been electronically shuffled around the governor's office, a jovial Jack Stroud came on the line. I identified myself from two nights earlier.

"Yeah. You was the guy hangin on to Redway's sister. Interesting article you wrote. Yeah, interesting. Ain't this a hell of thing? Here the guy gives that great speech, and right-on he was, too, and then winds up dead damn near the same way. Hell of a thing. Can't remember anything like it. What do you make of it, Mr. Alexander?" His manner was amiable, even friendly, but his last question had an edge on it. It seemed he used my name too easily. I was sure people underestimated Jack Stroud, the way flies underestimated the length and speed of a frog's tongue. Jack Stroud made his living with his tongue, of that I was sure, and I wasn't about to underestimate its range.

"Well, actually, that's why I was calling you. I really don't know what to make of it."

"Well, you know, son," he started, and I was thinking, *son, I'm probably only a good five years younger than you.* "You got me in a bit of trouble over quoting me on that hitch in the get-along thing in your story. Governor thought I might have spoken out of turn. Not been as sensitive as I should have been for all those bleedin hearts."

Stroud seemed genuinely hurt by this. If the governor had truly rebuked him, it would have been the height of unfairness. What Stroud had done, I now realized, was to put a form of backwoods damage control on a potentially disastrous event. I tried to work this to my advantage. "Look, Mr. Stroud, I used your words because I thought you put the situation in a proper perspective. What it could have been called was a real fuck-up. Your words brought the situation down a level or two."

"Well, son, you know that was exactly my intention. Exactly my intention, and I told the governor hisself, too."

I tried to build quickly on our new understanding. "Did you know Burwick personally?"

"Not really, seen him around. I mostly deal with the attorney general his own self. Ambitious man, he was. Everyone said so. Decent fellow though, had all the right ideas. It's a shame. That fellow would have gone far; had that pretty wife, too."

"Did he have any enemies you know of?"

"Well, he had at least one, Mr. Alexander, or don't they teach you boys country logic at Harvard?"

It seemed our brief camaraderie was over, and Halloran wasn't the only one who did his homework. There seemed little point in continuing the conversation, then he said: "Say, Ned, how was it

69

that you were so quick to get to the murder scene? I hear you beat everyone else there by a mile."

"Well, sir, we Harvard boys are taught Ivy league savvy."

He chuckled at this. "Touché, son. Touché." And he hung up.

While I was talking to Stroud, a message appeared on the screen of my word processor that I had a message at the front desk. The receptionist, who I knew as Mildred, greeted me and said that a fax had just come for me. She handed me two pages. The first had the heading **FAX** Cover with the message: *Nice job on your article. Let each act be as your own. More to follow. Kant's reckoning has just begun. Thought you could use a little help. One page to follow.*

It was signed, *BWWY.*

I looked at the next page to find it empty save a number writ large in the center.

.067

6

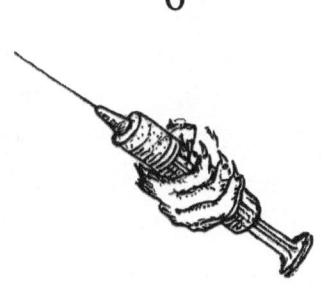

T for Texas

I stared at the number for quite a while and looked for other information as to who sent it. I found nothing, only the signature BWWY. It could have been a joke by some crank, but the arcane nature of it made it seem ominous. *More to follow, Kant's reckoning has just begun.* I was sure this fell into Hickey's German shepherd category. I was pretty sure it could not be considered a confidential source since I had no idea who had sent it. I'd run it by Halloran. Before I did anything, I first wanted to do some checking.

Mad Michael, of BMW fame, was the best mathematician I knew, so I put in a call and got him on my first try.

I gave him a thumbnail account of the situation and asked him if he could tell me anything about the number. Was it significant to any type of math formula? "It's not a number, strictly speaking," he said. "At least not an ordinal number, a counting number. It's a decimal fraction, and as such it is a relationship between two values. It says that you have sixty-seven one- thousandths. Or if you had something divided into one thousand parts you'd have sixty-seven of them."

"So whatever it stands for is in one thousand parts?" I asked.

"Not necessarily." Mad Michael was enjoying himself. "There could be an infinity of numbers that could resolve themselves into this relationship. If you multiply each of these values by two, the relationship would be the same, as it would be for three or four, all the way to infinity, the relationship would be the same."

"Great," I said.

Unaffected by my despondency, Mad Michael went on. "It could be a constant, though. A standard relationship in an equation like the gas constant."

"What?"

"You know, $PV=nRT$. R is the constant, 8.31, it makes both sides of the equation equal. Come on, you've had chemistry. Nothing comes to mind right now, but I'll check around. I like a mystery. You say this number is tied to a murder? Very cool."

"I thought this wasn't a number," I said sourly.

Michael laughed. "Very good! Who says you can't learn at your age? I'll do some checking and call you later tonight." He hung up in a state of happy excitement.

The telephone seemed to be a living thing. No sooner had Michael gone than it was ringing to Halloran's voice. "Hey, Harvard, they've picked your story up on both the AP and UPI wires and it's gone all over the country, and world for that matter. I just got a call from a buddy in New York and the *Times* carried it on the front page! They didn't even bother to rewrite it, just stuck your name right on it. Congratulations. Go out and get a copy and frame it for your den."

"I don't even have my own bedroom, much less a den," I said, trying to comprehend the implications.

Halloran chuckled. "Frame it anyway."

I was soon in his office, showing him the fax.

"Well, anyone in the country could have read your story by now," he said.

"Should I show it to Hickey? I think he'd be angry if I didn't."

"Yeah, I see no harm in it. Keep him informed—it will only help us in the long run. What the hell you figure Kant's reckoning is? And why is it that they think you need a little help?"

The phone rang and Halloran handed it to me. "It's Hickey." The difference between detectives and journalists, I suppose, is the perspective of suspicion. Halloran's last question was Hickey's first. Once again, I found myself a central character in this drama, and I had to tell him that I had no idea why someone should offer me help or what the nature of that help might be. Beginning to feel a bit irritated, I flashed back to the image of breaking into Burwick's car and stealing (not really an unfair word) Solomon's article. This image cooled me down considerably, giving me tolerance for Hickey's trolling. The harangue continued steadily for another few minutes or so, punctuated by periodic "I don't knows" from me until he said, "Hold on, there's someone who wants to say something to you."

The sound of deep breaths and then, "Ned, this is Kim. They brought me right over here from Florence in a Highway Patrol Car, and the glove they found on that attorney lawyer fellow is one of em from Redway."

"Are you sure?" I said, jumping up from my seat.

"Absolutely. No doubt about it." She started to say something else, but Hickey took the phone.

"OK? You have your information, and you got it from your own source. It didn't come from me or my department. Any other reporter can get the same confirmation as you, but they'll have to ask for it. Clear?"

"Yes," I said.

"Miss Richards wants to know what she should do with your hundred dollars."

"Tell her to hold on to it and we'll have dinner in a few days."

What kind of help, indeed? What was I doing that needed help? Less than forty-eight hours earlier, I was looking for a job, and now I had two bylines, one of which was frameable on the front page of the *New York Times*. OK, let's pretend that I'm a famous journalist, and it's twenty years later. I'm in my den, and in a place of pride next to my large brick fireplace hangs a framed copy of the front page of the *New York Times*. But what's next to it? Another framed article? *Arizona Reporter Solves Murder with Help of Mysterious Fax.* Or, *Esoteric Clue Decodes Murder.* Neither seemed possible, both seemed silly, but I left the framed copy of my article with an empty frame alongside it in my imaginary den, which looked much like my father's. I let the den dissolve but would return later to see what, if anything, had appeared in the empty frame.

Solomon and I had agreed to meet-up around five o'clock, and it was getting close. I picked up the file on Burwick, compiled by a university intern named Rachael, who worked as a part-time researcher whom Halloran had put at my disposal. Rachael's work was good. Burwick was a local boy who had gone to high school in Tucson and done his early education at the University of Arizona, also in Tucson. He graduated magna cum laude in political science and had gone off to Yale Law School. There, he was hot stuff, law review, later clerking for an Arizona Supreme Court justice. He met his wife, fellow law student Victoria Ramsfeld, who was from Athens, Georgia. They were married at the end of Burwick's second year. I calculated that Burwick had taken the same amount of time to complete his bachelor's and law degree at Yale as I had to get through my sophomore year at Harvard. Boola, boola. Anyway, shortly after graduation, the newlyweds moved to Phoenix, where Burwick worked in the governor's office and studied for the bar. He passed in the top three percent and was off and running as a golden boy through a number of positions at the DA's office, right up to assistant attorney general. While in this position, he was given several high-profile cases dealing with capital offenses.

I began sifting through the articles that Rachael had copied. Most were a review of Burwick's cases. The Redway case was not the first time he had tangled with Dr. Shirley Moran, but mostly he stayed above the fray, giving his comments in the form of news bites, press conferences, or private interviews. One article, however, was of more interest and was from what used to be called the society page. The article covered a scholarship fundraiser for Burwick's high school, and there was a large color picture of the guests of honor, Roger and Tory Burwick. The picture was three years old, taken not long after Burwick had returned from New Haven, but the photo held my gaze because Victoria "Tory" Ramsfeld Burwick was stunning! The photographer caught her in motion, looking regal and animated, her uplifted leg striding forward, her shoulder length auburn hair trailing behind her, as did a string of pearls yet to overcome inertia and share her body's momentum. Her eyes and smile focused on something beyond the camera. In contrast, Burwick was motionless, smiling confidently as his wife moved past him. Roger Burwick was indeed a handsome fellow, something I had missed, obscured until now by his pomposity and position. I realized that I had not liked him, but now somehow mitigated by the lovely creature by his side, I wondered for the first time, with genuine emotion, who would have wanted to kill him, and why. And why do it in a way so full of irony, a death meant not only to remove but also to disgrace.

I sought out Rachael and asked her to search for anything with Tory Ramsfeld's name in it. When I returned to my desk, Solomon was waiting for me. She had done considerable background work in her time away. Burwick and his wife lived in Tucson even though his main office was in Phoenix. He commuted and maintained a small apartment near the state capital. Solomon had met with two of Burwick's colleagues in the Tucson office and talked to one other in Phoenix. It seemed that Burwick had been well respected, if not particularly well liked. He seemed to have had no close friends in the office and was perceived to be aloof but not unfriendly. He was not what you would call a team player, by all accounts. Increasingly, he had been given the higher-profile cases and was often used by the attorney general as a spokesman. It was a common perception that the attorney general was preparing a run for the governorship, and Burwick was his logical successor.

"Anyone seem glad he's dead?" I asked.

"No, but no one seemed aggrieved, either," Solomon said. "The DA's office is a pretty competitive place, and the alpha male has just been eliminated."

"What about alpha females?" I asked, and Solomon shot a stern glance at me. I continued quickly, "Any close female colleagues?"

Lowering her gaze, she said, "There are a number of female lawyers in the office, but only one senior assistant, and she's out of town."

"That Sandra Warren?" I asked. "She was at the execution." "Yes, that's the one."

I told her what I had found out about the glove and the odd fax message. She seemed interested but asked few questions. I shared the biographical information from the archives but left out the part about the fundraiser article. She had set up a meeting with the attorney general and made arrangements to fly to Phoenix early in the morning. We left it that I would write an article incorporating the information we both had gathered. Declining my offer of a beer at Sam's, she left me with her notes.

I wrote the article in a little over an hour, integrating the biographical information from the archives with the comments furnished by his colleagues, and closing with the sinister pedigree of the glove found on Burwick. As I was finishing up, Rachael came in with a folder containing her Tory Ramsfeld research. I turned in the article and walked her to her car.

"Hey, Rachael, you're at the university, aren't you? See if you can get a hold of a yearbook for Burwick's senior year, will you?" She assured me that she could and drove off. I drove home, leaving the folder unopened on the front seat of my car. There would be plenty of time tomorrow.

No one was at home, my hosts being away on an extended camping trip. I felt exhausted but not sleepy, restless and yet somehow exhilarated. There were voices whispering in the back of my mind; I wasn't sure I wanted to listen harder or block them out. I tried to put my mind in neutral. *Solomon* ...

I was just drifting off when the phone rang. My "hello" was just a reflex. "Neyed," I heard my name in two soft syllables.

"Helen?"

"Yeayes, Neyed, it's me, your motha. Surely you rememba me."

"Hi," I said, trying to slip my idling mind back into drive. "How did you get this number?"

"I'm resourceful social scientist, rememba. I called the newspaper," she chuckled. "We've all been readin your articles up here at High-ridge, they've been carrin em in the Knoxville *Tennessean*. You got quite the little drama goin on, son. You be careful now."

"Yeah, you should talk." My mother had been in danger, beaten, and arrested in her sociology work more times than I had gone to the movies. *For a genteel woman, your mother spends an awful lot of her time in jail,* my father would say, as he hurried down to Georgia, Alabama, or Tennessee to help extricate my mother and her colleagues from whatever predicament they were in. These forays took the form of arranging bail, sometimes in person, and calling up old school chums at the FBI to throw a little federal weight around, at least when the infractions weren't federal. Pleading and cutting deals when they were.

"Listen," she said. "I've been holding this workshop on minin reclamation practices, or lack of em, with some students down from Columbia and Harvard as well as some local folks. I swear, those Ivy leaguers aren't as smart as you'd think. The Jallico students, once they lost their awe, said much brighter things."

"Yeah, well, Helen, I've been making the demystification of Harvard a personal crusade for some time now."

"Yeayes you have, dear, and made a proper job of it, too. Well one of the Columbia students is a girl from Texas who's active in the anti-capital- punishment movement, and we were discussin your articles over the last couple of days. Seems her brotha is a prison guard at a Texas prison that's fixin to execute a prisoner. The man's name is Willie Ruckles; he killed a Houston policeman during a robbery and escape, been on death row for about eighteen years, and the execution is set for the next few days. I swear, policemen are such babies, raisin such a fuss when one of their own is killed, as if they're more important than regular citizens. Imagine the military gettin angry because soldiers were killed in battle rather than civilians. Anyway, this girl's brotha and Ruckles have gotten to be friends, and he asked her if you could come down there and talk to him, Ruckles, that is."

"Me," I said. "Why?"

"Said they liked your articles, and they know who I am. They think you'd be sympathetic."

"Sympathetic to what?" I asked.

"I don't exactly know, but her name is Violet and she's right here, hold on."

A new voice came on the line. "Hello, Mr. Alexander." *Call him Neyed, for heaven's sake,* I heard Helen in the background. "Uh, Ned, like Dr. Alexander said, uh, like Helen said, my younger brother is a prison guard at Alamosa prison, and he and a prisoner on death row, Willie T Ruckles, have become good friends. There's always been just the two of us growing up, but when I went away to school in New York, Leo, that's my brother, began to develop a strong friendship with Willie. It sounds strange, but Willie's become like a father to him. He's really a remarkable man. He's earned three academic degrees while in prison and done quite a bit of scholarly writing.

"Well, in an incredibly bizarre role reversal, over the last five years, he's taken Leo under his wing. A couple of months ago, Leo was quite distraught, as all of Willie's appeals came back denied. But lately he's been quite calm. I am frankly very frightened Mr. Al, uh, Ned. We talk almost every night, and when he heard I was here with your mother and read your articles, he asked if you could speak to him and Mr. Ruckles. He said to tell you that it was very important and you would not be sorry if you came. Although I probed with all my training as a social scientist, and with all my sisterly wiles, he wouldn't tell me anything more."

I asked her a few more questions, and she said that she had been following the case and would fax me some of the news articles. "Look," she said finally, "the workshop here is over tomorrow, and I'm flying right to Houston. I could pick you up at the airport and we could drive to Alamosa. Ruckles is scheduled to die in three days." I said I would do what I could and get back to her.

By now, it was ten o'clock. I called the *Sun*, but the switchboard secretary didn't know me or my writing, and no, she didn't read the paper. After a five- minute merry-go-round, she agreed to call Halloran's home and deliver a message that I wanted him to call. Ten minutes later, he was on the line.

"What now, Jimmy Olsen?" Halloran sounded jovial, equating me with Superman's bumbling press pal. I told him my story, punctuated by his grunts of comprehension and an odd bubbling sound that I hoped was a large whiskey sour. "OK," he said at last, but it was too late to get me any up-front money. I would have to pay my way and keep an expense account and OK all charges above fifty bucks with him.

"Do you have a credit card? Is that OK?" he said. "Yes."

"You have three days, Harvard, and I want you checking in twice a day." I got his home phone number and hung up.

I called Southwest Airlines to book a flight, but as I suspected my credit card was denied. My next call was to the bus station. Houston was a sixteen- hour ride, but it was only fifty-two dollars, and one was leaving at twelve- thirty in the morning; I'd have to hurry. It wasn't posh, but it would get me in late the next afternoon. I'd call Halloran from the road. I didn't want him having second thoughts. I realized I was looking forward to this with some excitement.

I called Highridge and Violet answered, and we arranged for her to pick me up at the Houston Trailways station. Just before we ended our conversation, I asked, "Hey, Violet, what's your last name?" "Pink," she said and hung up.

Violet Pink. Imagine…

Middle-class America outgrew buses as a major mode of transportation sometime after the 1960s. The bus to Houston and other stops southeast was only half-full as it pulled out of its downtown Tucson station at exactly one half-hour past midnight. I looked around at the other passengers and felt like I'd stepped back twenty-five years: a young woman with a small child and a baby, a middle-aged rotund woman with an infant and a large wicker picnic basket, an elderly black man with a younger man I took to be his son, accompanied by two teenage children, a boy and a girl who talked quietly toward the back of the bus opposite where I sat. Several unaccompanied middle-aged men dressed in western garb rounded out the crew. I noticed that all the men with the exception of the black youth and me wore hats, which made me feel more like I had stumbled into a period movie. I was thankful that no one sat next to me. On the empty seat was my laptop and two folders, the one Rachael had prepared on Burwick and one with the articles faxed to the *Sun* by Violet that I'd managed to retrieve from the misanthropic night receptionist just before leaving. In the luggage compartment was my backpack with three changes of clothes, and in my pocket was two hundred and fifty dollars, my entire savings withdrawn from a cash machine minutes before departure. I felt strangely self-contained and complete as I stared through my reflection out the window as we moved away from the lights of Tucson east toward Texas in the growing darkness of east Highway 10.

I picked up the two folders and held them, each containing clues to be investigated, parts of mysteries yet unfolded. I gazed out the window and let the humming of the tires carry me along. I was unaware of falling asleep, only of waking up to an early sun throwing a red light on barren desert hills. The light, like the hum of the road, was soothing, and I drifted back to sleep. The sun was high above the hills when I awoke to a baby's crying.

I reached for the folder that contained the articles Violet had sent. It was a fairly extensive document for such short notice. Willie T Ruckles, 25, and a friend, Theodore Blount, 23, had held up a convenience store in Houston in the late '70s. After giving the robbers forty-five dollars in a paper bag, the store clerk had pulled a .367 magnum Colt from under the counter and fired at the fleeing Ruckles and Blount. Fire was returned as the robbers were pinned down behind an ice machine. A Houston policeman, Walter Stith, who had just left the store after making a purchase, came back in to investigate the gunshots and was caught in the crossfire. Leaving a wounded Blount behind, Ruckles ran right into the hands of Stith's partner. Stith lay dead on the floor, still clutching his purchase, a bag containing a box of doughnuts (no lie). Blount died in the ambulance on the way to the hospital. Both men were killed by bullets fired by store clerk, Roy Rogers (again, no lie). Although it was Rogers who fired the lethal shots, and it was never proved that Ruckles had fired any shots or even possessed a weapon, he was nevertheless tried and found guilty of the murder of Officer Stith. The Houston PD rallied behind the prosecutors in asking for the death penalty, which was awarded, but as there was a federal moratorium on executions at the time, Ruckles was remanded to the authorities at Alamosa State Prison until such time as capital punishment again became legal.

During the ensuing eighteen years, Ruckles had taken advantage of many education programs offered by the Department of Corrections, receiving his baccalaureate degree in English literature and history from San Marcos State College, as part of an outreach program between Alamosa Prison and San Marcos. Ruckles was, in fact, the only graduate of the program. During his studies, with the help of a young prison reformer, Jack Randolph, who had just become the new warden, Ruckles set up an educational program for prisoners to work toward their high school diplomas. Upon graduation, Ruckles enrolled in a special law school program at the University of California at Berkeley, and within three years he graduated with honors. He applied to the State of Texas to take the bar exam but was denied on the grounds that he was a felon awaiting execution, whereupon he began post-graduate work in the Berkeley Department of Philosophy, where he maintained continuous enrollment.

During his undergraduate work, Ruckles wrote a number of articles on black history, scholarly articles on Black English in prisons, and a textbook on teaching adults how to read, which was adopted by popular educators and a number of grassroots programs of adult literacy, as well as by the Alamosa program itself. During his law studies, he co-authored major articles with his law professor, Adam Zegura, that dealt with various issues of ethics, education, and prisoner's rights. After law school, his flow of scholarly writings slowed. Two things seemed to have contributed. First, Jack Randolph was transferred to another post and subsequently left the Department of Corrections for an academic job. The second factor was the rise of Walter Stith's younger brother, Robert, within the police union, becoming a ranking union official in the state of Texas. Robert Stith was young, personable, and aggressively political, making capital punishment a professional crusade and taking every opportunity to keep Ruckles' crime before the public. Each time an article about Ruckles' accomplishments appeared, it was followed by a passionate attack from Stith.

In the period that followed, capital punishment was again legalized and Texas, along with Arizona and Virginia, became a leader in the new and burgeoning industry of killing people within the framework of the U.S. Constitution. The new warden at Alamosa, Busby Van Zant, quickly made it clear that the days of reform and coddling were over. He now ran the circus; death row and "old sparky" were once again center ring.

With the reestablishment of capital punishment close on the horizon, several people and organizations took up the cause of an appeal for Ruckles, led by his law professor, Adam Zegura. The folder contained articles recounting appeals and requests for a new trial. Zegura referenced police- state-style tactics being used to silence Ruckles and asked for scrutiny from the federal Bureau of Prisons. Accompanying these were pleas from intellectuals around the country. The articles indicated that a showdown between Ruckles and Stith supporters appeared imminent, the rhetoric mounting with each article; then the furor abruptly stopped. A last article during this period said that the request for a new trial had been withdrawn, and Ruckles and his lawyers were pursuing an appeal within the structure of the corrections system itself. Then, there were years of nothing. One lone article a few months later stated that with budget problems the high school diploma program started by Ruckles and Randolph had been suspended. According to Warden Van Zant, the prisoners were given the choice of the closure of the high school program or the weight room. It was a problem of limited resources, Van Zant was quoted as saying.

Then, two years ago, a new and conservative governor was narrowly elected, replacing the charismatic liberal grandmother who had served but one term. A major supporter of the new governor was the slain policeman's brother, Robert Stith. An execution date was set, and short articles chronicled the denied appeals. Stith and the governor were quoted as they repeatedly played their cop-killing card, and though there was opposition from many anti-capital-punishment groups, Ruckles and his former advocates were strangely silent. It seemed that Ruckles was to die in three days' time.

I finished the final article, set down the folder, and picked up the one on Burwick. The two teenagers across from me listened to a transistor radio quietly. It was a country blues station from Dallas and played the song of an artist I was familiar with, Sonny Boy Powell, a guy who lived in my brother's hometown. The song seemed apropos, *T for Texas T for Tennessee.* The refrain went: "T for Texas T for Tennessee/ T for Texas T for Tennessee/ Ain't no woman gonna make a fat mouth of me." *What's a fat mouth?* I thought as I shut my eyes momentarily against the sting of eyestrain. When I opened them again, Sonny Boy was gone, the sun was behind us, and the bus moved into the outskirts of Houston, pulling into the station at dusk.

I stepped off the bus stiff and a little groggy to see a young woman coming toward me and waving. "Hi, Ned, I'm Violet," she said, stretching out the *o.* "I know you from your mother's pictures." Violet Pink was blonde and slim and appeared to be no more than about sixteen years old; she looked more like a waitress in a truck stop café than an Ivy League doctoral student.

"Thank you for coming," she said as she took hold my backpack. "You hungry?"

"Yes," I found myself saying as she threw my pack into the back of a well-used Ford pickup.

"There's a great little Mexican restaurant near my place. Just can't get good Mexican in New York, and it's good for vegetarians, too. Imagine a Texan who doesn't eat fried chicken, pork chops, and steak! I'm a bit of a freak here, for sure." Her cadence was confident and yet also nervous, and the surfeit of culinary information was no doubt a way of taming her nerves. She had a lot riding on me and my visit, it seemed. As we drove through Houston, exchanging the large buildings of downtown for the houses of the suburbs and then more open fields and dry pastures bordered by tilting and weathered posts, connected by scallops of sagging chicken wire, Violet continued on. She talked about New York and Tennessee, the workshops at Highridge, what an inspiring and dynamic woman my mother was. Her conversation had the metabolism of a hummingbird—it would hover stock still for just a second, then buzz off in a completely different direction. Still a little groggy, I was content to listen to the beat of the invisible wings that transported the ribbons of words that formed her sentences, until we pulled into the dirt lot in front of an amorphous adobe building that said Gonzales Family Restaurant over a mural of Our Lady of Guadalupe. "Here we are," she said as the hummingbird died.

Señorita Violeta," sang out an elderly mustachioed man who moved toward us. "Long time, no see."

"Long time no aqui, Enrique," Violet said from somewhere in the folds of the man as the two embraced. "Too long. It's good to see you."

"I've not seen the young señor also for quite some time. Is he well?"

"Yes, well, but going through some hard times." She introduced me to Mr. Gonzales, saying, "Enrique is like a father to Leo and me. Many times as children we took our meals in the kitchen here."

Enrique sat us at a table next to a beehive-shaped fireplace that burned happily.

"Dos cervazas, por favor," she said. With more beer and another lady across a table from me, I thought back to Solomon. It was just three days since I'd taken the last job in town.

"Why am I here?" I asked.

"Actually, I don't know exactly, only what I told you over the phone. Leo has been increasingly distraught over the past six months, as the final appeals for Mr. Ruckles all come back denied. We're very close, my brother and I, and talk over the telephone almost every day. Then, about a month ago, Leo became strangely calm and uncommunicative about how he was feeling, and about what was happening at the prison and with the appeals. When I would ask, he would just say everything was about the same, but there was little emotion in his voice, just a heaviness. I kept trying to probe what was going on, and he'd just say he was OK and not to worry. This went on until just a few days ago when he heard that I was at Highridge with your mother, and he asked me to call you with the request."

Enrique set down the two bottles, and when Violet did not take her eyes from me, he moved quietly away. "Like I said, my brother and I are very close, just three years difference between us. Our mother's name was Rose, and she said she married Daddy so she could be the Pink Rose. It was probably the only thing about the union that worked out for her. She died when I was eleven.

"Even at that age, I knew it was not a totally bad thing. She was tired— used up. She didn't sicken as much, as she just slipped away. Shortly before she died, I was walking home from school through a little stand of mesquite trees and there was this insect about half an inch long, clinging to a tree, and it caught my eye. At first, I didn't know why it looked so strange, but it was all hunched up and squirming, then I realized that it was crawling out of its skin. As I watched, a little brown beetle emerged through a little slit in its own back, leaving its skin still clinging to the tree. The insect crawled away, but I was fascinated with what it had left behind. Gently, I plucked it off the tree, and I remember it crackled at the touch, it was a perfect insect in every little detail except that it was clear and hollow with a little slit on its back. It's a statue of a ghost, I thought—like Mama. I brought the beetle skin home and kept it safe in a box. After that, I thought I could see my mother becoming more and more transparent, and within two weeks she was dead.

"At the funeral, I asked the funeral director if he saw my mother when she was dead. He said yes, that she looked beautiful. 'Did she have a slit in her back?' I asked.

"He looked at me so strangely and said, 'What a terrible thing to say,' as he walked off.

"My mother's sister, Aunt Anita, was standing nearby and said, 'She's such a strange and wicked child.' Ever since, Leo and I have been strange and wicked children, with only each other to count on."

She looked up at me and laughed. The sensitive and surreptitious Enrique had left two more bottles of Dos Equis and slipped quietly away unnoticed. "That night Leo and I formed the secret society Sock, spelled S-A-W-C, a secret society for *strange and wicked children*. Even today, we often sign our letters with that after our names.

"School was always a refuge for us, although in different ways. We were both smart children, and the schoolwork came easy. For me, intelligence was a security fence I put up between me and the rest of the world, but for Leo it was just one more thing to be angry about. He had never seen the beetle skin and never knew that Mama's passing was not a bad thing. At school, he was teased for being a teacher's pet, and so he compensated by being tough and talking back to his teachers. And in no time, he was just like all of the other boys, during the day. But at night, in the security of SWAC, things were the same between us."

"What about your father?" I asked.

"Our father was a force like the weather, something to be endured but not counted on. Sometimes pleasant, even bracing—sometimes bitter cold, and sometimes raging. He blew through our lives like wind through a doorless and windowless house, to be neither pitied nor loved, nor after a while, even to be feared." She laughed again. "I wrote that for a freshman composition, and I've never been able to improve on it."

Our bottles were empty again, and there stood Enrique with two more. Violet shook her head and waved her hands back and forth when she saw the beers, and Enrique's eyes twinkled as he looked at her from behind the bottlenecks. "Uno mas won't hurt you, mi Violeta," he said, and then looking to me, added, "I like her best just a little borracho," making the sign for little with his thumb and forefinger. "She's always so serious."

Violet smiled and accepted the beer with an exaggerated bow of her head. The affection and history between the two was evident. With a little dance step, Enrique left with our order.

Over dinner, Violet continued with her history. She and her brother lived pretty much on their own, living on what money their father left when he blew through, doing odd jobs around their school hours and in summer, all supplemented by dinners at the Gonzales family restaurant, where they both worked, more as family members than employees. When Violet was seventeen, their father blew through for the last time. Graduating at the top of her class and a full scholarship to the University of Texas, Violet commuted between Austin and their home as Leo ambled through high school, a bright but uninterested student.

"I loved college and graduated in three years," she said. "I knew I was being selfish, but I couldn't help myself. I met your mother at a workshop at Highridge during my second year and she's been my hero ever since. She's really like a mother to me, inspiring and ominous, encouraging and critical, and always on the other end of the telephone when I need someone. She was the one who arranged for me to go to Columbia, and for me to work with her during the summers at Highridge."

Violet, it seemed, was another person in a long line whom my mother was mother to.

7

The Flypaper Method

I woke up early, the sun just winking over the low adobe hills. Violet was in the kitchen, and the smell of coffee was everywhere. "Coffee?" she asked.

"Please," I said. She pointed to the stove and a large aluminum saucepan that held what looked like chocolate soup.

"Percolator's broke, had to boil it, tastes good though, once the grounds settle."

"My father made it the same way sometimes," I said. "Called it cowboy coffee."

"Everything around here's cowboy something," she said, smiling. "Leo's already gone, said I should bring you along when you're ready."

Ready? The past three days were about to catch up with me. I was about to meet Willie T Ruckles, who barring any sort of miracle would be dead within the next forty-eight hours.

"Would you like some breakfast?" she asked.

Yeah, if I want to throw up, I thought. But I was gracious: "Coffee will be fine, thanks."

I felt a terrific need to talk to my father. *Put this in perspective for me, Dad*, I wanted to say. Instead, I asked, "When will you see Helen again?" I was a bit ashamed to admit that just saying my mother's name out loud made me feel a little better. I realized that she was the one tether to my old life in this bizarre new wonderland of death.

"I'll stop by Highridge on my way back to Columbia after this is all over. I think Leo's going to need me for a while, maybe he'll even come back with me." Her answer startled me; deep in my reverie, I'd forgotten I'd asked a question.

"Leo says they keep the death row prisoners awaiting execution in a special prison away from the other inmates," Violet said as she drove her pickup farther outside of town. On our way, I realized I hadn't checked in with Halloran per his instructions, so we pulled into a convenience store and I phoned. *I do need to ante up for one of those cellphones*, I thought.

After being patched in by the switchboard, Halloran came on. "I am going in to see him now, and I'll give you a call when I'm out," I reported. I asked him if there was anything new in the Burwick case, and he said there wasn't. I asked him if Solomon was still working on the interview with Burwick's wife, and he said she was. He didn't seem talkative, so I hung up. The prison was a depressing collage of cinderblock, asphalt, chain-link fencing, and razor wire, the landscape broken only by one lone and gigantic cottonwood tree. The tree gave its name to the prison, alamosa, being Spanish for cottonwood. The tree was magnificent, labeled cynically by the prison workers as the "Hangin Tree." We drove through the first of a series of gates where our names appeared on the proper lists and forms. The last gate terminated into a small parking lot before an entrance into the prison. "You go on in and I'll wait for you here," said Violet.

"It might be a long time," I said. "Sure you want to wait?"

"I'm a grad student, remember, there's always something to read." She patted a stack of papers on the dashboard. "I'll be fine."

The procedures were a repeat of four days before, at Florence (God, was it really only four days ago?), with ID showings, pocket emptying, storage baskets, pat-downs, and metal detectors. This complete, I was passed to the last guard at the mouth of a small room with the introduction, "He's the one to see the Nigger." This was the first direct reference to Ruckles' race that I had been given. I had assumed he was black from the articles and the degree in African American studies, but neither the articles nor Violet had mentioned the fact. The room was bare save for a table placed in the center; seated at the table was a thin white man with a large head, dark curly hair cut short, and large green eyes. It was the eyes that held my gaze—they were simply the most intense eyes I had ever seen.

"Who's that?" I asked, looking at the man at the table. "Why, Ruckles, of course," said the surprised guard.

"I thought he was black," I said stupidly. But for an involuntary shake of his head and a sound made with spit and air from somewhere within his mouth, the guard ignored my comment.

In back of the table was a wall of Plexiglas (you could tell by the scratches) behind which two guards stood with what appeared to be shotguns. I spoke again to the guard who had escorted me, saying, "I was told that this interview would be confidential," as I nodded at the two guards.

"They can see, but they can't hear," he said. "See that red light on the wall? That shows the mike's turned off. You have your privacy. Two hours today, two hours tomorrow—that was the deal. Better get started because the time starts now." He looked up at the two guards and tapped his left wrist with his index finger, indicating to them that the time had started, and with that he turned and left the room.

I was now alone with Willie T Ruckles. I walked over and sat down on the other side of the table in front of him. He was smiling. "You we're expecting Mumia, or maybe Rubin 'Hurricane' Carter," he said with a chuckle referring to two other black prisoners of literary fame. "Race has always been a conceptual tangle. For all functional purposes I am as Black as the guard colloquially labeled me. Thank you for coming, Ned." He spoke with a deep voice that resonated with a hint of what sounded like a British accent. The effect was at once cultured and commanding.

"Thank you for inviting me, Mr. Ruckles," I said. "Although I still don't know exactly why I am here."

"I'll call you Ned, and you'll call me Willie, we have little time together and none for formality. Besides, I know your family well. I have read both your father's and mother's work and have corresponded with your brother for a decade now and..." He smiled broadly. "I have even read your book. You see, although you are just meeting me, we have been connected for some time. You are here through the aegis of your recent articles, Leo's sister's connection with your mother, and the fact that I needed someone who I could respect and trust, thus the duty fell to you, and again, I thank you for coming." I didn't know what to say, so brilliantly, I remained quiet and Willie continued. "In slightly less than two days, unless stopped by order of the President, which will patently not occur, I will be dead. And before that I have a story to tell, and after that a series of events to play out. For all of this to occur, I will need your help. Today, I will tell you a story the facts of which, while known to others, only you will have in sum total. I wish for you to document these facts in the form of a news story or stories immediately subsequent to my death, but not before. This is where trust comes in, and I am betting on your family integrity and your word. Do I have this?"

He paused, and I nodded meekly and uttered some type of squeaky noise that was interpreted as a yes.

"Good," he said. "I believe I can tell you this story in the time we have left today. Tomorrow, I will dictate to you a letter that I wish to be delivered in strict confidentiality and will not be subject to public display or knowledge, until such time as the recipients might wish it. And although I have no right, I would ask you to assist the recipients in all ways you can. Also, tomorrow you will be given a certain knowledge, and instruction on how to act on this knowledge. Now to my story. I have had much time to organize and practice, so this will be much less an interview than a dictation. Write fast, and please hold questions other than those to clarify a point until the end, or until tomorrow. However, we are being observed, so every once in a while, look up at me and say something nonsensical—like *what time is it?* Or *what's your favorite color?*—so the guards think it's a real interview."

With those instructions I wrote furiously while Willie T Ruckles told his story.

"My name is Willie T Ruckles, my mother named me Willie, not William, and the T stands for nothing, and at the time of my death I am forty-four years and one hundred and eleven days old. For the last eighteen years, I have been an inmate of Alamosa Prison, the year previous to this I resided in the Harris County Jail in Houston awaiting trial on a charge of murdering a police officer in the commission of a robbery. I was subsequently found guilty and sentenced to death. Before taking up residence in the Harris County Jail, I lived for twenty-four years in the house of my mother in an area of Houston called 'Four Corners,' in a specific neighborhood locally referred to as the Quarters, a collection of wooden-frame row houses that used to house slaves who worked in the various small farms in the area. Upon emancipation, the Quarters' dwellers acquired their homes by possession and default, and maintained them over the generations though contiguity of occupation. Thus, my home, about as sound as an abandoned railroad car, was passed down the generations like a bucket in a fire brigade, to rest in the hands of my mother.

"It has always seemed rather strange to me that I remember as little as I do about my life as a child and young adult in the Quarters. My strongest memory of it is the wind, and the musical sounds it produced, as it moved through the walls to wherever it was going. That, and the cold; to this day, when I hear some musical tones I feel cold. With the exception of my mother, and my brothers and sisters whose numbers increased with the passing years, people moved through the house much like the wind, though the chords they produced were more dissonant. My mother, as her people before her, upheld two longstanding traditions, the first being residence in the Quarters, while the second took its lead from the slave owners and concerned a progressive bleaching out of the pigment brought over in the genes and folds of the skin of our founding generation from Africa. We Ruckles have always had the dubious distinction of being the whitest residences of the Quarters. This distinction carried the twin burdens of pride and ridicule. Early on, I learned how to fight and I learned how to run. I was pretty good at both. Fighting and running, or usually some combination of the two, pretty much defined my pre-incarceration existence. Sandwiched in between the fighting and running were various admixtures of alcohol, drugs, talking smack, and sex, though far less of the latter than the smack talking would indicate. I remember almost nothing about school, though I did attend periodically, dictated by one emergency or another, usually a truant officer's visit or hiding out from someone I did not want to find me.

"For me, being good at fighting had almost exclusively to do with the use of my hands and my feet, in the old-style rumble notion of fighting. Somebody would call me whitey, honky, or red, and I'd immediately pop him in the nose, or dance around hitting and kicking. I was fast, and I was angry, but I wasn't mean, and this can be a tragic flaw when you live on the streets. Although I carried a knife, it was all for show and I never used it; guns I was simply afraid of, although I saw my share of them from the people moving through the house. Although I had literally thousands of fights and was involved in countless petty crimes, with the exception of the occasional truant officer, I managed to stay clear of the law. However, as I got older and the times and drugs got meaner, weapons assumed prominence, and my days were numbered.

"Increasingly, the people I hung around with carried guns and took drugs, because almost everybody in the Quarters carried guns and took drugs. I had some status because of my fighting ability and smack talking, but I was not thought of as a major player by the street elite, who ignored me, and mostly I just hung around.

"On the fateful day, a sometimes friend of mine, Theodore Blount, who was called Teddy Bear, and I were hanging out and wanted to buy some whiskey. In point of fact, we wanted to buy some more whiskey, and we needed money. In the fuzzy logic of the street, we decided to hold up a convenience store. Blount carried a gun as part of his standard wardrobe and took the lead. I was along for support and camaraderie, and was ready to run at the first sign of resistance or opposition. To my surprise, the store clerk, a wiry and wizened white man, seemed willing to give us the money, he put money from the cash register into a paper bag and held it out in his left hand for me to take it, which I did. I took it and turned to run, but almost in the same motion of handing me the bag with his left hand, the clerk's right hand came up with a huge handgun and began shooting. I did my running thing but got confused as to the way out and wound up behind an old-fashioned Coke machine—the newspaper articles incorrectly called it an ice machine—that was the only thing large and substantial enough to shield me from the bullets, which seemed to slap everywhere. We had entered from the back of the store through the delivery entrance so we hadn't seen the man who had left just before we entered, who as it happened was a highway patrolman. Blount had been hit in his left shoulder by the clerk's gunfire, and he howled in anger and pain as he fired his pistol in the direction of the clerk. The clerk, too, was screaming and had taken cover behind the counter and fired wildly with only his gun hand visible. It was then that the highway patrolman, a man by the name of Stith, entered the store his gun drawn. At that same moment, Teddy Bear pitched forward and the policeman screamed and fell backward, then everything was still and I ran out the front door right into the arms of Stith's partner, who handcuffed me and left me in the dirt parking lot and went inside. Both the patrolman and Blount were dead, the victims of the clerk's gun. The clerk was unharmed, Teddy Bear's marksmanship being as poor as his judgment."

Willie T Ruckles paused. "Ask me my favorite color and look interested," he said. I had been so intent on taking down his story word for word that I had forgotten the nonsense questions for the guards, who had not taken their eyes off us.

I looked up, "What's your favorite color, Willie?" I asked earnestly, observing the scrutiny behind him.

"Pink," he said, smiling, then continued. "I'm telling you all of this not only for autobiographical background but to set the context of what's to follow here.

"I lay face down in the dusty cinders of the parking lot, while patrolman Stith's partner entered the convenience store. My hands were cuffed behind me, and my feet secured together. I rolled over on my back and looked up at the sky, and then the most miraculous thing happened. It was like the sky and the whole world under it contracted, leaving only me intact. It was like I was looking at me, and only me, from way up above. Next, I was falling, falling right into myself, and then I was looking outward, seeing the sky, the clouds, and the light, hearing the noises around me. I remember thinking, 'I'm being born.' As indeed I was, right there rolling in the dirt of the grimy parking lot, amid the chaos of yells and sirens of police cars and ambulances, I was delivered at that moment, into the world fully conscious for the first time—awake and aware.

"There are a number of kinds of birth, you know," he said, looking up at me and smiling. "In fact, birth is just an arbitrary line that we draw to separate one set of events from others, in the same way what we call ourselves are arbitrary boundaries we draw around ourselves to define each of us as individuals, then becoming lonely, we seek to draw larger boundaries to include some while excluding others." He waved his bound hands back and forth above the table and laughed. "Sorry, I'm going philosophical on you and getting ahead of my story."

He went on. "Well, from that moment almost everything was heightened: colors, sounds, smells, movements. I became aware of patterns of all sorts: tiles on the floor, and the way a fly would move across a ceiling, the way a building was laid out, the grain in a wooden table top, and the rhythm of a ceiling fan all captured my complete attention. But most compelling were the patterns in the behavior of human beings. The way people talked, the things they said, and how they said them; the ways their eyes fixed and moved, the motions of their hands, all of these things captured my attention to a level that would crowd out everything else.

"The only things that weren't heightened were my feelings—from these, I was curiously detached. Those things that constituted the focus of my life before, the individual pleasures and comforts, were absent. Food lost its taste, acts of unkindness, and instances of physical discomfort and pain seemed to have little impact. It was as if from the time in the parking lot, I never completely got back into my body but stood partly outside myself— observing, analyzing.

"One of my memories of my mother was that she liked to do jigsaw puzzles, the kind with a thousand pieces. She would work for days completing one, and when it was finished she would glue the picture to a piece of cardboard and hang it on the wall. Shortly after my incarceration in the Houston jail, I had a vivid dream, which of itself was memorable, since to that time I had few dreams that I would remember. In the dream, I was at home in the Quarters and heard a knock on the door. I opened it to see a white man in work overalls. 'Delivery for Willie,' the man said and motioned in a large dump truck. As I stood at the doorstep, the dump truck raised its bed and I was buried in a load of a million jigsaw puzzle pieces that threw me to the ground. 'What am I supposed to do with these?' I asked, looking up at the deliveryman. 'Put em together,' he said as the dream ended. From then on, that was my life, looking for patterns, and putting pieces together.

"I remember little about the substance of my trial, but I recall all the surrounding detail in stark clarity. I can draw you the patterns of tiles on the floor, or the grain of the wood in the oak table I sat behind, the paths the insects took moving across the floor and the ceiling, the hand motions

of the judge, the jury, and others in the trial, everything. Most of all I was fascinated—mesmerized—by the way people talked.

"Teddy Bear Blount was dead and the law enforcement community enraged. Roy Rogers, whose gun had done all the killing on that day, was scared, he looked to me like a furtive vicious mammal. A hybrid, part human, part rodent, desperately afraid that someone might hold him accountable for the death of officer Stith. He needn't have worried. The police had me, and that was enough.

"I had a young public defender who, in retrospect, did a more than competent job, although she got little help from me. I was neither interested in the facts of the case nor its ultimate conclusion. This lack of interest had nothing to do with a cynical view of the American system of jurisprudence, but rather so many other things occupied my attention. In jail, for the first time in my life, I was safe and engaged in a predictable routine. My favorite word at the time was nice. 'This is nice,' I would say to myself a hundred times a day.

"My immediate attention, when not absorbed in observing patterns of interactions between things, focused first on my language. One of my earliest revelations was: 'Nobody here talks like me'. And I listened intently to everything that people said and the ways in which they said it. Some of it sounded like music, some of it like hammers chipping concrete. It was all so fascinating and engaged my total awareness. I listened to people talk, observed how they talked, how others reacted and adjusted to that talk, then talked themselves. From this, I made my very first discovery. Talk, my talk, and that of others, was the glue that would stick the puzzle pieces together, and I resolved to learn how to talk. After my mantra of 'this is nice' came 'I want to talk like music,' again, a hundred times a day. Although these things may sound a bit childish, these revelations remain among the most profound insights of my life.

"My study of language was aided by two sources. The first was by Sara Hawkins, J.D., my public defender. She came from Rhode Island, was educated at Brown and, of the only importance to me at the time, talked like music. Sara was arguing capably that I should not be tried and found guilty of first-degree murder, when I had killed no one and not even touched a weapon. And later, when I was found guilty, she worked to keep me from the electric chair, yet I was only interested in her vowel sounds, vocabulary, and cadence. It was all a frustrating and stressful experience for Sara that ended with little victory. If someone would have asked me what I most wanted at the time, I would have said: 'I would like it to be nice, and to learn to talk like music.' So, I had all the things that I wanted. I've given it considerable thought since, and I think that the development of the intellect, for that is what was going on, is like the development of an infant. At certain times, specific developmental processes are activated, causing great periods of growth in certain areas, while other processes remain static, until such time as they, in turn, are activated and others are stopped. I was discovering patterns and connections in the world and learning to talk like music. There was simply no defendant in my body for poor Sara to defend, but I couldn't have had a better music teacher, or she a better pupil. Over the years, we have corresponded and I have tried to make her aware of the great gift she gave to me.

"My other source came from a sadistic guard by the name of Griz. Griz was a night guard who staffed a community room where inmates were allowed to watch TV. Everyone was afraid of Griz, inmates and guards alike. He had been transferred around after numerous infractions and wound up in the community room to try to limit his liability. To get in the community room, you had to be on good behavior, and there were a number of other guards on duty at the same time. Deprived of his opportunities for sodomy and physical abuse, Griz engineered a plan to cause as much misery as he could under the circumstances. He decided with no opposition to make the official television channel the public education broadcasting system PPS. Under Griz's plan, it would be educational for the inmates to watch *Upstairs, Downstairs* on Masterpiece Theater. It was a series of the trials, triumphs, and adventures of the household servants in an early-1900s English Mansion. The inmates felt abused and complained. Which, of course, was the intention, but I thrilled to the sound of the language. It was, in fact, music, and I set out to talk just like they did. Later, I realized that I was learning a couple of different subtle idioms, as there were a variety of different social classes represented, but at the time it was all the same glorious sounds. I, being a cop killer, was not allowed access to the TV room, but by good luck my cell was placed up against the room and patrolled by the same guards, so the door was open between the two facilities and I could hear perfectly. I could even see a little bit if I stood at the front of the cell, but all I cared about was the sound. I'd lie in my bed, listen, and practice what I heard in a whisper. So that was my classroom, every night lying in my bed, listening to the music of *Upstairs, Downstairs*, practicing speaking like the people I heard, making long lists of words that I did not know. And all presided over by Griz, who would at regular intervals make lewd, chuckling comments about what he would do to one or another of the maids if he were lord of the manner.

"Oh, ho, lordy! What a primary education that was, Ned!" With that Willie rocked his head backed and laughed and laughed. I'd been scribbling like a mad man, intent on getting everything he was saying down on paper. My head snapped up to look at him, those green eyes that seconds earlier focused like lasers were now filled with tears and sparkled in the light like emeralds. The shift was so abrupt that the guards behind the Plexiglas stiffened to attention and the guard in the adjoining room put his hand on his holstered gun.

"Everything all right there?" he said.

"Oh, yeah," said Willie, still laughing, "everything's just fine." This came with just a slightly elevated hint of Masterpiece Theater. You could tell that the guard wasn't pleased, he'd been startled and didn't like it, however, they were rapidly running out of contingencies over Willie T Ruckles.

"Well, just keep it down, that's all," came the guard's response.

Willie's chuckles were slowly rolling to a halt. "How you holding out?" he asked, eyes still moist and flashing.

My hand could hardly move, and felt like it had been released from the mouth of a lion as I tried to rub the feeling back into it, "I'm fine," I said, and Willie chuckled gently. I glanced up at the clock. It had been just about an hour, and while it felt like I'd been in the story for days, half of our time for the day was already gone.

"We have a lot to cover, so I'll go on," said Willie, reading my mind. He continued. "Many of the words were new to me, and as I've said, I would make lists of them in my memory and confront Sara with them when I saw her. Sometimes I had as many as fifty. This frustrated her even more since it seemed to further demonstrate to her my complete uninterest in, and even lack of capacity to understand the proceedings. At one point she said, 'Look, Willie'—she had long since stopped calling me Mr. Ruckles, sounding as ludicrous on me as it would have on a five-year-old child—'I know these words are important to you, so just write them down and I'll write out the definitions later and give them to you so you can read them when you have time. That way we can focus on what we need to here.' Poor, tolerant Sara, it was a good idea, but I could barely read or write.

"Much like talking, I soon became aware that I could not read much more than signs or simple instructions. I had some rudimentary phonics skills and could stumble through words or perhaps even short written texts. Reading for me was only a form of direction, somebody or something telling me where to go or what to do. It occurred to me when Sara suggested that I write down the words that I hadn't known that everything that could be said could be written down. And it equally occurred to me that I could not do it. Along with spoken language, I now became fascinated with the written word, particularly those on a typewritten page. The words looked like bugs to me, the little black flying insects and the ants that crawled across the courtroom table or the walls of my cell. I thought of the helixes of flypaper that spiraled down from the doors and window of the Quarters where the insects became trapped like the words on a page. I looked closer at the insects and saw that they were of many kinds, just as the words were of many different kinds. I imagined that each insect was a word, and I resolved to learn all their names, both the words and the insects.

"I've pretty much kept my promise, too," said Willie, allowing himself to wander briefly, "I can tell you the name, both scientific and common, of every insect that flies or crawls through a prison door or window." This was his first, and only, show of pride.

It struck me that insects were assuming an important place in my narrative, what with Willie's word bugs and Violet's ghost beetles.

He continued. "So, I sat there in the courtroom, seated at the table with Sara, I looked at her papers, trying to make sense of the bugs that inched across the page. I would watch people talk, and see the words they spoke come out of their mouths like a stream of flying bugs, swirl around for a few seconds, and land plop on a sheet of fly paper, where they stopped moving ready to be read. This is how I taught myself to read—The Flypaper Method.

"I have likened my bourgeoning intellect to the development of an infant. I believe that the incident of Stith's death, and my incarceration, triggered a transformation in which I was made specifically receptive to certain features of my environment. This receptivity gave me a heightened sensitivity to certain things, both in my surroundings and within myself, while excluding most others. Because of this focus my learning was accelerated. Sara didn't know if I was depressed, schizophrenic, or simply stupid. And as the court would not entertain any plea of insanity, she did the best she could with what she had. She arranged that I be allowed to have a small pad of paper and a pencil the size of my little finger to write down words. I believe, in the beginning, this was done much like parents give a child a coloring book in a restaurant to keep them occupied while they eat dinner. But for me, it was like a mainframe computer.

"Words flew like swarms of locusts. My vowels sculpted themselves into an Albion wind, mine was a whole world of Masterpiece Theater, and flypaper. Patterns froze into concepts, and concepts into ideas, and ideas back into observations. One morning when Sara and I got together before the court proceedings, I asked her in my best *Upstairs, Downstairs* voice, 'What's a madrigal?'

"'What?!' she said, looking hard at me.

"'Is it music talk?' I asked. She continued to look hard at me with a puzzled expression.

"'I don't know exactly,' she said, 'it has something to with music.' She kept looking at me with this puzzled look. I remember this so fondly, for it was the first time anyone took my intellect seriously. The feeling was the most wonderful I'd yet experienced.

"'What you need is a dictionary,' she said.

"In my former life, I'd needed a dictionary about as much as I needed a textbook on brain surgery, but Sara said she would try and arrange it. I'm not really sure I knew what a dictionary was at the time, and I certainly had no idea of its implications. She asked the judge that I be allowed a dictionary, but the prosecutor objected. Sara then said that I needed a dictionary to clarify the words being used in order to understand the proceedings, and if denied, she would file a written motion that I was being denied due process. While the judge and prosecutor weren't buying any of it, threatened with a delay, they agreed. I could have a dictionary as long as it didn't have a hardcover.

"So now I was the ecstatic owner of a small, but replaceable, pad of paper, a pencil so short I could stick it in my ear without causing injury, and a paperback volume of the *Oxford Dictionary of the English Language*. Sara gave it to me with an inscription:

> *To Willie, give a man a fish and feed him for a day, teach a man to fish and feed him for a lifetime.*

"Fish? Sweet Jesus, I had the whole trolling fleet!

"The trial proceedings wound on, but I took little note of its progression. I was busy with my words, the music of language, and sticking it to flypaper. Roy Rogers gave his testimony; at one point, Sara asked me if I had any comments on what he was saying.

"'He talks like broken glass,' I said. She just sighed.

"That was my level of interaction. At the time, my greatest concern was working on my spelling, so I could look up the words I didn't know. My questions to Sara now concerned not the meaning of the words but their spelling. I had my dictionary with me at all times now, just reading it when I was not looking up a particular word. As the trial continued, all I would have to do is look over at Sara, she would sigh and write the word down that had just been said. Although I didn't understand the process, I was learning at a phenomenal rate. My *Upstairs, Downstairs* language was coming along, too. Few people talked to me, mostly Sara and the guards. Sara had some inkling of what was going on, but I was asked frequently by the guards if I was 'trying to be funny' or if I was 'gettin smart.'

"By the time the jury rendered its inevitable verdict, I could talk like music, read the bugs on the page at a phenomenal speed, and I could resolve what people said into a mental transcript of a printed page, and had read the *Oxford Dictionary* through the middle of the *S's*. My memory and observation powers continued to be clear and powerful. I observed in fine detail, and I remembered everything I saw, heard, or read.

"If you buy into the analogy of my intellectual growth as the development of a child, during the time of my initial arrest and trial I moved through my infant stage to that of a precocious toddler. The prosecutor asked for the death penalty, and even though there was a moratorium on executions, this extended the proceedings while Sara lodged an appeal. I was happy about this since it allowed me to continue my education with Sara, Griz, and Masterpiece Theater. As I developed, I was becoming more aware of the context of my immediate surroundings and their implications. But death, my death, was an abstraction that I gave little thought, for I was just barely becoming awake. During this time, however, I began to insert myself into the patterns I observed. I became aware that I was the central pivot around which the courtroom proceedings revolved. All the talk, whether music, or broken glass, was directed at me. Strange as it sounds, this came as somewhat of a surprise. This realization was indeed Paradise Lost. In the place of innocence was responsibility; in the place of solipsism was the beginning of compassion. Everything would now change, and everything was not nice. I now had things to do.

"This awareness was the waking up of adolescence, the dawning of manhood, if you will, the circumcision rite of passage. The puzzle pieces that had been so many colored building blocks in a child's sandbox became the harsh objects of reality, of power, anger, and retribution. The music of language became dissonant.

"The appeal phase of the trial moved quickly, and I was sentenced to die in the electric chair, and until such time as it became legal again, I was to live out the remainder of my life in the Alamosa State Prison in Houston. The old world of my new consciousness rapidly crumbled. My regular contact with Sara ended, as did the courtroom that was my classroom. Griz also moved on. He was found on the steps of a local police station with three bullet holes, one in each knee and one in the center of his forehead. The story was that he finally sodomized the wrong guy, the son of a Mexican Mafia don.

"There are few people in this world I owe more to than ol Griz. May he find peace in his next life, though there'll be some serious karma to work through, I should think," Willie said, shaking his head with a mirthless smile.

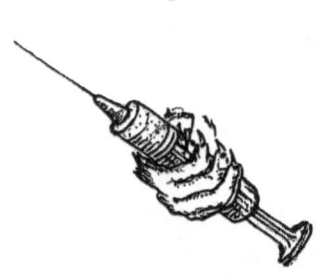

8

Sister Shashwati and L.T. Zegura

W illie went on. "My new life began with my transfer to to Alamosa and two incredible pieces of luck. The first was a new warden had just taken over, and he set about implementing a number of progressive ideas about prison management. At the center of these reforms was an educational program offered in conjunction with San Marcos State College that provided inmates the opportunity to work on two- and four-year degrees in a variety of liberal arts.

"Part of the new system was that Warden Jack Randolph met with every new prisoner for an interview. He was quite familiar with my case, and he asked me if I thought the verdict was unfair since I had not killed anyone. I told him that from what I had observed, that fact seemed to be irrelevant to everyone but Sara, and I really didn't give too much thought to it. I remember he looked at me and said, 'Interesting.' He asked me what my interests were. Nobody had ever asked me that. I told him I liked to study words and the way people talked. He asked if I liked to read, and I told him I did, but I hadn't read any books except the *Oxford Dictionary* in the Houston jail. 'Really?' he said, then told me about the college program, and that there was a small library where I could check out books. He said that while everyone could take part in some form of education, there were only ten slots for degree program students, and he asked if I was interested. This was my second piece of good fortune. When I told him yes, he said that there was a test to get in and would I be interested in taking it. I said yes again. Then he asked if I had any questions for him.

"Can I have my dictionary?' I had brought it with my things but I hadn't been allowed anything in my cell. He said he would arrange it. And the interview ended.

"Later that day, I was brought my dictionary. Two days later a guard came to my cell, saying, 'Warden wants you to take a test.' The test of all things was a test of reading and vocabulary. Vocabulary, another piece of luck! I took the test and a few days later I was called back to the warden's office, where I was told that I had scored one hundred percent and was to be given one of the ten San Marcos degree slots. Over the next few months, as I adjusted to the routine of prison life, I also received materials and attended meetings concerning the program. There were more tests, and I found out I knew nothing of mathematics. While my awareness extended to a basic geometry of forms and patterns, I knew next to nothing about numbers. I could add simple numbers mostly by counting on my fingers and do 'takeaways' by the same process. Of multiplication and division, I knew nothing. Algebra and calculus, I'd never even heard of.

"I now entered into my formal phase of learning. The centerpiece of which was the program at San Marcos State. The program was of two phases. The first was a two-year program of general education courses made up of undergraduate requirements in English, writing, mathematics, humanities, science, social science, and foreign language. It began with remedial courses on reading, writing, and mathematics, then moved to the college-level courses. It was a very tightly structured curriculum with a strict sequence of courses and tests that governed the progression through the program. And how I loved it, it was like living in a tight, cozy cottage, like the ones I imagined in an English village—no cracks in the walls to let in the cold or moaning winds.

"The courses were set up to let each student move at their own rate, teachers came intermittently for group sessions and less frequently met individually with each student. I virtually inhaled this part of the program. The instruction in reading and writing augmented and refined what I was learning with my flypaper approach. As a student in the college program, I had not only the course materials that I could keep in my cell but also unlimited access to books from both the prison and San Marcos libraries. As a death row inmate, I had additional restrictions, which was fine with me, since it meant I had more time for study.

"The only thing that I kept from my previous life was my fighting ability. My quick hands and feet, along with my limited access to most prison functions, protected me from the more serious internal prison abuses. I completed the program in a little over a year. My accelerated rate had the advantage that I had more individual sessions with the San Marcos faculty. This provided human interactions that I would not otherwise have had, and were extremely important for my development.

"The second phase of the program had to do with specializing in a major. They allowed me to choose two, although I would have preferred five or six. English Literature, and what was called at the time, Afro-American History."

I looked up at the clock; we had just forty minutes left. Willie again read my mind.

"I'll not go into as much detail during this period, as unlike my earlier learning, there are a number of people connected with this story who can provide you those details.

"My studies in English Literature were like being transported to outer space; it was *Upstairs, Downstairs* times one thousand. It gave me exposure to ideas that were at once completely foreign, and universal, transporting me to different times and cultures, while educating me to being human. If English Literature transported me to the apex of humanity, Afro-American history confronted me with my own cultural history, a history that was personal and threw me back into the soil of this country where I, despite all of the loftiness of my Albion diversions, was merely a Black man in a death row prison. This, shook my emerging intellectual psyche to its core, and was its first true test."

Willie looked up at me and lectured for a moment. "The worth of ideas," he said, "ideas in art and literature, or ideas in history, is their ability to transport one out of present circumstances into something more substantial— more worthy. It was a test of becoming fully human."

He continued. "I threw myself into the history of my people, its causes— its effects, the past, present, and the future. It was a time when much was happening, and from behind my walls I determined to be a part of it. From my readings, I was familiar with radical and poverty pedagogy, and developed a reading program based upon the emotional power of certain key words for the prisoners. Because of my familiarity with the British class systems and language styles, I wrote a book on Black English that became influential in the civil rights movement. With Warden Randolph, we constructed an education program that received national recognition. I wrote letters to civil rights leaders and those active in the movement. Surprisingly, many wrote me back, some of whom who had read my books and articles. It was during this time that I came to know your brother and the work of his father. I was the subject of a number of newspaper articles. These articles sparked negative reactions on the part of some citizens, most notably the dead officer's brother. More on that a little later.

"I wrote a number of articles on indigent education, and the social implications of speech, that were published in magazines and scholarly journals—my education rolled along. I was never so happy as I was during this time, studying, writing, and meeting at various times with my professors. I was dreading graduation, and as it quickly approached, I wondered where I would go from here. The thought of an end to my formal education, and all it had given me, filled me with a fear that capital punishment had not. I was contemplating applying for other majors when I was summoned to the office of Warden Randolph.

"With Warden Randolph, in a chair next to his desk, sat an enormous man. He had thick black hair, a full beard, and stood six-foot-six when he finally stood up. He looked to me like a resting bear as he held out his paw to shake my hand.

"'Willie, this is Dr. Adam Zegura, of the University of California at Berkeley.' All I could do was stare at the bear-like man with my mouth open. I must have made some kind of greeting and sat down.

"'Dr. Zegura is a professor of law at Berkeley and has traveled to Texas to meet you.' Stunned, all I could do was to continue my stare. My gaze moved toward the ceiling as Dr. Zegura stood up.

"'Mr. Ruckles, I've been studying your career for some time now, and I'm very impressed with your work. I know that you are getting ready to graduate soon, and I have traveled here to ask you if you've ever considered the study of law.'

"'But I'm in prison,' I managed to stammer.

"'You would not be the first prisoner to get his law degree, but there are many types of law. I am developing a discipline called social law. It is a mixture of the fields of law, political science, and philosophy. As a field, it looks at the social, cultural, and political implication of the law and its decisions, things your work already does. You would be on the ground floor of a new academic discipline and earn a traditional law degree at the same time. Based on your existing body of work, my university is prepared to offer you a full scholarship with all the necessary supports of conducting such a program from a Texas prison, and I will serve as your personal contact.'

"'Willie,' said warden Randolph, 'I'm concerned that when you graduate the prison board may decline your requests for further education. If you're already enrolled before graduation, it may circumvent any objection the board can make. I also believe my time at the prison will be ending soon. Robert Stith is becoming very influential due to his support of the new governor. I would like for you to be taken care of before I'm forced to leave.' "I couldn't believe my ears. A full scholarship to the University of California in an area that I was already working in before I even graduated was simply unbelievable. I was caught up with emotions I had heretofore not experienced. My eyes watered up and a tear rolled down my cheek. This was the first time in my life I remembered crying, though it would not be my last. "'There must be application and admission forms to fill out,'" I said, trying to regain my lost composure. Dr. Zegura walked over to the desk and retrieved a manila folder and brought it over to me.

"'I've taken the liberty to use your work to fill out the applications, and you've already been accepted on this basis. All it needs to become official is your signature.'

"I looked through the application and saw a list of my publications. The essay parts of the application were taken verbatim from my books and articles with no embellishment. It was like looking at a personal history of my thoughts, observations, and insights over the last two years.

"I reached for the pen Warden Randolph held out to me.

"'One more thing,' said Dr. Zegura. 'You're being admitted simultaneously to both a law degree program and to a doctoral program in the department of philosophy. The law degree typically takes three years, and we foresee your education lasting longer than that. The Ph.D. in philosophy will be overseen by my wife, Louise Taylor.'

"And just like that, I was a Cal Berkeley law and doctoral student behind the walls of Alamosa State Prison. I was to be the only graduate of the San Marcos program, which was dropped soon after my graduation, along with Warden Randolph and many of his educational reforms. But I was installed in two degree programs that would keep me in business for a long time. Along with my education, Adam Zegura pursued a retrial and reversal of my original conviction and enlisted the help of powerful groups and people. "As I approached the end of my law degree, everything was looking good for a retrial. Stith and the governor lost no opportunity to remind people of the heinous nature of my crime, but Zegura's people also proved influential, and they kept the case in front of the media.

"Adam and I published a number of papers together, and social law was becoming an accepted part of American academic jurisprudence. He was my first real friend, and my first and only colleague. I was on top of the world, having unlimited access to the Berkeley libraries; I was free to study, think, and write. I had everything I wanted out of life, and the governor and Stith were getting worried. I received my law degree after three years, and even though I had no desire to become a practicing lawyer behind bars, I applied to take the Texas bar exam.

"The Texas bar rejected my request on the grounds that I was a convicted felon serving time, and we appealed the decision. Then the powers struck back. On the basis of my bar exam appeal, the state prison board held a review of my educational program and decided that enough was enough. I'd finished my law degree, and they reasoned that was enough education for anyone, let alone a cop killer. They moved to terminate my doctoral program in philosophy.

"Zegura was furious and fired back with legal appeals from an army of his colleagues both within and outside of Texas, and a media blitz that said I was a major academic scholar and to deprive me of my educational status and access was cruel and unusual punishment and a disservice to all Americans. The battle lines were drawn, and a showdown was coming.

During this time, my access to my education was suspended and I was prohibited from publishing my work, so now I really was in prison. I still had access to Zegura as the head of my defense team and I wrote, of course, but at this time I was forced back into myself. I had not realized how important the outlet of my ideas had become, how fundamental this process was to my being. I used this time to reevaluate what my life had meant up to this time: the Quarters, my mother, Teddy Bear, Sara, Griz, Warden Randolph, the professors at San Marcos, Adam and his wife.

"I had done very little work on my philosophy degree up to then, but I had recently begun to study eastern religion. I had some knowledge from the non-violent philosophy employed in the Civil Rights movement, based upon Gandhi's techniques gained from eastern philosophic traditions. But of its specific principles and various forms I was ignorant. Zegura's wife, Louise Taylor, was a Buddhist scholar, and we had talked about my future studies. The link between Gandhi and American civil rights seemed to be a good entry point. I had no material on hand but was still allowed access to the prison library where I found a copy of *What the Buddha Taught,* a short treatise on the tenets of Buddhism, with which I spent a good deal of my time. Deprived of my academic work, I began to teach myself to meditate.

"I had thought I had matured intellectually, but it was in this process that I left the end of my intellectual adolescence and entered into full adulthood. Left alone in my cell with few diversions, my mind engaged itself as never before. As the world melted away, it also became accessible to me in full. In the three months of this period, I had never been more efficient in my thinking, my writing, and my work.

"I was able to smuggle my writing out through Zegura, who referred to it as legal correspondence and as such privileged information. The substance of this writing was published in the form of a little book on philosophy that was published under an assumed name. More on this later. In this period, I was also limited from corresponding with the outside world, which as I've said included publishing articles. To combat this we, Zegura, his wife, and I, came up with a strategy. Zegura's wife went by the name Louise Taylor and published her scholarly work under the same. I would publish my work under the name L. T. Zegura, submitted by Louise. Everyone assumed that L. T. stood for Louise Taylor and she was using her married name. This also made sense because many, though not all, of the pieces I was now writing were published in a wider venue than just scholarly journals. Louise continued to use her own name for her scholarly work.

"The various editors seemed not to mind this dichotomy, and I had my window to the world. I also published other books under my assumed name. This went on for a period of almost a year. The resolution was repeatedly delayed by motions made on the part of the state. Zegura felt the delays concerned fears that other appeals would be addressed at the same time. The governor and Stith had their names on the line and continued to be apprehensive and repeatedly took their case to the media and the court of public opinion. Zegura was animated and hopeful. I continued to write and meditate. Both sides were passionate, and on a few occasions, violence had broken out at public demonstrations. I was shielded from much of the news, but it came to me from Zegura and from letters I was allowed to receive from the public—they ran about fifty-fifty for and against.

"It was time for something to be done, and I had Zegura call a meeting of both sides. I was ready to cut a deal with the state. Adam was adamantly against this but finally ceded to my request.

"In the deal, I proposed that I be allowed to continue my doctoral program with all the access to personnel and scholarly resources until such time as I graduated or was put to death. The state would not oppose the extensions to my program that I applied for. This was prompted by Zegura. In return I would drop all requests for a retrial and to be admitted to the Texas Bar, and all appeals would be conducted through existing mechanisms. We would make no appeals to the media and I would not publish under my own name, but I could continue to transmit my work through Zegura to my doctoral committee. After some wrangling and direct opposition by Stith, the compromise was accepted and Zegura, despite his opposition to it, drew up the documents sealing the deal. I was back, happy and thriving. In full control of my life until such time as it was taken from me.

"How we doin?" asked Willie, using his Black voice and smiling, leaning back on his chair. In the diminished afternoon light, he indeed looked more like a black man than he had when I entered. "That's most of my story, and we even have five minutes to spare." I looked at him and rubbed the feeling back into my writing hand that was now numb and shaking.

"You've published more things under the name L. T. Zegura?"

"Yes, and it will be up to you to rescue the good lady's name after tomorrow," said Willie, still using his Black voice and chuckling. "There's about fifty of em. But mostly I wrote under the name of Sister Shashwati."

I stared at him incredulous. "You're Sister Shashwati?" I managed to say in a weak voice.

"In person," Willie said, bowing his head.

"Shit's gonna hit the fan when people find out that the state of Texas killed Sister Shashwati," I said.

"That's why they ain't gonna do it," said Willie.

The guards from the back of the room had materialized behind Willie and levitated him, one on each shackled arm. Willie was still chuckling as he was transported from the room. At the door, he turned over his shoulder and said, "And Ned, there really is no such thing as coincidence."

9

Saturn Kitty

*ister Shashwati, Sister Shashwati...*I continued to sit at the table as the room dissolved. I drifted back three years to Oxford, England, and the lowest point in my life. It was the end of December, cold, gray, and raining. On the heels of a miserable Christmas, I had just returned to my hostel after the closing of the Eagle and Child, a pub made famous by C.S. Lewis and J.R.R. Tolkien. I was drunk and gripped in a profound depression. I had recently broken up with a Canadian woman who had just finished up her fellowship in psychology and returned to Edmonton. The affair had been short but intense, and it had left me hollow and desperate, filling my emptiness with one pint after another in places we had frequented over the previous month.

I had been engaged in this regime for almost two weeks now as I returned to my hostel, cold and wet. The whole town was deserted, the result of the weather and the end of the term. After fumbling awhile with my key, I managed to gain entry and put on some water for tea in the common room. I sat down on the couch to wait for the water to boil. I stretched out and put up my sopping feet, and they dripped onto the coffee table. Lying almost flat on my back, I looked through my fingers at the room, playing a game with light and my impaired perception. I brought my gaze down to my feet, where I saw something blue. This was not curious since it was typical of the perception game. But the blue object continued to remain next to my dripping tennis shoes. I reached out for it and the object resolved itself into a book. A little blue book, bound in cloth. The title was *The Anatomy of Coincidence*, and the author was Sister Shashwati, published by the University of California Press. I opened the book to look for some sign of ownership, the pages looked new and gleamed white, and the smell of new ink greeted me. I was sure that the book was not on the coffee table when I had put my feet up. I got up and looked around the room and called out, but the hostel was as empty as my last beer glass at the Eagle and Child.

I made a cup of tea and committed to getting out of my wet clothes before I tackled the book, which seemed to carry the perfect title for a book found in an empty hostel. Getting out of wet clothes after a hard night at the pub is not as easy as it sounds. I rolled around on the floor of the common room. looking much like I was engaged in a wrestling match with myself, but after many tries I managing to change into a sweat suit, and there in the day room, still half drunk, depressed, despondent, and with my sweatshirt on inside out and backward, I was introduced to Sister Shashwati, who had mysteriously appeared to me.

The book seemed to speak directly to me in my present condition. It made the case that things that seem random and confused are really not the result of chance but part of a plan that we in some way control and are responsible for. It was not that we are part of a preplanned system, not that there was no free will, but that we were in control of major events, that things happened out of a higher order, an order that we ultimately determine. To make the case, Sister Shashwati used a variety of devices, including eastern philosophy, religion, history, baseball, and the stock market. Looking at my recent breakup, I began to put it into a perspective that I could begin to come to terms with. It was the beginning of my return to life. Dealing with the breakup, my father's death, and my finishing Harvard, all of it began with that book. Since that time, I have read all of Sister Shashwati's books, of which there are a number, and greet each new one with anticipation. In fact, I have built a personal philosophy of life on her works. Even now her newest book was in my backpack in Violet's truck, waiting to be read.

"You rent this place out for the weekend, pal?" said the guard. The room materialized again, I gathered up my notebook and left, finding Violet in her truck just as I had left her.

"Leo's been here and left this for you," she said, handing me a folder. "We're supposed to go home and wait for instructions." In the folder were three letters. The first was a copy of a letter written in a child's primary school hand to Willie from a Margret Hoag dated fifteen years earlier, the second was a letter typewritten from Willie to Margret Hoag dated a few days later, and the third was a long letter written to Willie from Margret dated two days ago. I put the letters back into the folder and asked.

"Hey, Violet, ever hear of Sister Shashwati?"

"The eastern philosopher? Sure," she said. "I've used her books as texts in a few of my classes."

"What's the academic take on her?"

"Well," she began thoughtfully, "the view is a bit divided. Some feel she's just who she says she is, an eastern woman, albeit an educated one, living the life of a sage and forwarding her writing to a contact at the University of California. Others think she is a pseudonym for an academic scholar. Still others think she's a composite of a variety of scholars collaborating to produce her books. Whatever's true, the work is universally held in high regard, which is amazing for someone with a popular following."

She looked at me suspiciously. "Why do you ask?"

"Just curious," I said as she stopped the truck on the side of the road. She looked straight at me and again asked why I was asking.

"I can't tell you until tomorrow," I said, knowing better than to lie. "I gave my word."

She took a long look at me then started the truck again and we moved on down the road.

"Thank you," I said.

Violet said nothing and stared straight ahead, her fierce intelligence already grinding out the truth.

I opened the folder and took out the first letter, written by a child.

Dear Mr. Ruckles,

My name is Margret Hoag and I am seven years old. I heard my daddy and Nancy talking about you and I think that they are right you should be punished and not let out of jail just because you are smart. Because I'm smart too and I still got hit with the belt when Saturn Kitty spilled the milk I gave her from my cereal bowl. I call her Saturn Kitty because she has a ring around the top of her head like the planet Saturn. Nancy yelled and daddy spanked me with the belt even though I know my times tables to the 12s, and the names of all the planets and how far they are away from the sun. My daddy is a policeman and killing a policeman is very bad. I think you should be hit with a belt too until you die.

Sincerely yours,

Margret Hoag

2nd Grade

Carrillo Elementary School

I moved on to the next letter, from Willie dated a few days later.

Dear Margret,

Thank you for taking the time to write to me. I am so very glad to hear that you are smart. I did not know my 12s times tables until after I was thirty, and I still don't know how far the planets are from the sun. I will look it up now that you have called my attention to them. Knowledge is a very powerful thing, and I am pleased to know that you have gone so far already in your education. Keep studying and it will take you to places you can only imagine. Please give my best to Saturn Kitty. I am sure someday you will become a great scientist.

Yours truly,

Willie T Ruckles

Alamosa Prison

The third letter was from an older Margret.

Dear Mr. Ruckles,

Fifteen years ago, I wrote you a terrible letter. You responded with a letter of your own that was kind and gracious, generous beyond measure. I think I know now why I wrote that letter: I was hurting and reaching out, why I reached out to you is still a bit of a mystery, although I have come to find out that there is no such thing as coincidence. It seems that your long battle with the barbaric state of Texas is coming to an end and I need to say some things to you while I still can.

I was living in abominable circumstances for a little girl. Just how abominable, I didn't know at the time. I remember when I got your letter. I checked the mailbox every day when I got home from school, and miraculously neither my father nor stepmother was home. It was the first letter I had ever received, and I took it into the shed where I played with Saturn Kitty. The letter was like magic, I read it over and over to Saturn Kitty saying, he thinks I'm smart kitty, that I will become a great scientist, he says he's sure Kitty, he says he's sure. This went on for two days. On the third day, I woke up to loud voices coming from the kitchen. "She's my daughter, god damn it, Nancy, I'm the one to decide," then the sound of a fist hitting the table.

"A quarter of a million dollars, John, it's a quarter of a million dollars." Then the sound of a slap and a muffled cry. "It's a quarter of million dollars, where else are you going to get that kind of money?" Nancy sobbed. "You're probably going to be fired from the force anyway." Whack, and another cry.

Then a third voice, a deep male voice saying, "Mr. Hoag, I am here with a serious offer, and you need to respond to it without recourse to violence." The voice was stern and commanding. It was time for me to make an entrance, so I came in rubbing my eyes as if I had just woken up, though I was wide awake.

"Hi, daddy," I said, and my father grunted.

"You must be Margret," said the giant man with kind eyes. "Hi, I'm Adam." He walked across the kitchen to shake my hand. I took his hand and I remember I had a feeling of safety that was not standard in my house.

The man turned from me to my father and said, "Mr. Hoag, I have a cashier's check and forms to be signed." "John…" pleaded Nancy in a breathy voice.

My father grunted again and reached for the pen being extended by the giant whose name was Adam. And just like that my freedom was bought for the exorbitant price of two hundred and fifty thousand dollars. You might think that a request to go off with a stranger would cause trepidation in a seven-year old girl, but that was not the case. With his handshake, Adam, hereafter Uncle Adam, had my complete trust, a trust that to date he has never violated. I was asked to pack all the things I wished to take with me, which took precious little time. I didn't even ask where I was going. I went to get Saturn Kitty, but she was nowhere to be found and I left without her.

We drove off through the neighborhoods of Houston into the countryside, the desert giving way to rolling lawns bordered by white wooden fences. We drove for about an hour until we came to a white fence and a sign that said Emma Callwell School for Young Women.

The school was an absolute haven. A farm with horses, and animals, ponds, with ducks and geese, trees, walking paths, outside tables for study, an amphitheater for group activities. I was placed in a sunny room overlooking a stable with a number of horses that spread over a pasture with a duck pond. The room was private and had a bed with a canopy, a desk with a light, and bookcases. My few possessions looked pathetic in these surroundings. Uncle Adam left me in the care of the dorm mother and said that he would return tomorrow when we would buy the things I would need for my stay.

The next day was the best day of my life. I began my studies. Science took place in a laboratory with microscopes. During music class, I selected an instrument that I would learn to play. A French horn of all things! I ate a fabulous lunch that would become standard, but certainly was not standard on that day, and I met the girls who would become my friends. Uncle Adam came in the afternoon and took me to go shopping. We bought more clothes than I had owned in my entire life. I had enough outfits that I would not have to repeat for two weeks. But best of all, at the end of the day we went to a bookstore where I bought three-dozen books everything from science to fiction to fill my waiting bookcase. At the end of my most perfect day, after dinner, I was called into the head mistress' office. Mrs. Stanley asked me how my day was, and I told her that everything was perfect. She then asked me if there was anything I needed. I told her the only thing that was missing was my kitty and would it be OK if I could have her with me. I had asked Uncle Adam earlier that day and he said he would see what he could do. She said that animals were not usually allowed since there were so many animals that were already part of the school, and I told her I understood. Even this could not dull the excitement of the day, though I was sad.

On the second day, after school was over, I was recalled to the head mistress' office and was told to wait as she exited the room. A folder was open on her desk, and I looked down on it. It said my guardian was the Sister Shashwati Foundation with Dr. Adam Zegura as its agent. The head mistress returned holding my kitty. I was so emotional all I could do was bury my face in her fur and cry. "I thought she was not allowed to be here," I sobbed.

"Well, we couldn't let you be without Saturn Kitty," she said. I'm sure you know, or at least knew, all of this at the time it happened, but there is something you may not know. The only person that knew my kitty was named Saturn Kitty was you. I told you in my original letter but never told anyone else. I kept the name my personal secret and never told anyone always referring to her as Kitty. The only way the head mistress could know her name was from you. From that time, early on, I knew it was you who was my benefactor, and shortly after that I became aware of Sister Shashwati and "her" books. So, I've known who you were almost from the start. I've kept the secret out of respect for your wishes.

But through your work, I've come to know you—to love you. Both for what you've done for me, and for who you are.

I'm sure you know that Uncle Adam has always been there for me. At times of graduation and transition, birthdays and special events, through all of my school changes. Orchestrating my time away from school, vacations to the Amazon, Kilimanjaro, school programs in Europe and Asia, study at CERN and Palomar, art history programs in Florence and the Louvre. When I would ask who was doing all this for me, he would just say someone who wished me well and wished to remain anonymous. But all the time I knew. All of these amazing experiences that you have provided me has made me who I am today. Currently, I am 23 and completing my Ph.D. in astronomy and particle physics at M.I.T. And if not yet a great scientist, at least a scientist, on the way to fulfilling your original prophesy.

While my life has been a wonderful combination of privilege and experiences, I have missed having a parent; even Uncle Adam couldn't fill this need. For this, I turned to your Sister Shashwati books adopting the information I found there as advice from a father. I may be the only one of your readers to read you with a male voice. Through this voice you became my father, the father that was always there, always listened, always supported me, and always understood. No child could have had a better one. On my eighteenth birthday, I went down to the Boston Court and changed my name to Margret Hoag Shashwati. It was my special birthday present to myself. Of course, I had to let Uncle Adam in on the change. I told him everything I knew about you at that time and asked him to use his discretion about telling you. He never did tell me if you knew, but he did say that I should still respect your request to remain anonymous. I have done that, but I have also followed your legal appeals and the execution process. When I heard the execution date was set, I told Adam I was coming out to be with you as best I could, and despite his objections, I came.

Uncle Adam said that if ever there was someone unafraid of death, someone who was well prepared to go, it was you. I believe this, too. I've read your work and I think I understand it well enough for that. But still I feel a profound loss of the best thing in my life.

I love you with all my heart. Thank you.
Your daughter,
Margret H. Shashwati
P.S. Saturn Kitty is still with me. She is 16 years old and maintains a frisky good health.

I put the letter away just as we were pulling up to the house. Violet was quiet as she stopped the truck. "Violet, I'm sorry," I said. She smiled and dismissed the apology with a wave of her hand.

I went inside, took out my laptop, and began writing what I thought would be the first of many articles on the death of Willie T Ruckles. I found it difficult to organize, and I was shaken by my revelations. I finally ended up writing two articles. The first was an account of Willie's achievements since his original incarceration, his battles with the prison board and the state of Texas, and his ultimate execution. The second described his literary personas of L.T. Zegura and Sister Shashwati. I had gone online and reviewed a number of articles of L.T. Zegura, and of Sister Shashwati, I was pretty well informed. Both articles were long, longer than your standard newspaper article, but I couldn't make them any shorter, though I tried. Although they lacked much of the detail, both were fairly faithful to the facts and the sequence of the story Willie had revealed to me. Violet remained silent and let me work without interruption, bringing me a cup of tea on two occasions.

I was just finishing up my second article when the phone rang. "It's for you," Violet said from the living room, and I went to answer it.

"Mr. Alexander," said a deep male voice. "My name is Adam Zegura, and I'd like to see you this afternoon." We made arrangements to meet at the Holiday Inn where he was staying. Violet let me take the truck, and I drove over to meet him. In the short winter days, it was already dark when I arrived.

Adam Zegura was a big man who did, in fact, resemble a bear. Indeed, he was a formidable presence, but it was his sad and kind eyes that seemed to define the man. He greeted me warmly when I entered the hotel. "You'd probably like a drink by this time," he said, smiling. "Let's go into the bar." It was still early, and the bar had few people in it. Adam chose a secluded booth in a dark corner. He ordered a whiskey, and uncharacteristically I ordered the same. After the day I'd spent, I figured I could use one.

"I'm sure you've found Willie to be a unique individual," said Zegura. "Individuals," I corrected.

"Yes, you've been introduced to Willie's other identities. I don't always agree with his decisions, but there is no one in the world I respect more. Up to this time, I have served as Willie's agent to the outside, managing his affairs. As a death row prisoner, he was not allowed to hold assets, but with his death all this will change. The value of the Sister Shashwati books is over a hundred million dollars, with revenues accruing every year. There are two books still to be published. The money exists in a foundation, untouched, with the exception of the educational and living expenses of Margret Hoag, Margret Shashwati. You've read the letters?" I nodded. "Willie wants to set up the foundation, and for reasons of his own, wants you to serve as its first president. The other members include Leo and Violet Pink, Margret Hoag Shashwati, Louise Taylor, and your brother Bob. I am to serve as its legal agent."

I looked into my whiskey glass and asked, "Why me?" "Willie says he trusts you and has known you for a long time." "But we've just met today."

"I know," said Adam. "Willie says stuff like that all the time. I've learned that he means different things by what he says than we do. But it's his request. Will you agree to it?"

I nodded again, thinking this was not the most bizarre thing that had happened today. "What does this foundation do?" I asked.

Zegura's smile broadened. "Other than take care of a few of its new members, it is to be determined by its board. Willie is a unique individual and not without a sense of humor. I am drawing up the legal documents now. They should be ready for signatures tomorrow, one of the many things that remain for us to do. Nice to have met you, Ned, and I'll be seeing you tomorrow," he said, leaving me alone with my whiskey glass.

10

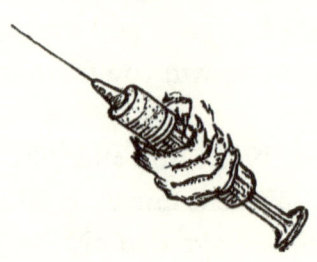

Say Hello to Your Brother for Me

I finished my whiskey, then another at the bar, while I reread the three letters. There was at least one more to follow that Willie would dictate to me the next day. I wondered what revelations that it might contain, and why nobody disclosed that Willie T Ruckles was really the beloved Sister Shashwati. Surely that would make a difference in the stay of execution. Then I thought that given the politics of the time, it wouldn't have, and anyway, it wasn't Willie's style. I wished I could talk to someone about all of this, but having been sworn to secrecy, I was left completely alone until the morrow. One more whiskey and I suddenly thought of Solomon and wondered what headway she was making with the Burwick story. Then I remembered the unread file I had received from Rachael before leaving Tucson. I reached in my backpack and retrieved it.

True to her word, Rachael had researched the yearbooks of Burwick's fraternity and made copies of several pages featuring the deceased assistant district attorney. Most of it was standard fraternity pap, this function or that, dances, dinners, flag football and volleyball games, but one dance riveted my attention. It was a homecoming dance, and the king was a smiling, somewhat glassy-eyed undergraduate, Roger Burwick, with his arm around his date. The queen was identified as B. Solomon. Staring out at me from the picture was a younger but unmistakable Barbara Solomon. I finished off my whiskey and stared at the photograph. Barbara Solomon and Roger Burwick were, for a short time at least, an item. I thought back to the shadowy figure I had seen in Burwick's BMW leaving the prison, the hard copy of the article faxed in by Solomon that I had taken from the glove compartment of Burwick's car after the murder, and the sudden and mysterious absence of Solomon after the execution. I thought of the anger she had shown when discussing capital punishment and her admission that she was not necessarily against killing, just killing done by the state.

I ordered another whiskey—that made four—to think these facts over. This was information I knew Lieutenant Hickey would deem important to his investigation, but Solomon's secret was safe with me. Still, this was a new and interesting addition to the story that would warrant watching. I looked through the remaining sheets that Rachael had provided but found no more pictures of Burwick and Solomon, though Burwick was pictured with other women, none of them his wife.

I drove back to Violet's carefully, being one whiskey over the line. The elusive Leo had already come and gone. And Violet and I made our way to the Gonzales Family Restaurant. The dinner was a quiet one; unlike the previous night, we were left alone with our thoughts. We didn't talk about the upcoming day though it was clearly on both our minds.

"You better get some sleep, Ned. Tomorrow, from what I can glean, will be quite a day."

"How's Leo doing?" I asked.

"I don't know," said Violet. "He seems so calm, he worries me." I took Violet's advice and lay down, and to my great surprise I slept like a dead man until morning.

The morning was a repeat of the day before, with Violet depositing me at the prison and waiting the two hours for me in the parking lot. I received a particularly thorough search, the state not taking any chances on Willie's last day. Willie on the day of his death was radiant, his skin glowed, and his eyes were on fire. "Hello, my old friend Ned and president of my foundation," Willie greeted me with his best English voice, and he laughed raucously, causing the guards to focus their attention closely.

"So yesterday you got most of my story, at least in outline form, so you can get the particulars from the principal characters. Flesh it out and document it in whatever medium you choose—a book or articles, it doesn't matter, but I want my story to be known. I want those people who are responsible for what, and who I am, to be acknowledged. That's really what the documentation is about, that and the worth of souls lost to society, all with the potential to become Sister Shashwatis. The book or articles are not to be about me but about the process of becoming me. Do you understand?"

"Yes," I said. "But are you sure I'm the right guy for the job? Surely there are more prominent authors who could do this better than I can."

"I am absolutely sure of my choice. You must believe me and promise me you will follow through no matter what else happens. Remember, there are no coincidences. That's why you were given the book. Document it all, leave nothing out, and use real names. If you need a model, use *The Anatomy of Coincidence*. It was my first book and my most powerful; in some way, everything I wrote since then uses it as foundation. Do I have your solemn word to complete this trust?" Willie shot me a look that said he was deadly serious.

I nodded.

"Good. Let's start our day. First order of business is a letter I want to dictate and have you to deliver to the parties concerned. You ready?" And with that, Willie began to dictate the content of his letter.

Dear Margret and Leo,

The two of you are my children; I write this letter to you both, as a father. You have in your different ways given me all that children can give to a parent. You have brought me joy and pride in the way you have lived out your lives thus far, and you have given me solace and serenity with which to live out mine. For this, I thank you.

Margret, we've never met face to face, but I know you well, through Uncle Adam, and through communications with your teachers, and trip counselors, I have come to know you quite well. There are few papers you have written that I have not read. Your brilliance has far exceeded even my predictions. I read your last paper on the curled dimensions of space and was thrilled. I had never dreamt of such a thing, but now knowing of their possible existence it makes perfect sense to me. Bravo!

Leo, we have known each other over the last three years, and I have seen your growth into manhood, your struggles with yourself and your world have been truly heroic, and in what a place and context! You have the makings of a truly gifted writer and scholar, a path not necessarily like Margret's path in science, but one filled with passions, emotions, compassion, empathy, and wisdom.

With my death, things are about to change. I am in control, through the grace of Uncle Adam, of a great deal of wealth. Just how much I was not aware of until recently. I was never very concerned with money outside of the need to provide for your education and life, Margret. That and a few small grants administered by the foundation. Sixteen years ago, I started writing what has become a series of books under the name of Sister Shashwati. In the beginning, it was merely a way to organize my thoughts and progress on my path through Eastern philosophy, religions, and spirituality. It has evolved over the years into a particular philosophy, one that has received a worldwide following, and in the process amassed a fortune that shows no sign of diminishing. This wealth and the foundation will need to be nurtured, guided, and managed. The two of you, as well as a few others, I hope will assume that duty.

Margret, by your letter I've come to know that you've stolen my thunder with respect to the present revelation. Uncle Adam kept your confidence and secret well, as did you continuing the use of the name Hoag on your scientific papers. I should have known your intellect would pierce the mystery, but so early on is quite impressive. My compliments to Saturn Kitty.

Leo, you have known about my nom de plume for a little while now, but not its implications. I will leave the running of the foundation to the principals with only a few directions. First, the foundation, or one arm of it, will continue to support Margret Hoag Shashwati in her education and life. It will be extended to her work as a scientist, funding her research and continuing travel by which to pursue her work. Leo, you will use funds to pursue your education. I suggest that you follow your sister, Violet, to Columbia. Funds will be provided for the living expenses for you and your sister. While you have the ability to become a great scholar and intellect, you are not yet an academic and I feel your education will be more of an individual enterprise. I suggest you travel a good deal, talk to a variety of people from all cultures and walks of life, and educate yourself on your own terms, but don't neglect the university, for it too has a part to play in your development.

Don't ever doubt your intelligence or your ability to compete in a formal institution of higher learning. Though the university will, I feel, play a secondary role in your development.

I entrust all of these provisions to Adam Zegura to carry them out in the letter and spirit in which they have been conceived. I have asked that Ned Alexander, a longtime friend, act as the president of the foundation. His good judgment and compassion make him the perfect choice.

I looked up at this, and Willie gave me a big smile and chuckle but did not lose his concentration.

It will be one of his particular duties to make sure that the needs of the board members are met. Beyond these directions, I leave the foundation to you, under the competent guidance of Adam.

The only thing left to discuss is the matter of my death. As you know, I am to be put to death by the state of Texas tonight at twelve midnight. This I will not allow to happen.

Although it may sound odd for a person living in a death row prison, for all intents and purposes, I have assumed full control over all of the important aspects of my life. This, of course, would not have been possible without the help of a few significant others who have aided me in this process. In all of the things important to being a human, I have had control, and the same is true for my death. I have countless letters that have said that execution by lethal injection is too good for me, and I tend to agree. The French writer and philosopher Albert Camus said that "Suicide is something planned in the silence of the heart, like a work of art." And I have planned just such a death. It is on the model of a Samurai ritual, and it will serve both to satisfy those who feel death by lethal injection is too good for me and will absolve the state of Texas from guilt in my death, and with this act release me from any deals I made with it. I have bribed a team of guards to place me in a room with a sharp knife before I am taken to the execution, and there I will end my life.

Because of you, it has been a full and productive life and it will be a good death, one for which I am totally in control. In the room is a concealed video camera, the videotape of which will be made available to the press. Hopefully, the many fans of Sister Shashwati will forgive her for this last act. See the evils of the system of capital punishment, and the worth of all individuals irrespective of their deeds and histories, and see the important role of forgiveness, and the futility of mindless punishment.

At some later time, if the board approves, I have arranged with Adam and the University of California for the publication of a book that will be the second to last in the Sister Shashwati series, Death and Release, should go a long way to explain to my readers the reasons for my actions. Leo, although you have no direct role to play in this last drama, I want you and your sister to leave Texas immediately after, drive to Highridge and make your way to New York.

Adam will assist you with the funds. Do not stay around for the investigations that are sure to follow. Adam will stay here to take care of all the loose ends.

My final request is that you two get to know each other as siblings and help each other throughout your lives. Margret, get to know Violet. You will find you have much in common and much to offer each other.

Go with love my children and regret nothing. And know there is no such thing as coincidence.
Willie T Ruckles

I looked up from the dictated letter. "You plan to kill yourself?" I asked. "I do indeed, and I need your help once again, Ned." I looked at him. His skin was still glowing, and his eyes still on fire as he smiled at me. "After I leave here, I will be taken to prearranged place where I will be locked in and commit a ritual suicide. I will have enough time before the guard secures the key to the cell. He will remove the videotape and someone will take it to you in the parking lot. I ask you to wait there until this happens. You will arrange for the tape to go to a news agency and be put on the air. Can you do this? Do you have an outlet?"

I had a former girlfriend, Robin, who was a producer for the Global News Network. I figured this would be an exclusive pearl just up their alley. Robin had a brief stint as a television correspondent, but while conducting an interview with a movie star and proponent of the Second Amendment, she let off a terrific sonic boom on live television of what my mother would politely call "breaking wind," and with this, along with the gun advocates startled reaction, she never seemed to recover. So, she went back to a career as a producer behind the camera.

"I have a friend at a cable news network in New York," and told Willie a breif version of the story.

"That will be fine," he chuckled. "Ask them to delay the presentation, giving you time to type the letter. Give it to Margret and Leo, meet with Zegura and arrange for Violet's and Leo's departure."

"Are you sure this is the right thing to do?"

"Absolutely. I'll leave it to you to redeem the good name of Sister Shashwati through your book or articles. Make it clear why I chose this way."

"I'm not sure I see it clearly." "You will, I'm sure," he said.

I had forgotten to give Willie a message Zegura had given me last night. "Adam Zegura asked me to tell you that it's a done deal, whatever that means."

"It means that my Ph.D. thesis has been accepted by the University of California at Berkeley, and I am now officially a doctor."

"Congratulations, Dr. Ruckles," I said, bowing my head.

"Just in time, eh?" Willie expelled his now familiar laugh. "You can put it on my tombstone," Willie said, his eyes ablaze.

"I'll put it in your book." I said. "You gonna do it now, not wait for this evening?"

"No time like the present." said Willie. "Besides, it would be harder to pull off the closer the execution time comes. Say hello to your brother for me, will you?"

"I haven't seen him in over a year."

"You will, and soon I suspect. Goodbye now, Ned, I cannot thank you enough."

With that, he motioned to the guards, who came to lead him away. Did I imagine that they led him away with a particular gentleness?

I gathered my notebooks and left for the parking lot. Strangely, I did not feel sad. I felt that Willie had exerted control over his life, and there was little cause for sorrow. I also realized that this feeling would soon evaporate. Violet was waiting for me.

"We need to wait here for a little while," I said. She nodded and returned to reading her papers.

I recognized that with the airing of the video, the *Sun* would be deprived of an exclusive. and I knew Halloran would not be happy. I went into my previously written stories and edited them on the basis of the new information. I also wrote an article about Willie's suicide, beating the great state of Texas to the punch. I did not wait to view the videotape, referring to the suicide as a ritual, based loosely on the Samurai tradition. It wasn't the best reporting, but it was what I needed at the time to get through the rest of the day. Halloran would at least have it a tad before it was all over the airwaves.

Three articles Halloran and the *Sun* should be ecstatic about. I began to type out the dictated letter to Margret and Leo when the guard who had frisked me so conscientiously handed me an envelope with what I took to be the videotape.

"It's over then?" I asked. The guard gave me the barest of nods, not meeting my eyes, and left as quickly as he had come.

Violet seemed not to be surprised by anything. "We're to go home and wait," she said.

"Violet," I said. "I can tell you now that Willie T Ruckles is really Sister Shashwati."

"I figured as much," she said and smiled. "You're not all that good with a secret."

This stung me slightly, but I continued on. "Willie's just committed suicide, and this is a videotape showing it."

She gave me a long, sad stare. "I'm not surprised, given Leo's current behavior. I was expecting something like this."

We arrived at Violet's, and I finished the letter and printed out four copies, one extra for Zegura and one for me. I used Violet's dial-up connection to send the three articles to Halloran along with a short note that said I would be in touch. I instructed him to get them on the wires immediately and to watch the Global News Network. I then called Robin. The secretary said she was in a meeting, and I told her to have Robin call me back. I had the story of her life and that she would never forgive her if she messed this one up. The secretary seemed nervous and assured me that Robin would call back soon. Violet and I waited for what would come next.

We didn't have long to wait. The phone rang, and it was Zegura saying we should all meet in his room at the Holiday Inn in a half-hour. I began to worry that Robin would not call me back in time. Just about the time the worry began to kick in, Robin called.

"Ned, it's been a while. How are you?" Robin began.

"Robin, good to hear you, too. I'm about to repay you for all of your past kindness," I said, and then I filled her in. I could tell she was excited, but she remained cool and professional. She gave me the name and address of the closest affiliate and the name of a contact person.

"If this is all you say it is, we'll be ready to air it in about an hour. I'll put together some footage from our previous coverage of the legal battles." We then rang off.

Violet had a videotape player that you could play one tape and record another, so I thought to make a copy of the tape before I gave it to the station. Violet couldn't find a blank tape, so we used a copy of *It's a Wonderful Life*. We put scotch tape over the two holes in the back so we could tape over it. I put the tape on and saw Willie sitting shirtless and cross-legged on the floor of an otherwise empty cell. There was a homemade knife in front of him, a shiv, substituting for a Samurai sword. I rewound the tape and copied it on high resolution over *It's a Wonderful Life*. I thought the irony would cause Willie to smile.

Violet and I dropped the original video at the designated affiliate. Robin already had the station mobilized, so the process took only a few minutes and we were on our way to the Holiday Inn.

11

BWWY

W e arrived at Zegura's room at the Holiday Inn. It was a suite, and there were already three people sitting in the living room besides Zegura. Given our errand at the GNN affiliate, we were about fifteen minutes late. Seated at the coffee table was a young man who was surely Leo. I could see from his resemblance to Violet. He had the body of a high school jock and the eyes of a Buddha. But it was his hands that were his most singular feature, long, strong, and delicate at the same time. One could imagine him sitting on a mountainside in the lotus position, his hands formed into an intricate mudra.

At his side on the love seat sat a young woman with short, thick brown hair and hazel eyes. She was short, but her muscled build and erect posture gave her an arresting presence. Her gaze was penetrating and her movements quick and precise. She gave the impression of a gymnast at rest.

The third member was a middle-aged woman who could have been a lawyer, businesswoman, or a professor, as she was. She, too, was slim and wore a smart gray suit, her blond hair at shoulder length. Her light eyes sparkled and reminded me slightly of Willie's.

Zegura introduced Leo, Margret, and his wife, Louise Taylor. I gave a copy of Willie's letter to Margret, Leo, and Zegura. I gave my copy to Violet, going on the assumption that the letter held information important to us all. They all read it, Margret brushed tears from her eyes, Leo's features did not move, Zegura nodded and gave his copy to his wife.

"Well," began Adam Zegura, "Willie is dead by his own hand. It's not the way I would have orchestrated it, but Willie was his own man, one not to be dissuaded from an action once decided. He was my best friend and colleague. We will all miss his presence in our own particular ways, and though he is now gone, he has left us with considerable assets and duties to be discharged. We have two orders of business before us this afternoon. The first is corporate— to form the Sister Shashwati Foundation as it will now exist.

"All of the principals are in this room with the exception of Ned's brother, Bob, who has been a longtime friend and confidant of Willie's. I have been in touch with him, and he has given his agreement to serve on the board. Ned, you are to serve as the foundation's president, an important position and one that Willie was adamant that you alone should fill. It seems to me that his choice is purely intuitive, but I have come to have great respect, and even awe, for Willie's intuition. As such, I respect Willie's choice with complete faith. Willie further designated Margret as the secretary of the foundation, I am proposing Louise as vice president, and I will be a non-voting member and treasurer. Violet, you, Leo, and Bob will complete the membership of the foundation. Is this agreeable to everyone here? Signify by saying ay or neigh."

We all looked at one another stunned and murmured ay.

"Done," said Zegura. "This is all I need along with your signatures to begin the foundation. I have drawn up its bylaws according to Willie's wishes and expressed in the letter to Margret and Leo. Everything else can be determined at some later date. Please read through the bylaws and sign on the master copy on the table by your name." I noticed that Bob's signature was already on the form.

"The next order of business is to get everyone out of Texas safely. There will be much scrutiny on us given the events of the day and the high profile given to this case by the governor. Leo, you are the most vulnerable, and though we have taken great care to have you out of the area with strong alibis, given the governor's predilection, you are not safe while still in Texas. It was Willie's strong feeling that you and Violet should travel immediately to Highridge in Tennessee, staying with Ned's mother until such time as you return to New York.

"Ned, you seem to be all over this mess." Zegura smiled at me, his big, bear-like presence making me feel safe, a feeling he had imparted fifteen years earlier in Margret's kitchen. "Leo and Violet, I've rented you a car down in the hotel parking lot so your truck won't be the object of pursuit on the way. You should leave immediately after this meeting.

"Ned, as a reporter, you should have a certain immunity, but as the video and your articles come out, you, too, will be the object of investigation. Use caution. Will your paper back you up?"

"Yes," I said, not knowing if it would or not. "Have you delivered the videotape to the station?" I gave a brief narrative of Violet's and my delivery.

"Good. Everything is done for the moment. We all have our parts to play." It was decided that Margret was to accompany Leo and Violet to Highridge, where I would meet them after things settled down and the stories were written. Adam would stay on and deal with the press.

When we were all leaving, the desk clerk came to the room with a fax, surprisingly addressed to me. I read its short text: *Ned, A little more help. Come to the San Carlos Hotel, room 345, at five thirty this afternoon.* The message was signed as was the previous fax sent to me in Tucson, BWWY. After the signature was another number, .071. I handed the fax to the curious Zegura.

"Do you know anything about this?" I asked.

He shook his shaggy head. "Not a clue," he said. I told him about the previous fax and the mysterious number. "You going to go?" he asked.

"Yes," I said. "I am a reporter, after all." It was now a quarter to five. "I'll go with you," said Adam, retrieving his coat.

"No," I said. "You need to be available for Willie. Whatever this is, I have a feeling that it may be messy. You shouldn't be involved in something else at this time. Stay here and watch the Global News Network story, and I'll check back with you when I find out what this means."

Zegura nodded again. "OK," he said.

Before I left the hotel, I made a copy of the fax and stuck it in my backpack with the original. I took the keys to Violet's truck and a set to her house. Violet, Leo, and Margret left in the rental car. Violet had to return home to get some of her things for the trip, then it was immediately on to Highridge. Leo and Margret were already packed and ready to go. We said goodbye in the parking lot, and I hugged Violet and Margret. Leo remained calm and aloof. We said we would all meet at Highridge.

It was now five o'clock, and the San Carlos Hotel was downtown near the courthouse. As I drove the distance to the hotel, I had a creepy feeling I'd been here before. I arrived about ten minutes early. The San Carlos was a stately historic hotel of orange stucco. I walked through a lobby with its rough-hewn beams and a frescoed ceiling. Nothing seemed out of the ordinary. There were a few people sitting around sofas and coffee tables, and a few people in the shops that rimmed the room. The lobby ended in two curving stairways that were mirror images, and I walked up the left one. *When in doubt always choose left* was a rule I lived by. I made my way up two flights decorated with black-and-white photos of the hotel's earlier years, cowboys and cattle, fancy dinners with fancy diners, railroad memorabilia. Room 345 was at the end of a long hallway, the door was closed, and I could hear nothing from within. I was ten minutes early, but I knocked on the door. There was no answer and no sound, so I knocked again—nothing. I looked around the hallway and saw nobody, so I tried the door.

It opened easily, and just like Yogi Berra said, it was déjà vu all over again. The lights in the room were on, and slumped in a lounge chair by a period oak end table was a shirtless man. On the wall behind the chair, three narrow cylinders were attached with duct tape. As with Burwick, lines from the bottom of each tube were connected to each other by a single line ending in the man's arm. There were bubbles in the tubes indicating that a liquid had passed through them. I had seen it all before. The man looked dead, but what did I know, so I lifted the line-free arm and felt for a pulse. There was nothing. His wrist felt a little colder than mine but seemed still warm. I looked around the room. His briefcase lay open on the bed, and in it were a change of clothes and what I took to be a bathing suit. There was an unopened bottle of whiskey on the table and a bucket full of ice on the floor. The ice was not melted, and the whiskey was a good one, Glen Fiddich, the same one I had drunk with Zegura. The man's shirt lay on the floor next to his feet. Along with the whiskey on the end table was a note written on a small, lined yellow notebook. I knew better than to touch anything, but I craned my neck and read: "Kant's Reckoning Continues…" Still nobody had arrived, and it was now the appointed five-thirty. I picked up the telephone using a hand towel I got from the bathroom, called the desk and delivered the message that they had a dead man in Room 345 and needed to call the police. I gave the guy at the desk my name, feeling it could do no more harm than my presence. Once again, twice in four days, I found myself in the middle of a murder investigation, and I waited in the room with the unknown dead man for what would happen next.

Within a minute after I put down the phone, there was a gentle knock at the door. *These Houston police are really fast*, I was thinking as I opened the door. Moving past me was a woman who carried a gym bag.

"Sorry I'm late," she said. Then she looked at the dead man and back to me. She dropped the gym bag on the floor and stood in the middle of the room, trying to comprehend the scene into which she had stepped. For what seemed a long time she was quiet, then she began to scream. It was a loud and continuous scream. I could hear doors opening in the hallway. I moved to her and took hold of her hands, she flung herself into my arms and buried her face in my shoulder and sobbed. The sobbing was a great improvement over the screams, and as they softened she managed to say: "Who are you?" "Ned Alexander," I said, and this seemed to reassure her though I was not quite sure why. I was going to say I was a reporter, but I waited, as my name seemed to be enough for the moment. "Do you know who the man is?"

I asked.

"Why, he's Robert Stith, special counsel to the governor."

Robert Stith, Willie's arch nemesis! Holy shit, I thought. *Bet you didn't think today would end up this way when you woke up, eh, Robert?* I said to myself.

"Who are you?" I asked the woman. "Emily Robinson," she answered.

"Are you his wife?" I knew Stith was married from articles I had read about him, and Emily had a gold band and diamond on her ring finger.

"No," said Emily, and for the first time she began to access her position in all this. "I'm, I'm a friend," she finally managed to say. "I work with him at the governor's office."

Yeah, well, Emily that hardly goes very far in explaining your "sorry I'm late," comment, your gym bag, and an assignation at the San Carlos Hotel, Room 345, now does it? But I said nothing. I now looked the woman over, she was early middle-aged, a little plump, but this served only to further round her out in all the right places. Her bleached blonde hair was cut short in what used to be called a pixie cut—maybe it still is. She was of medium height, about five-five, and her overall appearance was attractive. I could tell she was wondering what to do when the police arrived.

Four uniformed cops, all men, had just entered the room. The one with strips on his arm appeared to be in charge.

"Well, what have we got here? Ain't never seen anything like this," the lead officer said. His colleagues were going around the room inspecting the room and the body.

"Who are you?" asked the sergeant, who identified himself as Hart. "Ned Alexander, I'm a reporter. I'm the one who reported the crime." "Reporter…" moaned Emily. She was realizing that this was not going to be her day, either.

"Thought it was called in by the hotel desk clerk?" "Yes, but I'm the one who told him to do it."

"So I guess it wasn't you who reported the crime, now was it?" said sergeant Hart.

This important aspect of the crime being clarified, the sergeant continued his investigation.

"Who are you?" he asked Emily. Emily answered with her name.

"Why are you here, Miss Robinson?" Emily said that she was meeting him here on business, yes business, the governor's business. Hart looked at the whiskey bottle, gym bag and open briefcase and grunted. Almost as an afterthought, he asked if we knew who the dead man was, and Emily told him.

This knowledge seemed to enliven Sergeant Hart, as he turned to me. "And Mr. Alexander, what is a reporter doing here?"

"I was told to come." "Told by who?"

"I received a fax telling me to come to the San Carlos, Room 345, at five-thirty."

"A fax?" The sergeant said this like he had never heard the word. "A fax, was it?"

"Yes."

"Do you always do what faxes tell you to, Mr. Alexander?"

"This is the first fax that's told me to do anything. And yes, I'm a reporter and this seemed like an interesting lead. And as you can see it's turned out to be one."

The officer could see that I was getting impatient and took it as an insult. "Who do you work for, Mr. Alexander?" I told him.

"What's a reporter from Tucson doing in Houston?"

"I came here to do a series of interviews with Willie T Ruckles," I said. "The Ni...the prisoner they're set to kill tonight?"

"Yes." I was happy to see that Willie's death was not yet common knowledge. I wondered if Robin had put it on the television yet.

Again, almost as an afterthought, the sergeant asked to see the fax, and I retrieved it from my backpack and handed him the copy as a young Hispanic man in a business suit entered with two other men in plain clothes.

"Detective Escobar," he said and flashed an ID. "Sergeant, get these men out of here. You, too, and seal off this room. "

The sergeant called to his men and indignantly retreated from the room. "Who are you?" Escobar said to me. And I went through the story again with the aid of a few more competent questions.

After listening to my story, he said, "Willie Ruckles is dead, committed suicide this afternoon. Somehow, there was a videotape of it and some fucking idiot leaked to the press. It's all over the television. Seems he was a famous guru or something. Governor's mad as hell. People wanted a comment from Stith, but he couldn't be reached. Guess he was having his own little party." He looked over to Emily, then back to me.

"How did you know to come here?" I asked.

"We got a fax too at the station, but it told us to be here at six. We came as soon as we got the word. Why do you suppose they asked you to be here a half-hour before the police?" I had been wondering the same thing and said I had no idea. I also told him about Kant's Reckoning and my previous fax, and said I had no idea about who, or what, BWWY was.

"Do you think the two murders are connected?"

I told him the methods and equipment looked superficially the same and they were at least connected by the sender of the faxes.

"Yeah," he said.

"Detective," I said, "is it all right if I leave the state? I need to get back to Tucson." I didn't mention my plans to go to Tennessee.

"You're not a suspect, but just leave me your numbers where I can reach you, and let me know if you're contacted by these guys again."

I assured him I would, told him about Lieutenant Hickey, and gave him his number along with mine.

The lab guys had come and were busy collecting samples and doing the high-tech stuff they do. I asked if I could call in and get the results of their work and autopsy and was told I could.

"Say," said Escobar, "can I have that fax they sent you?" I told him that the sergeant had taken it.

"Fucking idiot," said Escobar. "Robles, go find the sergeant and get Mr. Alexander's fax back."

"What?" said Robles.

I left and was down in the lobby when someone touched my arm. It was Emily, looking miserable. She asked if there was any way I could leave her name out of the article as the whole affair had the potential to be destructive and embarrassing. I loathed Robert Stith and his politics, but I had nothing against Emily, so I told her I would keep her name out of my articles if I could.

She thanked me and left. I headed back to the Holiday Inn and Zegura. The Inn's lobby was a circus, with Zegura center ring. Lights blazed on and off and cameras whirred and everyone was talking at once. Zegura calmly answered, or tried to answer, the questions being fired at him from all sides. Did he know about the suicide? Why had Willie done it? How had it occurred? Did he know that Willie T Ruckles was really Sister Shashwati? What help had he given to Willie? What happened to all of the money generated by the Sister Shashwati books? Did he agree with the suicide? Wouldn't it have been different if people would have known he was really Sister Shashwati? I listened from the periphery for a little while and caught Zegura's attention and pantomimed drinking and went into the bar. I was now ready to see Willie's video, but first I needed to write an article on Stith's murder and get it to Halloran before I turned my attention to the suicide and the articles that it would engender. I pulled my laptop out onto the bar and ordered a Glen Fiddich and toasted Robert Stith's timely departure. I tried to feel some remorse for his death but could summon none. Still, I felt I wrote a fair but patently unsympathetic article.

I described the scene in the room, how the major principals got there, managing to keep Emily's name out of it, describing her as an unnamed woman—unnamed because I didn't name her—and compared it to the Burwick murder, told the story of the faxes, and recounted the history of Stith's crusade to execute Willie, even though he had fired no shots that killed his brother nor had any weapon at the time. For the sake of objectivity, I had to write this section over three times to overcome the emotion that surfaced. I ended the article with a speculation of what BWWY might be and what part it had played in Stith's killing. I thought this last section had a fifty-fifty chance of being edited out of the piece, so I tried to tie it closely to the few known facts.

Take it all around, I was pleased with the job I had done. It had taken me only forty-five minutes to write it. I had just ordered my third Glen when I finished, and under its influence I added a postscript to the article: *Goodbye Robert, it's a better world without you!* I took a sip of my whiskey and stared at my last sentence, and it most gave me the fantods, as my hero would say. It's a Better World Without You. BWWY.

12

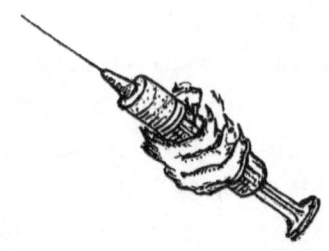

My Brother, the Hero

I finished my whiskey and continued to look at my last sentence. I rubbed my arms to quell the goose bumps that had formed on them. Could this really be right? That there was an organization, or at least individuals, that had as its mission the killing of people the world would be better off without. If that were true, why start here with Robert Stith? Surely there were more righteous killings than Robert. Then I figured, why not begin with Robert? The world was truly better off without his brand of poison. Anyway, I'd think more about it, but for now I needed to get my article, minus the last sentence, to Halloran. I went to the business center of the hotel, which was still open, and e-mailed my article to Halloran. I thought it was time to check in with him in person.

I was mostly out of money, but I had an old telephone credit card I had at Harvard that I would use to call my mother—and remarkably, it worked. I ordered another Glen Fiddich and used the pay phone in the bar. It was getting late, so I thought that I would just leave Halloran a message, but he answered with what would become his standard line: "Hey, Harvard, what's up?"

"Mr. Halloran, have you been getting my articles?"

"Yeah, all three have gone to press and will be in the paper tomorrow. They're already on the wires and online. Call me Mike, Mr. Halloran's my father. Great work, and good writing, no major edits, and so far, it's an exclusive. Sister Shashwati, for Christ's sake, a death row inmate. It's all over the news now, but we had it first. Have you seen it?"

"I haven't seen it yet, I've been busy, but I was the one that put it on the airwaves." I gave him a brief account of my last two days, the Sister Shashwati Foundation, and how the videotape got to GNN. I could tell he was excited and impressed.

"Did you get my last article, number four? I asked.

"Just got it, haven't read it yet. More on Ruckles-Shashwati, I'm thinking." "No, Mr. Ha—Mike. You're going to love this," which would become my standard answer to his "Hey, Harvard what's up?" And I told him of the Stith murder and its ties to the Burwick case.

He could hardly contain his joy. "Harvard, that's wonderful. Does anyone else have this?"

"Maybe now, but not when I wrote it, get on the wire, and I think we'll be first."

"Gonna move on it now. Great work—great work—Harvard."

I thought it was time to test out our new employer-employee relationship. "Mike, I want to stay here a few more days and follow up on these events, but," and here was the kicker, "I've run out of funds and need an advance." To my surprise, Mike laughed, gave me the go-ahead, and said that he was wiring me four hundred dollars tomorrow and keep the articles coming. I rang off to his exuberant chuckles and another "good work, Harvard." When I had hung up, I realized I hadn't asked about Solomon.

I went out to the lobby, where Zegura was just finishing up with the last of the television journalists. People were busy breaking down their cameras, sound equipment, and lights, having mined Adam Zegura dry. Zegura, for his part, still looked energetic and jovial.

"Let's get something to eat, Ned. Louise is spending the evening with family friends, and it'll be a chance for us to get to know each other."

We walked to Zegura's rented car, and I thought how different this night would be if Willie were to be executed at midnight. I thought of the agony his act had spared us, and silently I thanked him.

"I still haven't seen the videotape," I said.

"It was vintage Willie with a macabre twist," said Zegura with a wry smile. "He did it cleanly, just two slits along each sides of his rib cage, talking softly of forgiveness as he bled to death. Yep, the whole thing was vintage Willie." He shook his giant head.

Zegura drove us to a Japanese restaurant while I filled him in on Stith's demise. I also told him of my discovery of the possible meaning of BWWY. He seemed very interested and said he shared my lack of compassion, but he was quick to point out that Willie would not agree with us.

"Japanese food, in honor of the Samurai suicide?" I said as we pulled into the parking lot of Sushi Village.

"I thought it appropriate, and besides I love sushi, and Willie would have wanted us to celebrate this day," he said with a sad smile.

"Celebrate?"

"Yes. It was not easy being Willie T Ruckles, and I'm not referring to the prison, which was the easy part for him. Willie lived a full life grappling with its varied aspects. That's what the Sister Shashwati books, and their attendant philosophy, are about. They document his struggle with the nature of being human, and of human beings and the world they produce. Willie was a joyous soul, but his life was not a joyous enterprise, and again I'm not talking about the prison part. He viewed his death as a release from his duty as he saw it, to whatever is next. I don't mean to say that he didn't enjoy life—he did, every day—just that his life was not easy. He describes this process in his book, one of the two yet unpublished."

"*Death and Release?*" I asked. "That's the one."

"Will it be published soon?"

"That will be up to you and the other members of the foundation, but my advice is to publish it within the next year, and the final book a year or two after that, giving you time to write your chronicle. It will be a bit different from your Dylan Thomas book, I imagine."

I looked at him. "You've read that?" I asked.

"I've read almost everything you've written. It was Willie's request."

"There are really no such things as coincidences, are there, Adam?"

"No indeed, I've learned that one lesson well over the years. You know, Willie and I co-authored a seminal paper on social law that I presented at a conference at the University of Illinois School of Law. While I was delivering the paper, I looked up into the upper tier of the auditorium and saw Willie clear as life sitting in the first row. Shaken, I finished our paper and looked back to see only an empty seat, but I was sure that he was there. On my way back home, I stopped at the prison and told Willie of the occurrence. He just laughed his Willie laugh and said, 'Now you know, Adam, that is impossible,' and continued to laugh. I've told no one else of this other than my wife, who put it down to a kind of self-hypnosis. But to this day I'm not completely sure."

As we finished our tuna roll and sake, I could feel the goose bumps forming on my arms and neck as I thought of the book placed at my feet in my Oxford hostel. I said nothing.

"What will you do next?" asked Adam.

"I think it's time to pay a long-delayed visit to my brother," I said, forming the idea as I said it.

"I think that's a good idea. You may not be a suspect now, but that could change given the mood of the governor's office. They are badly in need of a scapegoat. I've heard they are trying to get the video pulled off the air. It was a good move to send it to New York, where they take the First Amendment more seriously than they do in Texas. When will you leave?" he asked.

"Right after dinner," I found myself saying. Then I remembered. "Well, maybe not until tomorrow," and I told him about Halloran's four-hundred- dollar wire.

Zegura opened his wallet and took out ten hundred-dollar bills and handed them to me. "Your expenses, courtesy of the Sister Shashwati Foundation."

"I can't take this, Adam."

"It's quite legitimate, let me assure you, and you will need funds for what comes next. Here, take this," he said as he handed me another four bills. "I believe I can retrieve your wire tomorrow. Ned, don't delay your trip. My best advice is to get the hell out of Texas. We'll all meet at Highridge in the next few days."

After a quick stop at Violet's house, I was on my way in her truck, speeding through Texas toward Louisiana and headed for Greenville, Mississippi, where my brother lived. Next to my father, my brother Bob was the person I could most easily talk to. He was actually my half- brother by my mother, but given the difference in our ages, fourteen years, we had grown up close. Bob would spend time with us in Boston, and I would, on occasion, travel down with him to Greenville. He did parts of seven years with us when he completed a real Harvard degree in public health, and he would go back home to Greenville on breaks and during the summer.

Bob was famous in the civil rights movement for acting alone in dangerous areas, registering folks to vote, and engaging in a variety of grassroots educational and community activities. His father, Amos Moore, was a longtime influential community leader. When a young man, Amos had traveled to Highridge for a weeklong workshop on the social aspects of farming in the south, and the young Helen became smitten with the charismatic local leader. Amos was married at the time and had several other children. There was never any talk, or thought for that matter, of marriage between the two. Love was enough, my mother once told me, but for several years Amos was a frequent visitor to Highridge.

About midway through their relationship, Helen became pregnant with Robert Baldwin Moore, and neither she nor Amos entertained thoughts of giving up the baby. And young Bob traveled between Mississippi and Tennessee on a regular basis. Amos' wife, Hattie Mae, accepted the baby as a full-fledged member of the family, and young Robert lived a mobile life with two mothers and a father. This went on for five years until my father came on the scene, and Bob now lived periodically in three households with two mothers and two fathers. After a number of years, a baby brother was added, and I began my relationship with my older brother.

Although there was no blood between them, Bob and my father had a very close relationship, Bob being a much better connoisseur of my father's wisdom than I. As a youth and young man, Bob pursued his public health degree at Harvard. It took him seven years but, unlike me, it wasn't from lack of application, for Bob continued his clandestine and heroic civil rights work wedged between his studies. There were many times when he went missing in the field, with rumors of his death, and each time he surfaced with a tale that excited the imagination of his younger white brother and carved out a mystic legend in the annals of the movement.

As the more dramatic parts of movement slowed, Bob completed his degree, began a masters, and founded several daycare centers and schools across the Mississippi Delta. He used his degree to develop and administer health clinics serving the rural areas of the South. The clinics were notable for serving both blacks and whites.

He had lately been tapped to run for congress but always declined, following his mother's bent for real work with real people. It was four hours and nearing midnight as I crossed Violet's truck into Louisiana from Texas, and I breathed a sigh of relief. It had been a long day. I crossed at Texarkana, which put me on the northwest end of Louisiana. Greenville was in the middle of the state of Mississippi, and I had about another four or five hours. I drove through one little sleepy town after another, until I reached a motel by the side of a small river with a grove of weeping willows. It seemed a pleasant place, and I was dead tired. I rang the bell, and it was answered by a smiling young woman I took to be Indian. As she was checking me in, I said, "When did all of the motels in the South become acquired by Hindus." I hoped it wasn't a racist remark.

The woman smiled. "I don't know; I'm not Hindu, I was born in Lucknow, India, and my family is Muslim. But I think the Indian takeover has been going on for quite some time now," she smiled a beautiful smile and my thoughts of racism were banished. I noticed she was wearing a T-shirt that spelled out something in a script that I was unfamiliar with, and I asked what it was.

It's Urdu and says, Advani School for Girls, and I asked her what it was. "It's a center for sexually abused young women and girls. Most have been rescued from brothels in North India and Nepal. I do some fundraising for them. It's a very good program."

"Do you take donations?" I asked. "Why, yes, that's what I do."

On impulse, I said, "Well I'd like to make a donation to the Advani School for Girls." I handed her the last four hundred dollars given to me by Zegura of Sister Shashwati Foundation money, or maybe it was Halloran's.

The woman, whose name was Laila, could only look at me. Finally, she said, "That is indeed a generous contribution. Most of the ones I get are in the one- to five-dollar range." She continued to shake her head and look at the money, and there were tears in her large eyes.

"Would you like a T-shirt?" she asked. "Very much."

She returned with a T-shirt and a brochure. "I only have a large," she apologized. "You may take an extra-large. I'm sorry."

"Don't worry," I said, "this will make me watch my diet." She smiled her beautiful smile, and we said goodnight.

The interaction made me strangely happy and I thought it an appropriate sendoff for Willie, whom I silently thanked. The room was cheerful and clean, and I lay down to bed in a shirt that said Advani School for Girls that fit me just fine.

13

Texas Duped

I woke up rested early the next morning, got dressed, and continued wearing my Advani T-shirt. I noticed a small envelope had been pushed under the door sometime in the night. It was a card with the same Urdu letters on my T-shirt. It was from Leila and read:

> *Dear Mr. Alexander,*
> *I am not used to the magnitude of your last night's generosity and I fear I was not appropriately thankful. Let me assure you that your kindness will result directly in making the lives of specific children better. I will probably not see you tomorrow, as I leave early to return to school in California at Berkeley.*

Berkeley, what a coincidence, I started to think, then caught myself and smiled and continued to read:

It was truly a pleasure to meet you. I hope to hear from you
in the future.
Leila Mohammed

She included her e-mail address, and I put the card in my backpack for safekeeping. I stopped on the way out of town for a southern breakfast of grits, hushpuppies, and eggs. A few more of those and my Advani T-shirt would be too small. I'd have to be careful. With a large to go coffee, I set out for Greenville and my brother Bob.

I hadn't been in Greenville in four years, and a few things had changed, more grocery stores, and fast-food restaurants, but its general quality seemed the same. Bob lived alone in a small wooden house in back of one of his clinics. There was a short wooden fence around it with a large dog inside. "Hello, John Lewis," I replied to the friendly greeting of the old dog, who was named after my brother's personal hero. I swung the gate open and Bob opened the front door and came with arms outstretched toward me. We hugged there in the front yard as John Lewis rubbed against our legs; I felt for the first time in a long time that I was home. Over coffee, I poured out the previous five days to my older brother, who listened like a father—like my father.

I finished up the pot of coffee and looked around the small, cozy house. The kitchen and living room were one large room. Everything was paneled in knotty pine, the walls were almost entirely covered, with the exception of the windows, with bookcases and shelves of all shapes and sizes, all Bob's work, as was the house itself. In addition to books, there was a space for an elaborate stereo and reel-to-reel tape deck, and spaces for his tapes and extensive record collection. In the corner was a desk with a microphone and turntable and wires going outside. For years, he had produced and DJed a once-weekly four-hour roots radio show, using his own records and tapes, some of which he had recorded in the field. He maintained a hook-up to the local radio station so he could do the show from home. Interspersed with the books, stereo equipment, and records were pieces of folk art, some of which I knew to be very valuable, and each piece had its own wooden cove. In the back of the house was a room that housed the bathroom, separated by a curtain, from the large room that served as a bedroom and study. Again, the walls were covered with bookcases, shelves, and cabinets. I searched the living room bookcases until I found a group of small books all bound in dark blue cloth and walked over and took out *The Anatomy of Coincidence*.

"Did you know Willie was Sister Shashwati?" I asked.

"Not until I was called a few days ago by Adam Zegura and asked to serve on the board of the foundation. It was a great surprise to me—and then it wasn't. I did know Adam before that and knew that Willie was writing as himself and with Adam under the name L.T. Zegura. Adam would send me drafts of some of their papers and ask for my comments, largely at Willie's request, I think."

"How did you meet him?"

"When I was working with the movement, he sent me a letter through our office. It was two months before I checked in and got it, but I was touched by the childlike genuineness of it. Willie was just beginning his academic career and was by no means as erudite as he was in his later stuff, but his intellect was as sharp and as penetrating as it always has been. He had just published his little book on reading instruction using fifty key emotionally charged words as its basis. I thought it was brilliant and started to use it in my trainings. I tried to order copies but found it hard; the publisher was small and had only printed a limited run. I wrote him back, nearly three months after his original letter, thanking him for his book and his interest in our work. I told him that his book was very useful and that I was using it in my training, but I couldn't seem to get any new copies. I asked if we could have permission to mimeograph it. He wrote back and said that our organization could have the book and the rights to it, that we could publish it on our own, collect the royalties, and apply them to our work. He also sent me a workbook that he also gave us the rights to. Ever since that letter, we have been friends and have corresponded regularly. I still use his books for our high school programs.

"In the beginning, it was easier to correspond directly, over the past years I have relied on Adam Zegura to broker our interactions. The Sister Shashwati books have made an impact on my life. I'm not sure how the knowledge that Willie was the author would have affected my consumption." My brother smiled. He smiled often but laughed rarely. "But knowing it now, I am not surprised. That Willie was, among other things, a sly one. From death row he rose to the forefront of social change. I think, little brother, your meeting was a bit more fantastic—that we're all being brought together in this way."

"Yeah, well, there is no such thing as coincidence," I said, smiling.

"So I've heard," he said, returning my smile. "Mom called, by the way, and wants us to meet her at Highridge. I told her we'd come tomorrow."

"That only gives me a day here. Will we have time to see your dad and Hattie Mae?" Despite the awkwardness of the situation, Hattie Mae had always treated me as a son along with my brother; despite the differences in our ages, I would often accompany him home and be part of the family. It was during the height of the movement, and I was kept out of the danger of the direct actions of my brother, Bob, and his friends, but I absorbed a lot of the times, and it was my mother's feeling that it was good for me.

"We'll have the barbecue tonight," said Bob. "I need to run out and meet with some clinic people. Do you want to come?"

"I think I should stay here and do a little work and check in with my paper," I said.

The first thing I needed to do was check in with Detective Escobar. I called the number at the station and got him on the first try. "How's the case coming, detective?" I asked.

"Autopsy's been done. It was the chemicals that killed him all right, but he was sedated first." He listed the chemicals that were in the tube and spelled them for me and gave me their concentrations. "They're exactly the same ones that would have been used on Ruckles."

I would have to check, but they did not seem the same ones used on Burwick.

"What was the sedative?" I asked.

"Chloroform. The coroner thinks that probably it was administered by a cloth over the face. There was a mild skin reaction and slight bruises that indicate that he was held down until he lost consciousness. Coroner speculates by the bruises that there were at least three people involved."

"Three people?" I said. I was thinking about the last moments of Robert Stith's life. Burwick was sedated as well, but he had his in his whiskey, which was much more civilized. Robert Stith's last moments must have been terrifying. I took a moment to see if I felt glad and decided I might be.

"Yeah, three people. We're looking for a group, it seems."

"Any leads?"

"Nothing so far. We're trying to find out where the chemicals came from, but so far nothing."

"Have there been any more faxes?" I asked, almost as an afterthought. "Ah, I'm afraid I am not at liberty to say," was his surprising answer. "Not at liberty, Detective Escobar? Would you be at liberty if there hadn't been one?" I probed.

"I'm not at liberty to say, but the governor is worried."

"What's the governor worried about?" Upon this question, Escobar was quiet for a moment, realizing that he'd said a bit too much.

"Have you been contacted further, Mr. Alexander?"

"No, but they would have had no way to reach me unless they had my address at the motel I stayed at in Louisiana."

Detective Escobar did not ask, but I just realized that I didn't even know how the fax came to be delivered to me at the Holiday Inn. Was I being surveilled by BWWY?

Breaking into my reverie Escobar said, "Louisiana? I thought you were going back to Tucson."

"I decided to visit my mother in Tennessee," and I gave him my mother's number at Highridge. I told him that if I were contacted, either through my paper or at Highridge, I would let him know immediately. He seemed reassured and asked where I was now, and I told him that I was calling from the road. It was maybe historical, but I didn't want to bring my brother into this. Escobar seemed to accept this, and I told him I would call when I reached Highridge, then we hung up.

Escobar had strongly suggested that there had been another fax and let slip that the governor was worried. Were the two connected? Was another fax sent that threatened the governor? I walked around Bob's front yard with John Lewis and thought things out. I wrote out my thoughts on a small notepad as I paced the yard.

Robert Stith was probably killed by at least three people. That suggested an organization was involved, not a single killer. The fax I received from BWWY after the Burwick killing was most likely from the same organization. But were they Burwick's killers?

The chemicals used to kill Stith and Burwick were not the same. I had gone back to my notes and checked. The apparatus on the wall appeared to me to be different, but I couldn't be sure. The methodology used to sedate the victims was different. It seemed to be important to the organization to keep me involved, even prominent. They had called me to Stith's room a half-hour before the police. *Why? Was the world a better place without the governor*, I wondered.

I looked down at the notes I had created. There were a few things

I could follow up on, but I realized I had not seen any television, not even Willie's suicide. I wondered what was happening in Houston, and I went inside to use the telephone. I first called Robin in New York. I got her secretary again. Did I imagine that she gave me her special attention when I told her who I was? Robin was in a meeting but should be out soon and would call me. I told her if the phone was busy to have her keep trying. The secretary, whose name was Stephanie, assured me that she would.

The phone was in the living room. I went into the bedroom-den, where there was a television and VHS. I knew that Bob didn't like television so had disconnected it from its antenna, but the VHS worked and I stuck in my special copy of *It's a Wonderful Life*. The movies credits came on initially, then faded to a dull gray scene of a jail cell. You could see the bars behind the figure of Willie sitting in a lotus position, bare at the waist and barefoot. There was a long naked shiv, just a bare strip of metal out in front of him. He first apologized to Officer Stith's family for his part in the killing. Then he went on to say that all killing was wrong, and the only way out of the suffering it caused was forgiveness. He then took the homemade knife and plunged it deep beneath his ribs and drew the knife slowly up along one side of his of his ribcage. He acknowledged all the letters he was sent that said execution was too good for him and said he hoped that his act would give some sort of peace to those who had written him, but it was only through forgiveness that peace could truly be achieved.

He told of how he arrived at the insights that led him to become Sister Shashwati, and he asked his readers to forgive those who had advocated for his death. And, indeed, the death by his own hand. By the time the knife had moved to his other side his voice was weak and a pool of blood flowed over his lap. He reminded the viewers that it was not Texas that had taken his life. He then just stopped speaking and moved no more. The videotape was then switched off, and a frenetic Jimmy Stewart filled the screen. I rewound the tape and switched off the VCR. The phone was ringing in the living room.

"Hi, Ned, this is Robin. Have you seen the coverage? Our ratings have gone through roof! I really owe you, buddy. I'm up for a promotion over this thing."

"Glad it's worked out so well for you," I said. "Listen, Robin, I haven't been around a TV for a while and I need to know what's been happening in Texas since the suicide. Can you tell me?"

"All hell's broken loose in Texas. The governor was ballistic about the suicide; they are looking for how he got into the cell and how the videotape was made and came to be delivered to us. They've been leaning on us to confiscate the tape and tried to make us remove it from the air, but so far the First Amendment is still intact and GNN is holding its ground. We've been leading with the story for a day now. There's been tremendous interest in Ruckles being Sister Shashwati. There's been a worldwide outcry against Texas. We've been interviewing academic and literary people, and they all say the same thing. That Sister Shashwati is held in the highest regard, both literarily and philosophically. They are universally taken by surprise. Nobody knew of the connection. We're busy preparing a special on the Sister Shashwati phenomenon that will probably air this evening. Zegura has been on the air mostly talking about Ruckles' legal battles and how the state of Texas, and how the governor's office in particular, had played it so punitive. He's not commenting much on the Sister Shashwati connection. He seems to have left the state."

"What about the death of Robert Stith?" I asked.

"Nothing much, just that he was found dead in a hotel room, the apparent victim of murder, but nothing specific."

"Listen, I wrote a story that should have at least gone to the wire services all ready. Have you seen it?" She hadn't. "Keep checking, and I'll email you a copy, but don't use it until you clear it with me, or see it on the wire, OK?" I knew I could trust Robin completely.

"Look, I'll be writing a follow-up in an hour or so and there'll be more information, look for that one, too." I said I'd also send her a copy.

"Listen, Ned, be careful," she said. "I was contacted by members of the Texas Capitol police, and they were asking about you and if you played a part in the videotape transmission." I assured her I would be prudent.

"We'll be in touch," I said, and we rang off.

I next phoned Halloran to ask why the Stith story hadn't been published yet. I was told that the governor's office had been asked by the senior editors of the *Sun* for a comment. Instead of a comment, the police from the governor's office had been intimidating and pressured the *Sun* to not publish it. It took time to work it through our legal department. But it had just been cleared.

"I've just submitted it to the wire and online edition. It should be there in a few minutes," said Halloran.

"I thought you were a senior editor," I said, mildly irritated.

Halloran caught my irritation but chose to ignore it. "Not senior enough, Harvard. And the Texas authorities were leaning pretty heavily." I felt bad that I had snapped at Mike.

"You can expect another article from me on Stith in an hour or so," I said, "and if things work out, maybe another one."

"I'll see if I can get this one out in a more timely fashion," said Halloran. "And Harvard, really nice work."

"Thanks Mike," I said in what I hoped was a somewhat apologetic tone, eassing my earlier remark. I thought of telling him of his donation to the Advani School for Girls but thought better of it, as I might need funds in the future.

"Keep in touch, Harvard."

My next call was to the Texas governor's office, playing a hunch. I asked for Emily Robinson, who was now back in Austin along with the governor. I was put right through.

"Emily, this is Ned Alexander—you remember, from Robert Stith's room." She needed no reminder. "I wrote my story and kept your name out of it," I said.

"Thank you," she said, then waited for what would happen next.

"I understand that the governor received a fax from the same people that alerted the police."

"Yes,' she said. "They threatened the governor, said the world would be a better place without him." Bingo!

"How did the governor respond?"

"Well, he was quite upset. They doubled his guard, and he went directly from Austin to his ranch." I smiled at the cowardly cowboy, doubling the size of his protection, and hightailing to his ranch. Great!

"Thanks Emily, I was just confirming facts I already had," I said in half- truth.

"Confirmed from whom?" said Emily as I rang off.

I called back to the governor's office and this time identified myself as the journalist who conducted the interviews with Willie Ruckles. I could tell the secretary knew who I was as she put me through to the governor's executive assistant, a Larry Buck.

"Do you recognize my name, Mr. Buck?" I asked.

"I certainly do," said Larry. "Are you in Texas, Mr. Alexander?"

I ignored his last question. "Larry," I said, using his name familiarly and hoping to piss him off. "Larry, I'm writing a series of articles on the execution, or near execution as it turns out, of the prisoner Willie Ruckles."

"Yes?" he said.

"The story's expanded to include the murder of the governor's special counsel, Robert Stith." Larry still waited. "I'm calling to see if you have any comment on the fax the governor received from the same people who faxed the police to come to the hotel room where Robert Stith had been murdered?" It was a mouthful. Was I a fat mouth? I waited for Mr. Buck to respond.

Rather than responding to my query, he said, "I understand that you also received a fax, Mr. Alexander."

"You are well informed, Larry," I said. "But would you like to make a comment about the fax that threatened the governor?"

"I have no comment on the fax," said Buck. Bingo.

"Was it from the same people who sent the fax to the police and me?" "I don't know if it was the same people," said Larry. "I've only seen the governor's fax." Bingo again.

"Did it have the signature BWWY?"

"I am afraid I cannot comment on that," said the retreating Mr. Buck. "Can you comment," I continued, hardly believing the fruitfulness of this interview, "that the governor was so unnerved by what was in the fax that he doubled his security guard and hightailed it to his ranch?" I bated him with the western cowboy movie word.

"It's not unusual for the governor to increase his security guard," said Larry, confirming that fact.

"Is it true that he was so scared of the statement that the world would be a better place without him that he retreated to his ranch to regroup?"

"Look Mr. Alexander," Larry said, now irritated. "The Governor is not scared of anyone, least of all a thug organization called BWWY." Bingo yet again. These Texas bureaucrats were not all that smart. It made me think that maybe Zegura was right when he said they should have fought the bastards in court.

"Mr. Alexander, are you in Texas?" he tried one more time. *I'm not the dumb one, Larry*, I thought. "Goodbye and thank you Mr. Buck" was what I said. And I did mean it.

I was so excited about the interview that I wrote the story immediately. It described how the governor was so unnerved by a fax that said the world would be a better place without him that he doubled his security and ran to hide out at his ranch, with little or no thought to his special counselor. I mentioned that the fax was signed BWWY and posed a few questions about who and what they were. It was a mean article, meant to embarrass the governor, but the facts supported it and I was feeling a bit mean.

Then I turned to the story that followed-up on Stith. I told the story of the chloroformed sedation and the fact that the Houston coroner speculated that there had been at least three people involved in the killing. In this article I recounted the part Stith had played in the pending execution and in the torment of Willie T Ruckles, now identified as the beloved Sister Shashwati. I reiterated how a fax was sent to the governor, causing him to double his security and run to his ranch.

This last story was not sympathetic to Stith, but it also was not as mean as the one I wrote on the governor. I emailed the stories to Halloran with copies to Robin using Bob's dial-up internet connection. Halloran would not be happy about the copies, but it wouldn't come back to haunt me if Robin used restraint, as I was sure she would. I went to the refrigerator, where I found a beer and I waited for Bob's return. I felt tired but energized by what I felt to be a good day's work.

14

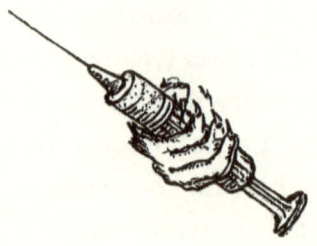

T for Tennessee

Bob returned home before I finished my beer. It was five-thirty, and the winter light was starting to fade. "Everything all right?" Bob asked as he greeted me.

"Everything's fine." I told him of the day's events and my stories.

"Well done. The governor is a bad man, and a little embarrassment will do him good," Bob said, smiling. "You ready to go to the barbecue? The family's waitin. Then we gotta get ourselves to Tennessee."

The barbecue was a real homecoming. Hattie Mae called me her son, and Amos, as always, called me "My Boy." I continued to wear my Advani T-shirt, but it was stretchin under the sweet potato pie, greens, and ribs. I saw stepbrothers and sisters, step aunts and uncles, and step cousins who all seemed glad to see me. The young ones had grown up in my absence, and I felt I'd been away too long. We drank beer, and some family members broke out instruments, including Bob on a steel guitar, and played music until it was early morning. Bob finally ended the party when he said we had an early morning tomorrow, traveling to Tennessee.

When we got home, it was nearly two o'clock. Bob insisted that I take his bed while he would sleep on the couch. I'd had this argument before and always lost, so I accepted gracefully. Before I went to bed, I asked him to play me the song "T for Texas T for Tennessee" that I had heard on the transistor radio on the bus. He went over to the bookcase and took out an album.

"Sonny Boy Powell—he lives here in Greenville, you know. He's in his eighties and will still play for people when they come over, but he refuses to play at events outside, says if he does the govment might take his assistance away." Bob put on the records and the refrain "T for Texas and T for Tennessee / T for Texas and T for Tennessee / Ain't no woman gonna make a fat mouth of me," blared out.

"What's a fat mouth?" I asked my brother. "Best you ask Sonny Boy."

"Perhaps I will. But for now, best go on enjoying working it out for myself." The song ended, and we hit the sack. I was dead tired but happier than I'd been in a long time. "Good night, Bob."

"Good night, little brother. It's really T for Tennessee tomorrow."

Five-thirty came too early when Bob woke me up. It was still dark, and coffee, scrambled eggs, and sausage were waiting for me. I dragged myself to the table—three and a half hours of sleep were just not enough. We took Violet's truck and were on historic Highway 61, headed toward Memphis, before the sun rose at our backs.

Despite it being winter, Mississippi was still green, and the cotton fields had been given over to legumes, beans, and other crops that put nitrogen back into the cotton-depleted soil. Driving steadily, we traveled three hours to Memphis, then stopped for gas and coffee at a country store. Memphis was near the Mississippi-Tennessee border, the flat bottom delta land that spawned the blues. Highridge was in another part of the state, both culturally and geographically, in the foothills of Appalachia, mostly poor white miners and dirt farmers, the music was old-timey, fiddles and banjos replacing guitars as the driving instruments. Highridge was just outside Murfreesboro, about an hour and a half east of Nashville. We still had a three-and-a half- hour trip to go. We continued driving over the flat delta country until it changed gently into rolling hills of grassland and cow pastures. Then the land changed again, into the eroded ancient hills that marked the emergence of the Appalachian chain. Murfreesboro was located in a dip in the landscape termed a hollow, or holler, depending upon who was doing the describing. We drove into it, gassed up, and traveled the few miles to Highridge, located on a small plateau nested in the Appalachian foothills.

The research and education center, as it was now called, had been rebuilt in its present form in the late 1960s after it had been burned down in a calculated bit of anarchy, engineered by local politicians unhappy with its role as an integrated training center for the civil rights movement. Its new form consisted of a series of circular prefab wooden buildings called rondettes, of which there were seven. Some were single-storied, others two. These housed an administration building, library, kitchen and dining hall, training facilities, dorms, and staff housing. The effect of the prefab rondettes on the Appalachian landscape was stunning, looking as if they were engineered specifically for the geography, and over the years a myth had grown up that this was precisely what had happened.

The center had begun as the vision of its founder, Milo Henderson, and articulated itself as a folk school initially filling the educational void of the surrounding mountain communities, and then the training needs of the CIO, who had just begun to unionize the local mine workers. When the civil rights movement began, Highridge found the transition a natural one. It was the one place where blacks and whites could meet together in the Jim Crow South, and over the years Highridge had paid a price, its almost total arson being the culmination. Through it all, my mother had been there, serving as its chief sociologist and training coordinator. She took time out to be my father's wife, and Bob's and my mother, but her priorities were always clear, and her family always adapted. None of us ever got in the way.

We drove to a house at the top of a small hill that was, until his death, Milo Henderson's. After his death, my mother as senior staff member inherited it. As we drove up, my mother came out to meet us. "Neyed, Robert, so good ta see you both. Finally, Neyed," my mother jabbed gently. Bob greeted his mother with "Momma," I with "Helen."

"Neyed, you've found yourself in the middle of quite a thing. There's a Detective Escobar that just called and wants you to call him as soon as possible. Professor Zegura talked to him."

We went into the single-story round house of my mother. The kitchen and living room were connected, taking up the diameter of the house, and to the left and right were bedrooms on one side and an office and a small meeting room-library on the other. The house was as tight as a wooden sailboat and looked like one with its wooden paneling. A woman I recognized as Margret was at the sink, washing dishes. She wiped her hands on her apron and came over to us.

"Margret Shashwati, these are my sons, Robert Moore and Ned Alexander, who I think you already know."

"Hello, Robert," she said as she extended her hand. "Yes, I've met Ned, but we haven't had a chance to talk."

"Well, if Highridge has anything to offer, it's time to talk. Violet and her brother are off for a walk, and Professor Zegura is down at the administration office talking to the director."

"Can I offer you two something to eat?" asked Margret.

"Margret's moved right in and taken control of the kitchen," Helen said, laughing. "And it's been quite an improvement, I can tell you."

"A particle physicist who cooks?" I joked.

"Cooking's all particles and physics. Besides, I'd starve if I didn't cook for myself," Margret said with a smile. "A Bunsen burner, a beaker, and a few ingredients, and pow, dinner."

I realized we'd skipped lunch and had only a cup of coffee since breakfast. "A little food sounds good."

"I'm OK with just something to drink," Bob said. "Let's sit out on the porch," said my mother.

Margret brought out a tray with three glasses of iced tea and for me a plate with a tuna sandwich and side salad. It was real tuna salad in the sandwich, complete with hardboiled egg.

"This tuna is great," I said.

"It was one of my favorites until I made the move to vegetarian," said Margret.

"I haven't quite made that move yet," I said.

"No, not by a long shot," my brother said, smiling. "Though I think I'm on my way," I countered.

"Yeah, I'll tell the pig whose ribs you ate last night and sausage this morning," said Bob in a rare laugh.

"I didn't do it all at once, either, and I slipped many times until I was able to stick to it," Margret said, coming to my defense as I stuck my tongue out at my brother. When she went back into the house I followed her, my lunch in hand.

"I am really so sorry about Willie," I said. "I only knew him for two days, but I feel a powerful closeness and connection to him. It's funny to say about someone you only just met, but he's left a terrible void in my life."

"Thank you for that. But it seems he knew you longer than you knew him.

At least you got to meet him," she said with longing.

"Yeah," I said, "but you got to know him through your insight and investigations. I think knowing him is more important than meeting him. And you met him through your letters. Although they were few, they were profound."

"You really are your mother's son," she said.

"No, I'm really my father's son. Bob's my mother's son," I found myself sharing.

"Well, thank you for saying those things. They mean a lot. I just can't get over the feeling that he was taken away from me just when I could have gotten to know him." She looked at me with tears in her eyes, and I put down the elegant tuna sandwich and hugged her. I could feel my shoulder getting wet and we just stood there in my mother's kitchen, and I realized I was crying in her hair.

"I've thought about it a lot since his death, and I think the lessons that Willie gave us was that it was his time to leave, by his own hand, and on his own terms. Remember, there is no such thing as coincidence." Margret hugged me tighter and cried harder. Bob came in, saw us, nodded at me, and left us alone. "You know Willie as well as anyone could, his books and articles and his letters were the important part of him, and you know that part of him intimately. The man that resided in the cell at Alamosa Prison was just the vehicle for all the things he thought, said, and did. And it seems to me that you were his greatest piece of work. That's what my father would have said to you, anyway."

Margret relaxed and pulled away slightly though still holding on to me. She straightened up and looked directly at me, her face braided with her tears. "I think I would like your father. Where is he?"

"He was killed by a terrorist's bomb in Lebanon three years ago," I said.

"I'm sorry," she said, her eyes tearing up again.

"Yeah, unlike Willie, I don't think it was time for him to go."

Like my mother would have, Bob came in again after giving us some time to recover ourselves. My father, I thought, would have waited until we came out. Hot on my brother's heels came Violet and Leo.

"We saw a herd of deer," Violet said excitedly. "I'm always amazed at how beautiful it is here. Hi, Ned, we were waiting for you." Leo nodded to me but said nothing, keeping faith with his taciturn ways.

They all met Bob and shook hands. Margret and I were mostly back to normal. There were about ten rocking chairs placed about the living room. The rocking chair was a symbol at Highridge, representing people sitting down together and discussing their problems rationally and coming to solutions. Its logo was two rocking chairs facing each other with a mountaintop behind. Zegura came in, filling the room, and he greeted Bob with a warm embrace, and we all sat down in a rocking chair.

"Glad you all made it intact from Texas," Adam began. "Things are starting to heat up there. You had a call from a Detective Escobar, Ned. Seems they are thinking of charging you."

"With what?" I asked.

"They identified the guards that we bribed. Willie handled the money, so I think I'm off the hook, but you were identified as the guy the videotape was passed to. I told him that even if that were true, which we're not admitting, it was not a crime. I told him as your lawyer my advice is not to return to Texas at present. Your article on the governor was published in your paper this morning, and the wire services picked it right up. GNN ran the story as its lead; governor's beside himself and looking for cover. It's nothing to worry about long-term, but I wouldn't go back to Texas until this blows-over."

"Don't worry, son, we have a long history of harboring outlaws here at Highridge," said my mother, who had taken a rocking chair and moved into our circle. "Makin an enemy of the governor of Texas, nice goin," she smiled her approval.

"Well, in any case, you should call him back," said Zegura. "And check with me before you do anything." I nodded.

"Well, all of you here, other than Helen, are members of the board of the Sister Shashwati Foundation. I can tell you that it commands a good deal of assets with more accumulating all of the time. The interest on the account at current rates brings in just over four million dollars a year. Willie's only stipulation was that you don't move too quickly in deciding how to spend it, and that funds are to be allocated for the educational and professional use of the board members; this includes living and travel expenses. Willie was adamant that the board members increase their awareness through travel. Margret's education and living expenses are handled separately by another part of the trust set up by Willie."

Margret looked into her lap, noticeably uncomfortable.

Zegura continued, "I would further recommend that for the first year we confine expenditures to the interest amount until we all decide what the major work of the foundation is."

Bob murmured, "Four million dollars? Whew!"

Violet was the first to speak out. "I think we should do something to fight capital punishment." We all nodded.

"Yeah, like a grant to BWWY," said Leo. It was the first words that anyone heard him utter, and it was said without anger or bitterness. He looked around the circle to show that he was completely serious in his suggestion. Everyone in the circle of rocking chairs now looked at Leo, who appeared little more than a powerfully built adolescent.

"Well," he continued, "who has better pointed out the barbarity of the system, first with Ned's murder of the DA in Tucson, and then with Stith. Like you all, I've read the articles. The death penalty is fine when it's applied to prisoners, vulnerable targets, mostly minority people." He couldn't help but look over at my brother, then, embarrassed, turned away. "But when the techniques are applied to powerful bastards, pillars of society, then it's murder."

Leo looked around the circle of wide eyes that now stared at him. "What did they call it in Ned's articles, Kant's Reckoning? Make every act as if it were your own. Well, that's just what they've done, to my way of thinking." He dropped his head and stared down at his folded hands in his lap. There was a lot of this going on in the meeting.

Everyone was quiet until my mother broke the silence with a loud clap and a full laugh. "Bravo, boy! What's good for the goose is good for the gander." She continued to laugh and applaud.

The truth and perceptiveness of Leo's statement struck me between my wide-open eyes. I had danced around this insight in my articles but never explicitly stated it, probably because it wasn't a fully formed thought. Kant's Universal Moral Axiom had been mentioned by BWWY in connection with both killings, the latter suggesting it had just begun. *Act in conformity with that maxim, and that maxim only, which you can at the same time will to be universal law.* The language was a bit archaic, but its meaning was clear, divined by both Leo and my mother. BWWY: What's good for the goose is good for the gander. Whatever Willie had done to jump-start young Leo's education it had taken off.

Zegura roused himself. "The idea to support anti-capital-punishment projects and organizations seems a rational response to the recent events. The idea to support BWWY seems less so. While I share Leo's sentiments and his analysis, we don't know who or what BWWY is. And if they, indeed, had anything to do with either or both murders, which seems likely, they're a terrorist organization, and it would be a crime to contribute to them. Let me suggest that I research a number of anti-capital-punishment organizations and projects and come up with a possible recipient of a grant funded by Sister Shashwati and bring it back for your comments and approval." We all nodded.

"Willie also charged Ned to set the record straight about his life, or should I say lives; to put it into perspective in a book or series of major articles. I would suggest that we undertake this immediately."

"I'm going to write it as a book," I said.

"It's going to be an important book," said Zegura, looking at me with a serious expression that I believed contained more than an element of doubt. "Do you know how to write a book of this magnitude?"

"I know how to keep a promise," I said with more conviction than I felt. Zegura smiled. "Well said, young man." It was a kind thing to say. Other than my brother, I was the senior member of this outfit of young superstars and Ph.D.s and was beginning to feel a bit old. "I've set up bank accounts for all the board members, with the exception of Margret, who already has one." Again, she looked to her lap as Zegura went on. "There is fifty thousand dollars in it for your use as I described it earlier. Please remember it was Willie's wish that this be used. Ned and Bob, I understand from your mother that you already have a sizable trust from your father's estate that neither of you has chosen to access. Please don't follow the same pattern with this one. It was Willie's wish, and as we all know, Willie's ways were not always directly discernable. Ned, your account has seventy-five thousand, the extra twenty-five is for expenses you will encounter in writing your book."

"Twenty-five thousand is a lot of ink cartridges," I said.

"It will take more than ink cartridges, Ned. You will need to travel and interview a large number of people who knew Willie, and many more who were familiar with his work. Many knew him only as Sister Shashwati, others only as L.T. Zegura. Make no mistake: This will be no little job—it's no little promise.

15

What's Good for the Goose

No little promise. I began to sweat, sitting there in a circle of rocking chairs, as I acknowledged the sheer size of the promise I had made. Hubris once again came to the rescue, as I told myself that hadn't I just written six or seven articles for a major newspaper, all of which were taken up by the wire services. Hadn't I already written a book about Dylan Thomas, small and personal as it was? *Yeah, I'll be up to the task,* I told myself, not believing a word, as I continued to review my life's pitiable output.

"Is there any other business before this group today?" asked Zegura. "Can we use the money to make contributions to other organizations?" asked Bob.

Zegura paused before he answered. "Bob, you can use it for anything that you all decide, but let me fulfill Willie's request to me, to impress upon you that the money is also meant for your personal development as a human being, your education in the greater sense, if you will. When you contribute, I would ask, but not tell you, to do so in a way that speaks to this issue."

My brother nodded. Zegura passed out bankbooks to each of us, complete with a bank machine card, and the meeting was over. It seemed we were all now being taken on as Margret had been so many years before. I looked over to her and hoped I'd meet with a similar result.

"You'd better call that detective back," said Adam. "While we don't want to give in to their whims, we don't want to overtly antagonize them, either."

"You can use the phone in my office. The number's right next to the phone," said Helen.

I figured Escobar would have gone home by now and I'd just have to leave a message, which was all right by me, but I was disappointed.

"Detective Escobar."

"What's up, detective, this is Ned Alexander?"

"Mr. Alexander, it seems you've not been playing fair with us."

"I've been completely fair with you, detective. How have I been unfair?" This recalled a conversation I'd had with Lieutenant Hickey. Did these guys learn this stuff in detective school?

"You've published facts that you've not been given officially, probably taken from conversations with the governor's staff," he said this haltingly, as if he were reviewing his words carefully.

"The important word, detective, is facts. Were any of the statements incorrect?"

"No," said the detective. "But the governor's office knew where the part about the probability of three killers came from, and I've had hell to pay for that."

"Sorry, detective, but I am going to use any information I get that's not off the record."

"Why in the hell did you write that nasty article on the governor being a coward?"

"Because I had facts to support it and inferences to embellish it," I said, another fat mouth full. "Besides, I never called him a coward."

"Not in so many words you didn't, but that was the effect." The statement was a true one, so I remained silent.

"You also gave the videotape of Ruckles' suicide to the media," he said, sounding a bit desperate. "You could be charged with obstructing a criminal investigation and receiving stolen property."

"I'm not admitting that I did any of that, but my lawyer tells me it's not a crime anyway."

"That that big guy that was on TV talking about the prisoner being Sister Shashwati?"

"Yeah, that's the guy. He's not only a big guy, he's also a world-renowned legal mind."

"Yeah, he looks to be plenty sharp. Look Ned, and this is *off* the record, OK?" He didn't even wait for my response. "I don't like the governor much, or his office, but they're talking about charging you with the murder of Stith, which is absurd. But you don't have to be convicted to have a lot of trouble, so I'd be careful with these guys. They've been known to play dirty."

Escobar was a good guy, and he opened himself to some risk for no other reason than concern for my wellbeing. I told him so. "Look, Detective, I really appreciate your concern. In the future I will not use anything in my articles you tell me to hold up on, and I will pass on any information I get to you." With that assurance, we hung up relatively amiably. Indeed, I would stay away from Texas.

Zegura concurred and said that I was to keep him closely informed. He was due to fly back to California, his wife already having left, and he would leave from Nashville later that night. I took the opportunity to conduct my first formal interview with him for Willie's book. We all had dinner together, mostly put together by Margret and my mother, and Violet helped in what was a sexist division of labor not standard at Highridge. It consisted of salad, black beans, and cheese enchiladas made with tofu substituting for the cheese.

As Adam drove his rented car toward Nashville, the members of our little party seemed to collapse. The ordeal of the past four days, significantly more for some, had with Zegura's departure achieved some closure. The drama of the execution-suicide; the flight from Texas to Tennessee; the constant media bombardment from GNN along with my stories; the founding of the Sister Shashwati Foundation and its first acts—all of this had, at least for the moment, come to rest. The three remaining men tried to even out the sexism score by doing the cleanup and dishes, after which we all slumped into the seats in the living room.

We all sat like zombies until Helen, in her best southern belle, said, "Y'all want a little drink?"

As it turned out, we y'all, did.

"You old enough, Mr. Kant?" my mother asked Leo. "Just," said Leo, in his first syllables since the circle.

"Just is gooda enough. In honor of the great state of Texas, I'm gonna make margaritas, I have all the fixins," she said as she pulled out a blender from a cupboard beneath the sink. "We'll work up to juleps later."

After two of Helen's margaritas, I began to relax and feel strangely energized, as you do with the initial effects of alcohol. And with the alcohol people had begun to talk more easily to each other. Margret sat slightly away from Violet and Bob, listening quietly to what they said. My mother was talking gently to Leo, who listened. I walked over to Margret. "Do you want to go for a walk?" She stood up and smiled, and we walked outside onto the porch, then onto a path. It seemed natural to hold her hand, and she reciprocated.

"Since we're becoming a family, I thought it would be nice to know something about you," I said.

"Yes, I've never been part of a family and it feels good. Uncle Adam was the only real family I've had, and he functions more like a loving guardian. Which is good, but not the same thing. You've read the letters—much of my history is contained in them. I came from a biological family that was very abusive. I never knew my mother; it was always my father and stepmother. The abuse was not so much physical, although there was a good deal of that, as it was emotional. I was a precocious child, and the abuse was targeted directly at my intellect and curiosity. I remember feeling like they were trying to suck the life right out of me. The way leeches in the creek I swam in sucked out my blood. It may seem strange, but this simile gave me a defense. When I was undergoing abuse from either of my parents, I would pretend to pull leeches from my arms and body, serving to keep what I had underneath intact. The behavior served me in two ways: Symbolically, it kept me safe, and the behavior frightened my father and stepmother a little. 'Whatever are you doing,' they would say? 'Stop that!' And sometimes they would discontinue their harangues. Of course, other times they would just beat me." She laughed with no sign of bitterness. "But you don't want to hear about this."

"This is precisely the kind of thing that I do want to hear about," I said as I squeezed her hand.

She looked up at me. "Well, to this day I continue to pull metaphorical leeches off of me. In the past, I've had a few professors who have been unkind, even ridiculing, of some of my more radical ideas, not many of them, but some, and I've pulled the leeches off, sometimes right in front of them, too. I tell you, it's unnerved more than one of them." She gave out another joyous laugh. "At six years old, I found this stray kitten who had come to the back door looking for something to eat. I gave it some meat and milk, and she stayed. This, of course, was Saturn Kitty, who before Willie really saved the young child's life. I kept her in a shed near the house. She was my closest confidant, my counselor, the one to whom I poured out my few joys and many sorrows. One day when Saturn was almost fully grown, I was playing with her outside the shed and Nancy, my stepmother, said I could bring her into the house. It was the only nice thing I can remember her doing for me that wasn't a duty, but it was a big one. She even went to bat for me with my father, which was unusual, saying, 'Let the girl have her cat, John, it does no harm, and it even goes to the bathroom outside.'" Margret laughed again. "So, things continued along until I wrote that despicable letter to Willie, when my whole life changed into Cinderella. You've read my last letter to Willie. My life has been an intellectual Disneyland, with every possible privilege and opportunity. And the travel! Uncle Adam really pushed the travel with me. At first, I was not ready for it, but he pushed. And he was right about it. My views would never have been what they are without the travel. It's been as important as the science in my development. I hope you guys will take advantage of the opportunity Willie has made possible, because he really knows what he is doing." She then corrected her tense with melancholy. "Knew."

"Tell me more," I said, and she obliged.

"I completed high school early, got a scholarship to MIT and graduated in three years with my BS and enrolled immediately in their Ph.D. program, finished the course work in two years, and am midway through my research and dissertation. I live on campus at MIT, make most of my meals at the lab, commiserate with Saturn Kitty, go out with friends every once in a while, and pull leeches off my body when I have to. That's me in a nutshell."

"Or a curled universe," I said.

"Or a curled dimension," she echoed. "What about boyfriends, your social life?"

"I've had a few boys—I've known about birth control for quite some time now, but no one I could really call a boyfriend. I've hooked up with people for a little while on my travels, but nothing serious." I tried not to look like a shocked old fart. "I've really been most interested in pursuing my science, trying to fulfill Willie's early prophecy. Though I've never been pushed."

"You seem to be on the cutting edge of things, I mean, alternate dimensions."

"I'd like to think so, but the field is highly competitive and it's difficult to come up with a truly original idea, much less any supporting experimental evidence. Because of the funds I have for my education, I spend time at CERNs super particle collider, so we'll see where that goes. What about you? Your mother says that you are quite an accomplished scholar and writer. She showed me a book you wrote about Dylan Thomas."

"My mother has a copy of that book?" I asked. I didn't know she'd ever read it.

"Oh, she's got more than one. In fact, she gave me a copy." "That was written quite a while ago."

"Don't worry, I won't hold you to it," she said, smiling.

We now sat on an upended log along the path as a half-moon rose over the Appalachian foothills. I wanted to kiss her, and I felt a mutual willingness, but I fought back the feeling. The idea of family had been implanted in me. Was Margret an emerging sister, or something else? I felt it was better to wait until I was sure. We walked back easy and comfortable, the momentary awkwardness behind us. I put the scholarship extolled by my mother into a more realistic context as I provided her with a brief personal history.

Margret and I said goodnight at the door of the dorm where she, Violet, and Leo were lodged, and I gave her what I hoped was a brotherly kiss. I returned to my mother's house wondering why she had given Margret such a positive account of her youngest son. She had copies of my little book and was giving them out? *Helen, you are a mystery to me for sure!*

What's good for the goose is good for the gander, you old sociologist! Doing what sociologists do best, reducing the complex interactions of larger groups into something that is understandable on a smaller scale.

Reducing confusing phenomena into bite-sized universal principles. Was that the methodology of BWWY? Was that their message? My brother and Helen had already gone to bed. I retrieved my laptop from the guest room that Bob and I shared, went into my mother's office, and began to write.

It was an article I provisionally titled *Facts and Speculations Concerning BWWY*. It began with an accounting of the behavior of the "organization" as represented by the words and actions orchestrated by the faxes. These included the fax sent on the occasion of Burwick's death, the faxes sent to me and the Houston police on the occasion of Stith's death, and the fax sent to the governor, threatening him. It recounted the details of the murders and the part the fax played in Stith's murder investigation, and it expressed the possibility that members of the organization could have been involved in the murder itself. It reproduced Kant's universal moral axiom and stated its presence in the note at Burwick's death. It discussed the implications of the axiom within the present contexts. It speculated that BWWY could stand for a Better World Without You, and discussed the possible implications. It further speculated that there could be more killings to follow based upon the quote that "Kant's Reckoning has begun." And it mentioned the mysterious numbers contained in the first two faxes, but did not state them. The article continued with Leo's assertion that BWWY and the killings, rather than dealing with revenge and retribution, were a moral lesson demonstrating the brutality of capital punishment. I closed with the quote from my mother, saying that a close watcher of the cases had summed it up as: *What's good for the goose is good for the gander*. It was only eleven o'clock in Tennessee, so it was a respectable nine in Tucson. I called the paper on the off chance that Halloran was still there, but no luck, so I called his home and got him. I told him about the article.

"A lot of it is speculation, but speculation based on facts. I think it's as good as anything else I've written and advances the story," I said.

He said he would review it from home, make any necessary changes and submit it for the morning paper. "If it's really good, I'll put it online and give it to the wires. Good night, Harvard." Good night was a good idea, and I accepted it.

I slept well for a few hours, then woke up. I went to my laptop and pulled up the *Sun*'s online edition and the article was there. It was mostly intact, but some of the wording was changed and there were a lot more qualifiers, but my mother's quote remained. Take it all around, I was pretty well satisfied, and I went back to sleep and slept till morning.

16

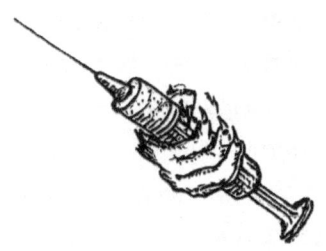

The Eradication of Smallpox

reakfast was a repeat of dinner, with Margret serving as the chief cook: whole-wheat banana pancakes, vegetarian sausage, fresh orange juice, and coffee. "Helen, I didn't know you kept all these healthy vegetarian options in your kitchen," I said.

"It's not me. Margret did the shopping before you came." Well, that explained it. My mother was southern fried all the way. I pulled up the morning copy of the *Sun* and the article was on the front page in the same form as it was on the online edition. I printed a copy and showed it to my mother and Leo.

Leo read the article seriously, then said, "Who do you think they are, Ned?"

"Don't know. All I know I put in the article. Actually, I put in more than I know. Although your analysis seems to be plausible, we'll just have to wait for more things to happen."

My mother chuckled at her quote. "A little downhome sociology," she said as we took our coffee out on the porch.

"Helen," I said. "Speaking as a sociologist, why do we have capital punishment?" It was a childish question, I knew, but a fundamental one to my thoughts and to the two investigations of the stories I was covering.

"Well, son, that's a toughie. As a sociologist, I can tell you that not all societies have it. Some countries, at least, have rejected it. We did, too, for a while, but that position was just too good for Americans, and we went back. I believe that it has to do with fear and control. Fear generates anger, and anger is used by those in power to control those who aren't, used as a tool by people seeking power. Angry people are easier to control, and they do some horrible things with that anger. It was why we had such a time down here with civil rights. When black and white farmers came together here, there was some uneasiness, even hostility, but when we sat down and figured things out, we found that we weren't all that different. But the people in power wouldn't have it, they kept people afraid and angry, and their acts of anger caused them more fear, and made them easier to manipulate. There are more technical mechanisms like choosing vulnerable targets and ways of dehumanizing the target so you don't feel empathy, but your question's a bit like asking, 'Why is the moon yellow?'"

"I know my question is childish," I apologized.

"Not childish," corrected my mother. "Childlike. They're not the same thing. Childlike questions go to the fundamental bedrock of an issue. They're hard to answer because the answer is often so simple, just complex to get there. They are, however, the most important questions we can ask." My mother gave me a serious look, and a smile that was just as serious. "You're starting to develop yourself into a real thinker, son."

"So I've been told by Margret," I said as I looked directly at her. "Oh that, just a little motherly pride."

To hear my mother associate me with the word *pride* was a new one. I could see that it also made her a little uncomfortable. I had always been her prodigal son.

Quickly changing the subject, she asked, "Have you ever heard of Dr. J. Erasmus Camp?"

"The man that cured smallpox?"

"Well, he didn't actually cure it. He and his team led a worldwide project to eradicate it, but yes, that's the man. He lives near here in Tennessee now.

Well, he's been trying to answer one of those childlike questions. I don't know if it made the news up in your part of the country, but his daughter was murdered about three years back. It was a big thing around here, I can tell you. Two young men kidnapped her from her high school, raped and shot her, and left her tied to a tree. This happened in Missouri.

"Erasmus' response to it was not your standard reaction. He holed up in his home for a couple of months, and when he came out, he visited us at Highridge. He was real interested in our work, asked a lot of questions, read our research papers, reviewed our projects, watched our videos, and listened to our tapes. Stayed with us for three weeks. When he went back home, he argued against the death penalty for the two men who had murdered his daughter and made a lot of people in his state furious at him. Since then, he's continued to argue against the death penalty and campaigned for gun control, two stances not real popular with a lot of Southerners.

"About a year ago, he took his Nobel Prize money and bought some land near here and started a laboratory that addresses why human beings are so aggressive, another of those fundamental childlike questions. I don't know much about his research, but he's a frequent visitor here, and we've gotten to be friends. Strange man, seems almost obsessed with his daughter's death and what can come from it. Might want to pay him a visit. He might have some answers for you, since you seem to have gotten so deeply into this death penalty thing."

"I'll think about it Helen. It would take the story in a different direction, though."

"Yeayes, it might do just that," said my mother as she got up and took her empty coffee cup into the house. "Might be a direction you could control, though."

This was an odd statement, and it made me think. Did I want to control the story? Scientists were concerned with control in their work, but were journalists? I'd think about that one, too.

I continued to sit on her porch. The day was beautiful, the Appalachians rose gently in the distance, on the rolling green of the Highridge landscape a few latent yellow butterflies played, the sounds of birds I could neither see nor identify were everywhere. Why, indeed, was there a need for capital punishment?

Violet and Leo were walking together over the path down below the porch, and Violet waved and yelled something, and Leo nodded. They were holding hands as they talked and strolled lazily. I thought of Margret and last night, and the urge to kiss her came over me again. I quickly shifted my mind to other places.

J. Erasmus Camp, smallpox; another murder? When did murder become so ubiquitous? The story was moving along too fast for me, I thought. In an attempt to slow it down, I thought of Solomon and the original case. I should really get back to it. I called the paper and asked for her. Not surprisingly, she wasn't there, so I left a message. I also wrote her an email. I had written her two short ones over the previous four days but had received no reply. In this one, I told her that I was almost through with the stories here and would be returning soon. I said I hadn't seen any further articles from her and was wondering how it was going. I tried not to say it as a criticism, but I was not unaware of that implication. I wanted to ask her about her relationship with Burwick, but I was already skating on thin ice, or whatever that metaphor is in Tucson. I asked how she was doing, said I looked forward to seeing her, closed, and sent it off. Still connected to the dial-up in the office, I heard the fax machine rumble.

Two pages followed. The first was a cover page with just my name and the fax number on it. It came from a machine with a 202 area code. The second page: "We just read your morning article. Well done. You really are our boy! More later." It was signed as the previous ones, BWWY. Under that however in parentheses was (Better World Without You) and the note: "You figured this one out without us giving you the hint that we gave the governor. Nice work!" I wondered again how they knew where I was, I would confirm later that it was originally faxed to the paper, who sent it on—probably Mildred.

I was reading it over again when my computer made a noise that indicated that I had an email. I opened it. The speed of the response supported what I had suspected—that Solomon was at the paper but chose not to take my call. It read:

Nice to hear from you.

Amiable but no mention of the previous two. She continued:

You seem to have stumbled onto a real cottage industry down there.

Stumbled and *cottage industry* were not the kindest words, but OK.

Been unable to connect with the widow Burwick, understand-able, but I think she's trying to avoid me.

Explanatory, with no attitude. Good.

The story and I will be here when you are back. Barbara.

Almost friendly.

I turned my attention back to the fax. I'd been expecting some type of communication after my article, and it seemed that everything in it was mostly, if not entirely, correct. That was good, but what was meant by *You really are our boy*? And what would being their boy entail? It gave me a creepy feeling, and I shivered there in the office. The fact that they were an organization seemed to be confirmed by the *we*, and since they didn't dispute my claim that they were probably involved at least in Stith's murder, I felt greater credence was given my reporting.

I'd need to do something with the fax. I'd told both Escobar and Hickey that I'd keep them informed, and I had no idea what being BWWY's favorite son would do to the pending charges contemplated by the Texas governor. I gave Zegura a call to ask his advice before I did anything with Escobar. He wasn't at the number. but I left a message for him to call me at Helen's. As I was thinking about Dr. J. Erasmus Camp and what it meant to control the story, Margret came in and took a seat by me at the desk.

"You look deep in your thoughts. I am I interrupting?"

"No, I could use a break," I said, and I handed her the fax. "This just came."

She read it over a few times, then handed it back to me. "Where's the 202 area code from?" she asked.

"Washington, D.C. My father spent significant time there, so I know it. The other faxes were from different parts of the country. The first one I got was from Atlanta, the last ones in Texas were from Illinois, Chicago area, and the numbers have all been traced to public copy centers. I'm sure this one will be, too."

"What do they mean, *you really are our boy*?"

"I don't know, but they're slowly moving me into a central place in the story, and I'm not sure I like it—I am sure I don't like it. I phoned Zegura. He wasn't there but I left a message for him to call me back.

"Your breakfast was really great. I don't remember when I have eaten so well as over the last few days," I said to change the subject.

"Well, thank you." She smiled at the compliment. "It's just simple stuff. I really liked our walk, and getting to know you last night," she said.

I could feel her closeness as she reached over and took my hand. I fought the powerful urge to lean over the short distance between us and kiss her.

"Margret, I'm finding myself very attracted to you." She squeezed my hand and said, "So am I, Ned."

I looked at her. "I'm not sure this is such a good idea."

"I'm not sure this isn't." She moved slightly away from me but went on holding my hand. A guy can only be so strong and restrained, and it never was one of my character traits.

Both of the office chairs were on wheels, and I rolled toward her, took her in my arms, and kissed her strong and deeply, and she responded in kind. We held on tight with our chairs rolling around the office floor. I felt the last days melting into her and for the first time since I had gotten the "last job in town," I felt my body relax. I moved to her neck, burying my face into her short thick hair, and she responded to my every little move.

The door to the office, which was shut, opened and my mother's voice filled the room. "Well there you are—" The two of us snapped immediately upright in our chairs like two children caught in the kindergarten coatroom. Helen, realizing what she had stumbled in on, took in a breath but continued: "I was looking for you two to see if you wanted to go with me. I have to teach a class in Jalico, thought it would give you a chance to visit one of the mountain communities and see some of the countryside." *My father*, I thought with an inward grin, *would have closed the door.*

"Sure, I'd really like that, Helen," I said, trying not to giggle. "What about you, Margret?"

Margret said she would like that, too, and my mother closed the door. We rolled together, grabbed on to each other and exploded into laughter until the tears rolled down our cheeks. I realized, as we separated and got ready for the journey to Jalico, that this was the first mutual affection I had experienced in over a year. And, good idea or not, it felt wonderful.

The Appalachians are old mountains, the eroded cores of an ancient chain, no match for their younger western brethren, but in this landscape, they were majestic, sitting atop vast reserves of coal that was the source of livelihood and the sorrow of its people. It was a beautiful winter day; the roads were clear, with just a remnant of snow on the shady sides. We traveled over the winding road as Helen talked about the crime of the mining practice called mountaintop removal. We drove for about an hour until we reached a little valley between the hilltops that was Jalico, a medium-sized mining town. We drove to the school and community center, and Helen stopped the car. It was the first day of her class. During the registration of her students, Helen took the time to get to know something about each one and to introduce each to the group. There were about thirty students taking the class called Community Mobilization. Margret and I stayed for the arrival of about half the students, watching my mother in her natural habitat, then moved out into the streets of the town.

We went looking for coffee and found it in the grocery store, a pot in the back with small Styrofoam cups. The store stocked a variety of goods, from diapers to shotgun shells, fishing gear to contact lens solution. Margret bought a red plaid hunting cap along with the acceptable coffee. "I know you, you're Helen's boy," said the clerk at the register. She shook my hand and said, "I'm Susan Jenkins. I saw you when I was at Highridge many years ago. It's nice ta see ya. Your motha means a lot to us round here. The coffee's on me," she said as she gave Margret her change from the cap.

We thanked her for the coffee and kind words and continued our walk. Everybody on the street smiled and greeted us. "It's a bit like being royalty," Margret said as we continued our journey.

"Yeah, my mother's a queen around here," I said, and heard the edge to my voice.

"Do I pick up that you have a little bit of a problem with her?"

"Not really," I lied. "Well, maybe a little. I don't think she's ever really fully approved of me."

"A little sibling rivalry?"

"Not really rivalry. Bob's always been my hero, so I've never been jealous of him. It's just that he's always been closer to my mother than I have. He's really famous, you know, they tell stories about him, even today, about his deeds during the height of the violence down here. It's hard to keep up with a mythic figure, so I never tried. I've been content just to float in his wake. I know that may sound like jealousy, but it's not. My mother's great and I love her, but I spent more time with my father living in Cambridge. My character, such as it is, developed more under his influence, my brother's more under Helen's."

We found ourselves at the end of a street that dead-ended into a small park, where miners' children too young for school played. "My mother spent time with us in Cambridge, but her heart was always at Highridge," I continued. "I spent a lot of time with her here, but I always had to compete for her attention, with her students, her workshops, dignitaries, her followers like Susan back at the store, and one day I when I was nine or ten, I just understood the way things were. I stopped calling her mother and began calling her Helen. It wasn't to create distance between us as everyone thinks but so I could compete on an equal basis with everyone who called her Helen. Since then, I've never called her anything else. And I like the fact that I call her something different from my brother. "

"Have you ever told her the origin of your name for her?"

"No, I've never gotten around to it. As time passed, it became a bit too intimate, I guess."

"Well, I think it may be time to share. You should have seen the pride with which she gave me your book. Pride with maybe just a hint of sadness. I think you should tell her."

"You know, somewhere along the line I got the realization that these children," I swept my hand across the children in the park, "were just as important to her as I was. And somewhere along the line it became all right. I think the time to tell her has passed."

"Maybe so, but I still think you should share it with her."

I looked down and noticed that we were holding hands. Still holding hands, we walked back to the community center. Helen was outside, and the students were slowly dispersing. On the way back home, I said, "We met Susan Jenkins, who thinks a lot of you," and I told her the coffee story. Margret nodded toward me, trying to catch my eye, but I pretended not to see. "Susan's a right smart community leader, took command of the miners' wives during a short strike we had here. The shortest strike on record, I believe. Yep, she's a smart one."

"Do you think Dr. Camp would see me?" I'd been thinking about our earlier conversation, the presence of the new fax, and having to explain it to Escobar, and I was feeling that exerting control by changing the direction of the story might not be a bad thing.

"Sure, he would. The man can talk, I can tell you that, and he enjoys talking about his work to those who take him seriously. I'll give him a call when we get home."

"Could you try to set something up for tomorrow?"

"I'll do that, son." During the remainder of the ride, I filled Margret in on Dr. J. Erasmus Camp, with Helen joyously providing additional details. When we got back home, Violet was waiting for me. Bob was out giving Leo a tour of the area.

"Professor Zegura called a little while ago and wants you to call him. He left a number," Violet said.

Adam asked me to fax him a copy and call back in twenty minutes.

After reading it, he said he saw no problem in sharing it with the detective. "Besides, it may give us a little cover seeing that it's them who are interested in you rather than the other way around. Taken together with your article, they almost admit to Stith's murder. Go ahead and share it with him. If nothing else, it shows your willingness to follow through with cooperation. Keep me posted." And we rang off.

My next call was to Escobar, who was a bit more skeptical in his approach. I read him the fax. He sounded tense, and I sympathized with what he must be going through with the investigation on one hand, the governor's office on the other, and being a nice guy on yet another. That made three hands! I'd need to find a better metaphor.

"What do they mean, *you really are our boy*? he asked immediately.

"I don't know," I answered simply.

"Where did the fax come from?"

I told him. "Why Washington?" he asked irritably. Again, I answered that I had no idea.

"But detective, if you take the fax along with my article, it says that it's mostly correct, that's like admitting to Stith's murder." I pressed Zegura's point.

"Yeah," he said. And the way he said it told me he'd already put it together. "The governor's not going to like this."

"Well, the governor doesn't like me to begin with, so this won't make much difference."

I also called Hickey and got him. He listened silently and asked me to send him a copy. Before we hung up, he asked me how they knew to send it to Highridge. As this had worried me, too, I'd checked that it had been indeed sent to the paper first and then forwarded. I told him so.

"Umm," said Hickey before the phone went dead.

It was getting on in the day and the light was beginning to fade. Margret had made a big salad and put out the fixings for sandwiches, roast beef, turkey, and peanut butter. I realized I was hungry, not having had anything since Susan Jenkin's coffee. I began to reach for the roast beef, gave Margret a look, and took up the peanut butter jar. She patted me on the hand. "Good boy," she said with a big smile and a nod.

Helen came out of the office. "It's all arranged. Dr. Camp will expect you at ten-thirty tomorrow morning. I'll draw you a map. It's not far." Bob and Leo had returned, and over dinner it was decided that Leo and Violet would take their truck and travel back to New York. Margret would travel with them, then take a train to Boston. Helen would drive me to Nashville and put me on a plane to Tucson, after my trip to visit Dr. Camp. Bob would stay on for a while with Helen at Highridge. Our new little family was breaking up.

After dinner, I spent some time interviewing Leo for Willie's book. Leo spoke of him as one would a father. Willie had seen something good and wholesome in the young man and began to develop it in their brief interactions. Over time Leo had begun to seek him out. Willie encouraged Leo to pursue his own directions.

"He never told me what to do, or what to think. Some of my early ideas were pretty naïve, some of them mean even, but he never told me I was wrong, that I should change the way I felt about things. He would suggest things for me to read, then we would talk about them. There wasn't much time in the prison routine, so Willie suggested that I keep a journal with my thoughts and ideas about the things that I read and other things too. I even began to write poems and essays about the things I was observing—the things I was thinking. I would write on every other line, leaving space for Willie's comments.

"Then one day he recommended a book called *The Anatomy of Coincidence* by Sister Shashwati." I had to smile at this. "It really changed my life—the way I viewed everyday occurrences, the way I dealt with people, but mostly the way I looked at myself. I believed I could really be someone, do something worthwhile. For two weeks, I couldn't think of anything else but that book, and I wrote a thirty-page essay on what I thought about it, how it changed me, and influenced the way I interpreted and reacted to things. When I showed it to Willie, he made some comments but said that what I wrote was pretty much the way he interpreted it. This pleased me greatly, though I didn't know it was Willie who had written the book.

"After this, our relationship changed, almost like I became his protégé; Willie was certainly my mentor. The other guards took to calling me Willie's dog, but I'm pretty big and strong, and after a few short scuffles the teasing stopped.

"At Willie's insistence, I submitted two of my poems to a regional poetry journal and both were accepted and published. I can't tell you what seeing my name in print did for my self-confidence. I wrote another article on the architecture of swallow's nests that was accepted by a Texas natural history magazine. I began to appreciate what my sister was doing with her life. And Willie and I began to talk about college. I said I didn't have the money for college and I wasn't in a position, like my sister, to get a scholarship, hell I had barely graduated from high school. He told me that Adam Zegura would help me. Then the execution began to be talked about again, and things looked serious. I became frantic and was totally consumed and depressed. It had been almost two years since Willie became my mentor. And I couldn't imagine a life without him. Then, at the worst of it, Adam Zegura came into the bar that I had begun to frequent after my shifts. He sat down where I was working on my third or fourth beer. I knew who he was from his visits to Willie, but I had never spoken to him.

"He said Willie had asked him to talk to me. I thought he was going to talk to me about college, and I told him I wasn't interested. He told me that was not the reason he was there. Said he was about to share a secret with me, one that was important to keep. Then he took out a large manuscript and handed it to me. It was titled *Death and Release*, and the author was Sister Shashwati. The manuscript was stamped: *Galleys—University of California Press.*

"When he told me Willie was the author, I was flabbergasted. Couldn't believe it. But he was, and Adam told me how it came to be and how Willie insisted that I read the new book then, before his death.

"So that's how I learned who he was. I read the book and it explained to me what Willie was going to do, and why it was all right. Reading it calmed me down, took away the panic and depression but not the sadness. It did allow me to function though over the last months through all this."

I looked at Leo as he closed his narrative. He looked older to me than he had before.

"What do you do now?" I asked.

"Follow Violet to New York. Professor Zegura's gotten me accepted to the Columbia writing program on the basis of my two published poems and my natural history article. But I suspect it has more to do with his contacts and good name than my literary accomplishments." He flashed me a smile that at the same time made him look wise and young. "And I'm going to follow Willie's advice and travel. First around the East Coast. I've never been out of Texas. Then I think to India and Nepal, see where some of Willie's ideas came from.

"What's that on your shirt?" he asked. I realized that I had put on the Advanti School for Girls shirt as I got ready for dinner, and I told him of its origin. He listened to the story closely. It was still early in the evening, though completely dark. Margret sat in a corner, reading my Dylan Thomas book. Everyone else was out on the porch.

"A little light reading?" I asked her. "Not so light. It's a little dark in places."

"Yeah, in some places," I agreed. "It seems a long time ago. How do you find it besides a little dark?"

"Sensitive, perceptive, and young, it's almost like it comes from the sixties."

"Late seventies," I said. "But with a strong sixties influence. Young?" I asked this twenty-three-year-old particle physicist and cosmologist?

"Yes, naïve in the best sense. Fresh. As if someone was pretending to be older than he was. An innocent marveling of the world, even—maybe especially—the dark parts."

"No fooling you is there, Margret?" I said. My father had said much the same thing with a certain reinforcing note in his voice the first time he read it. "A few years ago, I would have taken that as criticism, but now it sounds like a compliment," I said.

"Good," she said as she shut the book and sat down next to me on the couch.

Given our earlier intimacy, I was beginning to dread the coming decision that would have to be made tonight.

"Let's take a walk," she said, taking my hand.

The moon was waxing, coming up over the hills, the air was cool, and the little breeze made it cold. It felt good on my face as I tightened the sash on my sweater. The handholding had evolved into arms around each other's waist as we hugged and walked along. She leaned her face toward mine, and I kissed her. We walked for some time, then turned back in the direction of the dorm where she was staying. We had seen Leo and Violet enter earlier. We were both thinking the same thoughts, and Margret broke silence first.

"I have a whole room to myself, six beds, but it's all to myself. And as I told you, I've known about birth control for some time now." We were standing and facing with our arms around each other as she looked up into my face.

I was feeling our proximity was giving away too much physical information and I took a half step back, still holding her. "What happens after this?" I asked.

"Well, I go back to being a scientist, and you go off to the eradication of smallpox," she answered with a fetching smile. Her eyes sparkled.

"Margret, I think I would rather remain a member of your new family, although I don't know which member, than one of your traveling companions. I think we need to give it time and see what comes next."

"Is that your father talking? I think your mother would say go ahead," she said, laughing.

I laughed, too. "Yes, I think it just might be."

"I think I like your father." Her use of the present tense was moving.

My body had returned to normal, and I hugged her tight. "You should get some sleep. I heard you're going to get an early start tomorrow." We kissed for a long time, then said good night. I assured her I would be up to see her off.

17

The Intractability of Raccoons

True to form, if not my word, I was not up for Margret's departure. In my defense, I'd had a restless night, not falling asleep until four o'clock, the group having left at five-thirty. I was a bit upset with Helen, but she said Margret had asked her not to wake me. "She left you a note, though," said my mother. She handed me a folded piece of lab book paper with my name on it.

My Dear Ned, I've spent a sleepless night, as I know you have. Please forgive me for asking your mother not to waken you, as she wanted. I imagine you'll need your rest for handling the smallpox business. After going back and forth all night I believe your father was right, I would rather keep you as a family member for now (though just which member I don't know, either). I don't think you were ever in danger of becoming just another travel companion, but one can never tell. I feel closer to you than anyone I've ever met, excepting Saturn Kitty, of course. Let's continue to develop our friendship and see where it goes. Keep in touch by email and call often, and I will do the same. Love, Margret

I read the note over several times and reflected that my love life continued to be a collection of missed opportunities and self-sabotage. I wondered if Bob's was better. Helen lent me her station wagon and drew me a map to Dr. Camp's place. It was, as they say, just over the next rise, and I had no trouble finding it. The Camp farm, or research facility, was in a small depression similar to Highridge and consisted of a remodeled farmhouse and a newer building that looked more institutional, although in a gentle way. On the back of the institutional building was what appeared to be a series of chain link covered structures that looked like cages or kennels. Between the farmhouse and the newer building was a large barn that also looked to be recently remodeled. Its double doors were open and revealed bales of hay, various pieces of esoteric farm equipment, and a blue tractor. I drove up to the farmhouse and was greeted by a pair of friendly liver-colored hounds.

"You must be Helen's Ned," said an older man with thick, longish gray hair who had come onto the porch. He was coatless and wore black suspenders over a white shirt and a red bow tie. With his wire-rimmed glasses, the look was very distinguished. He came down the steps with his hand outstretched. "I'm Erasmus Camp. You can call me Raz," he said as he shook my hand and slapped me on the back. "Come on in. We have tea ready, or would you rather have coffee?" I said tea would be great, and we went into the house.

We sat in his comfortable living room and sipped tea. I caught him up with my last nine days, came around to my childlike question and Helen's suggestion that I come and see him. I had begun to doubt the wisdom of my coming. "Other than I understand that you are opposed to capital punishment, I'm not really sure why I'm here," I said.

"Well, let's start with that," he said simply.

With that, Dr. J. Erasmus Camp told his story. "As I'm sure you know, my daughter was killed, murdered, three years ago. The killing was brutal and senseless. My wife has been dead for the past ten years and Becca, Rebecca, was the only family I had, and I was devastated. This was in Missouri. I was teaching there at the University and conducting meaningless research. My major work was done when I was relatively young, heading up an international team that was successful in eradicating the virus responsible for the disease smallpox. It was the first time a disease had been fully eradicated, and the work earned me and another team member the Nobel Prize for medicine.

"At that time, I could write my own ticket at any university. My wife grew up in Missouri and had just been diagnosed with a rare form of leukemia and wanted to return home, so I chose Missouri, which provided me with a tenured position, a full lab, and the freedom to pursue whatever I wanted. All this in exchange for teaching a few classes in virology and the use of my name. They didn't even want the Nobel money. Their medical facility was excellent for my wife, and we moved into Missouri.

"After two pretty hard years, my wife died and it was just Becca and me. She was only ten at the time, and it was hard for both of us. The freedom I had at the university allowed me to be a present and attentive father. Our lives continued pretty much the same through her high school years. She was a pretty good student and wanted to follow me into medicine and public health, her grades were just good enough, and she was popular at school. Then, three months before she was to graduate, she was kidnapped and raped by two young men. They had a handgun and took her into the woods, tied her to a fallen tree, raped her, then shot her and left her there, still tied to the tree. It was a completely senseless crime. One of the young men was a classmate Becca had refused to go out with; the other was his older brother. The crime was savage, but the public outcry was equally savage, calling for the deaths of the two men and a lot more. Becca's classmate was only seventeen, not even an adult yet, but both were to stand trial as adults and face the death penalty. The letters I received were almost as brutal as the crime.

"As a medical man and scientist, it was always my intent to reduce the suffering of humankind. I was being pressured to make statements calling for the death penalty, and I found myself in an ultimate sorrow, and I just shut down. I went inside my house and just withdrew from the world. I tried to make some sense out of what happened, and I just couldn't. In the midst of my despondency I thought of all my colleagues who studied viruses. Viruses were then the least-understood organisms in biology. They were difficult to culture, their life cycles were extremely arcane, and there was a debate as to whether or not they were even alive. These things made the study of them difficult. Some were extremely virulent, and we made many mistakes in the beginning, lots of my colleagues died of the diseases they were studying. Cures were built literally on the dead bodies of researchers, and although it was sad, it was the way it was in the early years, and it was mostly all right. Those researchers died for something that was ultimately good. And that made their deaths sad but tolerable.

"I began to think of Rebecca's death like that—was there something good that could come from it? I knew it couldn't come from the ugliness that was in the letters I was receiving. I began to ask childlike questions like the one you asked your mother. It seemed that Becca died from two things, and neither of them were the men that committed the murder. The first was human aggression, and the second was from guns. I knew that my training in no way prepared me to address these problems, and I began to look around for direction.

"I began to emerge from my depression by looking at a number of organizations dealing with human welfare, anti-gun organizations, anti- capital-punishment organizations. All of these seemed to be more political than theoretical and seemed to offer little opportunity for a scientific direction. It was then I came across Highridge by accident. I went to their website and I found the first humanity and compassion tied to science that I had seen in the debate about capital punishment, though they weren't an anti-capital-punishment organization, per se, I began to find out more about the organization and its history. I was impressed by the part sociology played in the development of their policies and programs. It seemed the only organization I researched that had any kind of a scientific direction, and I began to correspond with your mother as Highridge's chief sociologist, and I found a home. I began the process to educate myself. This research institute is the result, funded by my Nobel money. Her life just had to count for something, Mr. Alexander!"

His voice and manner had been escalating as he continued his story, and with this last statement he seemed to lose control for the moment. He had taken off his glasses and his eyes glistened in the late-morning light that was flooding the bright room. He rubbed his eyes with his thumb and middle finger, and with this his distinguished demeanor vanished, replaced by sorrow and desperation. He quickly put his glasses back on and regained the persona of the Nobel Prize winner.

"Well, let's go see the facility," he said, standing up. "This house," he said, making a sweeping motion with his arm, "serves as offices and library. We have the latest electronics, computers, and video hookups for conferencing. In addition to sociology, one of the fields I found to be of potential benefit is behavioral psychology, as it employs a natural science and lawful approach to the subject matter, and relies heavily on evolutionary theory. This is something I knew a little bit about, and I undertook a formal study of it. The human tendency toward aggression seems to be locked up tight in the genetics of our species, governed by our evolutionary history. We have undertaken basic research into this process to come up with strategies to attack it." We had now entered the institutional building that was set up as a group of laboratories staffed with attendants in white coats who were all engaged with small animals.

"Are those foxes?" I asked about the bushy-tailed mammals with which the attendants were engaged.

"Raccoons."

"Raccoons?" I repeated as I looked at the masked animals.

"Yes," said Dr. Camp. "This is Dr. Richard Blake, who heads up our project. He can better explain the research to you." He directed me to a slim, bespectacled, curly-headed man coming forward. It was clear that Dr. Blake was expecting me.

"Welcome, Mr. Alexander," he greeted me without introduction. "Why raccoons, you ask?"

"Well, that would be my first question," I responded along with a handshake and a smile.

"Like you, we are asking childlike questions." I could see further evidence that my visit was anticipated. I was beginning to feel like an important guest.

"Why are humans so aggressive, and what can be done about it? Well, I'm sure Dr. Camp has told you our research has a heavy evolutionary component to its structure."

"Yes," I acknowledged, feeling again the preparation behind my tour. "Animals are prepared by evolution to be susceptible to engage in certain behaviors. Things like territoriality and aggression in mammals, songs and nest-building in birds. When an animal is prepared with little or no teaching or learning involved, animal behaviorists refer to the condition as preparedness—animals that are prepared by their evolutionary history behave in specific ways. Some of these behaviors are easily eliminated through conditioning, or teaching, through the applications of reward or aversive conditioning, punishment in lay language. Other behaviors are stubborn, and they resist these conditioning processes, and we refer to this state as contra-preparedness. Our working hypothesis is that aggression in humans is an example of a prepared behavior that also exhibits contra- preparedness.

"A classic example of a contra-prepared behavior is a raccoon's washing of its food. Evolutionarily, it confers the benefit of providing the raccoon with clean food. But while a raccoon will wash dirty food with clean water, it will also wash clean food in dirty water. It will even wash clean food in disease-ridden water. It seems to be a behavior that is incorporated deeply into the raccoon's behavioral repertoire, irrespective of the condition of the food or the water. Moreover, it resists reduction or modification through conditioning. We have an ongoing research program that attacks this behavior and attempts to modify it."

"You're attacking human aggression through raccoons washing their food?"

"Yes, exactly, Mr. Alexander, that's how science proceeds, from the simple to the complex."

"How are you specifically attacking washing behavior?" I followed.

"We have a number of projects and techniques to address it. Classical behavioral methods such as reinforcing the non-washing of food. Also, aversive conditioning: using loud noises and electro-shock to discourage it, using food availability and deprivation protocols, and stimulus control."

"Stimulus control?" I said. "I'm not familiar with that one."

"Managing the environmental factors around the animal to influence its behavior. Animals will act differently when in certain environments and not in others."

Like my interviews in bars, I thought.

"Lately, we've also been using chemical and pharmaceutical interventions," said Dr. Blake.

"Have you had any successes?"

"A few small ones, but nothing definitive yet," Dr. Blake conceded. "But the research is in the early stages."

We walked through the building where several people were engaged in various interactions with raccoons. None of the raccoons seemed happy. I couldn't bring myself to think any of the activities could affect the things that led to the executions of Willie Ruckles or Eugene Redway, or to the death of Robert Stith for that matter. *Maybe they should be working with grizzly bears,* I thought. I was quickly losing my faith in childlike questions. Maybe Margret would have a better feeling for this type of scientific research. "Where do the raccoons come from?" I asked, not being able to come up with a more relevant question.

"We previously trapped them from the wild, but now we raise most of our subjects in captivity."

"Do you think that domestication could be a factor?" I asked.

"Good question, Mr. Alexander, and yes it's a possibility of which we are aware."

I didn't know what would be worse if you were a raccoon, to be snatched from the wild or to be born into a life of harassment for an inborn behavior. Dr. Camp seemed to sense my ambivalence about the raccoons and took back the command of my tour. "We've recently begun work with songbirds," he said. "Songbirds exhibit a range of interesting behavior. Some are born with their songs intact note for note without even a model, much less a teacher, some need to be taught the entire song through repetition to reproduce it, while still others can sing the entire song when given just a few notes. We're investigating the genetic and social origins of each of these types of behavior."

"All of this to get a handle on human aggression?" I asked.

"Yes. When we attacked the problem of smallpox, we began at the beginning, with understanding the life cycle of the disease, it was only after this that we were in a position to develop the strategies that ultimately gave us the leverage to eradicate the disease."

We came to a lab room that looked like an aviary, where a young woman played bird songs to a pair of birds in a plastic box.

"You're addressing human aggression with birds and raccoons, but how are you addressing the problem of guns?" I asked Dr. Camp.

"At first we thought of them as two separate problems, but we've recently begun to think of guns as just one form of human aggression, one that we may be able to eradicate."

"Eradicate guns? There's just too many of them," I said, espousing a bit of conventional pop wisdom.

Raz seemed to come alive as he again took off his glasses, but this time his eyes blazed with fire. "Not more than there were smallpox viruses, Mr. Alexander—a lot less in fact. A lesson from smallpox was when we learned about the characteristics of the host, we had control of the disease. What we're engaged in here is learning about the evolutionary history of the host." His features softened. "Come, let's go back to the house for some lunch."

We walked back to the house: Dr. Camp, Richard Blake, and myself, and I couldn't stop thinking about grizzly bears and childlike questions, and I couldn't help but feel a bit sad. Maybe this was the way to attack human aggression, but maybe it was just a way to attack grief. It seemed a little too slow, a little too academic after my previous nine days. But then again, I wasn't a scientist, and with that thought I was missing Margret.

At the house, a lunch was laid out on a round oak table—home-baked bread, egg salad, butter, milk, and a salad with ranch dressing. "Everything here's from the farm," said Dr. Camp with pride. "Your mother tells me you're becoming a vegetarian. I hope not a vegan."

"No, not for now." *Helen, you old trickster!*

We sat down, and I asked a few more polite questions about the work, and more about the operation of the farm. We were almost done with lunch when the housekeeper-cook came out with a pitcher of beer. "You'll have to sample our beer before you leave us, Ned," said Dr. Camp. It was the first time he had called me by my name, since his first greeting of "You must be Helen's boy, Ned." As the beer was being poured, a woman in a lab coat came and asked for Dr. Camp and Dr. Blake to come to the lab. "Excuse us for a moment. Make yourself at home," I was told as they went out the door with the woman.

I picked up my beer and took them at their word and began to explore. I went into Erasmus Camp's office, sat behind his desk and looked at his Nobel Prize notification. A few pictures were on the wall, most were with comrades at rural outposts with a variety of thatched and jerry-rigged huts and hospitals. One was shaking hands with Kennedy; he was the only person I could identify. There was a picture on the desk of a pretty young girl I took to be Becca, hugging the liver-colored hound dogs with an arm around each. She was laughing and obviously full of life and energy.

"It's you who's powering this institution, girl," I said to the picture.

I moved from Camp's office to the library. It was an eclectic collection of books on virology, evolution, sociology, and behavioral psychology; there were journals and newsletters from a variety of institutions and organizations. I wandered into an office directly off the library that was the office of Dr. Richard Blake, with his name on the desk, and his Ph.D. degree in animal behavior from the University of Nevada at Reno framed on the wall. He seemed the right guy for this job. I was wondering what he knew about bears if he couldn't get the raccoons to eat their food dry.

I was nosing around his office when I happened to look at his in-box and recognized a letter with a familiar logo sitting on the top. The first time I had seen it I mistook it for a map that then resolved itself into the severed components of a human being. What was Richard Blake doing with correspondence from the Ying Lon

Society, whose stated mission was to intensify the death penalty? It was a letter about a page long addressed to Richard Blake from Jerry. I resisted snooping for a good ten seconds and then grabbed the letter and began to read.

Dear Dick, in response to your letter, things are moving along... was as far as I got when I heard voices coming my way from the library. I quickly put the letter back into its tray and pretended to be looking at the diploma when Richard Blake entered his office.

"So there you are," he said.

"Yes, I was making myself at home looking at your diploma. Reno, huh?" I tried to sound casual.

"Yeah, University of Nevada at Reno is one of the best behavioral programs in the country, along with Western Michigan. I interviewed with Dr. Camp right after graduation, and I liked his ideas and the chance to do some basic research. He offered me a position here, and I jumped at it."

"Have you been disappointed with your lack of results?" I asked undiplomatically.

"No, not at all. Raccoon behavior is intractable, but no more so than human aggression. I would have been disappointed if it were modified too easily. I feel there's more potential for the study this way."

"And Dr. Camp, does he feel the same?"

"Raz is looking for results, but he understands well the slow pace of science."

I was itching to get my hands on the Ying Lon letter but couldn't think of a way to do it. Dr. Blake settled down at his desk and turned on his computer, and I saw no opening. Obviously, the tour was over as far as he was concerned. I took my beer and drifted to back into the library. Dr. Camp sat in a comfortable chair, reading a book. He looked up when I came in and smiled. "Did you find anything helpful from your visit? I realize that we are in the initial stages of our research, and the link between the behavior of raccoons and the men who murdered my daughter is at best ambiguous at the moment. But I believe the approach has some promise; at least it's not mean." "Yes," I said, thinking that the raccoons being shocked with electricity

for washing their food might not agree. But mostly I agreed it was a civilized response to an untenable circumstance, and productive or not, I felt it was a courageous try. And if there were promise in grizzly bears, Erasmus Camp would probably be down for that, too. It was clearly time to go, but I wanted to hang around a little while to see if I could get back into Richard Blake's office. "You correspond regularly with anti-capital-punishment organizations?"

I asked him as a lead into my next question.

"Some of them, but they're mostly political organizations, but still we try to keep in contact. We've all been following your articles with interest, though. Do you remember that I told you I found Highridge by accident?"

"Yes," I said. I'd been meaning to ask about that but had forgotten. "Well, I was given a book by a friend in Missouri called *The Wisdom of Forgiveness*," Camp said, and I knew with an involuntary shiver what was coming. "It was at a time I was being inundated with savage letters, it made quite an impression on me, the author was a Sister Shashwati. On the inside cover of the book was a stamp that said Highridge Folk School Library. I asked my friend where he got it, and he said he didn't know, that he thought he'd always had it. I followed it up and discovered Highridge, and my life began to be put back together. Then I come to find out from your articles that Sister Shashwati was a death row prisoner in Texas. I took that as confirmation that we were on the right track."

Willie was just everywhere. There really was no such thing as a coincidence. Dr. J. Erasmus Camp was brought to Highridge and his raccoons by Willie T Ruckles. Maybe there was something here for me after all. I asked the question I was waiting for: "Do you correspond with organizations that are pro-capital-punishment?"

"Hell, no," was Raz's immediate answer as he looked straight into my eyes. "All they provide is poison."

I wondered again what the letter from the Ying Lon Society was doing in Richard Blake's in-box, using the familiar greeting *Dick* as the intro. It was one more in a continuing string of mysteries. Fighting to extend the visit a little longer, I seemed to remember that I had read an article about a troupe of monkeys in the Congo that served as a small reservoir for the smallpox virus, and that they were subject to periodic culling to protect the human population. I asked Dr. Camp about this phenomenon, and he confirmed that it was a little-known fact.

"Yep," he said, "the price of eradication is a few dead monkeys." His good humor seemed to vanish, his eyes and mouth cold and hard. I looked to see if he was joking, but clearly he was not. Richard Blake remained in his office, and this seemed a good time to leave.

18

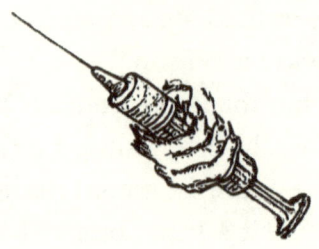

A Few Dead Monkeys

The short drive back to Highridge was an uneasy one. The visit had been disconcerting, leaving me with a range of conflicting emotions spanning sadness to perplexity to mistrust—a feeling that I had somehow been given a sleight of hand, that I'd only been shown the surface of what was going on at the institute. The letter from Jerry Boyle and the Ying Lon Society was troubling, as was my response to it. In retrospect, why hadn't I just asked Blake what he was doing with it, and told him that my eye was drawn to the familiar logo and I was familiar with the organization? It was a mild form of snooping, if it was snooping at all. Yet I had not asked. Why? Was I feeling that I was being sold a bill of goods? Dr. Camp had seemed open and genuine in his willingness to share his life and his research, even the most painful parts. Why these feelings of distrust?

Was human aggression locked somewhere inside the intractability

of raccoons and the music of songbirds? Did the techniques of eradicating smallpox hold the methodology for eradicating the world of
firearms? It seemed unlikely to me, yet here in the hills of Appalachia
was research that purported to address doing just that. How could
this visit help change the direction of my articles, and more important,
my place in it? As I drove back to Highridge, I couldn't shake my
uneasiness. I couldn't shake Dr. Camp's pronouncement, for that's
what it was, that smallpox's continued eradication was dependent
upon a "few dead monkeys." Was this just a statement of the reality
of the situation or did it have a metaphorical meaning? Another
question: Were Robert Stith and Roger Burwick a few of those dead
monkeys? I was sorry that I had neglected to ask Dr. Camp who it
was that killed these monkeys and how they did it. Was it too late
to ask? Probably, without giving away my suspicions. Suspicions?
What suspicions could I have? It was a legitimate research institute,
funded by Nobel Prize money, run by a friend of my mother's. What
suspicions? *Think...*

The letter from Jerry Boyle, addressed familiarly to *Dick*, wouldn't
go away. It was the first link between the Tucson events and the
newer events of the past eight, now nine days. It was too late to ask
Robert Blake about Jerry Boyle but not too late to ask Jerry Boyle
about Robert Blake. Which I would do as soon as I returned.

With these thoughts stinging like hornets in my brain, I walked
into Helen's house. My mother and brother were sitting and facing
each other in rocking chairs looking like the Highridge logo, "Hi
there, little brother," said Bob.

"How was your visit, son?" asked Helen.

"I don't exactly know." And I told them of the day, the raccoons
and songbirds, my nagging doubts, and the letter to Dr. Blake from
Jerry Boyle and the Ying Lon Society.

"That does seem a strange coincidence," said Helen. "I know
how Raz feels about the promoters of capital punishment, and I

can't believe he would knowingly correspond with them. Did you ask him about it?"

I felt a little embarrassed when I told them of my reticence to do that. It sounded like I was acting on a preconceived notion. But acting how?

"Wayell, it's been a quiet day around here, son, thank the Lawd." "Oh, Mama, you know you thrive on chaos," said my brother, and Helen chuckled.

Margret was gone, taking dinner along with her. I went into the refrigerator and got an apple and some cheese. I quartered the apple and cut off a few large chunks of what I took to be cheddar and put them on a plate. That and a glass of red wine would be dinner. I took the plate, glass, and my laptop and went into my mother's library-den.

It had been over twenty-four hours since my last article, and I began to write about my visit to the Rebecca Camp Research Institute for Behavior, mostly in the beginning as a way to organize my thoughts. I gave a background of J. Erasmus Camp's professional history and a brief account of his daughter's murder that led him to form the institute. The information for these two pieces came from an online encyclopedia and newspaper articles that were also online. I described the methodology and their hypotheses concerning evolution and the behavioral phenomena of preparedness and contra-preparedness. I described the eradication of smallpox, how it might be an optimistic metaphor for gun control, and the intractability of raccoons' washing behavior, and its promise for reducing human aggression.

I finished up the article with a personal observation of a man, with every reason to hate, who refused to give into the notion of taking a life, who battled ultimate sadness with science. Then I wrote another section of the article that told of the letter from the Ying Lon Society, and I speculated freely, giving free rein to all my barely conscious concerns. It felt good—cathartic. I told about the few dead monkeys and speculated from there. This part of the article was fantastic, even libelous, but I needed it for my own closure of the day. I made this portion of the article its own document and excised it from the whole. I titled it *A Few Dead Monkeys*.

I filed the Dead Monkeys article under the folder labeled "taxes," where I archive my most sensitive work, and printed out the first article. It had taken me just over two hours to research and write it, and it was now eight o'clock. I read it over and decided that it was pretty tolerable and took it to Helen for her comments. I don't usually let other people read my work prior to submission, but Erasmus Camp was her friend, and I wanted her views on the scientific content and organization. She read it and said it was a real fine job "considering your doubts." I asked her if she thought the article was fair, and she said that she did. "Nice work, son," she said, smiling at me with all of her Southern charm. I didn't know what to do with all of this new approval from my mother.

I asked for Dr. Camp's phone number. I would want his approval before I published anything, my visit not being ostensibly for journalistic purposes. I reached Dr. Camp on the first try. I told him I had written an article on my visit to his facility. I also told him of the content and read him a few quotes, and said I had shown it to my mother and she approved. I asked him if I could email the article for his approval.

"Well, Ned, that won't be necessary if Helen's given her seal of approval. I'll see it when it comes out. You can send it to me later." He sounded like he had been drinking, and there was a tiredness beneath his joviality.

"That's very gracious Dr. Camp."

"Call me Raz, doggonit," he said, and I was sure he had been drinking.

And why not? If anyone deserved a stiff drink, it was Raz Camp.

I took a deep breath and asked, "Raz, who is it that kills the monkeys?" "What monkeys?" he asked with a bit of confusion.

"The monkeys in the Congo that serve as a reservoir for smallpox."

"Oh those," he said, reorienting himself. "The World Health Organization contracts periodically with local snipers. Being part of the U.N., they couldn't contract with the military."

I thanked him again for my visit and rang off. The World Health Organization contracts with simian hit men. *Imagine…*

It was just six o'clock in Tucson. I emailed Halloran a copy of the article, titling it *Nobel Prize Winner Seeks Alternative to Capital Punishment Through Behavioral Science.* I went back out to the living room, grabbed another apple, some more cheese, and refilled my wine glass. I wanted to give Halloran a chance to read the article, as I knew he would if he were still there, before I gave him a call. I went to my backpack and retrieved my notes from the Burwick-Redway stories and found Jerry Boyle's number. Why wait until I got back to call? I dialed the number from Helen's library.

"Hello, is this Jerry Boyle?" I asked the voice that answered.

There was an obvious pause, and a latent "yes," followed by, "Who is this?"

"Mr. Boyle, my name is Ned Alexander. I'm a reporter for the *Sun.* We met at the Redway execution."

"Oh, yes, you called me a torturer, if I remember correctly," he said, chuckling.

"I don't think I called you a torturer. I said what you were talking about sounded like torture."

"Same thing, isn't it?" he asked. "What can I do for you, Mr. Alexander?" "Can you tell me if you know a Dr. Richard Blake?" I jumped in with both feet.

"Ah." That was followed by another long pause. This guy balked at really simple questions. "Ah, no, I don't think so," he answered finally.

"Can you tell me why he received a letter from you and the Ying Lon Society sent to the Camp Research Institute? Can you tell me the nature of that letter?" I continued relentlessly.

"Who are you asking about?" he answered. His poise was obviously shaken.

"Dr. Richard Blake," I repeated. "Can you tell me the nature of the letter you sent to him?"

"Oh, yes, Richard, we went to grad school together." "Where was that?"

"Yale," he said.

"I thought he graduated from the University of Nevada at Reno?" Another long pause. I thought we'd been cut off, then his voice returned.

"I'm having trouble with this connection. You'll have to call me back," he said over a perfectly clear line that suddenly went dead.

"Yeah, Jerry, you're having trouble, but it isn't with the line," I said into the dead receiver. The mystery letter was getting ever more interesting.

My next call was to Halloran. "Hey, Harvard, what's up?" "How did you know it was me, Mike?"

"Tennessee area code. You're the only person I know in Tennessee." "Right. Did you get my article?"

"Just read it and approved it for the morning edition. Well written and interesting, but it's a bit outside the scope of your other articles, isn't it?"

"The story's getting pretty broad, and it may not be that far outside," and I filled him in on the Jerry Boyle and his letter.

"You do find yourself in a world of coincidence, Harvard."

I thought about telling him the truth about coincidence but rather said, "It's coincidence city around here all right," and rang off.

I emailed Rachael, the university intern, and asked her to dig up anything on Jerry Boyle and the Ying Lon Society and that I'd be in at work tomorrow afternoon. I thanked her for her previous work and said it had been really helpful. I checked on flights and found one departing at nine o'clock the next morning that would get me in at three. If we left at five, I could make it, and with Zegura's cash I could pay for it. I asked Helen if she was game to take me. She said no problem, the earlier the bettah. My brother had gone to bed early, and it was just the two of us puttering around in the kitchen.

"Helen, I've never told you why I stopped calling you mother." And I told her the whole story, how I felt I could compete better for her affection, how it allowed me to step outside of competition with my brother, and the peace I finally made with my place in her life. "It was never to distance myself from you, it was to bring me closer," I said in finale.

Helen rubbed her glistening eyes. "I always knew that, son, but it's so nice ta hear you say it. I was aware you felt neglected at times, but I also knew it wasn't true, but you can't tell someone that their feelings are wrong. All I could do was show you, and I did try. In my way, I did try."

"I know my behavior didn't always make you proud, and I did some things for the negative attention they brought."

"Yeayes, you were right good at that. Your father understood that bettah than I. But you always had a good heart, and that was what was important to me."

Well, that wasn't quite true, but it was good enough for tonight. "Good night, Helen," I said.

19

A Few Dead Chickens

I arrived in Tucson at three, and it seemed like I'd been gone a lot longer than nine days with all that had happened. I had left the recipient of the last job in town and returned a published journalist, the president of a hundred-million-dollar charity, and the biographer of a death row prisoner who averted his own execution (or countermanded it) who was a world-famous international philosopher and guru. And to top it off, I was further assured of the transforming knowledge that there was no such thing as coincidence.

Life sure is tricky, I assured myself as I caught a taxi to the paper.

"Hello there, star reporter," I was greeted by Mildred Magee, the paper's flamboyant receptionist. "Glad you could make it into work. You quite the story round here," she said in her rich Louisiana musical lilt. Mildred Duvalier Magee was my first friend at the paper besides Halloran, who was not exactly my friend. She was six-foot-three and three hundred pounds of gladness and goodwill from New Orleans. I'd seen her only a few times, but we had this immediate understanding: Mildred knew I was a fuck-up trying to make good, and I felt that she took me on as her special project to look after. "Yes, sir, you the talk of everybody," she continued on, laughing as she talked.

"Good talk or bad talk, Mildred?"

"Oh, real good talk mostly, honey, except for Miss Solomon, who's been cranky and morose since you've been gone. I don't know, though, that it has anything directly to do with you, but I'd tread softly."

"Oh, Solomon's all right," I said with a confidence I did not feel. "Oh yeah! You can handle her." Mildred gave way to total laughter. I smiled sheepishly. "Is she in?"

"She's not been in today, submitted a story, though. It's probably online. You been having yourself quite a time; I understand the Texas po-lice want to arrest you." Mildred waited for my reaction.

"Where'd you hear that, Mildred?"

"Texas State Police called and talked to Halloran, I took the call and just happened to overhear the conversation." She gave me a wide-eyed smile and batted her eyelashes at me.

"You listened in on Halloran's conversation?" I said, returning her laughter.

Mildred gave me a deep, apologetic nod. "I do that occasionally." *Well, Mildred I'm glad you're my friend*, I thought.

"Listened to one from Lieutenant Hickey, too, told Halloran he wants to see you when you come back. Seems he thinks you've been involved with a few too many coincidences."

"He has no idea. What did Halloran say?"

"He said he'd tell you when you got back. Hickey said he'd better see to it that you came. Halloran told him again that he'd tell you, but it was not his place to ensure you went. You could tell Hickey didn't like it, but he left it there. Halloran's a good man, deed he is."

"Is he in?"

"Nope, but he'll be in a little later. You've got a new box, you know." "Box?" I said.

"Yeah, your own little cubicle got your name on it, a phone, and computer, bigger than your last one; just like a real reporter. Careful, though, it's right next to Solomon's."

"I'll be careful, Mildred," I assured her. "Is Rachael in?"

"Yeah, she's in, came in just before you. Hey, why don't you let me cook you dinner tonight? I get off at five. Cook you a nice Louisiana crawfish gumbo. You look like you could use a good meal, child."

"OK," I surprised myself by saying, putting my newly adorned vegetarianism on hold. I realized I hadn't eaten all day, passing up breakfast at Helen's for a cup of coffee, with a few more on the airplane. Louisiana gumbo was just the comfort food I needed—the apple and cheese spartan dinner seemed a long time ago. "Dinner at your place would be good."

I went to find my box and Rachael.

"Hi, Rach," I said to the youthful and energetic, auburn-haired girl sitting in front of a computer. "How's it going?"

"Hello, Mr. Alexander," she said. "I've been working on Jerry Boyle and the Ying Lon Society, and it's interesting. There is no record of a Jerry Boyle in the area. There's a Gerald Boyle who is a second-grade teacher in Globe, but he's in his late sixties, and no others. I've checked motor vehicles, and there is no record of a Jerry Boyle.

"What about the Ying Lon? And it's Ned, by the way."

"Well, that's another interesting thing. There is a Ying Lon Society, but it's a benevolent organization run for the Chinese community. They fund scholarships and medical care for the elderly, nothing to do with capital punishment. I talked to the chair of their board, a Mrs. Tang, and she's never heard of Jerry Boyle. I called the number you gave me in your email today, and it's been disconnected. But I got you the address of the house where the phone was."

"How'd you do that?"

"I called the phone company and I told them I needed them to disconnect my phone and gave them the number. They said it had already been disconnected, and I said, 'Really?' And asked them to double check the address and they told me it. I said yes, that was the right address and that my husband must have called it in."

"Nice work, really nice work, Rach." I marveled at the resourcefulness of this eighteen-year-old sophomore.

She giggled and looked up at me with pride. "I'm also running his name through the police computer database."

"How are you doing that?" I asked my young research assistant, becoming ever more impressed with her.

"I met this young cop the other night at Gentle Ben's, you know, the college bar?" I said I did. "He was trying to impress me and said if I ever needed it, he could get me into the police database. He was kind of cute, not at all coppy, so I called him up and asked him to run Jerry Boyle and the Ying Lon Society for me. We're meeting tonight at Ben's. I can call you tonight or let you know tomorrow."

"Rachael, you're eighteen. What are you doing in bars?" "False ID, boss," she said, smiling.

"Tomorrow will be fine," I said. "And Rachael, can you have him run the name Roger Burwick through the system?"

"Sure thing, boss," she said, basking in the praise for her good work. "Thanks for the work you did for me before I left, it was really helpful, particularly the stuff you got from the fraternity yearbook."

"Oh, that reminds me, I have some more stuff for you." She pulled out a manila folder from her desk. "I went back and made friends with the housemother, told her my little brother was hot to join the fraternity, and she opened up her library for me and let me borrow what I wanted."

"Your computer cop better watch himself." I said I would see her tomorrow and went back to my box to read the file.

Most of the photocopied pages were from newsletters, and Rachael had meticulously inscribed the date by hand on each. There were more pictures of events with Roger Burwick and Barbara Solomon, who was sometimes mentioned by name and other times referred to as his companion or escort. Then, in the last few months before his graduation, Barbara disappeared, replaced by a series of other companions. I went back to the files in my backpack and got the date of the first function presented in the yearbook and summed up the dates from the newsletters and came up with a year and two months as being the minimum length of Solomon's and Burwick's relationship—a significant amount of time. Roger had met Victoria Ramsfeld in law school at Yale, but I wondered if Mrs. Burwick was aware of Solomon's and her husband's prior relationship, and if that was why Solomon was having such a hard time getting an interview.

One thing was certain: Solomon was not keeping to the principle of full disclosure. I wondered why; it was certainly a risk for a journalist. I thought of the woman—yes, I was certain it was a woman in Burwick's car leaving the execution—and I had Barbara's article I'd taken from the glove box of Burwick's BMW in the parking lot of the El Palomino Resort. With the thought of stealing material evidence, Hickey came to mind. Halloran was still not back, so I figured I'd play dumb and call Hickey on my own. I called his direct line and he picked up.

He got right to it after I identified myself. "Mr. Alexander, you've been a busy man." Why did everyone greet me with that busy-man stuff? Didn't they do things with their days? *Yes, Hickey, you old slacker*, I felt like saying, but instead I said nothing and waited for what was next. "Did Halloran tell you I wanted to see you?"

No, sir, the receptionist did, she listens to all your conversations and then informs me. But instead I said, "No, sir, I just got back into town and I haven't seen Halloran yet. I figured I'd just check in and see if you had any leads in the Burwick case."

"My only lead at the moment, Mr. Alexander, is you." He waited to see how I reacted to this provocative remark. I remained silent, waiting for the next volley. "What do you think about that, Mr. Alexander?"

"I think it's pretty silly. I would have expected you to be further along than to suspect me." I chose the word *silly* on purpose, ratcheting it down from absurd.

"Oh you do, do you? Can you tell me why you're the only one who has been present at all of the killings?"

"The only killing I was present for was the Redway execution and you, or rather your employer, was the killer there." Hickey let that dig slide. "I came on the scenes of the Burwick and Stith killings after they were both dead, and I provided information helpful to the police on both occasions. I've also kept in touch with both the Tucson and Texas police departments and forwarded them all of the communications I've received from the organization that calls itself BWWY. You got the last fax I sent to you, I take it?"

Hickey seemed to soften a little. "Can you tell me why you were first on the scene at both murder sites?"

"Perhaps you should be asking why the police are slower to respond than I am. That would seem a more productive tack." I'd pushed him about as far as I felt I should. "To be fair, though, I did receive my fax telling me to go to the San Carlos Hotel in Houston a half hour earlier than the one sent the police. "I don't know why BWWY has chosen me to be a conduit, but I have passed along every bit of information from them." *From them, that was truthful enough*, I thought. "Have you made any progress in your investigation? Do you know where the chemicals that killed Burwick came from?" I asked him.

"They seem to have come from a local chemical supply house, sell mostly to schools and small businesses, some of these businesses resell them, and we haven't been able to trace the buyer. Slightly different than those used to kill Redway, but, in combination, just as lethal."

"Thank you, Lieutenant Hickey," I said by way of an apology. "Do you want me to come to your office?"

"Naw," he said. "This is good enough for now. Just keep me posted on anything new." I said I would and rang off.

"Hey, Harvard, I heard you were back," came Halloran's voice before his head and shoulders emerged from over the walls of my box. "Come on back to my office and we'll chat. Lieutenant Hickey wants you to come in and see him. I can't make you, but it would seem a good idea."

"I've already talked to him," I said, and I told him of our conversation. "How'd you know to call him?"

"I just figured it would be a good idea to check in with him. He told me you'd be telling me to anyway."

Was it my imagination or was he eyeing me suspiciously. It would seem nothing much got by Halloran.

"Let's go over to Sam's and have a beer and you can tell me of your adventures of the last week."

"You've got most of it in my articles and in my phone calls." "Tell it again. I want to hear it all at once."

"OK," I said. On the way out, I stopped at the reception desk and got directions to Mildred's place and a time for dinner.

Halloran watched the interaction. "What are you doing with Mildred?" "She's making me dinner tonight," I said causally.

"I like Mildred, but she's a crafty old girl. You watch out, Harvard." He eyed me suspiciously again. Why was everybody warning me to watch out for everybody else? Was my world such a hostile place?

Over beers, I told Halloran my story, Violet and Leo, Willie, Zegura and Sister Shashwati, the story of Margret; I let him read the letters between them, told him the story of Saturn Kitty and Margret's early detection of Willie's identity. I even told him of my feelings for Margret and our resolve to be friends for a while. I told him of the formation of the Sister Shashwati Foundation, leaving out the part about the money I received, thinking that might affect the speed and compensation of my now considerable receipts. I told him of my promise to write a biography of Willie Ruckles and said I would be using some of the information I gathered for the articles and hoped that would not be seen as a conflict of interest. Halloran said he didn't think so, but that I should write a statement describing it and he would take it to the paper's publisher.

I told him of the role my brother and mother had played in the drama. I related the facts about the faxes I had been sent, my conflict with the Texas State Police, and the part I had played in transporting the videotape of Willie's suicide. Finally, I told him about my visit to Erasmus Camp's research institute and the letter I found from Jerry Boyle and the Ying Lon Society, and about Rachael's revelations of today, of the address of the house that I would need to follow up, and Rachael's cop friend who was perusing the police database. At the end of my story, there were two empty pitchers and two empty mugs on our table.

"Quite the tale, Harvard, quite the tale. It seems your job is blossoming into a career. Get me your receipts tomorrow, and I'll get your reimbursement." Halloran drove me to where I was staying and my car so I could get ready for my dinner with Mildred. On the way, I asked about Solomon.

Halloran looked at me for a moment before he answered. Seemed to come to a decision and said, "To be honest, she's been a little off her game lately, preoccupied, distracted. Unhappy but won't admit to anything being wrong. She's had trouble getting into the Burwick story but refused any help. Maybe that will end with you back," he said with little conviction.

Mildred's house was located on Tucson's East side in a historic neighborhood called Old Fort Lowell, a series of low-slung adobe houses with a native desert vegetation between them. Hers was a modest square affair with a low stucco wall demarcating a front porch. I entered and knocked on the carved wooden door with an iron ring inset for that purpose. A barking dog immediately began to scratch on the inside. "Charbon!" called Mildred, as she opened the door, and I was set upon by a friendly, energetic standard French poodle. "Down, Charbon!" said Mildred, and she grabbed the dog by the collar. "She'll settle down in a moment, she's not used to visitors." I assured Mildred that I was familiar with the ways of dogs.

"Dinner's ready, but let's have a drink first."

I said a drink was a good idea. The dog calmed down and we took our drinks out into the backyard, where two large old mesquite trees held center stage among a cadre of wrought iron furniture that sat on the flagstone patio. "This is nice," I said, sitting in a comfortable chair with a black French poodle's head lodged between my legs.

"How'd you make out with the policeman?" Mildred asked.

I knew I had to tell the truth because Mildred was probably listening in. "Well, I don't think the lieutenant was entirely satisfied, but he's not going to arrest me just yet. I think he thinks I know more than I'm telling and he's leaning on me a bit."

"Do you?"

"A little. But nothing important yet." *No, not unless you think stealing evidence from Burwick's car is important,* I couldn't help thinking.

"You always in this much trouble?"

"I'm not in any trouble, Mildred," I responded.

"Oh, no, you're just present at the sites of two murders and one suicide, the Texas Police want to bring you back to Texas to find out how you were involved in giving an embarrassing videotape to national news, and a terrorist organization that kills people associated with executions has attached itself to you. Seems like trouble to me," she said, laughing.

"You've been following the stories closely." "Yes, baby, I have."

"Why?"

"Because you a good boy," she answered. "You have a nice light that surrounds you. You know that? I can see … what do white people call them, auras? I can see light around certain people, not everybody, so maybe it's not like auras exactly, but I see good light and bad light coming from people, and yours, honey, is definitely good. I saw it the first day you walked in and tricked Halloran into giving you that job."

"I didn't trick Halloran," I said in my defense. Mildred put her head down and looked at me from underneath her eyebrows with a steady gaze and held it until I broke. "OK, so I may have tricked him a little."

"I marked you from the first time you delivered your letters to the editor, looking the place over. What do they call it, casin the joint? Um, um, it was more than a little trick. And just because Halloran wanted to be tricked don't make it less of a trick. I noticed that light then and was pulling for you. Yes, I been followin you closely."

The conversation was getting a little too close, a little too intimate for comfort. "You see light around people?" I asked to divert the direction of the conversation.

"Oh yes, always have, even as a child. I'm a great-granddaughter of Marie Laveau, the great voodoo priestess of New Orleans and from way back when I was a child I was schooled in the family profession."

"You're a voodoo priestess?" I asked.

"Yes," she said, standing up and giving me a little bow. "And a good one, too."

"Mildred, I am indeed lucky to have you as my friend," I said, returning her bow.

"Deed you are baby, deed you are. Now let's eat us some gumbo."

The food was just fabulous; we ate the gumbo over dirty rice and with a white wine. Over dinner, we talked about our families and got to know one another. She told me of her life growing up in New

Orleans, her mother who was also a priestess, her two husbands and five children. I told her of my life shuffling among Boston, Highridge, and Mississippi, about my father's death, about my mother and brother. I filled in the blanks between my stories and even about Jerry Boyle and the Ying Lon Society, how I might have spooked him with my telephone call. The only thing I didn't tell her about was Solomon. Charbon and I were by now good buddies, and Mildred and I took our wine back out to the patio where I sat in the cool evening air, a glass of wine in my hand, and a dog's head and two forepaws in my lap.

"Mildred, about those lights you see, does Solomon have one?" I knew I was giving away information but decided to take the chance.

She looked at me a long time before answering. "Solomon doesn't always have a light. But when she does, it's a bad one. Good people can have bad lights, and Solomon's is one that congers up a sadness. It's hard to look at when it's there. But like I said, it's not always there."

The quiet between us was broken by a loud squawking noise. "It's that owl bothering my chickens," Mildred said as she got up shouting "shoo" and waving her arms. "Their house is safe, but the owl keeps trying, upsets the chickens terrible." My eyes were drawn to a small barn-like structure enclosed top to bottom in chicken wire. The structure did indeed look substantial.

"I keep a few chickens mostly for fresh eggs and a few other things," said Mildred.

"Like voodoo?" I asked naïvely.

"Chickens have a power." I waited for something more, but nothing more was forthcoming.

"You want some peach pie?" she asked, and I said I would love some.

We were enjoying our pie when I said, mostly to make conversation, "Do you think you could make me a mojo. I could use a little favorable luck about now." Mildred sat up straight up with an almost reflexive action and set her pie on the floor next to her chair. She stood up and, coming over to me, took my head, which felt about the size of a grapefruit, in her giant hands, tilted it so that my eyes stared directly into hers. "Oh, child," she said with a look of ultimate concern. "Oh, child," she repeated. "Don't you give those things a door into your house." I was immediately seized with an intense and creepy feeling and felt a shiver down my spine to my legs. "Don't you ever attach yourself to an object like that," she said in earnest, shaking her head to add to the effect.

"Mildred, I didn't know it was serious," I said, trying to regain some sense equanimity.

"A mojo gives yourself over to powers that you don't even want to know about, child." She shook her head again. "Do you feel you're in danger from anything?" She was deadly serious.

Despite the unsavory circumstances of my past week, I had felt no danger. "No," I said truthfully. "At least I hadn't until your talk of the mojo." "Good," she said, looking long at me, trying to determine the veracity of my answer. At last, she smiled. I said my goodnights to Charbon and Mildred, and I thanked her heartily for the best dinner I maybe ever had.

I went home and, despite the mojo talk, slept like a baby until morning having a pleasant dream about walking holding hands with Margret. I think we were looking for Jerry Boyle's house, but I couldn't be sure. But the overall effect was quite pleasurable. *Who needs a mojo?* I thought while waking up. I showered and got ready for work, putting on the clean clothes that Helen had washed for me while I was at Dr. Camp's. I put on the Advanti tee shirt, jeans, and Converse tennis shoes, organized my burgeoning files, put them in my backpack and left the house for the paper. There on the concrete porch was what looked like a Chinese character written in rust- colored paint. I knelt down to get a closer look, and the figure looked like a stick-figure of a person sheltered by a roof and in the paint was mingled some feathers. Someone during the night, and

I knew who, had drawn this figure in chicken's blood and feathers in front of my door.

The act and figure should have creeped me out, but it didn't. Rather, I felt a curious security—a feeling of safety. A mirror image of the Congo monkeys, the price of this safety was a few dead chickens.

20

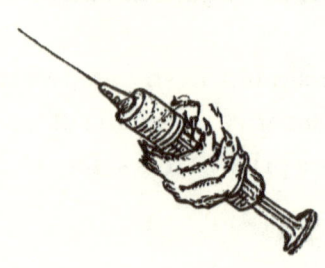

The Girl in the ER

I was excited to get to the paper, eager to see what Rachael's computer cop boyfriend had come up with, eager to see Solomon. I had emailed Solomon to see if we could meet, and she wrote me back that she would be in today, but she didn't specify a time. I emailed her back for a time but she hadn't yet responded. But still I was hopeful. Mildred was installed at the reception desk and greeted me warmly with "Mornin, honey." I wanted to say something about my front porch but hesitated, thinking it possibly bad form. Mildred said nothing, so I left it alone.

Neither Solomon nor Rachael was in. I went to my box and pulled up Solomon's most recent article on my desk computer. It was pretty much a rehashing of previous facts, written as an update, but it contained nothing that was really new. It appeared on Page Six. It used information from some of my articles, and I was just given credit for research, but I didn't take offense. Mildred had attributed my employment to a trick, but I attributed it to Barbara's petulance. I remembered how just about a week and a half ago her mounting fury extended the conversation between Halloran and me that ended with the last job in town. I remembered her impassioned and personal critique of capital punishment in the Giddy-Up bar.

I called the desk and told Mildred to alert me when Rachael came in. I need not have bothered, for while I was talking to Mildred, she put through a call from Rachael.

"Hey, boss, I'm coming in soon and I've got something for you. Something a little surprising," but that was all she said, and she rang off, leaving me wondering. Good sense of drama, Rach! I sat in my box and waited for her. I pulled out my notebook that documented the early stages of the Burwick murder and found the first fax that I'd been sent by BWWY, offering me a "little help" and the number .067. The fax was as confusing now as it had been when I first received it. I wondered if Mad Michael, my Harvard math wizard, had made any headway on finding out its meaning. I was operating under the hazy notion that the two murders were not committed by the same people, that Stith was killed by members of BWWY but Burwick was killed by someone else. Even though there were some links between the two crimes, namely the early fax and later a possible connection with Jerry Boyle, the chemicals used to kill the two victims were different, as was the methodology used by the killer. The apparatus was also different, although I didn't know exactly how. Even though these discrepancies could have been caused by regional differences in available materials and the killer's (or killers') learning curve, I still felt the investigation of the Burwick case should be pursued separately, so I returned to the first fax. I seemed to have some time on my hands, so I gave Mad Michael a call.

"Ned, Ned is that you?" he responded to my greeting excitedly. I began to get my hopes up that he had found out something, but they were soon dashed. "I'm so glad you called. Did you tell anyone about my BMW theory about the grille and Hitler's mustache?" he blurted out, his words tumbling over one another.

"I told Conway about it. Why?"

"Because I was almost killed, that's why," came his impassioned answer. "Killed?"

"Yes. I was run down by a black BMW outside the Harvard library. It dove on to the sidewalk at the last minute," he said. "The car swiped the side of the bordering wall! I was this far from being killed." I didn't have a physical reference for the distance "this far," but I could tell from the passion in his voice that it was close.

"Wow!" I said ineffectually and waited.

When nothing else was forthcoming, I said. "So, you think you've been targeted by post war Nazis?" It sounded pretty silly. "When did this happen?"

"Three days ago," he said, calming down a bit.

"Wow," I said again to show my sympathy. "Have you called the police?" "Yeah, they said it was probably an accident, a drunken student, but they said they would look into it."

"Did you tell them about your BMW theory?" "Hell, no. Then they'd really think I was crazy."

"Yeah. Wow. Well, I don't think it was Conway's inquiries, they were over three months ago, and if Bavarian Motor Works wanted you dead, they would have acted before this."

"Yeah, you're probably right, but it's still freaky. I don't feel safe walking the streets anymore."

"Yeah, that's tough, but it will probably get better. It probably was just an accident. Listen, before this happened did you have a chance to put in some time with my number or whatever it is?" I asked.

"Yeah, I did a little but haven't come up with anything yet, sorry, I've been a little preoccupied."

"Are you still interested?" "Sure I am."

Rachael stuck her head around the wall of my box, and I motioned that I would be with her in a moment.

"What did Conway say?" he asked.

"About what?" I had to ask as my attention was diverted to Rachael. "About my BMW theory, what have we just been talking about?"

"Sure. Sorry," I said. "He said it was possible. No, actually, he used the word probable."

"Great!" said Mad Michael.

"Don't worry, given his history, Conway's a bit of a conspiracy theorist. But I've got my own conspiracy theory going on here and I really could use your help. Listen, go to any of the anti-capital-punishment websites and play around with their statistics, see if you can make some sense out of it. Can you do that? I'm up against a wall here."

"Sure thing, buddy," said Mad Michael, sounding more like himself. "I'll give you a call tomorrow. What's your phone number anyway?"

I gave him the number at the paper and told him to keep me posted about the BMW thing, and rang off.

"Well," said Rachael, and I could tell that she was pleased with herself. "Beginning with Jerry Boyle, we got nothing. There was a DUI for a Gerald Boyle from Globe—that would be the second-grade teacher—but nothing else in the whole state. Then we ran the name Roger Burwick."

I noticed that the partnership had matured over the evening from *my cop friend* to *we*.

"And this is a little bit awkward, boss. Roger Burwick was implicated in an assault-and-battery charge with his girlfriend, who was treated at Tucson Medical Center for cuts and bruises consistent with domestic violence. The girl in question made a statement that she was assaulted by Mr. Burwick. The police examined him but could find no corroborating physical evidence that supported the claim that he had beaten the girl. He flatly denied the charge, and the next day and the charges were dropped."

"This is bad, Rachael, but why is it awkward?" "Because, boss, the girl was Barbara Solomon."

The name went through me like lightning. It took me a second to catch my breath.

"When was this?" I asked when I could speak.

The answer was pretty much the exact date I had determined for the time of their breakup, according to Rachael's newsletters.

"Solomon..." I said, still trying to comprehend the implications.

"Yes," said Rachael. "See what I mean about awkward?" And she handed me a folder.

I looked through the file with the original police report, and it said pretty much what Rachael had told me, but following the report were photos. A barely recognizable Barbara Solomon stared out defiantly from black eyes all but swollen shut, her nose and mouth showed a number of cuts, and there were bruises on her cheeks. Another photo showed bruises on her forearms from what were probably attempts to block his incoming blows. Still another showed large bruises on her back and neck.

"She said he hit her with gloves on so it wouldn't leave marks on his hands," said Rachael, as disgust blazoned her youthful features.

My eyes went out of focus, and I realized that they were filled with tears. I was overwhelmed with feelings of raw hatred for this guy and a wish to kill him, until I remembered he was already dead. I thought of Jerry Boyle and Ying Lon Society's statement about intensifying the death penalty, and it didn't seem so outrageous now. I realized that the difference between me and Robert Stith, Roger Burwick, and maybe even Eugene Redway wasn't that much. That maybe the research of J. Erasmus Camp wasn't so misguided after all. Then I caught myself and civilization reasserted itself and I returned to the present.

"Again, this is amazing work, Rachael, you and your computer cop friend. I don't need to tell you that this is really confidential, only you and I and your friend can know about this."

"Yeah, I realize that, boss. Also, Ryan is really taking a chance with this, so we really need to protect him as the source. Not even Solomon should know if you decide to show it to her. Ryan said that he had to go through four layers of security to get to this information. Usually, he said, it just takes just one or two. He worked real hard to get it for us."

"Yeah, I guess the governor doesn't want it known that the golden boy of the attorney general's office was a woman beater. Ryan, is it? He must like you a lot to do this for you."

"Yes, I think he does," she said, smiling and nodding. The police report came from the computer, but the pictures came from the actual file. This thing is really creepy, though, with the gloves and then the hand-in-glove thing." Rachael shook involuntarily as if she were trying to rid herself of something unsavory.

"Your boy's safe with me, Rachael," I said and gave her hand a little squeeze.

"What's next, boss?"

"I don't know, Rach, I need to think on it a bit. But I'll let you know when I do. And thank Ryan for me."

The first thing I did was to put all the material that dealt with Barbara into a single folder, including the article I had taken from Burwick's glove compartment. I labeled the folder "taxes" and set it aside and reread everything in it as I waited for Solomon. Taken together, the file was quite incriminating, added to the fact that the woman in Burwick's car was probably Solomon. I could see Lieutenant Hickey building a case for murder. Barbara's failure to declare a conflict of interest was beginning to look like more than a minor issue. I began to think about the evidence for the murder to have been committed by BWWY, and it certainly would have been consistent with their mission, but the evidence when compared with that on Solomon looked flimsy. I decided to wait an hour, and if Solomon didn't show, I would go to the address of Jerry Boyle's telephone.

I was preparing to go when I heard a rustling from Solomon's cubicle. I picked up the file and went next door. "No, I haven't gotten the interview with Burwick's widow," she greeted me before I could say anything.

"I'm not surprised."

"What the hell's that supposed to mean?" "It means we have to talk," I said softly.

"Spare me any lectures, Harvard, about how to go about doing my job. Other people may think you're God's gift to journalism, but I'm not one of them."

"You can spare me your defensiveness," I said. "I know a few things that may be important to you, and we need to talk." I still spoke softly. Either something in my manner or my face caused her to look at me and momentarily drop her attitude.

"OK, let's talk."

"Not here," I said. "We need to go somewhere private. Let's go over to Sam's."

"Sam's? It's eleven o'clock."

"Hence the privacy. Besides, I think we can both use a beer."

I could see the puzzlement in her face and that she was beginning to feel a little nervous.

"Fine. But I'm not drinking."

"OK, I'll do the drinking for the both of us."

We walked over to Sam's without a word. When we arrived, Barbara strode to the bar and ordered a Diet Coke and sat down. I ordered a pitcher of beer with two mugs and remained standing. "Come on, let's go to the back," I said. We sat opposite each other, and I poured myself a beer and left Solomon's glass empty. I passed her the folder.

She looked at the folder. "You're giving me your taxes?" she said sarcastically.

"It's just a code I use to provide an uninteresting title to curious eyes.

Look inside and realize I'm not judging you."

"Judging me..." she began, as she opened the folder, then fell silent as she moved through its contents. Midway through, she reached over for the pitcher and poured herself a beer. She continued to move through the folder, quietly sipping. She stopped when she came to her article and took it out from the folder: "Where did this come from?" she asked softly.

"The glove compartment of Burwick's car. I took it from the parking lot of El Palomino, before the police checked it. I was careful," I boasted, forgetting briefly the terror involved in the process.

"That's why..." she said to herself, as she poured another beer. The Diet Coke remained orphaned on the table. She returned to the folder, looking up at me periodically. She seemed to spend a lot of time over the pictures and articles in the newsletters. When she came to the photos of her beating, she sucked in her breath, took them out from the folder, and placed them face up on the table. She picked up each one in turn, scrutinizing it closely.

"Where did you get these?" she said.

"It doesn't matter. What matters is that if I can get them, so can the police."

She seemed to consider this for a moment, then said, "Roger Burwick was the worst kind of bastard. When I met him, it was the end of my freshman year, he was a junior and a big man on campus, handsome and charming and at first very attentive. I even forgave him his bit of fraternity arrogance, thinking it was just a phase. We went everywhere together until my life became just an ornament to his. At the end of my sophomore year, I realized what was happening and I took back control of my life, took my classes seriously, and did things with other friends whom I'd been neglecting. I'd seen a little of his dark side over the year we were together, but they were small things, at least I told myself they were small. He would hit me when he was upset or had been drinking, and it wasn't all that often. He was always apologetic and repentant, and I even talked myself into thinking I was partly to blame for it. Violent relationships work like that. Things really became intense, however, during the time I began to reassert my independence and our fights often ended with my getting hit.

"I was about to end the relationship when I decided to go on a school field trip with my class to Mexico. The trip coincided with a fraternity gathering of the national house, and he went berserk. I laughed at his behavior and said I was through with him. We were at his apartment at the time, and he went into his bedroom and came back wearing these leather gloves and began hitting me. I thought that this would be like so many times before, a little violence followed by crying and pleas for forgiveness. But this time it was different, the blows didn't stop, I raised my arms to block them, but they kept coming and coming through, and I really thought that I would be killed. I rolled myself into a little ball, put my head into my legs and hugged them with my arms."

She picked up the photo that showed bruises on her back. "Here," she said. "This was where he kept kicking me. I was crying and screaming, but nobody came. Finally, he said, 'Get out of here,' I picked up my purse and stumbled to my car. My eyes were all but swollen shut, but I managed to drive myself to the ER. At the emergency room, they immediately checked me into the hospital, and I told them my story, the police came and I filed a report.

"The next morning a police officer visited me and told me there was nothing they could do unless there was a witness, that there was no evidence at his apartment, or any physical evidence on his person. He said they had searched the apartment but found no gloves, and Roger was denying that anything had happened or that he had even seen me that night. That he didn't know why I would make up such a story other than he had broken up with me.

"That afternoon, Roger came to see me, said he was sorry, that he'd just been accepted to Yale Law School and he didn't want anything to get in the way, and if I would agree to drop the charges he would agree to leave me alone. By implication, if I didn't, he wouldn't. The police had just told me there was nothing they could do, and I was battered, in pain, and vulnerable. To my everlasting shame I dropped the charges." She said this bitterly. She motioned the waitress over and ordered another pitcher.

"I hadn't seen him since then until he became so visible on the Redway case, and then only a few times at press conferences, and while we saw each other, we never interacted. Not until I saw him in the bar in Florence—he left just before you came in." I remembered the figure leaving the bar and the empty glass at her table. "I told him what I thought of his politics, and we left it at that. He had to represent the execution. After the execution, he saw me at the prison gates walking back to my car that was parked at the prison store, and offered me a ride to my car. I accepted, mostly so I could give him a copy of my article that said in a roundabout way what a creep he was. He delivered me, saying that he'd made an earlier purchase at the store. And that was the last I saw of him, but the whole thing was so upsetting I went home and got drunk. Hence, you getting the call to El Palomino." The waitress brought the new pitcher. Solomon poured us each another glass.

"I saw you in his car, you know," I said.

"Yeah, I thought you did." She picked up the folder and dropped it on the table. "Do the police have this?"

"If they do, they don't have it from me. Look, Barbara, I'm glad the son of a bitch is dead, and I don't care how he got that way. The world's a better place without him."

"BWWY? I heard you were their boy." She smiled warmly at me.

"You don't think I did it, do you?"

"It has crossed my mind," I said, smiling over my beer.

"I'm changing my mind about you. You really are a very sweet man. Shielding a murder?" She tapped the file on the table. "There's a hell of article in that folder, Harvard."

"Not for me. And Harvard's Halloran's name for me. You can call me Ned."

"Well Ned, for your information I did not kill him. I don't have the chemistry background for one thing. If I wanted him dead, I would've bashed in his head with a beer mug." She smiled and took a sip from hers and saluted me with it.

"Well, it's really what Lieutenant Hickey thinks, and I think you're taking unnecessary chances by not coming clean with your past history with Burwick and fully disclosing it and taking yourself off the story. So far, you really haven't done anything with the Burwick story other than the recap that appeared today."

"Good point. I've been worrying about that myself, and it's why I've been so ambivalent about interviewing Burwick's widow," she admitted. "But she has been dodging me.

"OK," she went on. "I'll come clean as you say with Halloran and stay off the official parts of the story, but I still want to be involved with you on the research."

Barbara Solomon wants to help me with research. Who would have thought? I told her about Jerry Boyle, the Ying Lon Society, the letter to Richard Blake, and the address that Rachael scammed. We made plans to visit the Boyle house later that afternoon, and Barbara went off to come clean with Halloran. As she got up to go, I handed her the file.

"You hang on to it," she said. "I trust you."

I was not fully convinced that Barbara hadn't killed Burwick, but then again, I didn't care.

21

A Benevolent Heuristic

Jerry Boyle's house, at least his telephone's house, was on the Northwest side of the city, lots of desert surrounding each of the houses, many with horse corrals. On the way, I asked: "What did Halloran say when you told him about your relationship with Burwick?"

"Former relationship," she corrected. "He said I was doing a smart thing, that I shouldn't say anything to the police until I was asked. He wasn't wild about me helping you with research, but he just said to be careful and stay out of the limelight."

"Sounds like good advice to me."

We drove up the rocky driveway to find a one-story ranch house. There were no cars in the carport, and the place looked deserted. We parked and rang the bell on the front door anyway. Silence. I walked around the perimeter of the house looking for anything interesting, peering into the unshaded windows. The house looked immaculately empty, and the doors and windows were all locked. I worked my way back around to the front door, where I found Solomon holding a white envelope, which she handed to me. The envelope had my name handwritten on its cover. "I found it taped to the front door," she said.

I opened it and took out a typed sheet of paper.

Dear Mr. Alexander, We knew you would find your way here. You really are our boy. Who would have anticipated that you would discover me so quickly? By what fortune you discovered my letter to Richard Blake I may never know. But you have, and bravo! Besides, our work has taken a different turn lately. Ying Lon Society, as I'm sure you know by now, is a name I appropriated from a local Chinese benevolent society. I thought it an apt name for our purposes. You see, the Ying Lon Society, as you were exposed to it, was used as a heuristic, a teaching device that pointed out the barbarous nature of capital punishment—that and to identify the most pernicious of its advocates. Since its short inception, we have had queries from the governor's office, politicians, as well as other solid citizens. Not really hard to believe, is it?

But then we were confronted with a heuristic of our own, and have since taken a different direction, one I'm sure you can guess. So, the Ying Lon Society goes back into the Chinese community relatively unscathed. Wait for the next fax. Until then, know that we remain friends.
BWWY

I looked up from the letter. Solomon was staring at me, and I handed it to her. She read it and said: "Whoever these guys are, they sure seem to like you. I guess Jerry Boyle's not his real name, either."

"No, a false name, and a false organization," I said. "It sounds like it served as the precursor to BWWY, though. If Burwick's murder served as a heuristic to the formation of BWWY, it means his killer is definitely different from Stith's. And it looks like another fax is on the way. I wonder how much trouble that one will bring me?"

We returned to the paper and didn't have long to wait. Mildred greeted me with "Halloran wants to see you, and you have a fax I just put it in your box." I thought she meant my mailbox, but when we went there it was empty.

"I thought she just said she put a fax in here?" said Barbara. I smiled. "I think she means my cubicle."

"You mean your office?" she said indignantly.

"Yeah, my box. Loosen up, Solomon," I said, laughing.

"Box," she murmured under her breath, as we walked into my box. Solomon may have loosened up toward me a bit, but obviously that didn't extend to the world at large.

The fax was set face up on my desk and read merely:

Virginia, a little reciprocal information.

It was signed *BWWY.* There was nothing else on the page other than my name and a number of the fax sender with an area code I didn't recognize. "Virginia?" I said. "And what's reciprocal about it?" I looked blankly at Solomon.

"Maybe Virginia refers to the little girl who needed reassurance that there was a Santa Claus," she speculated dryly. "But the three states that execute the most prisoners are Arizona, Texas, and Virginia. Maybe they're going for the trilogy." I had forgotten that she had made an extensive study of the death penalty for a while now.

"Let's go see Halloran," I said. I picked up my phone and called Mildred and asked her to run down the area code. I also called Rachael and asked her to check on impending executions in Virginia.

"Hi, Harvard. Hi, Solomon," Halloran greeted us as we came into his office. "Find out anything from the Boyle place?" I handed him the letter. He read it and handed it back to me, and he sighed and sat way back in his chair.

"I'm going to have a hard time keeping the two of you out of jail," he said. "You going to show this to the police?"

"No," I said. "It mentions Richard Blake and by implication associates Dr. Camp and his research with a murder. I don't think it's fair to do that at this time. Besides, I haven't told Hickey about the Jerry Boyle connection. But I'm going to show him this," and I handed over the fax.

"Virginia? And what's reciprocal about it?" Halloran asked. I spared him Soloman's Santa Claus hypothesis.

"That's what I said. I have Rachael looking into impending executions in Virginia."

"Well, you two delinquents keep me posted," he said, and we left.

I figured I'd call Hickey after I had a few more facts, and they were quick in coming, if a little confusing. The area code was from Fairfax, Virginia, a suburb of Washington, D.C. Rachael was also quick on the draw. "The only execution they had scheduled in the next few months has already happened two days ago, boss. A woman by the name of Carla Rawlings, convicted of having her husband killed to collect an insurance policy. The woman had an extensive history of mental problems, and there was a great outcry from opponents of capital punishment."

"Anyone who championed the execution?"

"Yes, the attorney general himself," she said. "A tough-on-crime guy who's running for Congress. I copied you a few of the last news articles," and she handed me another folder.

"Thanks again, Rachael." After I read the articles, I dialed Lieutenant Hickey's number.

"Talk to me," Hickey said after I told him of the fax. I read him the sparse contents of the message and told him about the area code and the executed prisoner.

"It seems to me that the attorney general, a Lee Hoskins, would be a good candidate for a likely next victim," I ventured.

"Oh, he would, would he? When did you receive the fax?" he asked. I told him an hour ago.

"It took you an hour to call me?"

"I wanted to do some checking first." I sounded apologetic, I thought. "Mr. Alexander, you can let the police do the checking," he chided. "Yes, sir."

He thanked me and asked if I would fax over my fax and the articles on the attorney general copied by Rachael. I thought of asking why he needed my articles if I was to leave the checking to him, then thought better of it and said I would immediately. I could educate the lieutenant on the finer points of journalistic responsibility and the unavoidable overlaps with law enforcement some other time. Right now, it was more important that I keep the lines of communication with him open. "Anything else you want me to do?" I asked.

"Yeah," said Hickey. "If this guy gets murdered, don't you show up first on the scene," and he rang off.

My second call was to Detective Escobar and the Houston police, as I had also said that I would keep him posted. I thought it was politic to keep up a good, personal relationship with Houston.

"Mr. Alexander, you've been quiet for the last few days," he responded when I identified myself.

Yeah, quiet's when I'm dangerous, Detective, I thought but said: "I've just got back to Tucson."

"What can I do for you?"

"Well, I've just received another fax," and I gave him the information I had just given to Hickey. Escobar seemed happy to get the details and asked that I send him everything I had. He also didn't scold me for my research. I asked if I should put in a call to the Virginia police, and he said to leave it to him.

"Anything new on the Stith case?" I asked. He said that the state police were working with the FBI doing a check on all known terrorist organizations, but nothing new yet. The FBI was down rechecking the crime scene and being a nuisance to his investigation, but aside from that, nothing new. "Anything more about me?" I asked.

"They've decided not to issue an arrest warrant for you concerning the transmission of the videotape. They're still mad as hell, but the governor's office figured you'd be a bigger embarrassment to them as a captive. You're OK for now, but I still wouldn't come back to Texas anytime soon if I were you." I thanked him said I would stay in touch. It gave me a warm feeling to know that I was not a wanted man by the Texas Rangers. I told Halloran about my calls and asked if he thought I should go to Virginia.

"No. If there's to be a murder, this is one you can stay away from." "That's what Lieutenant Hickey said."

"Good man, that one," he said.

I faxed out the material to Hickey and Escobar and I sat in my cubicle to think about what should happen next. I wrote a short article about the fax, didn't name myself as the recipient but rather said it was sent to the paper, which it was—kind of—and told of a next possible crime in Virginia, and I gave a profile of the attorney general and candidate for U.S. representative, Lee Hoskins. I submitted it to Halloran, and he sent it on for the next day's press. I asked Halloran if I could list Solomon as a researcher, and he said no, but I listed Rachael Jones as a contributor to the story. Take it all around, I was pretty well exhausted and pretty well satisfied with the day and was making ready to leave when Solomon came into my box.

"How about a drink and maybe dinner?" she said. "You've never known me to turn down a drink."

We walked out of the paper, and Mildred gave me an appraising look. I said good night to her and we left the building. I could see "be careful" written in her eyes.

"Let's skip Sam's," said Solomon. "I know a little Greek restaurant on 4th Avenue, and it's also got a bar."

We walked to her car in the parking lot. It was a BMW, I noticed. "Get in, and I'll drive," she said. I thought of Mad Michael's dilemma. She noticed my hesitation. "Don't worry, I'm not going to kidnap you. I'm a murderer, not a kidnapper, remember," she said, laughing.

"No, it's not that. It's just that it's a BMW."

"What, you're offended by my yuppie tendencies, Harvard? I mean, Ned."

I laughed and told her about Mad Michael's theory and current problems. "Don't you think the grille looks a little like Hitler's mustache?"

"I'm Jewish, at least on my father's side. Do you think I'd drive a car that I thought looked like Hitler?"

"Doesn't the religion in Judaism follow the line of the mother?"

"Yeah, I think so, but still…" Despite her dismissal, I could tell she was thinking about it.

"Where are we going?"

"The Parthenon on 4th. I know the owners, a husband and wife, but the best part is that it has a patio with heaters and we can eat outside. The food is excellent, too."

Inside the restaurant, Barbara was greeted warmly by the female owner, whose name was Molly Avotatos. She ushered us ceremoniously over to the small bar. "It may be a little wait," she said, sweeping her arm around the filled restaurant.

"That's OK," said Barbara. "We want to eat on the patio and expected to wait."

"Alexis, drinks are on the house," said Molly to the young bartender.

It was déjà vu of Violet and the Gonzales Family Restaurant.

Over gratis drinks, a number of them, I told Barbara my story of the days since I had seen her at the Florence bar. It was a relief to tell someone about stealing the article from Burwick's car. I told her about the dirty trick I'd played on Ray Block, and she laughed until her eyes teared up, and that was good to see. I told her about Willie, Zegura and Sister Shashwati, Margret and the foundation, Violet, Leo, Helen and my brother Bob. She already knew the story of J. Erasmus Camp, Richard Blake and Jerry Boyle. I told her of my run-in with the Texas police over the videotape of Willie's suicide, Robin and GNN, and my presence at the hotel where Stith had been murdered. I told her my commitment to write a biography of Willie T Ruckles and the true origins of Sister Shashwati and *her* books. It was quite a story—three drinks' worth. We were taken to the patio and installed at a table with a bottle of Greek white wine. I ordered my favorite food ever, mussels—served over a Greek pasta. Barbara, a vegetarian as it turned out, ordered spanakopita, a spinach pastry. I was beginning to feel the effects of the alcohol of the day that had begun with beers at Sam's and an unsavory folder, that had morphed into dinner. I'd been talking steadily for most of an hour: "Enough about me. Tell me something about you," I said, looking into large brown eyes.

Barbara took a drink from her wine glass. "Well, my name is Barbara Sarah Solomon and I am not, contrary to popular belief, a murderer, though I have been subject to poor judgment concerning human character in my past. I am a reporter with the Tucson *Daily Sun*, and I try to conduct myself with honesty and integrity though I can, in the operation of my duties, rub people the wrong way. This has led to a general opinion among my professional colleagues that I am a competent reporter who is cold and aloof and without feeling." Her eyes filled with tears that ran down her cheeks, and I reached over and took her hand and kissed it, as our dinner came at precisely that moment. I looked up from her hand to my mussels and pasta, and Barbara dabbed her face with her napkin.

We ate our excellent meals in silence. The bill came with two generous glasses of ouzo. I reached for the bill, and Barbara took it from me, opened it up, and showed it to me. "No charge," it read.

"It's because I cried." She was smiling.

"It's because you're a good person," I answered, thinking of Mildred's auras. She reached across the table and took my hand and squeezed it. She left a generous tip, and we exited the restaurant. Did I imagine that the owners did not meet our gaze as we left?

"Would you like to come home with me?" she said tentatively as we drove away from the restaurant.

"Are you asking me this because I may think you're a murderer?" I asked her. Yet again, attempting to sabotage my love life.

"I am asking you because you don't care. And I don't want to be alone tonight."

"Yes," I answered.

22

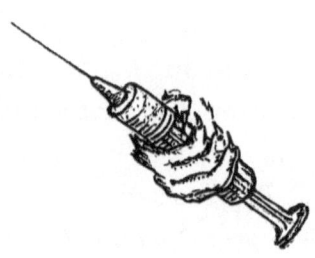

Married Life Is Not Enough

I woke up with an arm still around Solomon, her back to me. Her long dark hair covered her bare shoulders. My head felt a little fuzzy from the beer, drinks, Greek wine, and ouzo, I got up from the bed and worked my way to the kitchen and made coffee. Sipping from a large blue enamel mug, I went outdoors. I thought that Solomon would have lived in a trendy theme apartment building with a pool, gym, and party room, but instead her house was a small burnt adobe dwelling on a larger ranch, with grass fields and cottonwood trees. There was a corral with two black-and-white paint horses, a mother and baby, I thought. I walked over to them, and they both came over to me. I scratched the mother's ears, while the baby nuzzled my coffee cup, turning her upper lip inside out to me.

"It's an acquired taste," I told her. She looked like a she, although I didn't know. The interaction felt very calming. I said my goodbyes to the horses and returned to the house. On the porch, I noticed a now familiar sign, a rust-brown swatch with a few chicken feathers. I was beginning to worry about Mildred's egg production. Did she really feel I was in some kind of danger? I smiled, then the idea that I hadn't seen Solomon take the note from the door of Jerry Boyle's house popped into my head. I was the one who had rung the bell on the front door. I would have seen it behind the screen. Wouldn't I?

I went back into the house. Solomon was prowling around her bedroom. I waited in the kitchen until she came out, and I smiled and handed her a cup of coffee. I knew by my short time at the paper that she took it with milk and no sugar.

She accepted the coffee and said, "Don't think this makes us friends." "The coffee?" I said.

"Last night." Was she smiling? I couldn't tell, but it was good to see the old Solomon back.

"Wouldn't dream of it. I met your neighbors."

"Neighbors? Oh, the horses, a mare and her filly, they're my landlord's. I feed them apples and carrots."

"Good, because they don't like coffee." "You tried to feed them coffee?"

I told her about my encounter with the baby. "Filly?" I asked.

"A young female horse. I forgot you're a city boy. I like horses; they're completely honest with how they feel about things. No question with a horse."

"Unlike people in your life?" "Unlike people in general."

At the paper Barbara went off to her office, and I stopped by the reception desk to see Mildred.

"You wearin the same clothes as yesterday, and your car's not moved. You sleep in the parking lot, honey?"

I ignored her greeting. "How's your egg production these days, Mildred?" "Down little bit, come to think of it. You should come over for some fried chicken soon," she said, smiling.

"Mildred, do you really think I'm in danger?"

"Where there's smoke, there's liable to be fire, baby" was her answer. "They dropped those Texas charges, now didn't they?" she asked, a rhetorical question.

"How'd you know?" Mildred just looked at me from under her eyelashes and smiled.

"Anyway, how'd you know where Solomon lived?" I pressed. "Personnel files," she said, still smiling.

"Mildred, I'm glad you're my friend."

"Got that one right, baby," she said. And I left for my box to her chuckles that sounded like they could be coming from her chicken house.

Solomon was working on what I assumed to be another story when I came into her office.

"It's time we interviewed Burwick's widow," I said. "Mind if I try?" "No," she said.

"Mind if I try alone?"

She sucked in her breath. "No, it's a good idea," she said, and I exhaled in relief.

To my surprise, Victoria Burwick answered on the first ring.

"Mrs. Burwick," I started, "my name is Ned Alexander, and I'm—"

"I know who you are, Mr. Alexander," she said, interrupting my delivery. "You're the reporter who's been writing the articles about my husband's death. What can I do for you?"

"Mrs. Burwick, I am writing a new article about the death of your husband, and I'd like to have an interview with you before the article goes out." This all came out rather awkwardly, I thought.

To my surprise, she said, "Will you be coming alone?" "Yes."

"Well, I suppose it's inevitable that I talk to someone, so it might as well be you. I've been refusing other reporters."

I set an appointment at her house for two o'clock that afternoon.

I went next door to inform Solomon (this setup was really convenient), and when I heard my phone ring, I answered.

"Mr. Alexander, this is Lieutenant Hickey," came the voice. Not giving me time to respond, he continued, "I thought you'd like to know that your prediction about Virginia has come true. District attorney Lee Hoskins has been found dead in a hotel where he was staying on the campaign trail."

"How was he killed?" I asked, fearing I knew the answer.

"Same way as Burwick and Stith from the sounds of it. I don't have anything more, but thought you would like to know," he said.

"Thanks, Lieutenant."

He hesitated. "No new faxes?"

"Nothing. You'll have it as soon as I do, Lieutenant, be assured." I thanked him again for his courtesy, and he rang off. I went next door to tell Solomon and then went to Halloran's office. Solomon came with me, and I didn't object.

"Do you want me to go to Virginia?" was my salient question to him.

He hesitated a moment, looked up at the ceiling, and said: "Yes, I think it's a good idea considering what we know about the BWWY organization. Do you have enough funds to cover your travel?"

"Yes," I said. Thanks to Adam Zegura and the Sister Shashwati Foundation, I had plenty.

"You certainly know how to make four hundred dollars stretch," he said. "Comes from being a college student forever," I answered.

"Where was the murder?" "Alexandria."

"Alexandria, that should be easy," he said. "Get a plane ticket, choose a modest hotel, and get a compact rental car. I'm already battling Bob over your last expenses." Bob was the *Sun*'s chief accountant, and his approval was needed for any reimbursements.

"What's he questioning? I got free coffee in Jalico and stayed at my mother's and brother's houses," I said indignantly.

"Leave it alone, Harvard. It's my job."

I told him that I couldn't leave until late afternoon after my interview with Tory Burwick. He grunted, and I got up to leave.

"I want to go too," said Solomon. "My conflict is with Burwick, not BWWY per se."

Halloran for once seemed at a loss as to what to do. He hesitated and said finally: "BWWY is your story, Harvard. It's your call."

I hesitated only a moment and answered with my heart. "I would welcome the help," I said, realizing I was putting countless chickens in peril.

"OK, Barbara, but your role is only as a researcher. You're to have no formal journalistic role. That includes bylines. Is that OK with you?"

Barbara seemed less than happy but nodded and said, "Yes."

It was now twelve-thirty.

"I'll get the tickets and make reservations for us," Barbara told me. "You get yourself ready and take that interview and we'll meet back here at four- thirty. That should give us enough time."

Before I left, I went to see Rachael and asked her to search the wire for articles about the new killing and any background articles on the history of the execution. She said she was "on it, boss."

I ran into Mildred as I was leaving the building. "Goin to Virginia now, I see," she said.

"Yeah, and Mildred, you go easy on those chickens."

I went home, showered, and changed my clothes, and packed a few things that fit into my backpack and was off to the Burwick house. It was a little house in a historic part of downtown. I rang the doorbell, and Tory Burwick answered the door. It was a different persona from the one who had strode out of the newspaper photo where I had first met her. She wore a bulky knit sweater and jeans, you could tell that she was a stunner, but her eyes were dark and swollen, and her cheeks were an unhealthy red and puffy. Her hair was slightly wet, as if she'd just taken a shower. She wore white athletic socks but no shoes. I saw a sign at the door that told guests to remove their shoes before entering, and I complied. Her manner, however, was charming.

"Hello, Mr. Alexander," she said as she extended her hand. "I've made some tea, so please sit down." She ushered me over to the coffee table surrounded on three sides by a white suttee. When did Americans start drinking so much tea?

"Thank you for seeing me, Mrs. Burwick."

"Call me Tory, I'd appreciate that," she said. "Mr. Alexander, I agreed to see you because I've been reading your articles, all of them, not just the ones about my husband's death, and I've felt that they've been fair, if not always sympathetic." She smiled in a charming way that was reminiscent of the newspaper photo. "Except perhaps the one you wrote on the governor of Texas," she said, her smile becoming broader and even more charming.

"You are perceptive, Tory."

"What would you like to know?" she asked as she poured two cups of tea. "Just a little background to begin with. How did you meet your husband?"

"We met in law school at Yale during our second year. And were married shortly after."

"When was that?"

"About three years now, maybe a little more." "You didn't return for your third year?"

"No," said Tory. "Married life seemed enough." I thought of Solomon putting her life on hold for the guy.

"Are you from New Haven?" I asked, giving the home city of Yale. "No," she said, laughing. "I grew up in Athens, Georgia, went to the university there for my undergraduate." "How'd you come to go to Yale?"

"I followed my brother there. He was going to Yale Law, and I applied, got a scholarship, and followed him. He's a year older than me, but we were always close."

I looked around the apartment. It was a markedly feminine affair, and I could see no signs of a masculine presence. "You live in Tucson, yet your husband worked primarily in Phoenix?"

"The background questions over?" she asked rhetorically. "I prefer Tucson's smaller-town lifestyle. I never could get used to Phoenix, though I tried. Roger kept an apartment there and came down here periodically."

Periodically? I thought. A strange word, not on weekends, or often, but periodically. That explained the lack of masculine influence.

I decided to take a chance. "Tory, were you and your husband estranged— separated?"

"It is now you who are perceptive, Mr. Alexander." "Ned," I said.

"Ned," she repeated. "Yes, we were, as you say, estranged. Do you know the police have questioned me two times and never asked me that? Strange…"

"I think we're probably after different things." "What is it that you're after, Ned?"

"The meaning of all this," I found myself saying. "The meaning of all this," she repeated.

I continued to take chances. "Estranged is a long way from married life being enough."

"Yes, a very long way, Ned. Roger and I were going to get a divorce, but he wanted to wait until he was elected attorney general; he was sure it was going to happen." I had a déjà vu moment with Solomon's story of Burwick at the hospital.

"What did you think of that?"

"I thought it was the easiest way out," she said.

"You've been more than generous…Tory. One last question before I leave you alone. Did Roger Burwick have any enemies?"

"Everyone was Roger's enemy. He was competitive with everyone. He had allies at times, but no friends or even colleagues in a genuine sense. He was a purely political animal."

The interview hadn't gone the way I had expected, but I figured this was a good time to end it. "Thank you, Tory, for your time and candor," I said, standing up.

"I can't wait to see your article," she said, standing up with me. "It may be a while before this one is written."

I had slipped my shoes back on, and Tory came to the door. "Well, it's my turn to thank you," she said as she took my hand.

It was a little after three o'clock and I didn't have to meet Solomon for almost an hour and a half. I left my car parked where it was and walked to a downtown coffeeshop. I needed a quiet place to think. I ordered a coffee and sat down at a table. Tory Burwick looked the part of a grieving widow, but she didn't sound like one. What, then, accounted for her dark eyes and red face and swollen cheeks? I thought back to the photos of Solomon in the ER. What would they have looked like after a week and a half? Like Tory's, perhaps? I went to a pay phone, called the paper, and asked Mildred for Rachael and was told that Rachael had gone for the day but had left me a folder with Solomon. I went back to the coffeeshop and wrote her a note on my laptop.

Dear Rachael, Solomon and I are going to Virginia on the Lee Hoskins story, should be back in a day or two, and I need you to do a few things for me in my absence. Ask your computer cop friend for another favor—have him check the police database for Victoria Burwick or Victoria Ramsfeld. Also see if he can hack into the local hospitals in both Tucson and the Phoenix area for any information. I'm looking for anything similar to what you found on Solomon. Also check on Victoria Ramsfeld and see what information you can get from the University of Georgia at Athens, starting three or four years ago and extending back four years. Check on her time at Yale, too. Don't share this information with anyone. Don't communicate with me over the phone. Contact me via email, no other way. Thanks for everything. I'll get you back for sure. Ned.

I went back to the *Sun*. Mildred was away from her desk. I printed out my note to Rachael, put it into a sealed envelope, wrote my name over the flap, then taped it shut. That should do it, I thought. And I left it on her desk. Solomon said that she had booked tickets on the redeye for Washington, D.C., leaving from Phoenix. "I'll drive. We leave at midnight. It gets in at six o'clock in the morning," she said. "There wasn't anything leaving from Tucson this late. I've also booked us into the Capitol Holiday Inn and reserved a rental car." She handed me the folder that Rachael had compiled. "She was reluctant to give it to me," Barbara said. "She said it was for you. You really have a loyal assistant. I finally convinced her that we were working together, but I don't think she truly believed me. You do have a way with people." I wasn't sure this was meant as a compliment.

"In addition to the folder, Rachael gave me a wire article that lists a Lieutenant Owens as the officer in charge of the investigation. I called, and we have a meeting at one o'clock in the afternoon. Sorry I couldn't get it sooner. I couldn't get anything until I mentioned your name. They're really anxious to talk to you. Mildred says she had to go home early but to tell you the chickens are safe, whatever that means."

"It's good news," I said.

23

I Reckoned If They Could Stand It, I Could

We left for Phoenix right away, arriving at six o'clock, and got a cheap hotel by the airport, one room and two beds, to wait for our midnight flight. I held on to the extensive folder that Rachael had prepared for me. It made me feel good that she hadn't wanted to hand it over to Solomon, I had to admit. I read the wire article given to Solomon about the killing. The article was a short piece with limited information. Lee Hoskins, 53, the state attorney general, was found in his hotel room by an unidentified person—I read woman—attached to three long and slender plastic cylinders by a line that terminated in his arm. The unidentified chemicals found in the lines and cylinders were thought to be the cause of death. Police were called to the scene by the person who discovered Mr. Hoskins' body. The crime scene was sealed off immediately. There were bruises on his arms and an unusual red color was noted on his face. The article went on to describe the attorney general's bid for Congress and his advocacy of the death penalty for recently executed Carla Rawlings. The article ended with the statement from Lieutenant Owens that this crime was similar to a number of others thought to be perpetrated by an anti-capital-punishment terrorist organization. I was struck by the irony.

It didn't mention BWWY or the other murders, but the murder certainly sounded identical to Stith's, right down to the supposed woman in the room. "Don't these guys ever change their MO?" I said out loud, and I told Solomon of my speculation. She just grunted and kept on driving. The speculation would be confirmed the next day when I had the name of the woman and the fact that the only things in the room were his briefcase and her overnight bag.

I left the sealed contents of the folder to be read on the flight to D.C. I managed to get a couple of hours of fitful sleep. Solomon, on the other hand, slept like a baby, snoring softly. We were both up at ten, had a bad Mexican dinner, and checked in at the airport. In D.C., we took a cab to the Capitol Holiday Inn. The name referred to the hotel's proximity to the Capitol building, but the irony struck me and I mentioned it to Barbara.

She laughed and said, "It took you a while on that one, Harvard."

The room wasn't ready, but the desk guy, whose name was James, said he could have it ready for an early check-in after about an hour. I thanked him, and we went into the restaurant for breakfast. At the table, I looked over the complimentary map they had given us at the desk. "Hey, we're just two blocks away from the Air and Space Museum," I said.

"You really are an adolescent," said Barbara.

"No. This is good. I've never seen it and I want to go. They have the Wright Brothers' plane there and a whole lot of other stuff." I was sounding pretty childish, all right.

Barbara surprised me and laughed and said, "OK, let's go."

When we finished breakfast, the room was still not ready, so we walked the two blocks to the Air and Space Museum. The sun was shining and the air was crisp and cold, and I stuck my ungloved hands in the pockets of my down jacket. "This feels like we're on vacation," I said as we walked.

"Yeah, on vacation to see a guy who died with tubes stuck in his arm after being violently sedated," Barbara chided me.

This alerted me to the disturbing realization that these murders were becoming, for me, routine. It gave me a creepy feeling that I was becoming so indolent in such a short time. A week and a half ago, I would have felt outrage—or, if not outrage, at least compassion. But I felt nothing for either this guy or Stith. Burwick, on the other hand, I wanted dead. Did this make me a moral equal with those who championed capital punishment? I wasn't sure. I thought about my favorite book, *Huckleberry Finn*, and a scene when Huck tricks two would-be murderers on a sinking steamship, leaving them to die and thinks in a moment of compassion: "There ain't no telling but I might come to be a murderer myself, then how would I like it?" and he goes back in an act of conscience to save them.

Was I on my way to come to be a murderer myself? It made me feel uneasy. I returned to Huck Finn: He goes back to give them a way off the boat, but it's too late, the steamboat breaks up, and the murderers drown. Huck is feeling pretty down about it, too, until he thinks: "I reckoned if they could stand it, I could." Put in this perspective, he feels better.

I looked over at Solomon and said: "Well, I reckon if Hoskins could stand it, so can I."

She looked at me with her mouth open and just shook her head.

We walked in the mall side entrance and were greeted by the space capsules of Alan Shepard and John Glenn encased in clear plastic. I was amazed by their small size, particularly Shepard's; the bottom of the capsule was about the size of my arm span. They went up in the early in the mid-sixties at the same time my brother was surreptitiously moving about Mississippi, organizing and registering people to vote, an enterprise every bit as dangerous as Shepard's and Glenn's. *Maybe the world has gotten better*, I thought. We stayed about an hour, and Barbara withstood my exuberance.

"What do you think we should do next?" she said on our way back to the hotel.

"I want to see the hotel where he was found, see if there's anyone who was there when he was found, then I want to check out his campaign headquarters. I bet it's buzzing today." We checked into our room—one room, two beds seemed to be the rule. There was an internet connection in our room, and I pulled up the website for the Hoskins campaign. He was indeed a tough-on-crime, pro-gun, pro-capital-punishment, anti-abortion, far-right Republican. There were messages supporting the execution of Carla Rawlings alongside buttons to push to "make a donation" to his campaign. His major headquarters was in Alexandra, across the D.C. line.

We showered and got ourselves ready for the day. I had dressed in one of my two pairs of khaki slacks, one of my two Oxford dress shirts, and my one sport coat. Not quite preppy, but presentable. Barbara, however, emerged from the bathroom in stunning beauty. She wore a black suit with a mid-thigh tight black skirt, black simple tunic, and a black coat that terminated just above her waist; she wore a double strand of turquoise beads I took to be Navajo. In between the two strands, holding them together, was a piece of red coral. Her hair was blown dry and shiny and curled gently on her shoulders, and her darkly nyloned legs were slipped into moderate black high heels.

"Wow! Why aren't you an anchor on the national news somewhere?" I said. "I'm not sure I want to be seen alongside of you."

Barbara smiled at the attention, and I could tell she was pleased. "Get used to it, Ned," she said, smiling. I was glad she used my name.

Harvard, it seemed, was reserved for when I did something stupid.

We picked up our rental car from the parking lot and drove the short distance into Alexandria. "Why don't I drop you off at the hotel and I'll go on to the campaign headquarters? We might be more effective if we split up," she offered.

The idea sounded good to me. I was beginning to like conducting my investigations alone. "Good idea, you're certainly dressed to get the maximum information, at least from the male workers." Barbara smiled again.

She dropped me off at the hotel, imaginatively named the Alexandria. "I'll be back in an hour or so, and I'll meet you in the bar."

The Alexandria was a stately old hotel built along plantation lines. It seemed a quiet and sleepy place, one for the gentry rather than the business or casual traveler. True to my method, I began by sitting down at the bar. I was the only one there. A young woman by the name of Cindi came over to serve me, and I ordered a beer. "I guess you've had some excitement here," I said as she brought me my drink.

"Excitement?" she said, looking perplexed. "Yeah, the murder and all."

"Oh yeah, the politician guy. I was working the night when he came in.

He's running for governor or something. He comes in here quite often—well, I guess he came his last time."

"He came in here the night he was murdered?"

"Yeah, ordered a scotch. He seemed to be in a hurry, though, kept looking at his watch, and left after about ten minutes."

"You say he comes, came, in here often?"

"Yeah, about every two weeks, stays a day or two. Like I said, he's running for governor and has meetings. Brings people in here sometimes. They yak it up, very official, then everybody leaves and he stays on with the woman."

"The woman?"

"Yeah, the woman who works with him on his election," she said. "She was the one that found him last night."

"Do you know her name?"

"Nancy is what he called her, but I don't know her last name. Say, you aren't from the police, are you? They were in here last night asking questions, too."

"No, my name is Ned Alexander and I'm a reporter for a newspaper out of Tucson, Arizona."

"Cindi Johnson," she said, shaking my hand.

She thought about this for a while then said: "You're a long way from home. This news in Arizona?"

"Good question. It is only because I've been covering other murders similar to this one that I'm here."

"Huh," she said. "Alexander, like the hotel?"

"Sort of," I said. I put down a hundred-dollar bill on the bar. Cindi took it and brought back the change, setting it down on the bar. I reached over and pushed it into the little gutter behind the bar. She noticed but didn't say anything.

"Can you tell me anything else about Mr. Hoskins, the man running for governor?"

"I can tell you he was married, and not to Nancy. She came in a couple of weeks ago, his wife that is, and made a big show about being his wife. There was a big party here, and she was really quite obnoxious. He seemed embarrassed, though he didn't do anything about it. They, the politician guy and Nancy, that is, have been here a few times since then, not the wife, though. You should really talk to Ramona. She was in the room with the dead man. She didn't talk to the police, though, at least not yet."

She looked at me. "You sure you've got nothing to do with the police? When I assured her, she said, "Because she's illegal, what do you call it, undocumented. She left before the police got there, and it seems Nancy didn't rat her out, probably because she didn't think of it."

"Is Ramona here now?"

"Yeah. We're all having to work double shifts these days."

"Look, Cindi, could you ask Ramona if she would talk to me? Tell her I will keep it confidential and she won't be at risk from me. Also give her this." I took another hundred-dollar bill from my pocket.

"Sure. I'll see what I can do. This should help," she said as she waved at me with the bill. I wondered if this would be a reimbursable expense from Bob. As it turned out, this was one of the battles Halloran would lose. The first of many, I would come to learn.

"Wait here, and I'll be right back," she said as she deposited another beer in front of me. "On the house."

Cindi returned in about five minutes. An older, middle-aged couple had sat down at the end of the bar and looked around impatiently for the bartender. "She'll be right back," I told them. They looked right through me and didn't acknowledge my information but continued to look searchingly around the bar.

"She's waiting for you in the linen closet, that's on the second floor just to the left of the elevator," Cindi said when she came back. As she was telling me this, the man at the end of the bar had cleared his throat three times, each time getting louder. Cindi looked at me and smiled. "Regulars, but lousy tippers." She walked over to them with a syrupy "Well, what can I do for you two?"

I found the linen closet with Ramona inside. She was a nervous, middle- aged Hispanic woman who kept looking from side to side. "Thank you for talking to me, Ramona," I said. "I understand you were in the dead man's room last night before the police."

"Yes, housekeeping called me to say he had called because there were no towels in the bathroom. I finished up the room I was doing and took over a set of clean towels, and, oh my God, there he was dead in the chair, a woman was there and she was in quite a state, I can tell you. She was on the telephone when I came in, crying into it, telling the police to come quickly. I was very nervous because I don't want nothing to do with the police." "Did you know who the woman was?"

"I don't know her name, but I have seen her before. They often stay here."

"What was in the room?"

"Very little. There was a small suitcase on the bed along with the man's coat; his shoes were alongside of the bed. The woman had a little bag like you carry makeup in and a big purse. Oh, and there was a bottle of champagne with two glasses on the table beside the man. It was a good bottle of champagne, too, I can tell you that. I sometimes work in catering and it's one of the best, Don something."

"Dom Perignon?" I offered.

"Yes, that is the one." This was new information. "The woman was crying pitifully, so I went over to her and put my arms around her. But she just stiffened up, squealed like a pig, and stomped her feet up and down very fast, so I took my towels and put them in the bathroom and left her before the police came in. I'm not sure she even saw me, thanks God. That's all I saw."

"What about the man, how did he look?"

"Oh, he looked so horrible! His shirt was rolled up and he had a plastic tube in his arm, it was connected to these other bigger tubes that were taped to the wall behind him, and his mouth was open, it almost looked like he was trying to say something. Oh, it was horrible to see! I was glad to just get out of there. I was just getting off my shift, and I went down to see Cindi, and I even had a tequila—two tequilas, to settle my nerves."

I thanked her and gave her a card with the hotel phone and room number where we were staying. If she thought of anything else, I said, she could contact me there.

I returned to the bar and saw Solomon looking glorious, talking to Cindi. I picked up my waiting beer and went and sat down next to Barbara. "Barbara Solomon, this is Cindi Johnson. Barbara is a fellow reporter, and Cindi runs the hotel." Barbara extended her hand while Cindi looked at her sideways and seemed reluctant to take it. After an uncomfortable period, she took it and said, "Glad to meet you, Mrs. Solomon." It was Barbara's turn to give a sideways glance. *Yeah, Barbara, you're not the only fish in the sea*, I thought. Maybe the most glorious fish, but not the only one. The tension was palpable. "Could I get another beer? This one's a little hot," I said. Cindi brought me a new beer and things returned to normal.

"Was Ramona helpful?" Cindi asked. "Extremely," I said.

Cindi went off to serve some newcomers. "You certainly got friendly in a short time," Solomon said when Cindi departed.

"Names are important. I always get names."

"I think she's interested in more than your name," said the glorious fish.

I ignored the comment. "We better be getting to our next meeting. You get anything at the headquarters?"

"A little. I'll tell you on our way."

We settled up, I told Cindi I'd check in with her later, and I gave her the same card I had given Ramona. I left a ten-dollar tip, too, to equalize it with that of Ramona. I noticed that Barbara left no tip at all. I was secretly pleased. Barbara drove us to see Lieutenant Owens, and on the way she told me of her trip to the headquarters. "It was in shock and disarray. People were milling about without seeming direction, some people gathering up their things from desks others just wandering about, speculating about the murder. Most were asking what happens now. I was introduced to the campaign manager, a Mark Waller, who was guarded and careful when he heard I was a reporter, not at all like your friend Cindi." I stifled a smile and kept my attention focused.

"He said he didn't know why Hoskins was at the Alexandria, as he had booked him into a room at the Marriot downtown with the statewide traveling team, but that he often held meetings at the Alexandria and stayed there on occasion. He was called by the police and informed of the killing shortly after seven o'clock in the evening. He was thought to have been killed between four and five. The police interviewed him yesterday evening. He couldn't tell them much."

"That would be about two o'clock our time, not long before I got word from Hickey," I said.

"Yes," said Barbara.

"What about the woman who found him? Did he mention anything about her? Her first name is Nancy."

"Yes, Nancy Pretti." Solomon looked at me sideways. "Cindi," I said.

"Of course. Anyway, she's one of the few paid campaign workers, serves, or served, as Hoskins' personal assistant."

"I'll say," I said and waved off her inquiry. "Tell you later. Did you speak to her?"

"No. Waller said she didn't come in today—too upset."

"Did he have any idea who might have done it, any enemies?" I asked hopefully.

"I asked him that, and he said that a district attorney has a lot of enemies some that would like to see him dead, but none that would actually kill him. He did mention, however, the acrimonious interactions between Hoskins and the group Virginia Against the Death Penalty that was his greatest opposition to the execution of Carla Rawlings."

"Yeah, I read about them in the articles Rachael prepared for us. They seem to have a fairly active director, I recall."

"Yes, a Jim Campbell." Barbara seemed happy to produce a name I didn't have. "He publicly confronted him on a number of occasions and openly backed an anti-capital punishment opponent, raising money for his campaign against Hoskins."

I filled her in on what I had found at the hotel and could tell she was impressed, particularly with the use of two hundred dollars of personal funds. "It shows commitment if not good economic judgment. Bob will never approve those for reimbursement," she offered, but she didn't call me Harvard on this one. "These guys seem to top off their executions with affairs."

"Yep," I said. "And you can't get them to stop washing their food, either."

She gave me a quizzical look as we pulled into the police station but didn't say anything, which was good because I didn't have time to explain.

We checked in and were given visitor badges and taken to the office of Lieutenant Owens. Phil Owens was a short, balding, middle-aged man who looked like he could use a little time in the gym, but despite this, he had the bearing of a tough cop. "Mr. Alexander, Ms. Solomon, thank you for coming," he said, indicating the two chairs opposite his desk.

"Thank you for seeing us," said Solomon, flashing him a disarming smile. "Mr. Alexander, we're hopeful you can shed some light on this crime.

Detective Escobar said that you've been a great help to him, and Lieutenant Hickey was also complimentary."

I answered that it was nice to hear but that I was not sure I had been much help to their investigations. I shot Barbara a puzzled look. I had the feeling I was being played a bit by this detective.

"Come now, Mr. Alexander, you've developed a relationship with this organization, this BWWY. Lieutenant Hickey alerted the Virginia Police that Mr. Hoskins was in danger from information you passed on to him before there had even been a crime."

"It's true, I did receive a fax with the word *Virginia* from BWWY, and we did research about any executions to be conducted in your state and discovered the Carla Rawlings case. We checked to see who had championed it and further discovered district attorney Hoskins as a likely candidate. I passed that information along to both Lieutenant Hickey and Escobar. They did whatever else was done."

"Why do you think this organization has taken such an interest in you?" I'd been over this ground once or twice before. "I don't know, Lieutenant, other than they find me a convenient conduit to provide information to the public."

"Conduit." He mouthed the word like he was chewing it.

"I'm sure you've been provided copies of the faxes I've received, and have read my articles," I said.

"Yes, they have courteously provided me with those, Mr. Alexander."

"Then you know what I do," I said simply.

"No, Mr. Alexander, I think you may know more than you're telling me." "Lieutenant Owens, what can you tell us about the murder investigation?" said Solomon, a bit louder than our conversation.

"Ms. Solomon, I am in the middle of my interrogation here, and you're interrupting," answered Owens curtly.

"No, Lieutenant, you're not. You're having an interview with the press. You didn't ask us in. I set up this meeting with you on the phone yesterday, and you are dangerously close to a violation of the First Amendment." She stood up, her spectacular form bearing down over the pudgy Owens, who just stared up at her. "Come on, Ned, were leaving, unless Owens here wants to arrest us."

"Ms. Solomon, I meant no affront to your partner, or to you. Please sit down," Owens cajoled.

I made a motion for Barbara to sit down for the moment. "Let's hear the lieutenant out, I'm sure he didn't mean anything improper," I said, not at all feeling the truth of my statement. Barbara walked around her chair, but in the end, she sat.

"The perils of being a policeman, I'm afraid," said Owens. "Let me begin again. Can you in your own words tell me what you know about the organization that by your faxes have been implicated in the murder of our attorney general, and your relations with it? You must realize that this is for us a high-profile crime. Then I am sure, Ms. Solomon, I can answer all of your questions."

Barbara unwound slightly in her chair but remained haughty and vigilant. I went through my story of the cases and the bits of information offered to me by the faxes, sometimes orchestrating me to be a bit ahead of the police. I told of arriving on the scene before the police in the Burwick and Stith murders, how the crime scene looked, and the quote from Immanuel Kant and how I came to identify it. I told of my interactions with the police and information that I had passed on to them, and how I was committed to continuing to do that. Hence the fax and information on Lee Hoskins, and finally our editor's decision to send us to Virginia, as there was the possibility that this crime was related to the others. As for my relationship with BWWY, his guess as to why they chose to favor me with information was as good as mine, and the exchanges were strictly one way.

Owens listened attentively and took a few notes. When I was finished, he thanked me, asked a few follow-up questions mostly about the nature of the crime scene in Texas. Then he turned to Barbara. "Now, Ms. Solomon, for your question, we are proceeding in our investigation along two lines at the moment. The first is the organization BWWY, working closely with the Texas and Houston police. The second line has to do with a man called Jim Campbell."

"Of Virginia Against the Death Penalty," Barbara interrupted in what was poor journalistic form.

"Yes, you are well-informed," Owens said. "Mr. Campbell has an alibi for the afternoon and night of the murder, but we are interested in his organization and possible connections with your organization." Barbara noticeably stiffened at the last words and looked at Owens. Owens realized his mistake and was quick to rectify it. "The organization with which you are familiar, rather."

"What about the woman who found him? I asked.

"A Nancy Pretti, she was a campaign worker and went there for a meeting and found him. She is not a suspect at this time."

"Other than the apparatus used to kill him, did you find anything else in the room?" I asked.

Owens looked at me. "No," he finally said. I shot Solomon a furtive look. It would seem they were circling their wagons, nothing about a bottle of Dom Perignon, two glasses, and the woman with a makeup kit.

"Can you tell us why he was checked into the Alexandria when he was also checked into the downtown Marriott?" asked Solomon.

"You are well-informed, indeed, Ms. Solomon," said Lieutenant Owens. "Since we are becoming friends, Ms. Solomon, the official position is that he was at the Alexandria with Mrs. Pretti for a meeting. This will be our position until such time as it becomes an impediment to our investigation. You can treat the information at your discretion."

"Can you tell us how the murder was done?" I asked.

"I can do better than that, Mr. Alexander. I can show you. We'd like you to inspect the apparatus and tell us if it is the same as in the other killings. Would you please follow me," he said, standing up.

We followed him to the corridor, down several flights of stairs to what looked like a chemistry lab. I wondered briefly if we were going to see the body, but we stopped in front of a stainless-steel table enclosed by a hood.

"Do these look familiar?" said Lieutenant Owens as he pointed to three plastic tubes with what looked to be IV lines attached to them.

"I've never seen them this close before," I said, looking at the murder weapon. "But they sure look similar to the ones that were used in the previous killings, particularly the Stith murder. Can I pick them up?"

"Go ahead, they've been drained of their contents, dusted for prints and await further analysis. Watch out for the needle, though."

I picked up one of the tubes. It was about two feet long, perhaps a little less, and three inches in diameter, and the ends had been cut cleanly. Fastened to the bottom was a plastic cap with a little nipple protruding about a quarter of an inch. Attached to the nipple was a plastic tube about three feet long that merged with two others and joined a single line ending in an intravenous needle. Inside the tube was a smaller tube set up as a plunger, with a bottom piece that would force the liquid into the veins of the victim.

"What are those things?" I asked, pointing to three circular pieces of rubber tubing.

"Rubber bands. They fit into the notches in the top of the plunger and are attached to the two little arms that have been glued to the bottoms of the tubes. They provide the power to get the poison into the victim. Ingenious, don't you think?"

I looked at the base of the large tube and saw two plastic protrusions sticking out from the side. Lieutenant Owens took a tube and a rubber band looped one end around one of the protrusions, threaded it over the notch on the top of the plunger shaft and looped it over the second little arm. "Walla," he said in a bad French parody as he held it out for me to examine.

It was indeed an ingenious mechanism. *I wouldn't have thought of it,* I thought. I didn't say it, though. Given our recent history, it would have sounded solicitous. "This gives it enough power?" I asked. "The rubber bands seem to me a bit flaccid."

"Oh, yes, Mr. Alexander. They've done tests, and the tubes would have discharged their contents in less than a minute. Like I said, quite ingenious, and well-engineered, our technicians tell us. Whoever is responsible has had some scientific training."

"Where do they get this stuff?" I said as I marveled at the ingenuity. "The tubes from aquarium stores, the rubber bands are for model airplanes. I'm told that all of the materials are easily obtainable from aquarium or water landscape stores and hobby shops. Even the lines come from there, the IV needle comes from a medical supply house."

"Have you run any of it down?"

"We're working on it, but so far nothing specific." "What about the chemicals they used?"

Owens pulled out a drawer in a nearby desk and extracted a piece of paper and handed it to me. It was the chemical analysis of what was found in the tubes. "The chemicals are identical to those that killed Stith. I don't know about their concentrations, though, without checking my notebook," I said.

"No need, the chemicals and concentrations are identical to those in the Texas murder, as is the apparatus," Owens said.

If you already knew that, what did you need me for, I thought. I realized I was indeed being played. But why?

Barbara, too, caught the implication of Owens' last remark. "Well, thank you for your courtesy, Lieutenant Owens. We'll be leaving now," said Solomon, curtly putting an end to our collegial interactions.

I, too, thought this was a good time to leave. "We'll be in touch."

We turned to go. "Mr. Alexander," Owens said, "I would ask you not to leave the state without letting us know ahead of time."

At this Barbara pulled herself to her full height and walked to within a few inches of Owens. "Lieutenant," she said, virtually spitting out the word as she towered a good head above him in her three-inch high heels, "I don't know what you think you're playing at, but we are staying in Washington, D.C., which is clearly out of the state of Virginia, and we don't plan to move. We are Americans and will travel freely in our own country, and if you wish it otherwise you can issue a warrant."

"I may, Ms. Solomon, if it comes to that."

"I would expect nothing less of a state that chooses to execute a mentally defective woman," said Solomon. "We'll use our discretion liberally on this story, and we will be interviewing the attorney general's wife. We'll not be willing accomplices to the whitewash that's obviously your intent. If you wish to arrest us, you know where we'll be. Come on, Ned." I followed her out like an errant child in the wake his mother.

24

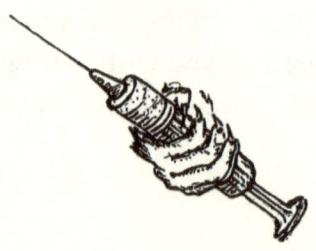

The Seed Crystal

I followed Barbara through the tangle of staircases and hallways that led us unerringly back to the reception room. She flipped her visitor's pass to the desk sergeant as she glided out the door, I handed my pass to him politely and expected to be stopped from leaving, but I also managed to exit without incident.

"Arrogant prig!" said Solomon as we gained the street.

"That was a marvelous show you put on, but you were a little reckless with the arrest parts."

"It wasn't a show. I meant every word. Let him arrest us if he wants." "Us? It's me he's going to arrest."

"Oh, buck up, Harvard, you're a big-time journalist now. Besides, he was only bluffing, trying to get you to divulge new information."

"Yeah, you're probably right, but this state executes mentally defective women, so they're liable to do anything, as you so poignantly stated."

"Believe me, you're all right," she said. So I did.

"Are we really going to interview Mrs. Hoskins?" I asked.

"We are now. If we can. The state of Virginia is into damage control, and we're not about to help them."

"There's that *we're* again. I'm the one with my name on the story." "Well, what do you think we should do, Ned?" she asked. It seemed like a genuine question.

"Did you read the articles in Rachael's file?" I asked. "Yeah."

"All of them?" "Yes."

"Well, he was a pretty bad guy from where I stand. Let's go expose him for what he was."

"Good man!" She flashed me a dazzling smile.

"We should try to get an interview with Jim Campbell of Virginia Against the Death Penalty," I said.

"I already have. Called after I left Hoskins' headquarters. I talked to his secretary. He wants to meet with us but can't do it until tomorrow. He's meeting us at the restaurant of the Air and Space Museum at 10:30 tomorrow."

"The Air and Space Museum?"

"Yeah. They have a nice restaurant, and I thought you'd like it. You were so excited on our first visit that I thought you would like a little more time there. It's big and public, and therefore anonymous. I think it's a good place to talk."

"You sound as if we're spies."

"We are kind of on this one," she said. "Unless you want to fess up all of your information to Lieutenant Owens." She looked at me. Another smile.

"I should get an article out to Halloran on what we already know," I said. We went back to our hotel. Barbara said she wanted to make some phone calls but would do it in the lounge, and she left me to my article. I was a little surprised, glad that she did not want to participate in the writing. She went off, and I sat down with my laptop.

I told the story of the murder of Virginia attorney general and U.S. Congress candidate, Lee Hoskins. I recounted the scene at the Alexandria, described the murder weapon in detail and how the materials could be purchased from any aquarium store, new information that I'd not previously written about. I told how Hoskins had been discovered by a woman who had gone there to meet him, about the scotch he had had at the bar, and the unopened bottle of Dom Perignon with two glasses. I gave a brief description of the professional relationship between Hoskins and Nancy Pretti, not shielding her as I had Emily, and that they had been guests on previous occasions. I told of Hoskins' championing of the execution of Carla Rawlings and of his public battles with Jim Campbell and Virginia Against the Death Penalty. I stated that the police investigation was headed by Lieutenant Phil Owens, and that they had no serious suspects at the moment. I described the similarities between this murder and the two others, stating that Owens had said that the apparatus and the chemicals, along with their concentrations, were identical to those of the Texas murder of Robert Stith. I finished up the article with a profile of Carla Rawlings with information collected from the stories Rachael had gathered. I left this section pretty sparse, as I wanted to write a specific article about Carla and her execution after I had met with Jim Campbell. I read the article through, made some minor edits, but was pretty well satisfied with it. It painted a picture of a man, probably engaged in an affair, who had used his power and influence to score political points in securing the execution of a mentally impaired woman.

Barbara was still not back, so I thought I would give Rachael a call to see if she'd come up with anything. I got Mildred at the front desk. "How you doin, honey?" she asked.

"It's a bit precarious here, I've got to say." I told her a little about the scene with Owens. "Is there anything you can do without killing a chicken?"

"Yeah, there's other ways," she answered. "Well, try one of those."

Mildred chuckled and connected me to Rachael. "Hi, boss," she greeted me. "Got something for you. I was just getting ready to write you an email, so you saved me some time."

"Hold up." I knew that Mildred was probably listening. I waited until I heard a click on the line. "Talk to me. What have you got?" I asked.

"Still working on the college stuff, but we did manage to get some things from the hospitals. Ryan's been working his ass off for us."

"Hospitals?"

"Yeah. Got stuff from Phoenix and Tucson both. All domestic violence stuff, but no charges filed. Only one for a Victoria Burwick, that was the first one, treated for a battered face and arms, no broken bones, just a lot of bruises. That was in Phoenix General in September of '95."

Shortly after they moved to Arizona, I noted. Rachael went on: "The rest of the hospital emergency room visits were under the name of Victoria Ramsfeld, at various Phoenix area hospitals, never the same one. There were three more: one in Mesa, one in Glendale, and one in Scottsdale. All similar symptoms, cuts and bruises on the face and extremities. The one in Mesa, November 95, was for bruises to the face—black eyes bruises on the neck, The one in Scottsdale in February of '96, she had a broken wrist and fractured cheek bone, the one in Glendale there was a fractured ankle. That was in September of '97. Ryan's really been working, I can tell you that.

"All the injuries were described as accidents, one was slipping in the shower, one was falling down the stairs; that was the fractured ankle, and the one in Scottsdale with the broken wrist was described as a rollerblading accident. There were also two in Tucson. The first was in November of last year and was attributed to a fall in the shower, and the last one was at Tucson Medical Center in December. Get this, boss, it was the same night, or morning, really, of the death of

Burwick. She had bruises on her face and arms. X-rays were taken, but there were no broken bones. It was attributed again to a fall down the stairs. No one's that clumsy, boss," Rachael said, stating the obvious. "Really nice work Rachael. Ryan, too. Can you fax me what you have to the hotel?" I gave her the number. "Sure thing, boss."

"And Rachael, we'll do something really nice for your boy when I get back," I said.

"Already have, boss, no worries. I'll be in touch," she said, then rang off.

I was resting on the bed with my eyes closed, thinking about the information Rachael had given me when Solomon came in the room.

"You taking a nap?"

"Just finished the article." I waved her over to the laptop.

She went over and read it, alternately grunting and chuckling. "You don't need me to get yourself arrested," she said, laughing. "This is good work, Ned. It'll certainly show Owens not to fuck with the press all right."

"We'll probably be gone before he sees it anyway," I said optimistically. "You send it off yet?"

"No, I was waiting for your comments."

"That is sweet, but my comment is: Send the sucker off."

I wrote Halloran a short note, sent him the article, and told him we'd be in touch after we met with Campbell. It was five-thirty, and I was feeling the need for a drink. "It's been a good day," I said. "Let's go downstairs to the bar."

"OK, let me freshen up."

Freshen up? I thought. *You already look like a queen.* But "OK" was what I said.

We took the elevator to the lounge, ordered drinks, and sat at a booth in the back. "Got an interview with Hoskins' wife in Richmond tomorrow at four," said Solomon as our drinks came.

"How'd you get her number?" "Mark Waller."

"Hoskins' campaign manager?" "Yeah," she said.

"How'd you get him to give it to you?"

"Had to promise to have a drink with him this evening. We're meeting at a capitol bar called the Hawk and Dove at nine. That'll give us time for dinner. I heard some people talking. They said the National Gallery is open tonight and they have a very nice restaurant in the basement, wine and everything. I thought you'd like it, another museum and all."

"I'm flattered," I said. "It sounds lovely."

I told her of the disturbing information Rachael had gathered about the frequent and secretive hospital visits of Tory Burwick and Victoria Ramsfeld. She listened with a grim expression. More drinks came, and I went to retrieve the faxes Rachael had sent. They said pretty much what I already had been told. I passed them over one by one to Barbara, who read them without a word. "I am glad the bastard's dead," she said finally. "Really glad."

"Yeah, me, too." Was I really coming to be a murderer myself, as Huckleberry Finn said? I shivered involuntarily.

She reached across the table and squeezed my hand. "Let's go over to the Art Museum and get us a shot of beauty," she said.

Two men had come into the bar while we were talking and sat kitty corner to us, and I thought their attention was bit too focused in our direction. They didn't look like cops, but who could tell? Our glasses sat empty on the table, and I noticed that they had finished theirs.

"Order two more drinks," I told Barbara.

"I thought you wanted to go to the museum." "I do, but order them anyway."

Our drinks came, and the two men called the waitress over. Two drinks appeared at their table.

"Let's go," I said, motioning to leave our drinks untouched. The men left immediately after we did also, leaving their drinks on the table. As we left the hotel, I could see the them behind us, keeping a discreet distance.

"We're being followed," I said.

We were now walking across the grassy mall that stretched the mile between the Capitol Building and the Washington Monument, and the two men were still following us. "Owens's goons, I'll bet," said Solomon.

"I don't know," I said. "It may be the good guys." "You are the optimist, Harvard," she said.

This time, I didn't think I was being stupid or naïve. Owens was trying to get me to divulge information that I hadn't published in my articles. In fact, that was astute, for I did have some. I could be nervous, but I couldn't fault him, because it was true. I was being played by both sides. These guys looked to me like eco-warriors rather than cops. I didn't say this to Solomon because I was enjoying the feeling that we were spies. I felt a little like James Bond beside the beautiful and stormy Barbara Solomon as we entered the National Art Gallery, lit up against the Washington night.

The two men kept a distance, though not an artful surveillance. We got our shot of beauty, and I viewed the portrait known as the *White Girl* by James Whistler, of *Whistler's Mother* fame. It was a six-foot portrait of a young, beautiful, brunette woman in a long white dress looking tentatively out of the canvas. I had viewed the painting as a teenager with my father. He had said that the woman was Joanna Hiffernan, who was a mistress of Whistler's whom he had treated badly. It was a sad but beautiful painting. I wondered what Whistler would have thought of BWWY and the Burwick killing—would he have been nicer to her?

We wound our way to the basement restaurant and had a good dinner of Maryland crab cakes and red wine. Our surveillance committee was nowhere to be seen. We talked on issues that had nothing to do with our present situation, got to know each other a little more. It was as if we gave ourselves permission to put our present reality on hold. We drank our wine and talked of our childhood and families. It was a nice little shot of beauty, as Barbara had described it.

The dinner over, we were back to our surreal reality. Barbara took a cab to the Hawk and Dove, and I wandered my way back to the hotel. I did not see any evidence of our tail. Either they had left or gotten a lot better at their job. My guess was the former. I was wound up from our dinner and the day. I didn't want to stay in the room, so I got my laptop and went into the bar, thinking I'd take a shot at a rough draft at my Carla Rawlings article. Along with the medical reports on Tory Ramsfeld, Rachael had included some more background articles dealing with the issues of executing people with mental deficiencies. There was good information that would be useful. I sat at the booth where Barbara and I had sat earlier. I ordered a beer and had just begun an outline for my article when someone slid into the seat across the table from me, and I was looking into the eyes of Jerry Boyle. "Hello, Ned," he said, smiling. I noticed that the two men who had followed us earlier were back at their table.

"Yours?" I asked, nodding over at the two men I had pegged as eco-warriors. "Yes, part of our team. I'm sorry if they have been an annoyance."

"Not an annoyance, but not very accomplished, either," I told him. "We spotted them from the beginning."

"Yeah, we're just beginning to learn our craft. It's a steep learning curve, but we meant no harm, and we'll get better."

"Just what is your craft?" I asked. But Jerry chose to ignore my question as rhetorical. "Who are you?" I asked and motioned to include the two men sitting kitty corner.

"My name really is Jerry, though not Boyle, and we are members of the Better World Without You organization, as you identified us a number of days ago. And we feel it's time to let you in on some more of the story, as you've kept our secret so far."

"Kept your secret? I've kept no secrets."

"Oh, but you have, though. You kept secret my letter to Richard Blake, and the possible relationship to J. Erasmus Camp's research institute. And you kept the letter I left you at my Tucson residence from the police. All things that could have proved awkward for us."

I listened to what he said and had to acknowledge the truth of it. I had been holding back information that could have been helpful to the police, though nothing that seemed crucial at the time. Taken together, it began to look like complicity. "What about Richard Blake?"

"Richard was only involved with the Ying Lon Society, but he was also intrigued with the heuristic idea and our attempt to identify the most virulent members of the capital punishment movement. That was the extent of his involvement with us. I don't think Camp was ever aware of it."

"Did you kill Hoskins?" I asked him simply.

"Personally, no, but collectively I'd have to say yes. The organization is growing at a fantastic rate. People who have been frustrated for years are now feeling empowered, and it's just the beginning of a movement."

"A movement to kill those who help to execute people?"

"A movement to make the world a better place. And we've captured the frustrations of many organizations and causes."

"Did you kill Burwick?"

"No, we didn't. Burwick was where it started, though. Burwick's death was a seed crystal serving to provide the structure for what followed."

"If you didn't kill Burwick, then who did?" I went on, asking all my basic questions.

"That we cannot say, only that they transformed the movement, and in so doing, created a new one."

"A new one…"

"There is more to come, Ned, and we'll be in touch," he said as he stood up to leave.

"Wait, I have more questions," I protested.

"Rest assured, all your questions will be answered. In the meantime, pay close attention to your meeting with Jim Campbell." The two men at the table had already left, as Jerry, last name unknown, exited the lounge.

The waitress came over. "Do you want your friend's beer on your tab?" she asked.

I looked at the retreating inchoate murderer, "Yeah, I'll cover my friend."

Roger Burwick, a seed crystal! Who would have thought? But now that the subject was broached, it did tie certain things together. It explained why the methodology was different between the Burwick murder and the other two. It also confirmed my suspicion that the killers were different. It confirmed what Boyle, or whatever his name was, said about a heuristic. Somebody killed Burwick, then it was essentially copied by BWWY, which was busy refining the technique and turning it into a movement. It also seemed to clear Solomon from planting the letter. Seemed to...

Jerry had just said there was *more to come*. That was a phrase off the first fax I had received. More had indeed followed, and it seemed that they weren't going to be satisfied with just completing Solomon's trilogy. I sat there at my table in the lounge, ordered a cup of coffee, and began to think of the number on the first fax: .067. What could it mean? It was delivered after Burwick's murder, so it couldn't have anything directly to do with the other murders, could it? There was another number attached to the fax that had sent me to the San Carlos Hotel: .071, a slightly bigger number. Something was getting bigger. What, besides the number of victims? I pulled out the last fax I had received with the word Virginia, and the message, *a little reciprocal information*, printed on it. I scrutinized the fax closely.

Yes! At the bottom of the page written in tiny letters was another number. The writing was so small and its placement on the bottom of the page caused me to think it was a function of the transmission of the page by the fax machine. That is, if I had noticed it at all. The police had obviously not noticed it, either, or they would have asked me about it. But there it was, a larger number still: .077. With each death came a number, or numeral, as Wild Michael had corrected me. I stared at the fax and then got very excited. I felt goose bumps forming on my arms. I went to my room and called Wild Michael's number. It was ten-thirty, getting late but still early enough to be respectable, but I was so excited I would have called him if it were three o'clock.

A sleepy voice came on the line. "You're going to bed early these days, son," I said to him.

"Got to teach an early class tomorrow," he said, "and didn't get much sleep last night." He was waking up now. "They caught the BMW driver who tried to kill me."

"Really?" I said. "Was it the Bavarian Motor Works Corporation?"

"No, it was the ex-boyfriend of a girl I've been seeing. Wasn't even German, an Irish lad from Southie," he said, laughing.

"What are they going to do to him?"

"Nothing, they gave him a ticket for reckless driving and let it go at that.

The cops were all Irishmen from Southie, too." "What about the girl?"

"Went back to her boyfriend." He sighed.

"Well, there's nothing like attempted murder of a rival as a declaration of love," I said and laughed.

"I was getting tired of her anyway."

"Listen, have you found out anything with that number—numeral, rather."

"I went to some anti-capital-punishment websites and played

around with some numbers but got nothing yet," he said. He sounded a little deflated.

"Listen, isn't there something in mathematics called a reciprocal?" "Yeah, it's the fraction you get when you divide a value into 1. It's a basic operation of fundamental importance to a whole lot of mathematical calculations." He started to wax on.

"Well," I cut him off, "it may be fundamental to our calculations as well. Go back to your websites and try to derive our number as a reciprocal. I've got a few more for you to try as well." I gave him the numbers and told him my theory that the numbers got bigger as the victims increased. He said he would begin tomorrow when his class was over.

I thanked him and gave a few words of encouragement. "Well, we've got one mystery under our belts, anyway," I said. "What's that?"

"The great BMW conspiracy," I said and rang off.

It was too late to call either Hickey or Escobar with the information about the new number. I thought I'd let them communicate it to Owens. I'd give them a call tomorrow since there was nothing they could do with the information anyway. I was all charged up with no place to go, so I sat down to wait for Barbara. I was pacing up and down the narrow thoroughfares of our one-room-two-beds floorplan, alternately looking out our seventh-floor window, when the phone rang.

"Ned, this is Michael," he said excitedly. "I couldn't get back to sleep after your call and I thought I'd try some numbers and I got it on my first try. I got all your numbers."

"Talk to me, brother," I said.

"Well, I went back to the website I'd been working with and looked around for statistics, and I saw one that I just knew would be right." He waited to up the drama level.

"And?" I said, not giving him a chance to inhale.

"It was the number of confirmed innocent people that have been executed since the modern death penalty has been instituted. I divided that into one and got our first number." Michael no longer acknowledged the difference between number and numeral. "Then I subtracted one, representing the first victim, from the total and divided that number into one and got the second number. I did the same for the third and got that number. The numbers are the reciprocal of the number of deaths of innocent people minus the number of people murdered. Cool, huh?"

"Yeah, cool," I said, the implications racing through my mind. "What happens now?" said Michael.

"Well, we solved our second mystery of the night, and for two of the three murders, we know who and we know why. Now what's next is an article that tells about it. Don't worry—you'll be credited as the math wizard who cracked the case. With any luck, the story will go out on the wire and you can read it in the *Boston Globe*."

"Cool," Michael said again, and I rang off.

I was halfway into my article when Solomon returned. "Have a good time?" I asked.

"Ugh," she said, and shook her hands. "What are you writing at this late hour?"

I told her of my meeting with Jerry Boyle, the pedigree of the two men who had followed us, my insight into the numbers, Wild Michael's calculations, and my inferences about BWWY and the murders. Barbara laughed, hugged me, and would periodically rub my neck and shoulders as I worked. It was her turn to pace the room.

I told the story of the seed crystal from the first murder, speculated, but did not give a source, for it serving as the model for a future methodology of murder based upon lethal injection, the current method of choice of the best executioners. I resurrected my mother's comment about what's good for the goose is good for the gander.

I told the story of the numbers that accompanied the killings and their meaning with respect to a reciprocal derived from the number of documented innocent victims of the death penalty, and I gave the number as fifteen confirmed innocents. I recounted that the idea for the reciprocal came from the fax itself and how Michael had used the information to solve the mystery. I speculated on the importance of the ironic double meaning of the word *reciprocal*. Describing the murders as the reciprocal of the deaths caused by execution, I described the construction and function of the killing apparatus, and I quoted Lieutenant Owens' remark that whoever was involved employed a knowledge of science and engineering to the task. I ended the article with the speculation that the killers of Stith and Burwick were not the same individuals, the killers of Stith and Hoskins likely being an organization. And that with fifteen innocent victims of the death penalty and three murders, that there would, in all likelihood, be more killings.

It was a long article, and I showed it to Solomon. She read it and nodded. "Good job, good writing, Ned. You've solved a good part of this mystery. You need to get this article out before there are more tangles with the police. I think you need to call Halloran on this one."

"It's almost one o'clock in Tucson," I protested.

"Call him anyway. The *Sun* doesn't go to final press until three-thirty, and I think he's going to want this story in paper and not let other papers pick it up off the wire first."

I dialed Halloran's number with some trepidation. "Hello," he answered sleepily.

"Hey, boss," I said, sounding like Rachael. "Talk to me, Harvard," he said, not unkindly.

I told him of my evening and its revelations. I told him of my latest article and Barbara's insistence that I call him. He said that I did the right thing, and that my first article should be in the morning edition. He asked if I had emailed the second article yet, I told him I would do it now. He said that he would go down to the paper and ensure the article's publication, then put it on the wire. I thanked him, apologized again for waking him, and went to ring off, but Halloran stopped me.

"Let me offer a little advice, Harvard."

"Sir?"

"Before you turn in tonight, call the Tucson and Houston police departments and leave a message for Lieutenant Hickey and Detective Escobar telling them you have some information and ask them to call you when they get in. You don't want them to find this information out via the newspaper or other media."

"I'll do that," I said.

"And Harvard, I read your first article, and that advice goes double for Lieutenant Owens. You two need to be careful on this one. The First Amendment only goes so far, and it only goes so far with litigation. The paper will stand behind you, but we don't want to get in a legal tangle if we don't have to. Tell Solomon I said for her to be careful, too. You guys get to your interviews tomorrow and then get the hell home." He rang off.

"What did he say?" asked Solomon, who had been listening to my half of the conversation.

"He said that I should tell you to be careful." "Shit," she said.

I made my obligatory calls to the three policemen, getting only voicemail, and sent Hickey and Escobar a copy of my article, but not Owens.

"Enough about me," I said. "How did your date go with Waller?" "Ugh," Solomon said again. "It was so skeevy." She shook her arms and put her hands into her hair and ruffled it as if she were trying to divest herself of lice. "His only reason for the meeting was to hit on me. I haven't been in a groping situation like that since high school. The place, though meant to be hip, was skeevy, too. Young men in thousand-dollar suits trying to power network with other thirty-somethings; dapper-looking old men with young girls using their power and position for their own advantage—for their own reasons. It was really the worst of what this town has to offer."

"Did you get any information from him?"

"Damn little for the effort," she said. "I found out that Hoskins was way ahead in the polls. Although it was ten months to the election, he was considered to be a sure thing for Congress. And they sure hated Jim Campbell, thought that he was the only stumbling block to overcome. The candidate he was backing was not doing too well, and Waller said Campbell was considering running against Hoskins himself. Campbell has been received positively in polls. It made his conflicts with Hoskins more of a political issue to the campaign."

"Well, we can ask him about it tomorrow," I said. "I'm finally getting a bit tired."

"Me, too," she said as she took her bed clothes into the bathroom.

I sleep in a T-shirt and my boxers. It seemed modest enough, and I saw no reason to change. When Barbara came out wearing a blue flannel nightgown, I was already installed in my bed. She got into her bed and left the side of it turned down.

"Why don't you come over here and help me get the skeeve off," she said.

25

A Goodbye to Cindi

Morning broke, and with it my chance of an anonymous departure back to Tucson. At six o'clock Barbara opened the door to go for a majestic run on the Washington Mall and was greeted by a complimentary copy of the *Washington Post* with my article on the front page. Barbara came back, paper in hand, and roused me into full wakefulness. "Look," she said delightedly, "we've made the *Post*." It was the first of my two articles; the second would have arrived after their paper went to press but was sure to be on the wire by now. Shit was about to hit the fan, I was sure.

"I wonder how long I have before Owens decides to arrest me," I said. "He's not going to arrest you," she said, still in jubilation. "They haven't changed a word. I'm going for my run with our founding fathers, then let's do breakfast." She left the perfect picture of health and happiness.

Having barely enough time to pee, I heard the phone ring, and

I picked it up to Lieutenant Owens' voice.

"What the hell is this?" he began.

"What the hell is what?" I decided to play dumb. "This article in the *Washington Post*," he said irritably. "You get that paper out there?" I said.

"Listen smartass, you better start talking," he snarled.

"It's an article I wrote for my hometown newspaper that obviously went out on the AP wire and was picked up by the *Post*, who thought it warranted the front page," I said with a touch of pride, and a fat mouth.

"How'd you know about the champagne bottle and glasses?"

"An anonymous source, it's privileged, but ask your men," I said to throw him off Ramona. I waited for the explosion to follow.

"Well, you get your ass in here as quick as you can, and if you don't, I swear to God I'll have you arrested. I'm giving you an hour." I could hear his wheels turning trying to identify which of his men had betrayed him.

"Did you get the message I left you at your office?" I said to break into his acrimony.

"What message? I haven't been in yet." He seemed to calm down a notch. "I left you a message that I had some information, and for you call me this morning when you got in." "What information?"

"I'll tell you when I see you in an hour," I said and rang off. I stared at the dormant telephone, expecting it to ring with more of his vitriol, but the phone remained mercifully silent. I was coming out of the shower when Solomon returned, flushed, sweaty, and glowing like the sunrise.

"You'll have to find another breakfast partner. Waller, maybe?" "Ugh," she said, doing that shaking thing with her hands.

I told her about Owens' call and my need to meet him in an hour. "I'll take the car and you keep the meeting with Campbell," I said. "If I don't get back or wind up in jail, you come and get me out. Should I leave you bail money?"

"I'm going with you," she said.

"No, no offense but I think I'll be safer without you, and if something happens it will be good if one of us is on the outside. Owens hasn't seen the second article that essentially solves the murders without providing any arrestable individuals. He may think I know more than I'm telling, and that some time in the cooler might pry something loose. I'll need you to be outside. Really, trust me on this one."

Barbara wasn't happy but acquiesced. "OK," she said finally. "This is getting serious, Ned."

"As you said, I'm a big-time journalist now," I said, smiling. "Fuck you." She smiled back.

I realized as I drove out to see Owens that I loved this shit. It struck me that since I took the last job in town, I had meaning in my life for the first time. I loved the mystery, I loved the doubt, loved the ambivalence that making the world a better place brought with it. I loved the dark side where my feelings of gladness for Burwick's, Stith's and Hoskins' deaths resided. I loved the people I had come to meet—who had become family: Willie, Margret, Violet, Leo, Adam, Halloran, Rachael, Mildred, Barbara Solomon, all of them added to the love I've always felt for my brother Bob. I realized the enormous love I felt for Helen that had become, at some point on my journey, equal to the love I felt for my father. Driving to the Alexandria police station, surrounded by feelings of love, I knew who had killed Roger Burwick, as surely as if I had seen it—I did see it behind my eyelids as I pulled into the station.

"Ned Alexander to see Lieutenant Owens," I said to the desk sergeant with a confidence that was certainly new to me.

Mr. Alexander, sit down," said Owens, standing above my seated form in a ridiculous attempt to intimidate me. "You have some information for me?"

I handed him a copy of the second article I had run off at the hotel's business office before I came.

"What's this?" he said as he took the copy.

"It's who killed Hoskins, and Stith as well, but I doubt you'll ever catch them."

He went to his desk and read the copy. He completed it and looked steadily at me for a long time, another vain attempt to intimidate me. "This tells me nothing about who killed the Attorney General," he said, slapping the article viciously with the back of his hand.

"That's because you're looking for an individual, Lieutenant," I said. "Hoskins and Stith weren't killed by individuals, they were killed collectively, as collectively as were Eugene Redway, Carla Rawlings, and Willie T Ruckles, for that matter. They were killed by a new consciousness that originated in the killing of Roger Burwick."

"The seed crystal?" sneered Owens.

"Yes, the seed crystal. But the crystal has grown and is still growing. It's not an individual, any more than the American Cancer Society is. Those innocent victims of capital punishment will be redeemed in time, and there's nothing you can do about it." This last part, I realized, was included to bait him. Was I crazy or just high on my knowledge of who killed Burwick?

"You seem sympathetic to this group, Mr. Alexander."

My father told me once when I was in trouble at school, that when I was in a tight place, that all things being equal, truth is always the best gamble. Employing my father's gambit, I said, "It really doesn't matter what I think, Lieutenant, but I'll tell you anyway. Carla Rawlings was a mentally impaired woman charged with contracting the killing of her husband with an ex-lover for a hundred-thousand-dollar insurance policy. She went to her death, a white woman, singing a Negro spiritual, as the state pumped poison into her veins. Lee Hoskins championed her execution for personal political gain. I don't know if the world is better with Carla Rawlings dead rather than in prison for life, but I do think the world's a better place without Lee Hoskins in Congress. So, yes, I'm sympathetic."

Lieutenant listened to my little speech. "Do you know who killed Burwick?"

"No," I lied for the first time.

"Well, Mr. Alexander, your sentiments aside, I'm arresting you as an accessory to murder. I'm betting you know more than you're telling me."

"Lieutenant, you can be certain I know a lot more than you." I stood up, smiled, and held out my arms to be handcuffed.

My hands remained uncuffed, but I was taken, checked in and put into a cell. I sat down to wait for Solomon to connect the dots. I was really glad that I had the foresight to leave my laptop and critical files in my backpack at the hotel. All the cops had here was my wallet and a blank notebook. It was about ten o'clock, and Solomon was about to keep her date with Jim Campbell. I hoped she would listen closely for me as Jerry said I should. I had few worries.

I had nothing to write with, but I spent my time composing an article on Carla Rawlings to be supplemented with information from Solomon's interview with Campbell, a fine example of an oral history if I did say so myself. It was four o'clock when Owens came down. "Anything you want to tell me, Mr. Alexander?"

"Nothing you don't already know."

He signaled for the door to be unlocked and motioned me to follow him.

Once we were in his office, he motioned me to sit once more.

You have a good many friends, Mr. Alexander, some in high places— the head of the Associated Press for one, the Governor of Virginia for a significant other, but these two requests to have my charges dropped were the most important for me." He handed me two faxes, one from Lieutenant Hickey and one from Detective

Escobar, both urging Owens to let me go. Hickey's said: "He's not the most savvy reporter around, but the boy's got integrity."

"I still think they're all wrong about you, Mr. Alexander. You still know more things than you're telling, and the name of a killer may be one of them, but the governor thinks that a battle with the press isn't in the best interest of Virginia on top of the Hoskins murder, along with the parts of his character that are coming to light."

"Well, I'm sure obliged to the governor. Can I leave here now?" "Yeah. Get the hell out of here," he said as he turned his back to me. I went out to the lobby to find Solomon sitting in the waiting room. "It's good to see you," I said. "Are you responsible for this?"

"Only indirectly. When you didn't show up for Campbell, I made some calls and found you'd been arrested, as you predicted. I called Halloran, and he took it from there. Owens was a real asshole, but in the end the governor trumped him."

"Did you keep the interview with Campbell?" "Yeah, got a few good things for you."

"You should be meeting with Hoskins' wife about now," I said.

"I conducted the interview over the phone. Got a shitload of information from her. Turns out that she really hated the son of a bitch. It'll make a good article."

"Do you think you could write that one?" I asked pathetically. "Yes," she said, smiling. "Already cleared it with Halloran." "Let's get out of here. I need a drink."

"You've certainly earned one," she said.

Barbara surprised me by driving to the Alexandra.

"You stood up Cindi last night, so the least you can do is say goodbye to her."

Cindi was in her place behind the bar. We ordered drinks, and Solomon went down to the end of the bar and struck up a conversation with a young man. I apologized about not coming back last night. Cindi smiled and said it was all right, but it was nice that I'd come to say goodbye.

"One lifetime's just not enough," I said as a lame excuse. "Yes," she said, and she smiled sweetly at me.

I told her to tell Ramona to deny everything if the police came around, though I didn't think they would, that I'd done my best to protect her. Solomon came back after a time, we said our goodbyes, and Solomon paid the tab, leaving a hefty tip.

"I stiffed her the last time," she acknowledged. "I know," I said, "but I had you covered."

"Yes, Ned, it seems you're always covering me."

On the way back to our hotel, Barbara told me of her interview with Jim Campbell. It seemed he was going to run for Congress. "What do you think we were supposed to listen closely to?" I asked.

"Carla Rawlings hired her ex-lover to do the killing of her husband. The prosecutor said that Carla was the mastermind of the crime and a representative of what he called pure evil. It turns out he suppressed testimony from the lover of his complicity, who admitted that he had, in fact, engineered the killing. He got life and Carla got the lethal injection. He committed suicide before her execution." She looked at me poignantly.

"You think the prosecutor's been targeted by BWWY?" Barbara looked at me and simply nodded.

"What do you think we should do?"

"I think you write your story, then alert Hickey and Escobar and leave it to them. You owe nothing to Owens, or Virginia, for that matter."

It was five-thirty by the time we returned to our hotel room, and we each had an article to get out. I told the story of Carla Rawlings, about the murder of her husband by a lover who ended up confessing to the primary blame that was suppressed by the prosecutor and the attorney general. I gave a synopsis of the case against executing people with mental impairments and told how she went to her death singing the Negro spiritual *It Would Take a Miracle*. It told the story of a pathetic human being who was never dealt from the top of the deck. That she was the victim of individual greed, and a social and political policy that exploited human weakness for its own reasons. I finished up with a caution for Prosecutor Steven Spitch to watch his back. I finished up and interrupted Solomon in her article to read it before I sent it along. It was selfish, I knew, but I needed the support at that time. Graciously, she read it and said that it told a story that needed to be told, that she had no suggestions and to send it off, which I did.

I called Lieutenant Hickey and left an extensive and probably confusing message on his voicemail. I did the same for Detective Escobar, but the second time was a bit more organized and coherent. Solomon still worked on her article about Hoskins' wife.

"I'll meet you at the lounge," I said. Barbara nodded, and I left.

I took a seat at *my table* and ordered a whiskey, which I hadn't done since my meeting with Adam Zegura at the Holiday Inn, and then I realized I hadn't eaten anything all day, having refused the jail lunch. I ordered a basket of fried zucchini; I looked up to see Jerry "Boyle" reaching for one.

"You guys are really improving on this surveillance thing," I said.

Nothing surprised me anymore.

"I told you we're adjusting to the learning curve," he said, smiling. "I hear you've had quite a day."

"Heard from whom?"

He just continued his smile and reached for another zucchini. The waitress came over. "I'll have what he's having," Jerry said.

I looked at him and not for the first time thought there was something familiar about him.

"I know who killed Burwick," I said.

"Good for you," he said, appearing uninterested. "Is Erasmus

Camp any part of this? I asked him.

"Not directly. Richard Blake and I were, indeed, college friends at Yale, and he was peripherally involved with the Ying Lon Society, but not BWWY, and not the murders. As I told you before, I don't think Camp had any knowledge of our dealings."

"Good," I said. The waitress brought him his drink.

"If you know who killed Burwick, then you know the whole story. You're important to us, Ned. It was never our intention to put you in danger, but today we came close. I'm here to tell you to get out of town before the close of this evening to avoid any further trouble."

"Spitch?"

"You really don't want that information," he said. "We leave at nine-thirty tonight."

"Yes, that's soon enough." He finished his drink and signaled for the waitress, who brought us over the bill. I reached in my pocket for some cash since we'd already checked out.

Jerry put out his hand.

"I'll get this, Ned. it's the least I can do," he said, handing the waitress a credit card.

"It's time for you to get out of this town. You can reach us with this number when you need us." he handed me a piece of paper with a telephone number with a 202 area code. "We'll be changing it periodically, and we'll update you through various means. Keep up the good work." He reached over the table and shook my hand and took another zucchini. I looked at the number then up to the table and he was already gone.

The learning curve ascended again when the waitress brought his receipt.

I read the name of the card imprint: Gerald Ramsfeld.

26

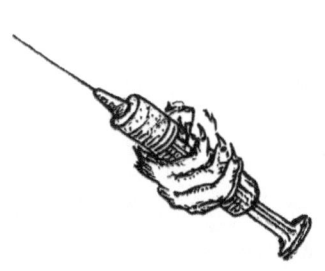

I Won't Tell If You Don't

Our flight went through Chicago and Las Vegas, all to avoid connections through Texas. Solomon was taking no chances. Though it added five hours to our flight time, I thought it was sweet. It didn't matter to me, as I slept like a dead man, holding Solomon's hand the whole way, and sleeping on her shoulder. I hadn't told her that I knew who Burwick's killer was. But I needed a good sleep for the coming day.

The eleven-hour trip got us into Tucson about six in the morning. Uncharacteristically, I awoke from the three-plane trip fresh and rested. Solomon, on the other hand, had slept only sporadically and was feeling a little ragged. We took a taxi to the paper and retrieved my car; Solomon's was still in the Phoenix airport parking lot. I drove her home. At my place, I took a shower and put on the clothes I didn't wear in D.C. and told her to call me when she woke up, then drove back to the paper. I had put in a call to Rachael last thing before we left D.C., and she'd agreed to meet me at nine.

I already knew what I would find, though I didn't know the exact details. I stopped for coffee and a bagel, I walked through the doors at a quarter till, to find Mildred already installed at her desk.

"Well, you made it back, honey. Lawdy, it's good to see you," she said, smiling seriously and shaking her head.

"Hi, Mildred. It's good to see you, too. How the chickens?"

"Down one," she said, continuing to shake her head. "When I heard you was in jail I just had to do it, Ned. Just no getting 'round it. You the hardest boy on chickens I ever seen."

"Sorry. I'll get you some new ones."

"Oh, don't you worry, I've got me lots of chickens," she said, chuckling. "Rachael's waitin for you."

I found the researcher sitting on the other chair in my box and holding a file folder. She got up when I entered, and we hugged.

"You got something for me?"

She nodded and opened the folder. "Victoria Ramsfeld's an interesting gal," she said. "I got her university transcripts." I'd ceased asking this eighteen-year-old whiz kid how she did the things she did. "Seems she was a bit of a child prodigy, graduated early from the University of Georgia at Athens, her hometown, with a degree in chemistry and a minor in philosophy." She looked up at me. "Fits, huh?"

I nodded, seeing that Rachael, too, had solved the mystery. "When she graduated, magna cum laude, she followed her brother, Gerald or Jerry, to Yale Law School, where he'd been accepted for the following year. He was a year older and they were very close." I wanted to ask her how she knew that, but it really didn't matter.

"Victoria took the law boards and topped them out. They made a special place for her, boss." At my look, she said, "Talked to the head of the admissions committee, and she said that they'd never seen a score like that and just had to make room for her. She was a good student, too, but at the end of her second year she got married to Burwick, a fellow law student, and dropped out of law school at the beginning of her third year, but not the university. She switched her major back to chemistry and took some graduate courses. She also took a philosophy class: twentieth-century religious activists." She looked up at me again. "That's probably where the Kant quote came from, huh?"

I nodded sadly.

"But here's the kicker, boss. I went back a few years prior to college." Rachael now pulled a copy of a newspaper article from the folder and handed it to me. It showed a picture of a teenage Victoria Ramsfeld holding three plastic tubes with lines all descending from the bottom of each. About halfway up, each tube was filled with a substance. The caption on the picture said: *Local girl captures top National Science Foundation Prize.* The article told the story of how high school junior Victoria Ramsfeld had analyzed three samples of local soils and isolated toxic chemicals from each, using a column fraction distillation. The article went on to say that this added proof to claims that toxic chemicals used in agriculture were stored in the environment. The experiments and their ecological implications earned her the top prize in the National Science Foundation competition for 1989, as well as a check for thirty thousand dollars. I finished reading the article and looked at Rachael. "Those tubes are what were used to kill Burwick, weren't they, boss?" she said.

I nodded again. "Yes, I think so," I said. "It also explains why there were small amounts dirt and sand found in the chemicals analyzed by the Tucson police and not the others."

"Boss," said Rachael tentatively. "I'm glad Burwick is dead. He was a really bad guy with what he did to Solomon and Victoria. I won't tell if you don't."

"Rachael, you have an excellent heart to go along with your exceptional brain." I handed her back the article.

Rachael gave a little sniffle, looked down at the folder, and said, "That's all I have, boss."

"It's enough," I said, taking the folder from her. "You take the rest of the day off. I'll fix it with the powers. Go see Ryan if he's around."

"He doesn't know about any of this, boss, and he won't. I got it all myself."

Thanks to Rachael's work, the mystery had virtually solved itself. Barbara was off the hook, but the problem was what to do now. I had heard the bustle that signaled Halloran's arrival earlier, and I went in to see him.

"Hi, Harvard, you've had yourself quite a time. Arrested, your first articles in the *Washington Post*, second one went in this morning."

"Thanks for all you did. The president of the Associated Press?" "Yeah, an old friend of mine. The governor was his doing."

"I know who killed Burwick, but I don't want to tell," I said simply. Halloran looked at me a long time. "Why?" he said finally. "Because Burwick was a bad guy, and his killer's a good person."

"I see," said Halloran. "It's a knotty problem. How did you find out?" "Intuition and then research," I said, remembering how it came to me in a flash of certainty on my way to see Owens. "Research? Rachael?" he asked.

I nodded.

"So, the source is not confidential," he stated. "She needs to be protected in this thing."

"I understand."

"You know Solomon and Burwick had that thing in college?" "Yes."

"You know that he beat her?"

"Yes," I said again, wondering if Barbara had told him everything. "OK, Harvard, I'll back you on this one, but if Hickey or the police find out I won't be able to help you out to the extent I did with Owens." "I know."

"You know this would be a hell of a story. It looks like no Pulitzer on this one, Harvard," he said with a smile.

I got up to leave thinking what a good man Halloran was. "Sir," I said, turning around at the door, "Solomon didn't do it."

"Thanks for that, Harvard."

I drove downtown and parked near Tory Burwick's house—Tory Ramsfeld's house, I corrected myself. She'd gone a long way toward reclaiming her name. I rang the bell and she answered, coming to the door holding on to a dog's collar.

"Come in, Mr. Alexander. Down, Benny," she said to the dog. "I've been expecting you today. My brother said he left you last night and to tell you that sometimes the learning curve is too steep."

"Tell him it is for all of us." I smiled.

She sat on the couch with her feet up, hugging the long-haired dog that looked a bit like a greyhound. She saw me trying to place the dog. "Borzoi puppy," she said, answering my gaze. "So, you're here for my story?" "I already know most of it."

She began: "Roger Burwick was a bit of a monster, handsome, charming, witty, but a monster nonetheless. It was not just because he beat me and your friend." She caught my look and said: "Oh, yes, I know all about Barbara Solomon. Roger was fond of recounting tales about her. Not because he was a wife, or partner beater but because he was a full-fledged sadist in everything he did. His job was perfect for him—handling the death penalty cases allowed him full access to the procedure, of which he took part at every opportunity. He would come home and tell me the details of the execution with a relish that he knew sickened me. He would get pumped up with his sadism and then the beatings would start. He used this trick of wearing gloves so his hands wouldn't show the effects of the violence. The first time he put me in the hospital, we used the name Burwick but he got worried that someone would find out, so he insisted I use my maiden name. The worst of the beatings occurred after executions. They seemed to do something emotional to him. He liked it best when the victims cried or whimpered. One day he brought home a video of one of the executions and insisted I watch it. I didn't want to, but I was fascinated with the process, the chemicals, the tubes that delivered the chemicals into the bloodstream, and their resemblance to an apparatus I had made for a science project in high school."

"The one that you won the National Science Foundation competition and a thirty-thousand-dollar scholarship?

"You are well informed, Mr. Alexander." I reached into the file and handed her the copy of the newspaper article. She smiled.

"Yes, of course. Well, it was after I had seen the video that the idea crystallized to provide an execution of my own. You see, in a bit of perversity, I began to want retribution as well as a way out, some kind of poetic justice. Roger was climbing his way up the ladder of politics, and I could think of no one worse for public office. So, I conducted death penalty research of my own into the chemicals and found that they were easily derivable from simple compounds I could purchase locally. I did it over time and at different stores and paid cash so they couldn't be traced. I synthesized the compounds in a small laboratory I had assembled in the shed in the backyard. And I waited with a pleasure that made me worry about myself."

She paused, then continued. "The only problem I hadn't solved was the intravenous needles. I was thinking I would just sharpen the ends of the tubes when I was sent to the hospital for the second to last time. In the emergency room I was put on an IV and saw where the needles and lines were stored. When I was alone in the room, I slipped three into my purse. I was pleased with the irony that it was Roger who, through his violence, had delivered the final component to me.

"On the night of the Redway execution, Roger came in higher than usual on the aftermath of the execution. He described how the board had slipped and the lines had gotten tangled around the victim's neck three times looking just like a noose. He had a pair of gloves made by Redway, and he marched around the house saying how the punishment fit like a hand in a glove—that it was his hand that had killed him. I told him I thought he was disgusting and then he beat me, as I knew was inevitable. I knew he had reservations for El Palomino—he went there after executions to calm down. I often wondered if there was a sexual component to this behavior, there was to some of the beatings, at least in the beginning.

"I had stored the apparatus and the chemicals in a gym bag I kept in the shed. I got the bag, packed a flimsy nightie, and went to El Palomino wearing a slinky cocktail dress, which made quite a contrast to my bruised face and arms. I knew the room number from the reservation notice Roger had left in the house.

"He was surprised to see me at the door of his cottage. I told him that I didn't care about the beating, that I wanted him. Men are so stupid. He didn't even question my behavior. Sorry, Mr. Alexander."

"No objection from me," I said. She continued: "I went into the bathroom, put on my nightie, and took out a vial with a strong sedative. I think he found my bruises arousing. While I was kissing him, trying not to flinch from my wounds, I poured the vial into his drink and in a few minutes he was fast asleep. I undressed him down to his boxers. I assembled the equipment, but I realized that I hadn't made preparations to fasten the cylinders to the wall. I took some yarn from my purse, looped them around the cylinders, and fastened them with safety pins to the curtain at the back of his chair. The three lines came together into a reducing mechanism I had bought at an aquarium store that merged the three lines into one; I attached the IV line and needle to the single nipple of the reducing unit, then stuck the needle in the large vein in his arm. I used the plungers I had made and, one by one, emptied the contents of the cylinders into Roger's body. He gave a few short spasms but then was quiet. I went to the bathroom, took off the surgical gloves I was wearing, and changed back into my cocktail dress. Before I left, I slipped the glove, with which he had beaten me, back on his hand. I had been careful to remove my blood from it with a solvent. I left the card that I had prepared a number of months previously as his epitaph. It was always a favorite Kant quote of mine. At the door, I looked back at the scene, and I walked back over to him and looped the main line three times around his neck. I picked up my gym bag and drove myself to the hospital."

Halloran was right, this would make a hell of an article. Tory leaned back on the couch, hugged her Borzoi puppy, and said: "Well, is that pretty much what you expected?" Her face had healed considerably in two days, and she gazed out at me with beautiful, if sad, eyes.

"Pretty much," I said.

"I don't care how you use this information in your article," said Tory, "but what I tell you now has got to be strictly confidential. Do I have your word?"

I told her she did.

"The next day my brother picked me up from the hospital, and I told him everything. He was the one that had introduced me to Roger in the first place and had never forgiven himself. He said he was glad the bastard was dead, but we had to clean up the evidence. We went home and cleaned up and broke down the chemistry lab; Jerry got rid of all the equipment and chemicals and things left over from the killing. By the time the police came and searched the place, everything was clean. I don't think Lieutenant Hickey fully believed me, but so far he hasn't been back." She leaned back on the couch and hugged her dog.

"Tory," I said. "I'm glad the bastard's dead, too. Everything you've told me is in the strictest confidence. Nothing you said will find its way into any article of mine. If you lay low, the police might just think your husband was another victim of BWWY."

"You said in your articles you thought the killers were different."

"Yeah, but who listens to me?"

At the door, I bent down and pet the puppy. I wanted to say something that was reassuring, but I could think of nothing. As I left her house, she stood at the open door holding her puppy and held back the tears filling her eyes.

With Tory Ramsfeld's statement, the saga that had begun as the last job in town was over, as far as I was concerned. It was now a waiting game. I went back to the *Sun* and picked up the morning paper and found my article about Carla Rawlings on Page Two. Solomon's article on Marie Hoskins was on Page Four. I checked the online edition of the *Washington Post* and found my article on Page Four. Solomon's, however, had made the front page. I checked on the previous day's edition and found my article on who killed Hoskins and Stith on the front page. Take it all around, we had comported ourselves pretty well in Washington, if not in Virginia.

I hadn't heard from either Hickey or Escobar, as I was in the Virginia slammer, so I called Hickey ostensibly to touch base but in reality wanting some news on Prosecutor Spitch. I got Hickey and thanked him for his support with Owens, and he grunted a "you're welcome" and seemed a bit embarrassed. I asked if he had gotten my confused message. Along with my second article. He said he had and alerted Owens, who had dismissed the information as paranoid delusion. "He's a real hard case, that one," he said.

"Tell me about it," I said in an attempt at camaraderie.

"We all think you're holding out on us, Ned, but Escobar and I agree you're not a criminal." I thanked him for his backhanded compliment and didn't say anything else because it was true.

"I hear you interviewed the widow Burwick."

Actually, I'd interviewed her twice, and I didn't know which time Hickey was referring to. "Yeah, grieving widow stuff, nothing that added anything to the story, so I left it alone."

"Grieving, huh?"

"Yeah, you should have seen her eyes." "I did see her eyes," he answered.

I figured that this was getting a little too close. "Well, Lieutenant, let me know if you hear anything about Spitch."

He said he would, and I rang off.

Barbara called, and I picked her up and took her to the airport. I bought a ticket for myself and went with her so she wouldn't have to drive back alone. Driving back, she said: "I hear you know who killed Burwick but aren't telling."

I knew better than to lie to her. "Yeah," I said. "It's a friend of yours, but you don't want to know the name."

"You thought that I did it for the longest time," she said.

"Yeah. You could kill a hundred Burwicks, as far as I'm concerned."

She reached across the seat and took my hand. We held hands all the way home.

I think holding hands is just the best thing. Don't you?

27

Nothing More to Write

It took BWWY three days to kill Steven Spitch. He was found dead in his office by the morning cleaning crew. The methodology was exactly the same as for Hoskins and Stith, but the steep learning curve was flattening, expanding from hotel rooms to places of business. It made quite a splash in all the local papers, but I kept silent. I'd already written everything I had to say. My articles were quoted by a number of reporters, so I was well represented. Lieutenant Owens tried to reach me a number of times, but I ignored his calls until they stopped. The paper also ignored his threats until they, too, stopped. I received a fax with the next number in the reciprocal sequence .083 as it inched itself toward 1. I passed the information on to Hickey and Escobar.

It took three days to kill Spitch, but only two for Tory to confess. She cited Kant's universal moral axiom as the reason. Hickey was close to an arrest. I found out about her confession from an article written in the *Times Review* by Ray Block. Hickey had given him the story as an exclusive. I asked him why he had done it when he called to tell me about Spitch's murder.

"It's your special punishment for holding out on us," he said. "And just be glad that's all it was."

I was indeed.

I wrote a story that chronicled the history of abuse Burwick had perpetrated on Tory and on an unnamed other, ceding to Barbara's request, who said I could use her name if necessary. I also reiterated how Tory's crime was the seed crystal for the ongoing BWWY murders and suggested that any attempt to seek the death penalty would probably not escape the organization's notice. The governor's office was busy combating charges that he took a series of kickbacks and bribes on government contracts and wanted Roger Burwick to go away as soon as possible. That, taken with the documented instances of domestic violence, and the fact that his colleagues all hated him, led to a charge of second-degree murder that carried a sentence of twenty years. Tory would be eligible for parole in seven, maybe sooner. I wrote the story of the trial, but it was all rather perfunctory.

After my article, I got a request to visit Tory in the minimum-security prison that housed her. She thanked me for my articles, saying she thought they had some effect on mitigating her sentence. And she asked me if I would consider taking her Borzoi puppy, Benny. It seemed that she liked the way he had responded to my petting at the door. I answered with my heart rather than my head and said I would, that he would be awaiting her return. It was time for me to get my own place, and I found a small place on a ranch right next door to Solomon's. Imagine!... She watches Benny when I'm away on travels and seems not to mind.

BWWY continued to grow and to thrive, with a killing after every execution. I periodically checked their roving website. They seemed to be gathering support from multiple contacts. The FBI became involved, but no one was ever caught. They showed a mild interest in me for a time, and when each visit was followed by an article directed at their incompetence to get closer to the organization, in time they lost interest. The organization expanded for a time with a public mock trial and real execution of a CEO of a large tobacco company that was transporting defective cigarettes abroad. I was sent information on the trial and their utilization of the *aggravating factors* used by the judicial system to establish the appropriateness of the death penalty. I passed on the information I received and wrote the series of articles but stayed away from the characters in this drama who were primarily in Virginia, of all places. The CEO, whose name was Harry Balch, was found dead four months after his death sentence was delivered to me in a fax. He was killed at his condo in Jamaica. It seemed he was suffocated by cigarette smoke confined in a bucket placed over his head—another example of ironic justice. Executions and cigarette exports were reduced for a short time.

True to its word, BWWY keeps me informed with respect to its phone number, sometimes through email, sometimes through a phone call. Once, it even came in a Christmas card. I haven't called them yet, but it does give me a secure feeling to have a terrorist organization at my back.

I continue to work on Willie's biography with the help of Robin and GNN video clips and stories. I publish it periodically in articles in a variety of newspapers, magazines, and professional journals. They've earned a couple of honors and awards. In the end, they will all be compiled in a book. The *Sun*'s legal department found no conflict of interest. With any luck, it will be out soon. The work makes me feel close to Willie and his life, but it makes me sad, too. I often travel to conduct interviews. I went back to Houston for an interview with his mother. She seemed not to grasp his importance—his influence. Instead, she directed me to her newest jigsaw puzzle, not knowing that her son was the king of puzzle pieces.

His second-to-last book, *Death and Release*, was published not long ago and was widely received as his best to date, although I know nothing can exceed *The Anatomy of Coincidence*. His many fans seemed to derive some degree of solace from it, as had Leo.

I continue to build a strong relationship with my extended family. We meet periodically for the Sister Shashwati Foundation, making a social event of it. I asked Zegura to research the Virginia Against the Death Penalty organization, as a possible grant recipient, and also the Avanti School for Girls in India. Zegura came back with a positive report on both organizations, and we made a substantial donation to each. We also briefly formed a political action committee to support the election of Jim Campbell, who won his election and is waiting to be seated as an anti-death-penalty member of Congress.

In other political news, P. Wellington Simon, the governor of Arizona, was found guilty of fraud, kickbacks, and a shitload of other crimes. A number of us called for him to be put on the chain gangs he had reinstated. Rather, he was given a sentence at a Phoenix white-collar prison and sent to a prestigious cooking school as his rehabilitation. He's already lined up a chef's position at a posh Scottsdale resort upon his release. Here's to Harvard.

The Texas governor came out of hiding and is preparing to be the next President of the United States. Imagine...

Violet graduated with her doctorate from Columbia and moved to Highridge, where she has become my mother's right hand, and in time will probably become my mother's replacement. Leo took to the writing program like an elephant seal to his harem and has become a poet, his work appearing in various journals. He even got one published in the holy of holies: *The New Yorker*. He kept his promise to Willie to travel and is now in India, on a tour of spiritual places. He still writes more than he talks.

Margret delayed her graduation to continue to do work at CERN in Switzerland. She's busy discovering particles that may be doors the size of protons to alternate universes, drinking red wine at night, and continuing to not eat animals. I visited her a few months ago. It was great to see her, and we began again, as always, where we last left off. I stayed with her, but mostly as a brother, even though we still hold hands while walking. Our lives still look too complicated. Besides, she had a traveling companion at the time.

Zegura went back to being a professor, albeit an unconventional one. He continues to develop the field of social law. He is busy collecting Willie's papers. We wanted to establish a Willie T Ruckles prison library, but the powers wouldn't have it. So we established it at San Marcos State College with another substantial grant through Sister Shashwati. The library will be a social justice resource supporting the rural South with cultural workshops and documentary projects. He's been of immeasurable help to me on my book. As of this writing, BMW has changed the style of its grille, morphing Hitler's mustache into Clark Gable's or maybe Zorro's and ensuring Wild Michael's continued safety.

Halloran, as perceptive as he is, was wrong. I did win the Pulitzer Prize for my work on the executions and murders, and the immediate follow-up articles on Willie. There was jubilation at the paper until a number of lucrative offers from some prominent organizations began to roll in. I sat down with the *Sun*'s ownership and after several meetings we worked out a deal. I would be installed in a position called Reporter at Large, which meant I would be free to follow stories of my own choosing, international as well as local and national, as they came up. In turn, I would agree not to work for the competition. They were particularly happy when I did not insist that they match some of the larger monetary offers I had received from other papers, although I did get a good raise. The one thing I did insist on, which was not negotiable, was that Rachael be hired as my full-time research assistant and be given a travel budget. Rach was elated and upon graduation will enroll herself in a master's degree program in journalism. She does my research and often shares a byline with me for her work. Lately, she's also handled some stories solo. She still sees Ryan, but we haven't asked him to break any confidences, or laws for that matter. At least I haven't.

It strikes me that most of us are following in someone else's footsteps: Violet in my mother's, Rachael in mine, Leo in Willie's. Margret and Bob, however, continue to follow their own music. Bob is building two new community high schools with a Sister Shashwati grant, and you know about Margret.

Barbara and I still go out sometimes. I guess we're friends now. But she also goes out with a few others, too. We're colleagues mostly, but good colleagues, and she watches my dog.

The *Washington Post* asked me to write a guest article on the death penalty, and I reluctantly agreed, mostly at Rachael's urging. The article, as it turned out, was in large part Rachael's research. We gave a history of the death penalty and its use in the United States, told how it had been mostly abandoned in *civilized* countries around the world. We described the aggravating factors necessary for the imposition of a death sentence. And we told of the method employed by BWWY when these factors were extended to society as a whole and made reciprocal. I closed the article with a critique of the historic defense of the death penalty—that it was cost-effective and served as a deterrent to future crimes. I presented the overwhelming evidence that it was neither. Then I gave my opinion that there was no rational good reason for the procedure. It was not cheaper and did not act to prevent any new crime. Its justification resided simply in the need for retribution. I described J. Erasmus Camp's program and presented that the reason for the death penalty's continuation was locked tight in the *intractability of raccoons* and its hope of redemption with the optimism provided by the *eradication of smallpox*. We'll see.

Acknowledgments

To: Pat Ghezzi, for first introducing me to raccoon behavior, and the complexities of preparedness and contra-preparedness; Helen Lewis, sociologist, Highlander Research and Education Center. I hope I've not taken too many liberties; Doug Peacock, who first read the novel, saw some merit, and hooked me up with my first editor; Andrea Peacock, my first editor, who guided me through my initial education with writing and the editing process; Craig Lancaster, my present editor, who stuck with the project through a second edition; Ren Blanco, who created the cover design of the first edition back in 2010; Ned Gittings, who created the present cover illustration; Paul Palmer-Edwards, book designer, who puts the magic in the current edition; Edward Giordano, media engineer, who places that magic out there, and to my publicist David Carriere who orchestrates its notice; Bill Halloran, of the U.S. Department of Education; Steve Zegura, old professor, old friend, who serves as both the physical and moral model for a major character. I'm sure you'll be able to tell which one.

And to Jane Anderson. I finally read White Lotus.

Thanks to all. Your fingerprints are throughout.

JG, 2021

Jamey Gittings is a fiction writer who splits his time between Arivaca, Arizona and Big Sur, California. Gittings was a problematic high school student who ultimately annexed a Ph.D. degree in areas of behavior disorders, mental retardation, and behavior psychology from the University of Arizona. He has founded a school for youth and adults with disabilities, worked for the United Nations, the Government of Afghanistan, and with the Government of India on projects focusing on disability, gender equality and international development. Jamey is the author of three subsequent novels, including the sequel *Meat of the Horse*.

For additional information,
please visit: **jameygittings.com**

www.ingramcontent.com/pod-product-compliance
Lightning Source LLC
Chambersburg PA
CBHW050010120726
47903CB00006B/1718